Dragon's Breath
Revised

Lee Kohn

Author's Tranquility Press
ATLANTA, GEORGIA

Lee Kohn/Author's Tranquility Press
3900 N Commerce Dr. Suite 300 #1255
Atlanta, GA 30344, USA
www.authorstranquilitypress.com

Ordering Information:
Quantity sales. Special discounts are available on quantity purchases by corporations, associations, and others. For details, contact the "Special Sales Department" at the address above.

Dragon's Breath Revised / Lee Kohn
Hardback: 978-1-965075-66-1
Paperback: 978-1-965075-38-8
eBook: 978-1-965075-39-5

O'Malley Series

(**Wind and Steel Revised**) is not related to the series

Crude comedy, Detective, Police drama, Sexual situations, Violence, Profanity, Strong, and Sensitive situations not suitable for all ages.

ACKNOWLEDGEMENT

I would like to dedicate this book to my two main characters, Lt. Jake O'Malley and Sergeant Theodore Williams, who have brought great joy to my writing. I had a lot of fun telling their stories and allowing the reader into their world. There is a lot of Jake O'Malley in all of us, whether we agree or not. He sees the world in one color and one dimension. I like him for his straight-forward, out-spoken, simple and honest way of looking at humanity. Although bitter, foul mouth and full of crude humor at times, he still manages to strike a chord in all of us. A very highly intelligent detective, but often sidetracked by everything and anything. I originally intended to kill off his character in 'Badge 13,' part 1, but could not bring myself to do it. It would break my heart if he was to leave this world before going on to yet another adventure. I also intended to erase Theodore's character off at the end of 'Dark Shadows of Rage,' part II, but what would the world be like without our black, overweight, creampuff-eating and loveable Shadow. 'Dragon's Breath Revised' is my favorite. A thank you, to all the people who read my books with an open mind.

I look at them as anti-heroes. Police officers and fire fighters are not heroes because they work for wages and know very well of the dangers involved. When police officers do what they are paid to do, it's called doing your job. A firefighter goes into a burning building, because it's his job. It's called employment. Without a paycheck they wouldn't even be there. Now if a person puts his life on the line for no gain whatsoever... ... That's the definition of a hero.

A sincere thank you to Lance Boggan, a master at what he does who took the pictures and laid out the cover and a thank you Sadie Cox for modeling for the front cover again ... Both are the only ones to put any effort into these projects....

PROLOGUE

Twenty-one hundred hours, five miles from the outskirts of Fairmont, Alabama, a vehicle slowly comes to a stop in an old cornfield that had been taken over by pecan trees from years gone by. The man turns the engine off and slightly tilts his head toward the young, beautiful high school girl lying in the back. She's passed out and is wearing a very short red plaid skirt and white blouse. He glances through the windshield, checking out the night sky, "Full moon tonight, perfect timing. It's time to awaken the Dragon." He drags her limp body from the vehicle, throws her over his shoulder and carries her to a tall dilapidated, abandoned, corn silo. He opens a small flap in the side of the structure just large enough for a grown man and drags her through the opening, picks her up and throws her on her back over two bales of hay stacked side by side as she started to slowly come around.

Barely awake and still groggy, she struggles to open her eyes. She sees through blurred vision a figure standing over her wearing a red sheet and red hood.

She asks, "Where… am… I?"

"The Dragon's den."

"Dragon's den? What dragon?"

"The Red Dragon."

"You're crazy, there are no Dragons."

"Well, before this night is over you will believe. Legend has it, the great, and powerful Dragon will rise and take what is rightfully his and become one with you, and then the Dragon slayer will come with his sword in hand, but the Dragon slayer is no match for this mighty Dragon."

"What?"

"It's just an old proverb."

She tilts her head slowly and nervously ganders around the large room.

"Who are you and why are you wearing a red sheet?"

"Oh, sweet angel, I am the Red Dragon, and this is my den." The man with a chuckle, lifts the sheet up and takes his pants off leaving the hood over his head. He walks over and snatches a red heart shaped locket from around her neck and drops it next to her limp body. He reaches under her short red skirt and pulls her white panties down and proceeds to push her legs apart.

1

She struggles again to speak, "I… wanna… go home."

"You are home, and the Dragon must get his fill. Oh, sweet thing, you are mine forever."

About this time, seven men wearing white sheets crawl through the opening one by one and stood behind the Dragon. He turns to them with a smile and then lies between her legs and starts raping her. She lies there with her white panties still hanging on her ankle and moans as he starts out slowly, and then, ripping her blouse open works himself into a violent, sexual frenzy.

Minutes later he stands, backs off and with yet another smile, "Ok boys, there's enough midazolam in her system to keep her from struggling and screaming. Do anything and everything you wish but leave no bite marks, or DNA. When you have all had a turn, I will strangle what's left of her, then y'all take her to the woods and dump the body. Make sure you burn her clothes. Lay her in a comfortable position. This makes three. That should be enough to bring the Dragon slayer up here. He has a soft spot for young victims." He takes a seat and watches as his men took turns pleasuring themselves. Each one rougher than the next.

An hour later, one by one they back off, pull their sheets up and place their pants back on. The Dragon walks over and stands there staring into the girl's haft opened eyes, "Now you've met the Dragon, and it's time for me to find another. I have no use for you anymore. There are plenty more good-looking girls at that school to keep me busy for the next six months, and I aim to rape and kill every girl on that soccer team then the cheerleaders." He turns to the other men, "You boys will get a turn on each one after I have gotten what I want but remember one thing; this Dragon slayer cannot be toyed with. I have had a run in with him before and he's no candy ass. When his left eye starts blinking, he will not hesitate to kill anyone who stands in his way." The man gets between her legs again and starts raping her again, but this time he places his hands around her neck and with every stroke he strangles her to death.

CHAPTER 1

In a large, abandoned warehouse near the Alabama State Docks on the west side of the Mobile River, Jake is wearing his black combat fatigue pants and a tight black t-shirt with sweat dripping from his temples brought on by the mid-June heat. He slowly eases around the corner, stalking his pray like a lion making his way to an unsuspecting black, water buffalo. Being careful not to be seen, he slowly peeks around some large wooden crates and then checks above every container.

He yells, "Just give up hoe, it's hot as hell in here! I know where you are, my fat worthless piece of black goo!" His voice echoed throughout the structure as if he was standing on the ledge overlooking a deep canyon.

Theo eases his head up to peek over some boxes and yells, "You don't have a clue to where I am you wop-ass redneck!" He wipes the sweat from his brow that's slowly traveling down his forehead, "Damn, you're right, it's hotter than hell in here! I'm melting like a two-hundred-and-sixty-pound chocolate candy bar."

Jake, "With nuts or without? Why don't you just give up and we'll go get some ice cream with fudge topping and sprinkles just like you like it."

"I'm all in…. wait a freakin minute, as good as that sounds, I'm not falling for it."

Theo's voice gave his position away as Jake yells, "Actually I didn't know where you were at first, but I do now chunky butt. You talk too much." He jumps up and cuts loose with ten rounds, peppering the wall with red paint just missing Theo's head by inches.

"You missed me you white-bread illegal immigrant!" Jake eases around a few more crates as he drops more red paintballs into the gun magazine mounted above the receiver of his weapon.

Theo grasp for air and thinks aloud to himself, "Okay, all I need is for him to expose himself one good time." He yells, "Hey Jake! That Ann sure has a nice, round, smooth, plump white ass!"

Jake yells again, "Yes, she does have a nice smooth, round, plump ass! So, you want to step this game up a notch or two, huh fat-ass? Okay my spear-chunking friend, let's get it on." He takes off for another crate trying to outflank him, when suddenly Theo opens fire, splattering blue paint on the wall behind Jake just missing him by inches.

Jake yells, "You missed me you stupid inebriated African reject! You know what day it is!?"

"The day I win this match you scrum sucking bottom feeder!"

"Well, that's a little harsh. Today is the eighth anniversary of me tearing Donna up in the cab of my truck! It seems like only yesterday! Yeah, I can still hear her screaming, 'Oh Jake, you are so big, go deeper, spank my smooth brown ass you big wang, white knight!"

Theo gets angry, stands and blindly fires like a madman and yelling, "I'll teach you to do those things to my wife, you drunk cracker bastard!"

Jake takes two shots, striking Theo in the arm. He yells across the room, "I got you asshole; I win again!"

"You hit me in the arm; it's just a flesh wound!!"

"The rules specifically say that if you get hit anywhere on your body, you lose moron!"

"Thirty years of breaking the rules and now you've decided to follow them, you arrogant, foul mouth pervert!"

Jake glances in every direction trying to figure out where he could get a clean shot. He yells back, "I'm coming for ya, porch monkey!"

"Bring it on you, white bread cracker, douche bag!" Jake slides around a few more boxes and takes out half a cigar and lights it. Theo slowly peeks over the top, sees the smoke, smiles, then snickers, and in a low voice to himself, "Now I know where you are, you Italian, Irish, low life piece of whore chasing, wife stealing garbage." He makes his way around four large crates and jumps out only to find Jake's cigar lying on a crate with smoke floating gently into the air.

"Shit! I've been had!" He dives for cover as Jake steps out from behind some large fifty-five-gallon drums and fires away. He misses Theo by inches allowing him to take off running for cover across a large open space.

Jake yells, "You can run fatso, but you can't hide! Well, not actually a run but more of a quick, rough looking wobble." Jake moves in closer and yells, "I can smell the sweet odor of victory, my overweight tub of chocolate toxic waste!"

Theo yells back, "Well, thank you, ass wipe, you were smart coming up with that cigar trick. I won't fall for that again!"

4

"Yes, you will! You fell for it last week, you fell for it this week and you'll fall far it again next week, you worthless fat orangutan!"

Theo notices a small conveyor belt running along the wall that will allow him to bypass Jake and come up behind him without being seen. He gently crawls up the wide rubber belt allowing his protruding belly to rest flat against the surface as he makes his way parallel to the wall. Jake listens closely waiting for the clumsy oaf to stumble or knock something over. He suddenly hears Theo's belly making a scrubbing sound.

Theo is laughing to himself thinking that Jake didn't have a clue as to where he was.

He quietly whispers, "I'm coming for you Jakey-poo." A few seconds later he steps into a pile of dog shit. "Now how in the hell did dog shit get in here!?"

Jake yells, "I heard that!" Silence takes over as he peeks around the corner and sees nothing. He was going to have to bring out the big guns.

"Hey Theo, I know you used that conveyer belt against that wall. Did I ever tell you about the time Donna and I went parking not far from here! I was relaxing looking out across the peaceful river as that human vacuum cleaner was bobbing that head up and down making them long strokes. Boy that girl can suck the paint off an oil tanker and when it was time to explode, she just took it like a trooper! For years she called me 'Jake the snake'."

Theo gets angry and yells, "You're cheating, that's not fair!"

Jake laughs and then yells back, "Yea, like you mentioned Ann's round ass. All's fair in love and war you village idiot! All that crawling around on your fat gut is for nothing. Your anger gave your position away young black Shit-Talker. The dark side has let you down."

"That's okay Wop Vader; I know your plans for building a whorehouse without me!" Theo slowly sneaks around a forklift making his way behind some more crates. "Hey Jake, did I ever tell you my cousin wants to take Princess Jackie out on a date? He's so black that if it wasn't for his eyeballs and teeth, he'd disappear at night."

Jake gets really pissed, stands and sprays the walls with wild scattered shots. "You tell your cousin that if he so much as looks at my daughter, I will shove my lightsaber so far up his black ass that more than his eyes and teeth will glow! You're cheating when you bring sensitive things to the table like my daughter!"

Theo starts laughing, "Look whose anger is giving himself away. The dark side is taking over Wop Vader, but I am sorry for bringing your daughter into it. I can see in my mind that ponytail covered with blue paint and hanging on my wall as we speak!"

Jake listens as he slowly walks along a large steel pipe. "O-me-big Wang has taught you well puke."

Theo yells again, "It's Luke, asshole!"

"Nope, violation of copyright laws stupid ass! You gave your position away again!"

"There are no copy rights on a first name old wise degenerate. I would have had to use his whole name A-hole."

"So much college for a man who takes thirty minutes to tie his shoes."

"For your information, I can't see my shoes smartass!"

Jake peeks over a large tank and can see a shadow on the wall of Theo's facial profile, that looked a lot like Alfred Hitchcock, "I can hear every step you make lard-ass! What made you think for one minute that you, stomping around, wearing size thirteen boots that you couldn't be heard." Jake slowly keeps walking and watching for any and every slip-up Theo might make. "Come on big ass, you know very well you just can't wait to raise that ugly mug of yours. It's just a matter of time before you show yourself and I get you right between the eyes, just above those goggles and boy is it gonna sting, that's if that wide ass nose and thick lips you inherited from that lazy, fat, ass great grandpappy in the slums of Africa doesn't block my target!"

Theo eases around to a perfect firing position waiting for Jake to get within range.

He looks over a stack of palettes and sees another lite cigar and a half empty bottle of Scotch whiskey.

In a low whisper, "I got you now, you cigar smoking, drunk bastard." He eases towards the bottle and smoldering cigar. "You are all mine, like a cheap Swahili hoe. I know where you are now bitch!" He peeks over the standing crate and starts firing over the top when suddenly he hears Jake's voice behind him.

Jake, "I'm right here, you low life, commercial for Slim-Fast!"

Theo slowly turns to him, and yells, "Not in the face, not in the face!!" Jake fires a shot and hits him on the forehead just above the nose, missing the goggles by a half inch. Theo falls back and hits the floor.

"Damn that stings, you snow-white bread-hoe chaser!!"

Jake walks over to where Theo's lying on the floor, "You can bet your ugly black ass that's not a flesh wound." He fires ten more rounds into his chest.

Theo screams, "Okay asshole, I'm dead already!"

Minutes later, they're walking across the parking lot toward there black unmarked unit with Jake emptying the bottle of Scotch. He opens the trunk, and they throw their paintball equipment in the back. He looks over at Theo sporting a red mark between his eyes, and ten red splash spots on his chest. "That's thirty-three wins for me and a fat black zero for you. This is what you get for bringing my daughter into the game."

"What you said about Donna was not right either."

"Well, I didn't tell a lie. That girls throat is deeper than the Mariana trench."

"Enough about my wife, and you had no right to shoot me ten times in the chest."

"It's called, 'coup de grace'. French for, 'had to be sure'. You know the cigar and bottle of Scotch were not what spoiled your plans. You farted a few minutes before."

"If I hadn't farted, I would have gotten you this time."

"I knew right where you were the whole time Humpty Dumpty. Did you really think you could hide three hundred pounds of black cow shit behind those little bitty crates? And you didn't think for one minute I didn't know you were going to use that conveyor belt? Dragging that belly across that belt sounded like somebody's muffler was dragging the highway."

"Next time I won't eat Mexican beans before the game." He glances around at the city skyline, "Whatta we do for fun now?"

Jake responds, "The girls are waiting on the beach for us and if we don't show, they won't speak to us for a solid week."

"Like I wanna hear, 'Not tonight, Theo, I have a migraine, or did you take out the garbage or did you vacuum the crumbs off the couch from eating all those banana creampuffs.? Like I leave any."

"They won't have sex either."

"Good point. I have an idea, why can't we do this paintball thing at night when I can have a clear advantage over you?"

"You think because you're black I won't be able to see you?"

"No, that's not what I meant at all. Hey, let me change the subject here; I saw some cute women playing Tennis at the park yesterday and I bet they're at it again. Something about short tennis skirts gives me a boner. Why don't we go play with them?"

"You'll have a heart attack trying to play tennis with those young, dark tanned honeys."

"I didn't mean play, I meant sit on the bleachers and wait for the wind to blow in the right direction while I rub my two fuzzy balls. I know for a fact some of them don't wear panties."

"You haven't been married a year yet and you're already trying to fool around."

"Hell yeah! You were right. Once you're married; they cut you down to once a month."

"Tried to tell you, but you wouldn't listen to me. When it comes to women, I know my shit. One day I'm gonna write an encyclopedia on the female species."

"Will it have naked pictures?"

"Damn straight, that's a given!"

"Well, I'll get the laptop fired up and you gather the pictures. Hey, let's go get something to eat before going to the beach."

"You gonna wipe that paint off your face first?" Jake asks as he takes the empty Scotch bottle and throws it as far as he could in the river and accidently hits a man in a small fishing boat.

"Oh shit! Get in the car Theo! Get in the car fast!!" They both quickly jumped into the marked unit and flew out of the parking lot.

CHAPTER 2

The scorching hot sun at Gulf shores glared down over their tanned bodies as the whole gang laid out on the beach drinking Piña Coladas and Margaritas. The intense heat is causing beads of sweat to run down their bodies, mixing in with the slick tropical tanning oil.

Theo turns to Jake, "I'm not sure this will interest you, but I have sand crammed all up in the crack of my black ass. My rectum is sanded so smooth my farts have lost that special sound they use to make. Never did get that sandcastle to look right."

"Wow! Thanks for putting that image in my brain, and I assure you, it does not interest me at all. If it makes you feel any better, it did look like a crack house in the hood. The sand wasn't wet enough."

"I think I'm gonna go in the water and wash it out."

Ann, Jackie, and Donna jump up also and take off running toward the ever-rolling blue greenish gulf waters, crashing in and then receding only to repeat the journey over and over.

Jake yells, "Watch out for jellyfish, they'll sting that black ass of yours and take your mind right off that gritty sand in that big ass crack you got!"

Theo slows to a stop, scans the surrounding waters and the crashing whitecaps and then turns toward him. "Jellyfish?"

Ann yells from ten feet out, "I haven't seen any jellyfish! Just because he doesn't like the water, he feels he needs to spoil it for everybody else!"

Jake shakes his head and yells above the sound of crashing waves, "That's not true and you know it! If his black ass gets stung, we will never hear the end of it!"

Theo stands there wondering who to believe. He turns to Donna, "Whatta you think my little, delicious, floating, chocolate bar?"

"Ann's right, we haven't seen any jellyfish all afternoon."

Theo turns and gives him a nasty look, "Always trying to mess it up for everybody else."

He walks back toward the on-rushing water and wades out until the waves crash against his chest. He places his hands around his mouth, magnifying his voice and yells, "The water feels great Jake…come on in!!" And then lowers his voice, "Asshole, always screwing with me when I'm trying to have some fun. I'm not scared of any jellyfish. If it screws with me, I'll slap his ass with peanut butter and eat the little bastard."

Ten minutes later he's lying on the beach screaming in pain as a large crowd gathers around him.

Ann yells, "Someone please call a paramedic!"

Jake makes his way through the crowd, "Ok, stand back people, he's not a beached whale, I think. It was most likely just a small Man of War. All I need to do is piss on the place where he was stung, and the pain will instantly go away."

Ann gives him a dirty look, "You're not urinating on him in front of all these people."

Theo yells, "I'm hurting real bad, let him piss on me! I'll do anything to ease this horrible agonizing pain!"

Jake smiles, "Okay people, y'all heard the man, turn the other way so I can ease my friends suffering and unload some of those Pinacolatos."

The crowd turns as he pulls his oversize penis out and urinates on the back part of Theo's thigh.

Theo yells, "Wrong leg you asshole!"

As Jake's relieving himself he mumbles, "Wow! That feels good." He shakes and places it back in his shorts.

A few seconds later Donna asks, "Does it feel better my big bag of brown sugar?"

Theo replies, "Hell no, it's still stinging like crazy!"

Ann gives Jake a look.

He can see where this is going, shrugs his shoulders and fires back, "Don't give me that look. Maybe it wasn't a Man of War. It could have been another species that's immune to piss or maybe they're not putting enough alcohol in the Pinacolatos. I guess next time I'll pack a bottle of chloroform and let him sleep through it."

Ann, "You always do this to him."

He places the cigar and mumbles, "Yeah right; like, I made the jellyfish show up too huh? He should be pissed at you three for telling him there wasn't any out there, and thankfully it wasn't a shark; I don't think piss works on them either."

An hour later Theo is resting in the beach chair. "This is just great. I smell like a stinking wino."

Jake says with a smile, "Go back in the water and wash it off, my big bag of brown sugar. You two have the worse pet names."

"Screw you! I'm never going back in the water. They should have damn flags up warning people of such shit."

Jake laughs, "I was the flag. I was trying to warn you asshole. You think I don't go out there because I don't like seeing seaweed stuck in the crack of Ann and Donna's ass. That gulf is swarming with shit they don't even have names for yet."

"You do this to me so much; I never know when you're joking or not, asshole yourself."

"Piss on you Theo! Wait a minute, I already have."

Jake starts laughing when Theo turns to him, "Always being funny at my expense…I can't stand it when you…when you…." He suddenly grabs his chest and starts trying to yell, "Oh my God, I'm having a heart attack!" He falls off the chair and onto the packed sand grasping for air.

Donna screams, "Oh my God!"

Ann screams out, "Call the paramedic Jake, fast! I think he's having a heart attack!" Jake grabs his cellphone then not thinking takes off running, but after about a hundred yards Ann yells, "There's not enough time Jake! Where are you going?"

He runs back, "I was going to find me an alibi. Shit! Whatta, I do?"

She watches as Theo struggles with chest pains, clinching his left side with a tight grip, and then suddenly sees him tilt his head sideways and gives her a wink without Jake knowing.

She looks up at Jake, "You're going to have to give him mouth to mouth."

Jake glances around at all the strange, horrified faces and replies, "I won't even kiss a dying white man, what makes you think I'm gonna put my mouth on those thick ass lips? And he's got that slobber or druid thing going on. I would rather shoot him and put him out of his misery. And what happened to the beating on his chest shit? I don't think mouth to mouth works on a heart attack."

"He's dying Jake, he needs mouth to mouth. He's your best friend."

"He was my best friend; now I gotta go find a new one." Jake gets sick and drops to his knees, "I need sex with Demi Moore too, but that's not gonna happen either, why can't I drag him back to the car and rush him to the hospital? And how am I going to explain kissing him at the next damn K. K. K. meeting?"

Donna screams, "He'll be dead by then! Do something fast before I lose my giant snickers bar!"

"Ok you two have got to stop with the pet names, it's starting to get on my last nerve."

Donna, "Please Jake!"

"But there's people watching and I'm okay with having sex with two girls tonight."

Ann yells, "You didn't mind them watching when you urinated on him!"

Jake shakes his head and leans over to give him mouth to mouth when suddenly Theo places his right hand on Jake's face, "That's far enough you wop bastard; I would rather you piss on me again than give me mouth to mouth." He starts laughing with Donna, Ann and Jackie joining in.

Jake gets pissed, "Very funny, and to think I just miss out on an orgy tonight."

Theo, "It serves you right for what you did too me."

"I told you about the damn jellyfish bitch! And... this... day... isn't... over... yet... best friend!" He gives him a wink.

"Ok, I'm sorry for the fake heart attack and a thank you for warning me about the jellyfish. Let's call it even old wise one."

An hour later Jake had his eyes closed but was snickering to himself after thinking about how to get revenge on Theo. So many choices when suddenly Theo sees a Gulf shores police officer walking down the beach looking for someone.

Theo, "Wonder who he's looking for?"

Jake opens one eye, turns and nods, "Looks like he's coming this way. I got a bad feeling about this. I bet it has something to do with me hitting that fisherman with that empty bottle of Scotch; try to remember that we have been over here all day. Look the other way and maybe he'll pass us by."

Ann jumps up and yells, "Last one in the water is a rotten egg." Donna and Jackie race her to the waterline.

Jake watches as the girls run for the gulf, "That Donna is using dental floss for a bikini."

Theo, "Stop looking at my wife's ass."

The officer strolls up and takes a seat on the footrest of Ann's empty lounge chair but says nothing.

Theo gives Jake a glance then back at the man, "That was not us skinny dipping in the pool last night, and we weren't anywhere around the docks when that Scotch bottle flew out in the river, but go on, we're listening. If this is about our little jellyfish and heart attack performance, you're too late, we only do one show a day unless it's funny."

He holds his hand out for a shake, "I'm officer William O'Shea with the Gulf Shores P.D."

Jake, with no expression on his face grabs Theo's arm to stop the handshake, "Hold on right there Theo, he hasn't read us our rights yet and I wanna know his business before we go any further. He could be running an errand for the I.R.S."

The officer nods his head, "Nope! Do not wanna speak to them either. I was sent by my chief to deliver a message from your chief. Apparently, you two have your cellphones off."

Jake, "So far, you're batting a hundred. There are good reasons why our cellphones are off. We're on vacation which you are screwing up as we speak."

"Didn't think I would ever find you two. The ponytail threw me off."

"Well, you found us, now un-find us."

Ann was standing in waist deep water next to Donna. Jackie was riding a small boogie board. She turns to Donna, "Whatta think that officer wants with them?"

Donna replies, "Most likely one of their old drinking buddies or Jake screwed his wife before you came into the picture and they're negotiating terms for child support."

Back on the beach, the officer stands and walks off as Jake turns to Theo, "No matter where you go to hide, they can find you. He should be working for missing person on our department."

"Let's quit; we can start that private detective business you're always talking about."

"What will we call it?"

"We can call it, 'Theo and Jake's Private Detective Agency'."

"Who's gonna hire a detective agency with a name like that? And I think you mean, 'Jake and Theo's Private Detective Agency.'"

"I said it right the first time."

Jake nods, "Forget all that. I just spoke to an investor, not more than seven hours ago, who can take the money we won at the boats and triple it."

"What kind of investment?"

"Seashore property. They have hundreds of these huts in the Virgin Islands and we can buy them cheap and rent them out to tourist who can't afford a thousand-dollar-a-night penthouse."

"Sounds pretty damn good to me."

Two days later Jake is driving back to Mobile. Theo is sitting shotgun, with a pissed expression on his face. Donna, Ann and Jackie are sitting in the backseat not saying a word.

Suddenly Ann blurts out, "You happy now, Jake?"

"You must be able to read my mind and know I have a boner? How was I supposed to know a hurricane was going to take out the whole damn beach? And in less than three hours after getting off the phone. I had no idea there was a hurricane out there. You three have been mad at me for two days, enough is enough."

Theo being sarcastic, "I know, why don't we buy some land in Kansas and Oklahoma's tornado alley and build some paper-mâché houses and rent those out too."

Ann snaps back, "Can't believe you two transferred money to that guy before consulting us."

Theo starts to say something when Donna interrupts, "Not a word Theo! You were behind his money-making scheme from the start."

"I have you know my ancestors lived in huts, so what makes you think I wanted to invest in that shit."

"It took Jake one minute to talk you into it."

"Well, you bet your sweet damn brown ass from now on, he won't talk me into anything again."

Jake, "Hey Theo, I ran across this guy who owns a bar out on Airport Blvd, and he's relocating because of a retiring issue, and wants to sale the bar for one third what it's worth."

"Well hell, I'm in, let's go check it out."

CHAPTER 3

Back at headquarters, they're sitting in two chairs facing the chief who's flipping pages, reading over some paperwork.

The Chief, "They found you two days ago. You two were supposed to be here an hour after they found you."

Jake places a cigar between his teeth, "We had two more days left on our vacation and if it wasn't for that hurricane in the Caribbean we wouldn't be having this conversation. You gonna give us the rundown on this Fairmont case or not? I have jetlag."

The Chief, "Jetlag from driving from Gulf shores to Mobile?"

"Ok, I stand corrected, call it a damn hangover."

"I see you still have that ponytail, but we will discuss that at another time in the future when I might give a shit. I have a complaint about a Italian and obese black man throwing a whiskey bottle in the river and hitting a fisherman in the head. They say he had to have six stitches."

"Wasn't us!" Jake snaps back with a grin on his face.

"The man said it was a black unmarked unit with a blue tag."

"Unless he can I.D. us better than that or a tag number, he has no case. Besides there are ten units on this department that uses a black unmarked unit, again, unless somebody got the tag number, he has no case."

"Forget that crap liar, the mayor of Fairmont requested you two by name. It seems they have had two murders over the last two months they can't solve."

Theo, "That wasn't us either. Do we need an attorney before this goes any further?"

The chief bows his head and rubs his eyes, "You know what I mean assholes."

Jake, "Why don't they call in the F.B.I.? Those lazy bitches have nothing to do but collect a check and violate people's rights."

"It's not a federal case and apparently, the town mayor has heard of your great profiling skills."

"Well, obvious he hasn't heard of my foul mouth, drinking, whore chasing, don't give a shit qualities, bottle throwing ass and bad investment skills."

Theo jumps in, "I have a question, just where the hell is this Fairmont you speak of?"

"Twenty miles northwest of Alexander city." The chief replied.

"Still lost."

The Chief, "Oh my God Theo! You two drive north to Montgomery, take a damn right and go northeast for about seventy miles or so, then take a left in Alexander, and go about twenty miles until you two stop seeing anything to do with civilization and bingo! You are there. Should be a pig trough on the left and an outhouse on the right."

Jake, "And what if we don't wanna go to this hillbilly shindig you speak of?"

"The town mayor is offering you degenerates two hundred thousand dollars if you can solve the case."

Theo, "How is it legal to take that if we're still on the payroll of the police department."

"They can give a reward to anyone they please. There's no conflict of interest in question."

Jake, "We're gonna need a city credit card from them for gas, food and hotel and we use our unmarked unit. We will leave on Friday. Call them and tell them I will need all the paperwork and photos of the crime scenes."

"They have already sent said credit card, and you two can leave today. The county sheriff will swear y'all in, when you get there."

Jake, "Can't leave until Friday. Theo and I have a very important business matter to take care of."

Chief, "Three weeks ago, my neighbor saw a black unmarked unit parked in my driveway."

"Did your wife get hit in the head with a whiskey bottle too?"

"Ha, ha. When I got home my bed was all messed up and my wife was jumping around the house like she had snorted ten ounces of cocaine."

Jake, "What makes you think it was me?"

"She was having butt troubles like someone had shoved a watermelon up her ass."

"Ok, I'm going to say this right up front, your wife is so ugly that I would come up with twenty alibies before confessing to that shit, but you might wanna check with stuttering Freddy in I.D. He drives a black unmarked unit and I heard he's very gifted in that area also. They say when he sticks it in and says, "'You, you, you are so, so, so tight ba.. ba... baby,' that the vibration from the stuttering drives her crazy."

16

"What the hell does that mean?"

"It means, it … it … it … was … was … was, most likely … him … him, him!"

Theo starts laughing so hard he had to get up and walk out.

The next night, the two sit at the end of the bar at Pat's place, with weathered looks on their faces. Theo is about to pass out when he looks over at Jake, "So you tore … the chief's wife's ass up?"

"I was telling the truth. If it were me, she would be at the doctor getting that throat re-sleave." He lights up a cigar and starts shaking an empty glass of ice, pondering over the things that had gone wrong over the last few days, and thinking hard about what if he had done it all differently. His first marriage was a disaster and now Ann is angry over the money investment disaster and has now separated and went to spend time with her mother in Dothan taking Jackie with her.

He leans back on the stool and takes a deep breath before glancing up and yelling at the barmaid at the other end, "Hey Brenda! What does two sorry ass excuses for businessmen have to do to get another drink around here?"

Pat's niece, a short, young, pretty, redheaded Irish woman, wiping the other end of the bar gives him a dirty look. She grabs a bottle of Crown in one hand and a Coke in the other and walks toward him with a disgusted expression on her face, "I be have an idea, Jake, next time, just be yell something rude across the room …. asrehole!"

"I've been shaking a glass of ice for a good ten seconds. I've seen possums frozen in headlights take the hint quicker or a sloth climbing a tree looking to bang another sloth."

She starts to mix the drinks when Jake says, "Straight please. You can pour that coke out in the sink and save the bottle."

Brenda, "Why me be save the bottle?"

"Because I wanna use it on you in a few hours."

"Very funny. You be have something in ya jeans bigger than a damn coke bottle."

Jake, "You know here lately I've been wanting to stick shit in there for fun."

"What be ya do when they be replace me with a A.I. female humanoid robot?"

"Will it have a better ass than you?"

"Not unless you be like wires and printout boards."

17

"Well, if it doesn't and I can't screw it or cuss it out, I guess we'll have to find a new bar, preferably one that has hired you. The fembot thing will rule out any storage room activities, or maybe not. I can just hear that fembot now in the storage going, 'YOU ARE TOO BIG, THIS DOES NOT COMPUTE, YOU ARE TOO BIG, WHERE ARE YOU STICKING THAT NOW? THIS DOES NOT COMPUTE, I REPEAT, YOU ARE TOO BIG, YOU ARE A STUD FOR SURE, YOU ARE KNOCKING MY BATTERIES OUT!"

She pours two drinks and just stands there nodding her head back and forth trying not to laugh.

Jake, seeing Theo passed out with his head on the bar, downs the drink at one time and then takes Theo's drink and downs it. He then notices Brenda just standing there staring at him.

"Okay, what's going on in that empty Irish redhead of yours? I'm sure there's enough room to make a field goal attempt between those leprechaun ears of yours. That gives you some hope."

"Ya be a drinking too much. Anyone can be make a bad investment fer sure. The lassie will be come back as soon as she be over the loosing-money shit. I be bet, at this very moment, she be lying in bed crying her eyes out fer ya. No lassie that be in her right mind would be give up a nine-inch crowd pleaser fer money. At lease me wouldn't."

"Bullshit Brenda, she's crying her eyes out alright, but it's over the money. She better not come around until I throw this crowd pleaser around a bit. Nobody cuts me off."

"Ya beat all Jake; all the lassies yer be managed to violate over the last forty year or so and yer still don't be understand 'em."

"Look Brenda, I have an idea; stop playing psychiatrist, shut the hell up and keep the drinks coming. I have enough on my mind without having to listen to your shit. I have an idea, being Ann and I have separated for a while, why don't you and I take this conversation to the storage room, and I'll plug that overbearing Irish pie hole up for three minutes."

"What about Theo?"

"Be let the lad be find his own blowjob."

They both look over at him as he sways back and forth and falls to the floor. Jake with a chuckle, "Problem solved."

"Shit, you be think he be hurt?"

"He has a hundred-pound airbag around his waist; I doubt it."

Ten minutes later they come from the storage room with Jake zipping up. Jake, "Where the hell is Pat? Is he still at the elf convention?"

"He be out fer another week fer sure."

"I guess he's still milking that hemorrhoid operation for all it's worth."

She stands there for a few minutes staring into his eyes and asks, "Can I be ask yer one question?"

"You just did, and one is all you get; so, take your ass to the other end of the bar, fix yourself a drink to wash your mouth out, and pretend you're actually serving a purpose here besides relieving my stress."

"I be know yer been around the block, rude arse, but me be wondering why yer never tried to be have a relationship with me. Me don't care if yer have money or not."

"You're a redhead and you always have that angry ass frown on your face, and you jump into men's shit all the time. Men screw other women to forget the one that bitches at home. That's why I know my way around the storage room better than Pat."

"So that be why yer never be ask me out fer sure?"

Jake shakes his head, "Hello! You just now figuring that out? You should have asked me sooner and I would have saved you the trouble. That's not all Brenda; have you looked in a mirror lately?"

"Why, something be wrong with me face?"

"Your make-up looks like you stuck it to a wall and then walked into it."

"That be because yer just smeared it in the storage room arsehole! Ya be have any idea how hard it be to aim something that long?"

"I have been doing it all my life as long as you draw a circle around your lips with lipstick. I like red gloss and your red hair has that 'I stuck my finger in a lightbulb socket' look, and your personality sucks."

"Yer don't be mind sticking me all the time, and again, me hair be going in every direction because ya be just pulled it in every direction. I can only be go just so deep no matter how hard you pull me hair. So, what me do to get the lads to be take me more seriously?"

Jake hesitates a minute or two and looks her over. "Spend more time in the storage room."

"I be, every time ya come by. Me be serious!"

"You really wanna know?"

"Yes stud, I be like to know fer sure."

"A lot of bourbon, and with that sour looking pus, you need to brighten up that personality; it be the Irish in ya fer sure lassie."

"Be tell me more."

"Okay, let's use the old hundred-point system."

"What be the old hundred-point system?"

"I'm getting there and wipe that from the corner of your eye. It's where we men add up the bad things about you women and decide how much money we need to hammer y'all and how long it will take.

"How be it work?"

"Okay…each part of your body can be worth between one to ten percent. For example: I would rate your face a 'six' and your hair a 'one.'"

She interrupts, "Other than yer just be messed it up, why be it get rated a one?"

"Because it be red Brenda, and men know that's from Irish breeding which makes your temper a bad thing and they don't need you calling them up every damn day from a cookie tree yelling and chewing on their ass with that Irish accent."

"You be do it all the time."

"I can get away with it because of what you just had in your mouth ten minutes ago, now let me finish. I rate your ass a seven because you cover it up so much, I can't see your cheeks hanging out. It's like Theo farting and I can't find a window to open. Your legs a six, because you fight me every time I try to place them behind your ears."

"I can be bend them just so fer…. Me not be a gymnast."

"Are you gonna interrupt me every time I say something? Now I rate your boobs a five, because I'm a leg and ass man, and I will rate your vagina a ten…"

She interrupts again, "And why do me vagina rate a ten?"

"Because all vaginas are rated ten with me, Brenda, now stop interrupting me. I would rate your personality a one, because you give me a whole lot of shit every time I need another drink. I rate your energy level at a ten and your willingness to please a man sexually at another ten." He leans closer and says, "Stick out your tongue."

She sticks her tongue out and holds it there for a second while he examines it. He reaches over, grabs it and moves it from side to side.

"Okay Brenda, I be see a bump back there at the base of your tongue that's causing that strong Irish accent, but I'm gonna rate that tongue at a ten because you know how to use it. Another ten because you do have all your teeth. Now all that adds up to 56%."

"That be 66% ya drunk bastard!"

"You just proved my point, now shut that stick sucker up and listen; okay, that gives you a 66% rating which we know from that damn math test we took in the fifth grade that it's not better than 100%. So, taking that figure into consideration, and how much alcohol it will take to improve it … a man's going to lose money and waste his whole damn night."

Taking every word seriously she says in a loud voice, "Shit! What be me do to be change me percentage rating?"

"Well, being that I'll take anything over five percent, I wouldn't change a damn thing, but if you wanna raise the percentage rate, mix the damn drinks stronger, get the hint?"

"Me still not be understand."

Jake slams his empty glass down on the bar. "Look Brenda don't let it bother you. Now stop worrying about it, I'm making myself horny again with all the dirty talk."

"Yer be lost me fer sure Jake."

"I figured I did when I first mention the old percentage thing. Okay, I didn't wanna have to go there, but I was talking to Vince in Narcotics a few weeks ago and he said he spent two hundred dollars taking you out wining and dining your ass and you got angry because he didn't say something right and cursed him out. He said you went from hottie to bitch faster than a F-18 hornet in a high-speed pass. He said it was the worst date he had ever been on."

"That arsehole be say that about me?"

"Yep!"

"Damn that, Vince. You be see his big arse nose?"

"That is one big ass nose, but that's not all, Mark in traffic said you kicked him in the nuts because he told you an Irish joke. Look Brenda, women are like vegetables and flowers. Now flowers are pretty and all, but they served no purpose other than to smell and look good. You can't eat 'em or smoke 'em."

"But…"

"All I can get, I'm getting there. Now a cabbage is an ugly plant, but cooked just right with some real cornbread, you'll have lovers coming out of the woodwork."

"So, yer be saying that if me wanna get laid, me be need to look like cabbage?"

"I was using a metaphor. Don't go off the deep end every time somebody says something you don't agree with. Just give them the best sex they ever had. It's like riding a merry-go-round. The horses are no good unless they go around and around and around then up and down and up and down…Break some shit, Brenda! Knock a few ceiling fan blades off! Tear the slats from under the bed! Get down and get dirty girl! Wear those fishnets, a garter belt and lacy panties. Scream some bad language! Yell shit like, 'yer be so big baby! Oh yeah, that be right! Knock me red Irish bush around', you know, shit like that!"

"Yer say me should look and be act like a whour."

"Bingo! Look Brenda, men think with their penises, sorry, but that's the way life is. You see, a woman is thinking about the meal, how much did the wine cost, how romantic is this date going to be, but a man is looking at your mouth wondering how much wine it will take for you to crawl under the table."

"Okay, me be try it next time."

"Don't try Brenda; just do it and your life will get thirty four percent better. Now let's go back in the storage room so I can soften that red sponge thing you got going on down there, and this time hold on to a case of whiskey, so I don't have to chase you around the room dodging beer bottles."

Ten minutes later, Brenda could be heard in the storage room yelling, "I be a gymnast fer sure Laddy! Harder, harder make it hurt me fer sure!"

Another ten minutes later, they came from the storage room with her walking very uncomfortable.

"Wow, that be awesome."

"Let's see how a female android handles that. And I was awesome because I gave a hundred percent. See how that works! Now help me get lard ass to the car. He's staying with me for a few days."

"Why the lad be staying with yer fer?"

"Donna's mad at him because he didn't save any money to buy her a house. She blames me for talking him into a bad investment."

As they drive back to Jake's place Theo wakes up and ask, "What happen?"

"You passed out, but if it makes you feel any better, I batted a hundred percent."

"You had your way with Brenda again?"

"Twice, she be needed a math lesson. I think I stopped that strong Irish accent when I smooth out that bump at the base of that tongue." Jake slowly turns to him, "Changing the subject, you hear about Charley?"

"Drunken Charley with no legs?"

"That's the one."

"I heard he married Rhonda."

"I guess you did hear then."

"I wonder what she sees in an old foul-mouthed, drunken vet with no legs and bad breath?"

Jake nods, "I think it was because she saw him lick an ice cream cone."

"So, what, anyone can do that."

"From a foot away? Dilemma solved."

"Even a double amputee drunk is getting more than me."

"What about that fat black chick with the eye patch?"

"Damn you! Will you stop bringing her up. I can't tell you anything!"

"The chief call me about two hours ago and told me he got a call from Sheriff Ray Henderson in Tallapoosa County."

"Let me guess; they're investigating a missing pig, and they think we took it when we went through there last year. Well, I'm not squealing…get it." Theo snickers.

"It seems they had another homicide in Fairmont yesterday and they need us up there tomorrow morning."

"I have too many personal problems to think about that shit. I think I'm gonna sit this one out. Donna's mad enough to leave me."

"One hundred thousand dollars will be a big down payment on a house and that will have her back licking that black thumb in no time."

"Ok, you talk me into it, I'm in. Now how do we start this case off when we get there?"

"We start with the highest official and work our way down to the troop leader of the boy scouts. It's always some high-ranking, power-hungry official who nobody believes would do such shit as that. We've been batting a hundred here in Mobile."

"Well, it can't be the boy scout's leader, it was girls raped, so stop joking. I'm serious."

Jake gets angry, "That's what I miss about the old Theo. He never took anything seriously and was always joking."

"They must need our help pretty bad to offer us two hundred thousand dollars."

"I still have homicides right here in Mobile pending back five years I haven't gotten to yet."

"You are a lying ass dog. You're caught up and you know it. You should be flattered that you're that well known."

Jake, "I'm having second thoughts myself. I have a bad feeling about taking on a case in Hicksville."

"You can use the hundred thousand too. And I bet we will run into a lot of pea picking girls wearing them short shorts with cowboy boots." Theo makes an adjustment to his crotch.

Jake thinks for a few more seconds and replies, "Okay, we'll do it. And since you brought it up let me tell you about this twenty-two-year-old girl that I met a few years back that worked at a petting zoo. She had those denim shorts crammed up her ass. I knock those cowboy boots right off her feet and...."

CHAPTER 4

Friday morning they're traveling north on I-65. The morning sun shines brightly through the right-side window of their black Crown Vic. Jake has his head buried in a pillow with his face partially hanging out the window. The warm breeze felt good and allowed him to drift off into a soothing nap. Theo is laughing and telling jokes as Jake falls victim to another dream about when he was just a young lad in middle school.

He stood there at the end of the gravel driveway waiting for the school bus to make its last stop of the morning. He's holding a small brown paper bag containing two peanut butter sandwiches, a banana, and a small bag of barbecue potato chips. He takes a gander over his shoulder and could see Spencer trying to hide behind an azalea bush. He was peeking over the top ever so often to make sure Jake got on the bus. He gives him a wave from the hip causing Spencer to throw up his hands knowing he had been discovered. It was the first day of a new school and Jake's first day in the eighth grade. Spencer walks over to where he's standing and places his hand on his shoulder.

"You gonna be, okay?"

"Yeah, I'll do just fine. Why don't you go back and drink another cup of coffee?"

"I will after I see that you get on the bus."

Jake shakes his head, "Will you stop watching over me so much. I've made it this far in school without you holding my hand."

"Well, excuse me for giving a shit. You've been tossed out of three schools already."

Jake, with a nod, "Relax, I can take care of myself. I promise no fighting."

"And what else?"

"Oh, come on, it's in my nature to look up skirts. How else will I know what color their panties are?" Spencer gives him a look.

Jake nods, "Okay, no looking up skirts."

Spencer glances down the road as the large, yellow school bus makes the corner at the intersection. A swishing noise can be heard coming from the airbrakes as the bus comes to a halt. The door opens and Jake grabs the roll bar and steps up. He gives the cute but slightly overweight bus driver a wink, turns and walks down the center aisle. He tilts his head to look up two skirts sitting in the front seat and then gives the girls a smile, "Nice panties; love the color." They give him a smile as they close their legs. He continues glancing from one end of the bus to the other and sees that every seat is taken but one and it had a very large mean-looking boy with a crew cut leaning against the sliding window. Green mucus is running from the boy's nose, and he had grits stuck between his five yellow teeth. Before he could take a seat, the boy placed his hand on the unoccupied space.

"This seat is saved."

Jake, not cracking a smile, "This is the last bus stop you ugly-ass moron. What happen… did a jackass kick you in the face while you were trying to milk him?"

The large angry boy gave him a look, "You don't hear so good dude, I said this seat is saved."

"No, you only think it's saved." Jake snaps back.

The large boy stood up, standing a head taller and looked down into Jake's eyes, "How would you like your ass whipped?"

Jake smiles, "You sure that empty space is worth what I'm about to give you? And buy a damn toothbrush for God shake before you lose those last few teeth."

The boy grins from ear to ear, "You can stand until we get to school, greaser." Suddenly without warning, Jake slaps the boy with his lunch bag, so fast and hard, snot, peanut butter sandwiches, banana and potato chips flew in every direction. The boy stands back up and swings, but Jake ducts and comes up with an upper cut striking him between the legs. The large bully falls back in the seat as Jake takes the empty place next to him.

"You owe me two peanut butter sandwiches, a banana, and a bag of potato chips; I'll collect tomorrow and if I even think you spit on them, I will pop that ugly ass mug again. So, how long have you had that green shit running from your nose?"

Jake sits out in the school's main lobby watching the other middle schoolers walk past the large glass window. The bus driver walks out of the principal's office, followed by a tall man wearing a gray three-piece suit. He gives him a hand jester. Jake stands and walks into the office and takes a seat. The clean-cut man takes a seat in a brown leather chair and throws a folder across the desk.

Jake with a smirk says, "My folder?"

"Yep, how'd you guess?"

"There are only two things that thick, ones in my pants and the other isn't Spencer's cornbread."

Then with a grin, "I was just going over it with the bus driver and you have built up quite a resume on your first day."

Jake tilts his head, "Would it make much difference if I told you that most of that was just a bunch of lies placed in there by people with wild imaginations in an attempt to slander my good name?"

"Nope."

"Didn't think so."

The principal drags the folder back toward him and opens it. "Jake O'Malley, well, well, it says here that you've been kicked out of three schools for fighting and making sexual advances toward girls."

"Well, the complaints did come from the girls."

"How you made it to the eighth grade I'll never know."

Jake with a nod replies, "The fights were no accident for sure. The sexual advances are not true. My hand slipped."

"One girl said she fell, and you help her up by grabbing her between the legs."

"Have you ever tried to pick up a bowling ball with one hand and not use the holes." *He leans forward,* "In my defense, that was one nice-looking bowling ball coach."

"I'm not your coach, I'm the principal and I will not tolerate your kind of behavior. Now what do you have to say about hurting Ruben on the bus this morning?"

"Ruben!? I never got a chance to ask his name, but the answer to your question is, you win a few, you lose a few."

"He's in first aid as we speak getting his testicles looked at. His mother wants to press charges."

"She should be at a drug store buying him some snot medicine and a toothbrush. He's gonna hurt a lot worse if he doesn't make up for my lunch I destroyed when I hit that skinned back pumpkin head of his."

"Wise guy huh?"

"Look, I just have this thing about bullies. Now I'm not sure how the rest of the year is going to go, but you can bet one thing, that snot nose lima-bean-fed pile of crap won't be saving anymore seats for an imaginary friend. You see, I accomplished in five seconds what the bus driver couldn't do in five damn years."

The man leans back in his chair, *"I won't stand for foul language in my school, so cut it out right now."* The principal stands, walks around the desk and takes a seat on the corner.

"You like taking matters in your own hands don't you boy?"

"Yep! Look, I know where you're going with this, so let me say this. Last year I told the teachers and the principal about a black kid taking lunch money from all the younger white kids and diplomacy didn't work. They didn't wanna cause a lawsuit for racial discrimination, so they just let him go on and on and on until he caught me in the bathroom and tried that shit with me. The funny thing about that was my stepfather is a cop and doesn't have the money for my lunch and he's too proud to ask for the free lunch the government gives out to lazy people who have too many damn kids. I kicked the hell out of his ass. Now I'm not sure if I cured him of robbing kids of their lunch money, but he took a wide berth when he crossed paths with me in the hallway."

The principal smiles, then walks over to a file cabinet and takes a short, sawed-off, wooden boat paddle from the lower drawer. *"Let me ask you something O'Malley, don't you wanna graduate and go to college and become a teacher, accountant, or a lawyer?"*

"A lawyer, that's funny, no I think I wanna become a cop, because that doesn't require a shovel or I wanna be coach for the Dallas Cheerleaders."

"You have two choices; I can suspend you for two weeks and call your stepfather or you can take three licks from my rule enforcer. So, which will it be?"

Jake thinks for a second; stands and bends over the desk. *"I'll take the three licks. I would like to kill this matter right now if it's alright with you."*

The man smiles, *"Brace yourself smart guy, these are gonna hurt."*

Jake looks back over his shoulder, *"Would you like me to lower my pants so you can kiss my ass? Now if it will end this boring conversation, please give it your best shot."*

The man takes a big swing and pops him on the rear end three times so hard the slapping noise could be heard down the hallway. With a grunt and a sigh of joy the man lays the paddle on his desk, "How did those feel tough guy?"

"Like you really did kiss my ass. You hit like a girl. I bet you struck out in baseball every time you came up to bat."

The man gets angry and stands straight, "From now own you're going to get a lick for every word of profanity that I hear coming from your mouth starting right now. Bend over; you have two more coming to you."

Jake laughs, "Make it three asshole."

Jake awakens from his dream of memories gone by and stretches back placing his hands behind his head.

He looks at the windshield covered with lovebugs. "Damn what a life; you eat, screw and end up with your ass smeared on somebody's windshield. That sounds just about right." He turns to Theo who's struggling to unfold a map and drive at the same time.

"That map whipping yo ass walrus butt?"

"It wouldn't hurt you to read the freaking damn thing for me. I think I'm lost."

"Did you turn right off 231 north onto 22 east then left on 280 like I said?" Jake asks.

"I thought you said right off 22 onto 231 then right on 280 after we left Montgomery."

"I have no idea how you got to 22, then 231 north, but it works for me! Stop at that truck stop up ahead; I gotta drain my oversized lizard."

"Yea, we could use some petrol."

He eases over in front of the pumps of an old country self-serve. Jake steps out and stretches back as Theo walks around the car, takes the nozzle from the pump and places it in the gas spout. As he leans over, his coat slightly rises above his waist exposing his 9mm shoved down in a brown leather holster attached to his belt. A thin young white male in his twenties is pumping gas into an old pickup truck when he notices the gun. He quickly hangs the nozzle up and runs inside the store.

He tells the young female cashier, "Hey Bobbie Sue!"

"Yeah Budda?"

"You see that big fat black niggra pumping gas in that fancy car out there?"

"What about him?"

"He bent over, and I saw a gun."

"Was it hanging out his ass?" with a chuckle.

"No, he bent over, and it was hanging off his belt. I think he's gonna rob you."

"Shit! Whatta, I do?"

"Call 911."

She takes the phone in hand and starts dialing the number.

Back in the bathroom Jake is using the urinal and reading the typical graffiti written across the nasty gray walls in front of him, "*Call Betty Lu at 467-8576. She can suck the green off a John Deer tractor.*" A few inches away, another group of words is drawn out. "*Linda Sue gave me crabs.*" Jake laughs when suddenly the door flies open and in comes a large trucker wearing a black Stetson and black pointed toe cowboy boots. He steps up to the urinal next to him and casually leans over to look, as Jake is finishing up.

"That there sure is a mighty big tool you got there. You wanna me to shake that monster for you?"

"Not unless you want your nuts kicked in your throat."

The man laughs as Jake zips up and starts to turn. Suddenly the big man grabs him on the shoulder, "You wanna go out to my truck and let me stroke that big thang a little?"

Jake gets piss, "First mistake, you just touch me. The second mistake, you didn't wash your hands before making first mistake."

"What's wrong with you dude? I can show you a good time."

Jake smiles, "I'm going to have a good time by breaking every finger on that nasty hand of yours if you don't remove it from my shoulder right now, you redneck broke back mountain cowboy faggot."

"Is that right?" The man responds.

"That is correct. I can already see that we are going to have a major misunderstanding."

"I might decide to bust your ass and take that wonder worm."

"Well go right ahead and be my guest, then after you get out of the hospital you can ponder over the three mistakes that got you there in the first place."

Theo walks in the store and smiles at the cashier and the young man standing next to the counter.

He asks the cashier, "You carry those extra thick banana creampuffs?"

Very frightened she answers, "Look Mister, take whatever you want and let us be. You'll get no trouble from us."

Theo is puzzled and glances around the store before asking, "Pardon me!"

The young man in a broken voice of fear, "Just take what you want and leave dude. There's no reason to shoot anybody."

"Did I just walk into cracker valley or something? All I wanna know is do you carry the extra thick banana creampuffs?"

The young girl starts crying, "We don't have any drugs here." She takes the money from the register and throws it on the counter. About this time Jake comes walking through the front doors with a short cigar stub hanging from his mouth wearing a black Stetson and black cowboy boots.

Theo asks, "Where the hell did you get the hat and the boots?"

"A big ass redneck gave them to me. I don't think he will be needing them anymore."

Theo, "That's nice, but can you interpret redneck for me?"

"I sure can; why just five minutes ago I had to interpret life's ups and downs to that distressed trucker in the bathroom. Poor bastard, I guess his delivery is gonna be late." He turns to the cashier and says, "You might wanna call an ambulance."

The young man at the counter starts to shake, "An ambulance!? Y'all gonna shoot us, ain't ya?"

Jake turns to Theo, "What the hell is he talking about?"

Theo shrugs his shoulders, "I have no idea, but they must hold third grade in a marijuana patch. All I ask was, 'do they carry extra thick banana creampuffs."

Jake snickers, "That's stupid; the regular ones are just as thick. They just print extra thick on the wrapper to fool idiots like you."

"That's bullshit! Whatta, you need an ambulance for anyway?"

"There's two hundred and thirty pounds of gay shit around back in the bathroom with all his fingers broke. How many times do I have to explain that?"

"Why does he need an ambulance for broken fingers?"

"In the process of getting his fingers broke, he slipped and fell, and I think he broke a hip." About this time the screeching sound of brakes can be heard as two police units fly up in front of the store and stop. Two officers in gray uniforms jump out and squat behind the doors with pistols drawn.

Theo stares out the front glass at the officers and then turns back to Jake, "Wow, they sure are in a hurry." He walks to the door, opens it and yells, "Something wrong officers!?"

One yells back, "Throw the gun on the ground nig#*&!!"

Theo turns to Jake, "Did he just call me what I think he called me?"

Jake nods, "So far that's the only thing that I've heard that makes any sense around here."

The young man says, "You might as well give up."

Jake turns and asks, "You call the police dude?"

"Yep, I sure did. Y'all was gonna rob us."

"Now what made you think that?"

"I saw a gun under that niggra's coat."

Theo's head quickly snaps around, "Look you little redneck bastard, you call me that one more time and it will be murder not robbery."

Jake thinks for a second and tells Theo, "Walk outside and place your pistol on the sidewalk."

Theo's eyes open wide, "You've got to be kidding. You hear what they called me which means that haven't heard of the civil rights movement up here. I'm sure that guy on the mule hasn't brought the newspaper yet, especially if he used the same map I used. They'll shoot first and then read me my rights, that's if they can even read."

"Do it Theo." Jake turns to the cashier and the young man, "You two get on the floor and stay there…now!" They jump on the floor as he walks to the back of the store. Theo takes out his pistol and opens the front glass door real slow, "Okay, now don't shoot."

An officer yells as Theo steps out, "Throw the gun on the asphalt, or we will kill your black ass right where you stand!!"

Theo starts to lay his pistol gently down on the sidewalk when the officer yells again, "You heard me spook, I said throw it over here!!"

Theo stands back up straight, "This pistol cost me five hundred dollars. I'm not throwing it on the asphalt and why do you keep calling me names?......I'm a…."

The officers moved closer as one takes aim, "I guess I'm gonna have to blow your damn brains all over that glass door!"

Theo reluctantly tosses his gun a few feet, when they suddenly grab him and throw him on the walkway. One officer grabs his hands cuffs and starts to place them on Theo's wrist.

One officer says, "We got us a fat one this time."

Theo slightly turns his head, "Hey, hey, come on dude there's no reason to go with that fat shit."

About this time the slide and barrel of a seven-inch polished stainless 460 Rowland pushes up against the back of one officer's head just behind the ear.

A deep voice can be heard as the officer freezes, "One of you should have taken the rear door. Now throw your gun on the hard asphalt, or I will blow your brains out which I could do with a 22." The officer nervously drops his gun allowing it to hit the pavement as Jake yells to the other officer, "You too asshole!" The other officer drops his also. Theo reaches down, grabs his pistol.

"Look at that Jake, a scratch!" He places it back under his coat.

Jake shoves the muzzle into the officer's right nostril, "You wanna tell us what's going on here before I paint the asphalt with your brains?"

"We got a call that they were being robbed by a black man with a gun."

Jake places his gun back in its shoulder holster. "Well, he is black and has a gun, but we are police officers, you idiots. What kind of robbers wears suits and drives an unmarked Crown Victoria with damn antennas all over the top and trunk lid?"

"Sorry, we didn't know. Where y'all from?"

"Mobile. Now if you two need something to do, there's a big ass queer lying in the bathroom who needs some attention. You boys should have taken that second grade more seriously." Jake and Theo stroll back to the car and drive off.

Theo is so angered he could hardly speak.

Jake snickers, "Hey, I found us two dates. I'll take Betty Lu and you can have Linda Sue."

Theo starts laughing.

Jake smiles, "You thought that was funny huh?"

"No, I just remembered, we drove off without paying for sixty dollars in gas. That'll teach them to call me names."

Jake nods, "I have that beat." He pulls three packs of extra-thick banana creampuffs from his coat pocket and throws them on the seat. "Hey, you were right, they are extra thick."

Theo glances down, "Screw their creampuffs; they hurt my feelings calling me names like that."

"You're right; what was I thinking?" He takes the creampuffs, rolls down the window, and throws them out. Theo slams on brakes doing a complete spin-around in the middle of the highway.

Jake starts laughing, "I thought you didn't want 'em after they called you names."

"I'm starving to death. Thanks for buying them for me."

"I didn't buy them, I picked them off the self when I went out the back. Scratch my buddy's gun, my ass."

"I can see this trip is gonna be another name calling adventure. I hate it when we need to work a case in bum-freaking-Egypt. It's like working around a bunch of hillbillies with their thought patterns no better than a carton of milk lying in the sun for three weeks."

"What?"

"Ok, I meant, no higher than a gopher's ass."

"What are you trying to say?'

"Let me put it in simple English for you. I hate dealing with rednecks, clodhoppers, yokels, hicks, and country bumkins that had seven tater diggers by their sister."

"What's a tater nigger?"

"I said tater diggers!"

"What's with the 'Sue' and the 'Lu' shit? It's like they're not sure of their last names."

"Maybe they can't say it without whistling through those two front teeth. Now I know exactly where the blacks got the idea with that big ass gap."

"Let's speak of it no more, I can't work on but one case at a time."

CHAPTER 5

They unload the car at the motel and after throwing everything on the bed, they settle in.

Jake glances around the shabby room, "Wow, this looks like home. Let's get down to the sheriff's office and get the rundown on the homicides."

"What's the hurry dude?"

"The quicker we solve these crimes, the faster we can get back to Mobile."

"Yeah, like Mobile is special."

"You wanna live up here?"

"Hell no, have you seen my sister?"

"I can run a tab there."

"I say let's get a shower first and grab something to eat and then get to the sheriff's office."

"It's always about food with you."

"Look, I've had three road-kill banana creampuffs in the last four hours and I'm hungry."

"Okay, we'll get a shower then something to eat."

An hour later they're sitting at a table in Mama's Country Kitchen. Everyone in the place was staring at them.

Theo, "What the hell is wrong with everybody? We fit in."

"What's this 'we' shit? You got a rat in your pocket? I fit in, but you don't. They're waiting for you to go all ghetto up in here or they have never seen a black man wearing a suit. I bet everybody in here is carrying a firearm including that infant over there. It's holding a pacifier in one hand and a 357 in the other and I bet that old man sitting in the corner over there can't wait to shoot you with his old flintlock pistol."

The waitress walks over and asks, "What can I get y'all fine gents today?"

Jake ganders at the menu and then looks up and sees her nametag, "Linda Sue'. Well, I'll pass on the crab soup, what's the special?"

"We have country fried steak with our homemade white gravy, white hominy and cornbread with a glass of sweet tea."

"That sounds delicious. How about you, Theo?"

Theo looks closer at the menu then looks up at her, "Do you have anything without the word, 'white' in it?"

She giggles, "Mama burnt some chitlins."

"What's a chitlin?"

"Cooked pig guts."

Theo gives her a puzzled look, "I have the fried chicken, dark meat only, black eyed peas and cornbread slightly burnt on the top. Do y'all have any homemade banana pudding?"

"We have the best in Alabama. Real bananas and pudding made from scratch."

"I'll take the biggest bucket you got of that.'

Two hours later they drove up in front of the town hall and stepped from the vehicle. Theo takes a gander at the large three-story redbrick building near the town square and turns to Jake, "Crap; their town hall is bigger than ours."

"I think it's the Tallapoosa County seat. Looks like they spent more on their offices than they did on those bumpy ass backroads."

Theo snickers.

"What's funny?"

"That name always cracks me up. Tallapoosa! Who comes up with that shit?"

"I think it's an old Indian name."

"Sounds like a nut disease, "Sir, you have a bad case of Tallapoosa nut begone."

Jake, "Tallapoosa nut begone! Damn, you have come up with a title to another country song, Theo."

"I know right. It can also be used on a date, 'Hey sugar, can I have some of that Tallapoosa you are hiding between those thighs?"

They enter the building and into the main lobby and sitting to their right behind a large oak counter is an older woman in her mid to late sixties sporting bright red lipstick and hair done up in a bun. They stroll over and just stand there for a few seconds when she glances up, "Can I help you two?"

With a grin, Jakes replies, "We need to see the sheriff."

"You have an appointment?"

Jake, with a smirk stretching across his face, "Always with the appointment shit. Look lady, your town is so small the *Welcome to Fairmont'* sign a hundred yards from here has the same damn thing written on the backside and you say we need an appointment?"

Theo snickers.

The woman, not finding anything funny, "You can make an appointment, or you two clowns can leave our little one-horse town the same way you came."

Jake nods, "Is that on the applications for all receptionists?"

She responds, "Is what on the application?"

Jake, "Your qualifications... Old bitch with an ugly puss, bad attitude and a habit of smearing red lipstick across your wrinkled up lips. I'm pretty damn sure you're not married. I bet you looked rough when you got up this morning."

"You wanna leave or do I have to call security?"

Jake turns to find an old gray-haired security guard in a wrinkled uniform sitting in a chair by the door with his aged hat pulled over his eyes and taking a nap.

"I think you might wanna tape that crime scene off and draw a chalk line around his ass. He looks like he's been dead for three days."

She gives him a sarcastic look.

He laughs and throws his badge up on the desk, "Is everybody in this chicken-shit town as rude as you?"

"Next time, just lead with the badges. We don't much take to outsiders."

"I never lead with the badges. I miss out on all the entertainment. I bet two hundred years ago you were an outsider. Look prune face; your damn town called us, not the other way around. We drove five hours to get here; almost got shot over some creampuffs by two of the dumbest-ass police officers I've ever met and was propositioned by a truck driver who now has to eat chicken with his feet and can't flip anybody off for two months. Now we're tired and could use a few drinks, so if you are not serving alcohol, I would like to look over the paperwork on the three homicides you people can't solve and find a bar. I might need to investigate that dead security guard why I'm at it."

"Why didn't you say you were the officers from Mobile? We've been expecting y'all."

"We didn't know it was a matter of national security to see the sheriff."

The woman picks up the phone, "Sheriff, you have two Mobile police officers waiting out here to see you and one's black."

Theo turns to Jake and then back, "What difference does it make whether I'm black or white?"

The lady smiles, "We've never seen a black officer before. We don't hire 'em up here." She leans forward and partially covers her mouth, "Nothing personal, but the little black boogers steal anything that's not fastened down."

Jake, "As you can see, my partner is black, but a far cry from being the size of a little booger."

Theo frowns, "I assure you madam, I don't steal, thank you very much."

Jake laughs, "What about the gas you didn't pay for and the creampuffs I took? And I was wondering how you pumped gas without a card."

"I used the card they sent us."

"But you said we didn't pay for the gas."

Theo thinks for a second, "That's right, I did pay for gas which makes you a thief. Wow that's a load off my mind."

The old woman, "You two finished?" She shows them to the sheriff's office. She knocks and then opens the door. There, sitting behind the desk, was a large-sized man in his late fifties with a pronounced gut, sporting wire-framed glasses. They stroll over to the desk as the Sheriff stands, reaches out to shake Jake's hand, and then hesitates when Theo puts his hand out.

Jake grins, "It's okay Sheriff, it won't rub off; if it did, his penis would be white as snow."

Theo quickly turns, "No you didn't."

Jake smiles, "Oh, yes I did."

The Sheriff, with a smirk, "Please have a seat gentlemen. Forgive me; we're not used to seeing black officers around here."

Theo, being sarcastic, "That's okay Sheriff. I bet you haven't seen a full set of teeth around here either. I bet there isn't a dental office within a hundred miles of here."

"I'm Sheriff Raymond Henderson. You can call me Ray. I'm not gonna try to hide the fact that I'm not happy that the mayor and town council brought in some outside help. We're a small department, but I think we can solve our own crimes ourselves."

Jake leans forward, "I'm Lt. Jake O'Malley and this here is Sgt Theodore Williams and we're not real happy about being here either. And if somebody thought for one second y'all could solve these murders, my partner and I would be sitting at Pat O'Donnell's place at this very moment."

The sheriff nods, "Let me swear y'all in first. Raise your right hand."

They raise their left hand.

"You two swear to uphold the law in this county...."

Jake, "Maybe."

The sheriff continues, "And abide by the laws of said county…"

Theo, "Maybe."

The sheriff continues, "You swear to not indulge in any immoral unauthorized activity…"

Jake, "Maybe not."

"I now swear that you two are authorized to carry a firearm and carry out any law enforcement duties. And with that being done, I'm gonna say, we have enough smartasses around here without two new ones showing up."

Jake leans forward again, "We're not just any smartasses, Ray; we pride ourselves on being two of the best smartasses in the south. And be very careful, I have a blinking left eye condition that normally means I have a bad side about to show itself."

The Sheriff frowns, "No, you be careful. I have a bad side too; especially with outsiders."

Jake leans back, "Unlike you, my bad side slaps the shit out of people insiders or outsiders! So, do you wanna start our relationship off with you lying on the damn floor in a horizonal position looking up as we go over the reports?"

"My bad side has been known to slap a few to the floor also."

"Yeah Ray, but my bad side doesn't know when to stop. Now if you don't want our help, you just say the damn word and me and my black ass partner or booger here will take our smartasses back to Mobile and let y'all get back to finding out who killed ten chickens in a barn out on highway 57. But I can help you even with that……it was the possum with the shit eating grin, full belly dragging the ground and chicken feathers on his face, you're welcome."

"Okay Lieutenant O'Malley, maybe I was just a little out of line. We've always been able to handle things ourselves around here. Ask me some questions and I'll try to help."

"When was the first girl's body found?"

"The first girl was found three months ago."

"And the second?"

"Two months ago."

"The third one?"

Three days ago."

"Wow, I bet they were all found a few days after a full moon?"

"Yeah, what does that mean?"

"According to my partner who stays up all night watching those horror films, it could be a werewolf. You have any hairy ass suspects?"

"Nope."

"Any leads at all?"

"Nope."

"Any DNA on the bodies and where can we find the coroner who did the autopsies?"

"No lab work has come back yet. We don't have a coroner here. The bodies were examined by our local doctor Jerry. We sent the lab work off to Birmingham."

"One murdered three months ago, and still no lab work? The mayor and town council were right, you can't solve 'em yourselves. Now tell me something about the victims."

The Sheriff pulls out several folders and flips them open.

"All three were white females, eighteen years of age, seniors, discovered nude and in the same location. They were on the honor roll last year and they would have graduated next year. All three were attractive girls, well known and played for the high school soccer team. The bodies were found strangled, across the road near a dense patch of timbers a thousand yards from the soccer field. It ties into thirty thousand acres of state land. I'll have my brother in I.D. bring the photographs out this evening. We have six officers on payroll and three reserves. It's a small department O'Malley, but I'll give you whatever help we can."

"Any evidence of sexual intercourse before or after they were killed?"

"Oh, they were raped alright. Again, no lab work is back yet. Like I said all lab work was sent off to Birmingham."

Jake, "Birmingham, England?"

"Very funny."

"Where are the victim's clothes?"

"No clothing was found. He must have taken the clothes to keep us from finding any hairs or other evidence."

"You said 'he'."

"They were strangled. It would have had to be a man. The girls were athletes, so only a man could have overpowered them, forced them in the woods, rape and strangle them."

Theo snickers, "Obviously you haven't met Sara the nutcracker."

The Sheriff gives Theo a look, "Pardon me."

Jake laughs, "Nothing Ray, just an old customer. Who said they were killed in the woods?"

"I believe they were forced into the woods, raped and strangled and left for the wild animals to devour."

"Signs of a struggle?"

"Not sure."

"How do you know they were raped?"

"Three good looking girls found naked bleeding from between their legs. Even an old country sheriff can tell that."

"They could have been abducted, raped and strangled in a residence, a car, or anywhere for that matter, and then thrown out in the woods. Where can I see these bodies?"

"Two have already been buried and the third, the funeral home has already embalmed her, and the wake is next Saturday."

"Well so much for looking over the victims. These crimes have already been compromised."

"What?"

"The crime scenes have been made vulnerable by unauthorized, access, or revelation, or exposure."

"I'm not following you, Lieutenant."

Theo interrupts, "What my highly skilled, intelligent, lead detective is trying to say is, you guys screwed up the crime scene and any evidence. It means we must start from scratch."

The Sheriff leans forward and says in a low voice, "If you decide to check out the crime scene, be careful not to stray too far off the path. A lot of people think that those woods are haunted. Hunters have claimed to have seen a creature so foul that the stench it gives off has been called Dragon's Breath. Over the years there has been many a camper venture too far and never to return. Witnesses say that this monster stands ten feet tall and is as big and strong as a Grizzly bear."

Jake laughs aloud, "I guess we should have brought our ray guns with us uh Theo."

"Can't, I used them to fry my beacon and they're empty."

"It's not a laughing matter. People take those woods very seriously."

"That's a good one Ray. Another boogie man story. Listen, I don't believe that shit for one second. Obvious you all get the Si-fi channel up here. It's a monster we're looking for alright. A sick son of a bitch and I'll find him, catch 'em or kill 'em, bag 'em up and deliver him to your front doorstep. It's a human being I'm after, if you can call him that, so don't even start with that spooky shit."

The Sheriff nods, "How long will you two be with us?"

Jake leans back, "Until we solve the cases."

"That could take a while. I've read some articles in the Alabama Police Gazette and you're quite a legend down there."

"That's just hungry journalist looking for stories, that's all. I'm laid back and I like everything simple as possible. In other words, I was almost the laziest bastard in the country, with Theo here bringing in first place, until I came up here."

Theo laughs, "Okay, you got me on that one."

The Sheriff leans back in his chair and props his feet up. "You think it could be a transit passing through?"

"Three murders in the past three months; a transit wouldn't stay here for more than a day, and if he did, someone would have picked up on him by now in a close-knit community like this. It would be very hard for him to get around. No, I would say it's going to be a white male, someone we least suspect like a farmer, bartender, preacher or it could even be a sheriff or mayor or one of the few corn growing commissioners."

They stand and start to walk out when the Sheriff yells across the room, "O'Malley!"

"Yeah?"

"I would be careful about how you talk to people around here. They don't like strangers, especially ones who hang round with blacks. These murders have the whole county uptight."

Jake, with a smirk, "Theo here is the not just black, but is the smartest shadow I have ever had, and you people need to be careful how you throw that 'N' around. He's okay with it to a certain point, but it pisses me off, and I will personally slap the first son-of-a-bitch who uses it unless it's a funny joke."

"I didn't mean any harm about the black thang. I'm just trying to forewarn you."

"Yeah, just looking out for our welfare I bet. Before I walk out of here, let me ask who the best person would be to talk with about your so-called haunted forest?"

"That would be crazy, old lady Harper. She's a widower and lives a few miles out on route seven near the county line. I can take you out there if you want."

"That's okay Ray, my partner has a road map. He can read it just fine, but has hell trying to fold it, so I believe we can find it ourselves. Text me the address." Jake writes his number down on a piece of paper, hands it to sheriff Ray and they walk out the door.

CHAPTER 6

Our two detectives slowly ease up in front of an old run-down shack out on route seven where an old woman in her early eighties with thinning gray hair sat quietly in a rocking chair surrounded by a dozen or so assorted cats. The porch had a ragged wooden swing with some missing slats and next to it was a rusted, broken-down refrigerator.

Theo starts laughing when he sees how rundown the house is, "Wow, talking about going back in time. Looks like that shack from, *'Tobacco Road'*. I bet that old lady was born in that dump."

Jake nods, "Let me do the talking; she has that crazy look on her face."

"Why, I know how to handle old crazy people."

"Look Theo, that old hag is old enough to have lost sons in the Civil War. She still might be a little upset about them taking her slaves away, and most likely furnish the rope at the last hanging up here."

Theo responds, "I think I can handle one old lady."

They exit the car and walk up to a dingy, broken-down white picket gate with a broken hinge.

Jake grabs the handle and gives it a little tug, causing the gate to come off the remaining hinge with his hand still holding the handle.

Theo shakes his head, "We haven't been here more than a few seconds and you've already broke shit."

Jake pushes him through the opening and yells before making it to the steps, "Mrs. Harper!"

The old woman stops rocking and yells, "Who goes there!?"

"It's Lieutenant Jake O'Malley and Sergeant Williams with the Mobile Police Homicide. Is it okay if we ask you some questions?"

The old lady spits some snuff on the wooden floor planks and answers, "Speak up boys; I'm about blind and my ears don't work so good!!"

They step closer to the front steps as Jake, in a loud voice responds, "I said my partner and I are police officers from Mobile! Do you mind if we ask you some questions!?"

"Come on up here on the porch young fellas. I'm pert-near bored out of my gourd, so I could use some visiting. Watch for cat shit."

They walk up on the porch and have a seat on the old swing. The old woman laughs showing her three rotten front teeth, "You can't sit in that swang."

Theo asks, "Why not? Are you saving it for someone special?"

Jake, "Daja vu." About this time the swing breaks and hits the porch catching a cat by the tail causing it to let out a loud hideous and haunting cry. Jake looks over at Theo who had a funny expression on his face.

Theo, "I think I broke my ass bone."

"Couldn't have, you have two thick black pillows between the porch and the ass bone."

The old lady continues to laugh, "That's why. I wish I could have seen that. Been ages since I saw any funny shit." She leans over and opens the rusted refrigerator and takes out a jug of moonshine, "Can I offer you boys a drink? I also got some lemonade in here, but the refrigerator doesn't work so it's hot as hell."

Jake nods his head, "If it doesn't work, it's just dry storage."

Theo stands, brushes his pants off and places his hand on the leaning rotten porch support. Flies were swarming everywhere. He sees one land on the backside of his hand.

"Psst, psst, Jake."

"What?"

"Check out the size of this fly."

Jake takes a gander, "That's not a fly, that's a hornet."

Theo snatches his hand away as the old woman asks, "What brings y'all city folks out here in the middle of nowhere to my place. If it's sex you be a wantn', too many year have gone by. I'm like that swang; I'm too broken down to spread my legs anymore. I used to love humping 'like a hog on a sow' until my late husband Vern was killed. No big deal though, he couldn't keep up with me. May the bastard rot in hell!"

Theo asks, "You humped his ass to death?"

"Hell no, he came home at three o'clock on a Friday night with the smell of rotten catfish on his breath, so I knew he'd been out with that bleached-blonde whore that runs the liquor store in town. I hit 'em over the head with an iron skillet until he quit moving. It didn't help his looks any, but it sure cured him of fooling around."

Jake smiles, "That'll teach him to brush his teeth before coming home."

Old lady Harper giggles, "Woutn' helped; he had one less tooth than I do."

Jake grunts, "I stand corrected. That will teach him to use some mint mouth wash before coming home. What'd the law do about that?"

"They arrested me, but I got one of them-there crazy pleads because I stripped naked and tried to give ole Judge Davis one of them-there lap dances. I fooled 'em good. You boys sound nice enough; you want me to show y'all a good time. I can still suck a bone from a pork chop. Cost you five dollars. I was saving myself for that special beau, but I'm plum tired of wait'n."

Theo swallows hard, "I'll pass if it's alright with you. I'm broker than a twenty-year-old blue-tick hound and I've lost my appetite for pork chops."

Jake gives him a look, "What the hell does that mean?"

"It's just a redneck saying I picked up at the rest stop. It means I don't have a five for a blow, but you're welcome to have a taste if you want. I'll just walk over to the end of the porch and throw up while she takes you on a wild nasty ride."

Mrs. Harper places a hand behind her left ear and yells, "What' he say?"

Jake responds, "He wants to know if you'll take a debit card!"

Theo lets out a loud fake laugh, "Sooo funny."

Jake laughs and turns back to the old lady, "Normally Mrs. Harper I would take a fine lady like you up on that offer but we're investigating the murders of three young girls."

"Oh, that was just awful what happened to those young pretty fillies. So, you two are gonna go after the old Dragon huh?"

Jake answers, "We might; it depends on what you can tell us about the Dragon."

The old lady leans over closer, "Is anyone here besides you two?" They look around and then Jake turns back to her, "Just a few chickens, lots of cats and there are flies coming out the ass."

She nods, leans even closer, again spitting snuff on the porch and wiggling her index finger for them to come closer, "Come closer young fellas, and I'll tell you a story about the meanest beast this side of the Tallapoosa River. The damn thing prowls through them there timberlands."

They lean closer. She says, "Closer, so y'all can understand the words I be a saying." They lean even closer when she suddenly grabs Theo by the ears and slaps a big sloppy kiss on his lips.

Theo jerks back and yells, "Shit!! What the freaking hell!?" He jumps up and runs to the end of the porch and throws up. After catching his breath he screams, "Why you crazy old bitch!" He throws up again wiping his mouth with his sleeve. "Oh my God, I'm dying!"

Jake just stares, watching him spew his lunch on the ground. He was about to burst out in laughter, but the site of her placing her lips over Theo's was just too sickening.

Jake, "I guess you were right; you can handle one old lady." He turns back to old lady harper, "Mrs. Harper, I know my partner could use the loving and all, but can you tell us more about this creature that wanders the woods down the road from here?"

She smiles, "That partner of yours sure is a good kisser, but he doesn't like to use his tongue much do he?"

Jake can't hold it in any longer and starts laughing like crazy.

Theo was still leaning off the porch with the dry heaves, scrubbing his teeth and lips with his sleeve.

Jake grabs his ribcage and catches his breath, "He would have used his tongue Mrs. Harper, but he just met you. Give him a little time to adjust to y'all's new relationship."

Theo yells, "Yeah like maybe a hundred or more years from now after I've dead and gone! That was by far the nastiest thing that has ever happen to me!" He spits several more times, "Damn! Taste like snuff."

Jake snickers, "Even worse than that time you slept with Janet Barnes over near the Waterfront Motel?"

"Okay, maybe it wasn't the worst, but it's the second worst thing that has ever happened to me. And I was drunk, so stop bringing that shit up."

Jake turns back to the old worn-out woman, "Can you tell me more about the woods?"

"Well, it all started about thirty or so year ago after the fire. There was a woman moved here from somewhere in, in, what's that place that looks like a bull's dong on the map?" They yell at the same time, "California!"

"That's it, now this here woman had a retarded baby not long after she got here and they kind of stayed to demselves'. They lived way up in the woods in an old shack and a few years later she couldn't take it anymore and set a torch to the place and burned it to the ground with the young boy tied to the iron bedposts."

Theo mumbles, "Yeah… mother of the year. Where's DHR when you need those assholes."

Jake turns to him, "Will you let her finish the story. Please continue Mrs. Harper."

"I will if yo partner there will give me another kiss."

Theo quickly turns and gives her a look before saying, "When hell freezes... ..." He turns and throws up again.

Jake glances down on the porch and sees a small kitten licking herself and has an idea.

"He didn't mean that, Mrs. Harper; I'll be glad to give you some sugar. They say I'm quite a kisser myself." He takes the cat in hand, turns his rectum toward her, "Pucker up, here I come." She puckers up and Jake, holding the cat's tail up, presses the kitten's rear end against her wrinkled snuff covered lips.

She smiles, "That's a good kiss, but you need to brush your teeth and shave that mustache off. Your breath smells like cat shit. Now where was I?"

Theo was shocked at the chain of events and watched as the cat ran under the shack.

Jake, "You were saying the mother tied the boy to the bedposts and then..."

"Oh yeah, you could have heard that there poor boy hollering clear to the next county. The screaming was terrible they say. The woman came down here and confessed her sins to me and then went back and jumped off Hell's Gorge. That's where they found her body. They never found the boy's body. I wrote it all down in my diary. They say the boy's ghost returned to haunt the woods and they say he searches for his mama to this day. He grew up and became 'The Dragon' who gives off a foul smell so bad that us old people call it Dragon's Breath. They say it will burn the hair from yo nose. That boy's ghost grew into a full-grown monster. Stands ten feet tall and weighs more than a round bale of hay; that's about four hundred pounds to you city folk. He eats the skin of his victims replacing the burned skin he lost in the fire."

Theo shakes his head, "Okay, it's official now. This horny ass woman has broken the Guinness book of records for being the craziest old lady in the world."

The woman snaps back, "Is that right? Well, ya partner here kisses a lot better than you do. He was nice enough to let me stick my tongue inside his mouth."

Theo makes a snorting sound, "Well, well, look who's being picky. I'm sure the cat enjoyed that."

Jake shakes his head, stands and walks down the steps with Theo right behind him.

He stops and turns, "Mrs. Harper."

"Yea?"

"You did know that first kiss was from a black man, right?" Jake turns to Theo, "Say something in negro."

Theo smiles, "It wuz goods talking wif yo old crazy white bread cracker ass Mrs. Harper."

The old lady yells, "Old my God, I've kissed niggra lips! Old my God!" She jumps from the rocker and staggers to the edge of the porch and starts puking.

Theo turns to Jake and gives him a high five. "That'll teach the bitch to ask before kissing."

Jake snickers and makes a hand motion to his lips.

Theo stops laughing, "What?"

"You have snuff running down your chin." Theo takes off towards the vehicle but throws up before making to the broken gate.

CHAPTER 7

As the sun rises to high noon, they ease to the side of the road coming to a stop in the gravel built up on the edge of the highway. They stared intently into the woods across a ten-acre cotton field.

Theo nods, "Look at all that damn cotton."

"Looks like a snowstorm hit last night in that one place." Jake responded.

Theo nods again, "Sure brings back some bad memories."

Jake slowly turns and gives him a look. "Memories? How much damn cotton did you pick Theo?"

"Well, I actually never picked any, but my ancestors sure picked a lot of that shit."

"I thought your great grand-pappy was a lumberjack."

"Well, that would explain why those pine trees bring back bad memories too. What's the point you're getting at?"

"I'm just tired of hearing about all that damn cotton those slaves used to pick. They should have been grateful it wasn't watermelons, steel cannonballs or crossties."

"Cannonballs. Why the hell would anyone pick cannonballs?"

"It's a metaphor or pun as in look at the positive side of it or just forget it."

"You know, I was thinking last night about growing an afro, maybe bring it back in style."

"Yea, and you could go out and buy some green plaid bell bottoms. You would look like a three hundred pound burnt stalk of broccoli."

Theo turns to the woods and breaks out in a sweat as he attempts to look deep into the thick, dark pine forest. "That ugly old lady wasn't kidding; looks haunted and spooky as hell to me."

Jake, without turning, "I can't believe you would believe horseshit like that. That old nag is as crazy as your cousin Erwin."

"Erwin's not crazy, just smoked too much crack over the years. But he hadn't tried to kiss me yet."

Jake fires back, "You know Theo; we're due for a little R & R."

"Roast and red potatoes?"

"Why do you have to relate everything with food? I'm talking about rest and relaxation. I say we camp out tonight and find out why everyone believes there's a monster living there."

Theo's eyes get as big as cueballs, "Hey! I say let's just take their word for it. And if my memory serves me right, we just got off vacation."

"Man, I'm getting that feeling again."

"What feeling?"

"Like somebody's pissing down my back and telling me it's raining. Yep, we're just need to spend a night in there."

"You are as crazy as old lady Harper if you think for one freaking second, you're gonna talk me into staying in those woods tonight."

"I have told you once; I have told you a thousand times, there are no such things as monsters and ghosts. Dead people are dead and that's all there is to it. You people kill me with that voodoo monster shit."

"What do you mean, 'you people'?"

"You people, as in black people. What's with y'all with that damn, 'you people' shit!?"

"Don't change the subject. It's not the dead people who frighten me; it's the ones that just can't except the fact that they're dead."

"Baloney."

"Yeah, I guess the headless horseman was baloney too?"

"Yes, he was. All fiction dumb ass. At the worst, we could get eaten by a black bear, bitten by a diamondback, or gored by a wild boar."

"See! It's crap like that that reaffirms me about your so-called wilderness camping plans. Last time you said that shit; I was almost eaten by a cat on steroids. I say we get some law enforcement personnel and search every square inch, and I mean in daylight hours."

Jake fires back, "You're just not going to let the bobcat incident go, are you?"

"That's just some shit you never forget. I still wake up in the middle of the night in cold sweats and dodging those claws."

Jake laughs, "I can still hear you calling that damn thing, 'here kitty, kitty, here kitty'. There are thousands of acres there."

"You think you and I can do a better job of covering it by ourselves?" Theo blurts out.

"It will draw less attention."

"The only way you're gonna get me into those creepy ass woods, is for me to be armed to the teeth and Janet Jackson as my guild."

"That's funny Theo; bullets won't kill monsters and they go right through ghost."

Theo snaps back, "It makes me feel better to shoot holes through their asses anyway. And I thought you said there are no monsters and ghost."

"It's a joke asshole."

"What about those black bears? Is that a joke, because I hear they can get up to four hundred pounds?"

"So what, you're black and you weigh over three hundred pounds."

"Ha, ha, ha, stop it! You're killing me with the jokes. You must stay up all night thinking up crap like that. I'm down to two sixty I have you know."

"I would be more scared of snakes if I was you. They say an eastern diamond-back can get up to seven feet up here and as big around as my you know what."

"Every time you open your mouth, you reaffirm my opinion about the woods. It's the wrong thing to say if you want a black man to camp out. And you know how black folks are about those damn snakes and why do you have to compare everything with your penis?"

"I'm not sure; you think I should compare everything with yours?"

"Stop trying to change the subject. Again, black folks just aren't into the camping shit."

"Y'all thought the same thing about the beach, now y'all flock down there like seagulls. Looks like thousands of baby seals lying out on the sand."

"Look Jake, that crazy lady says that there's a monster in there that stands ten feet tall and can rip a man's head off with these large green stained fangs."

"She said nothing about large green fangs. Listen to yourself. That old lady has you believing in all kinds of shit."

"So, I filled in the blanks, okay ... what about Bigfoot? I guess that's made up too."

"Oh my God, some asshole who's been smoking wacky weed sees a bear taking a dump in the woods and runs all over the country yelling Bigfoot! Bigfoot! This world is full of idiots starting with you."

"What about the tracks people have found in the woods of Washington State? Huh! What about that smart guy? They say they're over fifteen inches in length."

"You leave tracks that damn big!"

"Not in the woods I don't!"

Jake just stares deep into the forest and then smiles, "Let's go and pick up a few cans of spam and beans, a couple of blankets, a poncho and bring some mosquito repellant."

"Look, why don't you spend the night by yourself, being that you spent all that time in the jungles of Vietnam, and I'll sleep in the car?"

Jake laughs, "It's funny you should mention that; I saw this horror film the other night and this screwed up looking creature killed the one that was waiting in the car and left the one sleeping in the woods alone, because he was too busy eating the poor bastard in the car. So, are you sure you wanna stay next to the road in the car?"

"Who the hell said anything about parking it here? I was talking about leaving it parked back at the motel."

"I spent five days in the jungle with thousands of gooks looking for me and I never batted an eye. Did I ever tell you the story about Carla Longmire in the nineth grade?"

"Yes, two hundred times. It's times like this that I sure miss Carlos. We could make our escape while it's eating his Mexican ass."

"Yeah, I know what you mean. Let's go, I'm getting bored."

CHAPTER 8

Later that evening the sheriff shows them the crime scene. Jake, wearing his black combat fatigues with his gold shield hooked to his belt, black T-shirt with his brown shoulder holster sporting his polished 1911 460 Rowland resting in it, walks around the area and sees a few burnt spots. He leans over and puts his finger on the ground.

"This is where our monster burnt the girls' clothing to prevent any DNA from being found. Of course, we all know from every horror flick we've ever seen, a monster or ghost doesn't give a shit about DNA, he normally leaves slaver and teeth marks on the victim's ass, so like I have already mention in past conversations, it's a man we're looking for and a smart one at that."

The Sheriff, "Well, what's next lieutenant?"

"Who found the bodies?'

"Some anonymous caller called in on all three. Gave us the directions and it lead us right here."

"What's that bad odor I smell?"

"They say it's Dragon's Breath. It gets worse the further you get into the woods."

"I think I know that odor but can't put my finger on it. Well, you can go back to town for now. Sergeant Williams and I will stay here and look around the area for more evidence."

Sheriff, "Well if you need me for anything just call me." He walks down a path to where the cars are parked.

Jake turns to Theo, "Must have rain after the third victim was found. No tracks. Even the foot prints the officers left are gone."

They stroll back to the car as Theo gives him that look, "What do we do from here?"

Jake opens the car door and takes a folder from the seat. He lays it up on the car hood and starts reading.

"Did you hear me, Jake! And why are we dressed in black fatigues?"

"Look Theo, we're in the country now and I don't want us to stick out like a queer at a K.K.K. rally."

Theo, "I haven't seen anyone wearing black combat fatigues. We should be wearing blue jeans and shirts with sleeves cut off and spitting chewing tobaccer on the ground. And how can you tell if he's queer at a KKK rally if they're all wearing sheets?"

"He will be the one with the oversized hole cut in the mouth of the hood. We're wearing fatigues because you and I are going camping. Wow whoever wrote this report is worse than I am, and the pictures must have been taken with a cellphone. They're out of focus too."

Theo asks, "What did I say about that camping shit?"

"I wanna see what's out there. Been a long time since I've camped out."

"If you're having second thoughts, feel free to call it off."

"Can't do it Theo, I wanna find this myth and prove to the people they're full of shit."

Theo reaches over and grabs the folder, "Let me see those photos." He scans through the pictures, "I see naked girls with strangle marks and blood between their legs. Well, case solved, so let's forget all this camping shit you been speaking of and go home."

"This is gonna happen Theo. We need to check out these woods and see what we can find."

"What if we get lost?"

"Oh, I know my way around the woods my friend."

"Damn you, it's spooky as hell out there and after seeing those pictures, I say we don't, and tell them we did."

Jake laughs as he thinks of something funny. Theo laughs also not knowing why Jake was laughing, so he asks, "Okay, you're laughing; what's so funny?"

"I was thinking about when I was a kid and would stay up and watch those horror films late at night and after everyone went to sleep, I would get my little Swiss-made army knife and sneak outside in the dark and go looking in the woods behind the house hunting for a monster to kill."

Theo just stares and shakes his head, "Damn! You were one disturbed little shit. I remember staying up one night after watching *Dracula's search for Blood* and before I went to sleep, I hung Garlic, crucifix and towel around my neck to keep him from getting his fangs into me."

Jake lets out a chuckle, "Did it work?"

"I woke up the next morning smelling like an Italian salad and the towel got hung up on the bedpost and I damn near hung myself jumping off the top bunk, but on the lighter side, Dracula didn't get his fangs into me."

Jake starts laughing and decides it was time to screw with him, so he asked, "Hey Theo, what was the worse looking monster you ever saw in a movie?"

"I guess it would have been…wait a damn minute; I know what you're trying to do here, and it won't work, or will it?"

"I have no idea what you're talking about. We were talking about horror films, and I was just wondering what creature you thought was the most horrible looking creature of all time."

"Screw you, I'm not even going there."

"I always thought, '*Pumpkin head* was the worst, or maybe it was *Raw Head Rex* or maybe that deformed bear in *Prophecy* or…or… that damn creature from *Jeepers Creepers*…"

Theo sticks his fingers in his ears and yells, "Nan, nan, nan, nan…can't hear you!"

"Okay, no more talk of monsters."

Theo takes his fingers from his ears and says, "You know better than to talk that shit before we go on a camping trip."

"I'm sorry." Silence comes for a few minutes when Jake slowly turns, "That creature in *'Aliens'* was pretty damn scary."

"That did it; take me back to the motel!!"

"Okay, I promise no more about 'you know what.'"

They step from the vehicle and Theo stretches his arms back over his head, "Pop the trunk, my little cracker."

Jake shakes his head as he opens the trunk, "I can't believe you packed all that shit. All you need is your pistol, a knife, poncho, and a can of beans."

"I only brought the bare necessities."

"Is that right? You brought a three hundred dollar sleeping bag, a one-hundred-dollar tent, twenty-two banana creampuffs all on the town of Fairmont's credit card, and why are you grabbing Big Bertha?"

Theo interrupts, "Twenty Jake! And if I gotta go in there I want a whole lot of fire power."

"You ate two before you left the store smartass, and you brought ten rolls of toilet paper. You got the shits? Leave Bertha here, she needs her rest, and her weight alone will have you bitching in an hour."

Theo places Bertha back in the trunk and interrupts again, "I like my ass clean. I'm not using a leaf. I had an uncle who wiped his ass with poison ivy by accident. Do you know how hard it is to scratch your rectum?"

"You have the most dumb-ass relatives. Now as I was saying, you brought six of those fire logs. Now how stupid is that? We're in the woods; all you need to do is gather some sticks and logs. The shit is lying around everywhere."

"I'm not stomping around in the dark with a ten-foot-tall creature looking for a quick meal."

"Look Theo, even if this creature did exist, you wouldn't be a quick meal."

"You will appreciate all this fat if we get a hard freeze tonight."

"It's mid-June and even if it was the dead of winter how will you being fat benefit me?"

"You can cut me open and crawl inside to get warm like they do in the movies."

"Yeah, that'll work; digested creampuffs and gas should keep me alive." Jake reaches in the trunk and pulls out a large skillet. "What's this for?"

"So, I can fry my bacon and eggs. Go ahead Jake, make fun of me all you want. I came prepared."

"I hope you brought a mule to carry all that shit, because I'm not helping you drag that crap through the woods."

"Good!! You can eat those two small cans of pork & beans, while I lay out a spread fit for a king."

Jake grabs his tiny backpack and grabs the bag of creampuffs. "I'll carry the creampuffs for you. That will take some of the burden off your lazy ass." He takes off through the woods.

Theo throws a large duffle bag over his back and stuffs the rest under his arms and yells, "Wait up!! I can carry my own food. You can carry my sleeping bag, tent, skillet and eating utensils ... "

Three hours later and a few miles deeper in the woods, Jake comes to a stop in a small clearing near a creek and throws his blanket and backpack down near a large oak log. He scans the forest, then takes a seat on the ground and leans against the log and closes his eyes for a quick nap.

An hour later he could hear Theo yelling, "Hey Jake!! I'm lost!"
With out opening his eyes, "Hey, follow my voice!!"

A few minutes later Theo came staggering into the campsite carrying his tent, one roll of toilet paper and his rolled up sleeping bag. He was pouring sweat and could hardly catch his breath. He throws the stuff on the ground and falls out flat on his belly. "Good thing you left those creampuffs crumbs to show me the way."

"You picked them up off the ground and brushed the ants off and ate them, didn't you?"

Theo, "Yep…. I thought for sure that when I went to homicide, I would just be sitting around eating creampuffs, drinking coffee, watching porn on my PC and shooting the shit at my desk."

Jake opens one eye, "That's all you did do until you met me. Where's the skillet and the other rolls of toilet paper?"

"Somewhere back on the trail right next to those fire logs. Shit gets heavy when you walk that far. This is why I can't play the part of a native in a Tarzan movie. Let that lazy ass, white hunter carry his own shit."

Jake snickers and closes his eyes, "You're a real outdoorsman."

"I never said I was an outdoorsman. I'm a city boy. The closest thing to the woods for me is walking Donna through the park and if it wasn't for her, I would manage to get lost then." He drags himself over next to Jake. "Why so far? A few hundred yards from the crime scene would have been sufficient. Now what if we need to flee back to the car quickly?"

"I wanted to get the feel of things. Be in harmony with my surroundings."

"You're gonna look mighty stupid when that harmony tries to eat our asses. And that brings up another question. Why didn't you let me bring old Bertha? We might need that bitch encase our pistols don't bring him down."

"Don't call her a bitch! There is nothing to fear but fear itself."

"You are so full of crap." Theo looks into the sky, "Looks like it may rain tonight. Good thing I brought the tent…hellooo, you hear me, Jake? A tent!"

"You candy ass. I can make a rain cover out of pine needles, that's better than that nylon piece of shit you have there. I have never seen a tent that didn't leak."

"The man at the camping store said he guaranteed it not to leak."

He looks around and asks, "Where's the firewood?"

"What firewood?"

"The firewood you were supposed to gather while I was chopping my way through the forest like little black riding hood."

"When you're in the woods, you sleep in total darkness. And I thought you were bringing your own fire logs?"

"Oh my God! For the third time, I unloaded the fire logs two miles ago and here's a million-dollar question, why would you sleep in total darkness?"

"So no one can sneak up on us."

"What if this creature has night vision?"

Jake chuckles, "Like that Monster in, *It crawls in the night*?

"Don't start that shit again, and I mean that. But what if he has night vision?"

"Then you're screwed! Look Theo, there is no creature. The people in this county including horny and crazy old lady Harper are full of shit. And now that I brought the subject up; how was that lip lock she planted on you?"

"Gross! If that witch had slipped me the tongue, I would have had you run me over with the car. I do know one thing...if I had not let you talk me into this trip, my ass would be planted between Donna's legs right now." He leans back on a fallen tree, "I think I'll catch me about forty winks and when I awaken, I'm building that damn fire."

"If you want a fire, you better gather the wood. It will be dark in an hour."

Theo leans back resting his head on a small limb sticking out from a downed tree. "I'm just gonna take a short nap before dark. I need to catch my breath." He closes his eyes and drifts off.

Two hours later Theo opens his eyes only to stare into darkness in every direction. Jake had a flashlight pen stuck between his teeth going through photographs and other paperwork pertaining to the homicides.

Theo yells, "What the hell, you let me oversleep!"

"So?"

"So now I have to gather firewood and then set my tent up in the dark."

"I told you to do that shit before you took a nap."

One hour later, the whole area around them was absent of any and every small branch. Theo is rubbing two sticks together trying to start a fire over some dried branches and straw he had gathered. He gets frustrated and throws the two sticks down. "What kind of asshole came up with this shit?"

Jake, still studying the paperwork says without glancing over, "Most likely the same asshole that forgot to bring matches. You should have left that camping shit and brought a box." Jake reaches into his pocket and throws a Bic lighter at him. "Here, try this."

Theo gives him a menacing stare and grits his teeth, "You had that lighter the whole time I was rubbing two damn sticks together like some village idiot?"

"Of course, you don't think I rub two sticks together to light my cigars, do ya? And I was having too much fun watching you. From this angle it looked like you were beating your little black baby thumb." Jake grins and continues to read over the reports.

Twenty minutes later Theo was sitting near the fire struggling with the tent. He throws the small aluminum rods down on the ground, "You just gonna sit there while I struggle to put our shelter together?"

"You mean your shelter. If I needed a tent, I would have brought one. I was just thinking about these photos. These girls were raped and strangled somewhere else. The ground around the bodies wasn't disturbed. If they had been strangled there would have been some evidence of a struggle."

"Maybe he doped them up and you did say it rained the night before."

"Wow, sometimes you can hit the nail right on the head."

"Look, in a few hours the bottom is going to fall out of the sky, and I slapped a mosquito a few minutes ago and that bitch could have stood flat footed and raped a turkey."

"I'm sitting here looking at these photos and I'm getting that feeling again. I would say these girls knew who their killer was. Someone they trusted."

"Well, it's not you. Damn you Jake, I'm serious, I need help here."

Another hour goes by and Theo's biting into a banana creampuff and Jake's using his knife to rake the last few beans from a can.

"Hey Theo?"

"If it has anything to do with horror films, I'm not listening."

"No, seriously, why do they call it Pork & Beans when I can't find the pork?"

Theo rubs his belly and says with a smile, "I have no idea, but when we get back to Mobile, I will open a full investigation into it. Thanks for helping with the tent. I knew when I saw more than three pieces I was lost."

"You're welcome. Next time I tell you to travel light you listen to me. You do know that those creampuffs you have smeared all over your face will attract every ant in the forest for ten miles?"

Theo takes a deep breath, "Ants I can handle, but you were right, it is kind of quite out here. I feel like I'm one with nature." Suddenly a loud screeching noise can be heard coming from the darkness.

Theo yells, "What the hell!?"

Jake says, as he tries to stab the last bean running around the bottom of the tin can, avoiding the point of his large Bowie knife, "That sounded like a male owl's mating call."

Theo snaps back, "Sounds like he's the one getting it up the ass too me."

It gets quiet again when suddenly a loud scratching sound comes from the darkness.

Theo, in a loud whisper asks, "What the hell was that?"

Jake replies, "That sounded like a raccoon scratching for grubworms."

"Sounds like he found one." He tries to swallow the lump in his throat, glancing in every direction when another loud noise comes from the woods.

"Okay, now what was that? And don't tell me its two squirrels humping."

"That's a big buck, sharpening his horns on a tree, getting ready to whip some ass over some deer pudding."

"I thought they did that shit in the winter."

"Just guessing Shadow."

Then a loud moaning noise can be heard in the distance. Again, Theo gets a scared look in his eyes, "Tell me that's a possum whacking himself off."

"Nope, I have no idea what that was. Sounded like Pumpkin head coming this way."

Theo reaches over and grabs his 9mm lying next to his sleeping bag. "If he so much as takes a step into this camp, I will shoot his ass full of holes."

"Yea, like that 9mm is gonna stop Pumpkin head."

"Oh, when they fine my dead haft eaten ass, they gonna find an empty gun and empty clips."

"Just lean back and relax Theo. Here, occupy your mind and have a look at the murder victims and tell me what you think."

"You must have lost your freaking mind. That's all I need to do right now is look at that stuff." Theo stands, grabs his pistol and a roll of toilet paper and walks a few yards.

Jake glances over and asks, "Where the hell do you think you're going?"

"I'm through processing those creampuffs and I'm gonna check the results out, if it's alright with you, and I don't need the lab to check it."

"The hell you say. You're not going to have the campsite stinking of banana shit."

"Well, I'm not going to take a dump out there."

Jake holds his finger up and checks the direction of the cool breeze. Go fifty yards south of here. Call me if you see that bear from, '***Prophecy***.'"

Theo hesitates and slowly starts walking in that direction. He yells, "Which way is south and is this far enough?"

"Nope, further than that!" Theo walks twenty more yards, stops and checks the ground out before seeing a pine stump.

"Just right." He looks in every direction before pulling his pants down and then his briefs. He places his pistol near the stump and begins his journey into the land of relief. "I sure wish I have brought a newspaper."

Back at camp Jake takes a sniff of the air and smells a strong odor, "Asshole didn't go far enough." He then takes notice that the odor wasn't coming from Theo. It was the odor of someone who hasn't had a bath in a long time.

Theo was still using the bathroom and looking in every direction when the odor struck his nose. "Wow!! Those creampuffs sure took on a personality of their own." He hears breaking branches and someone or something walking on dry leaves. He fires up Jake's lighter.

He turns around and glances toward the campsite, "Jake! Is that you? This is not funny, so stop trying to scare me!" He glances back into the darkness and sees nothing. "Okay Jake, if you don't say something right now, I'm going back to Mobile." Still, he sees nothing. He stands with his pants around his ankles, looks over a bush and tries to see into the camp. He turns around to stare into the woods and suddenly he's facing a creature so large and repulsive that he becomes speechless. The lighter gave a glow to the large creature. The size of the thing is enormous, and it was wearing worn out coveralls with no shirt. Its skin was a two-tone brown with a pink tint to it. It had no ears, green teeth and druid was pouring from the corner of its mouth. Theo froze for a few seconds then stumbled back over the stump. He tried to scream but only made the Lou Costello sound.

Back in front of the fire, Jake was puzzled over the strong odor and says to himself out loud, "That old lady wasn't kidding about the smell." Suddenly shots are fired, not one or two, but fourteen shots.

Theo comes hopping back into camp as fast as he can with his pants and underwear still down around his ankles.

He fell flat on his face twice before looking up and yelling, "Oh my God Jake, I just came face to face with Pumpkin head!! He was ten feet tall, five hundred pounds and had three-inch fangs. It had no ears and smelled of raw eggs or something!!"

Jake starts laughing as Theo drags himself over to the log. Jake, still laughing, stands and walks out into the woods, but Theo sees that he has forgotten his gun. "Have you lost your mind?" He quickly pulls his pants up and slowly walks to the edge of the woods as Jake disappeared into the night. He yells in a loud whisper, "Jake, come back! Jake, come back!" Theo thinks really hard, "**Shane**." He comes back to his senses, "Jake, you forgot your gun!! Hey, if you run across my 9mm and a roll of toilet paper, it belongs to me!"

Ten minutes later Jake comes walking back into camp with a 9mm in hand. Theo's almost sitting in the fire with Jake's 460 Rowland cocked back. Jake takes his pistol and hands him his.

Theo watches as Jake just sat back down and leaned against the log. "Well? Did you get a glimpse of the ugly bastard?"

"All I found was your pistol, a pine tree with a whole bunch of holes in it and a huge pile of stinking shit next to a stump. The roll of toilet paper is missing though."

"I'm telling the truth; it was standing there ready to rip me into chunks of food! It was the devil himself I tell ya! Its eyes were all bloodshot and its pupils glowed like fire in the night. The smell, it was just like old lady Harper said."

"That old lady has you seeing things."

Theo slides over toward him, "I saw it, I tell you. It had no ears and if it wasn't for my quick thinking, I wouldn't be here right now to tell the story."

"Yeah, now that you mention it, I think I did catch some of your cat-like reflexes especially when you came hopping in here with your pants and underwear around your ankles."

"Make fun all you want. In the morning I'm heading back to Mobile."

"What about the homicides?"

"This killer isn't human. This a job for Van Helsing, not two lazy ass cops out of shape and worn out."

"You listen to me, and you listen well; it's a human we're after. A low life murdering son-of-a-bitch that will bleed like any other man. He's most likely staring at us at this very moment. This campfire has our faces glowing like two full moons, so take your black ass back to Mobile and into the safety of your wife's arms. I was doing this shit long before you came along. I fear no man or monster and if it's the devil, then so be it. I've been battling that bastard all my life."

Theo, with a sad look, "You have no right to talk to me like that. I've stayed with you through some bad shit over the years and not once have I ever let you down. Now I can stand toe to toe with any man, but this thing isn't human. And at least I have a wife to go home to."

Jake clams up and turns the other way. Theo thinks about what he said for a second, "I'm sorry for that last remark. That was totally uncalled for and I'm not sure I can even go home to mine."

"You're right, when it comes to relationships, I suck. I want you to think about something."

"What's that?"

"I don't have the luxury of leaving when I want. I have a job to do and it's the only job I know how to do. Being a car salesman with my foul langue and temper is out of the question. It's not about the two hundred grand; it's about stopping the killer before he takes somebody else's child. I say bring it on." He stands and walks to the edge of the woods and yells at the top of his lungs, "Screw you!! I'm coming after you, you foul smelling piece of murdering shit!!"

Theo walks up behind him and places his hand on his shoulder, "Okay, I'll stay, but do you have to piss it off?"

"I want the killer to make just one small mistake and I will be on him like stink on shit or in your case, shit on a stump."

They start laughing as he rubs Jake's neck, "I'm going to crawl in my tent and sleep good knowing I have the great Jake O'Malley on my side. Super Jake!! Able to slap a crooked politician without bending his elbow, able to spit into the devil's eyes and able to call and get an extra month on his cable bill and…"

Jake interrupts, "Okay, I get it. Go crawl in your hundred-dollar tent, your three hundred dollar sleeping bag and rest that five-dollar ass of yours."

Theo smiles and walks away, but stops and turns, "If you decided you wanna sleep in the tent, knock first because I'm a light sleeper and my gun will be cocked."

"Light sleeper my ass!"

CHAPTER 9

The fire had burned down to smothering amber and Jake had not been asleep for more than an hour when he was awakened by the sound of smacking and mumbling coming from the tent.

"That asshole will eat every one of those creampuffs." He quietly and slowly throws his dark green poncho over to the side and taking easy steps, works himself over to the entrance of the flapping doorway of the tent. Easing the flap back, and with the help of the moonlight, he peeks inside, only to find a small black bear straddling Theo. The dark hairy beast was licking tasty creampuff crumbs from his face as Theo mumbled, "Who's your daddy baby…oh yeah, treat daddy bad…you go girl…what a freaking tongue you have sweetie."

Jake, in a loud whisper, "Psst…psst…Theo, wake up, that's not Donna, you three-hundred-pound stick of butter."

Theo laughs in his sleep as the bear kept licking away at the yummy sugar treats scattered over his face.

Suddenly, Theo opens an eye and sees the bear's tongue lashing out with a river of druid dripping on his cheeks. He freezes, and in a low girly whisper says, "Oh shit!"

Jake, again in a loud whisper, "Don't move a muscle. This is one of those times you just close your eyes and let Mother Nature finish what the bitch is doing."

He thought the situation over and gently places the flap back over the opening and walks backwards coming to rest near his poncho. He changes to the backside of the log and mumbles as he pulls his poncho back over his head, "Stupid ass, serves him right for not cleaning his face." He could hear Theo's heavy breathing and could swear he could hear his heart beating rapidly. Jake closes his eyes.

Thirty minutes later the bear walks from the tent and into the woods. Seconds later Theo comes running from the tent firing a blast of fourteen rounds from his 9mm into the night.

Jake starts laughing and peeks over the log, "It's okay, he's gone."

Theo, almost in tears and in a broken voice, "You son-of-a-bitch; you were just gonna let him eat me!!"

"That's not true. I knew he would leave once he had finished licking all that sugar from your face and I also knew when he left, you were coming out of that tent shooting everything in sight. That was why I got on the outside of this log...so funny. Your eyeballs looked like two cueballs. You know something; you have used more ammunition on this camping trip than thirty hunters in the first month of hunting season."

Theo fires back, "I'll never get back to sleep now. My blood pressure is maxed out." He pops another clip in the grip of his pistol and backs into the tent mumbling, "Some damn guard you are. You let that big bastard slip right in on top of me. What a damn night this has turned out to be. I'm surprise that bastard didn't rape my black ass. What else could possibly go wrong?" He zips the front of the tent up.

Ten minutes later they're in a downpour. Jake looking from under the poncho and could barely see the tent but could hear Theo inside bitching about the leaks dripping from every corner. Suddenly Theo comes running out, dragging his sleeping bag behind him. He yells, "Make room for me under that poncho!"

Jake could not hold it in and broke out in laughter as Theo made his way partially under the poncho.

Theo frowns, "You're enjoying all this aren't you?"

Jake lays his head back down, "And to think I wanted to go to Disney World this year. You just back that fat black ass right up against old Jakey poo and no spooning!"

The next morning, Jake throws the poncho to the side, sits up and stretches his arms over his head. There scrunched up behind him was Theo, snoring away all cozy in his sleeping bag.

He shakes his head, "So sleeping beauty finally fell asleep." He starts to stand as the sun raked through the dense pine forest when he notices something moving in the sleeping bag between Theo's legs. "You dog you. Now I wonder what my fat jungle bunny is dreaming about." Suddenly the expression left his face. He slowly eases his large bowie knife from the sheath. Theo grunts and opens his eyes only to find Jake standing over him with his large knife in hand.

"Good morning, Jake, now what are you going to do with that?"

"Don't move. I'm going to slowly cut your sleeping bag open."

"The hell you say! You're not going to cut my three hundred dollar sleeping bag open. I can use the zipper."

"I said don't move a muscle. Unless your little black nub grew five feet last night, and I know for a fact it didn't, you have a bed partner."

"Have you lost your mind?"

"Shut the hell up and don't move a muscle! A snake crawled in your bag sometime this morning."

Theo freezes again. Jake slowly and gently cuts the bag with the razor edge of the knife.

Theo whispers, "Just stab the bastard, please!"

"I can't; I might miss and hit your wee little toothpick."

"Okay, new plan; just leave me here until he dies of old age."

"If you keep talking, he's gonna sink those fangs right into your Velcro nut sack."

Jake is cutting a foot-long slit when he suddenly hears the snake's tail start to rattle.

Theo, not moving a muscle whispers, "I think he's really pissed."

Jake quickly reaches in and grabs it by the vibrating tail, pulls it out and slings it into the woods. Theo swallows the lump in his throat and passes out.

On the hike back to the car, Theo is bitching. "That was the worst night of my fucking life. Don't you ever talk me into going on another camping trip again."

"Stop your whining and look at the good side of it."

"Your ass can look from every damn angle, all year long and you won't find a good side to this crazy adventure."

"It can't get any worse Theo." About this time a skunk, forging for food, steps from the bushes.

Theo snickers, "Well would you look at that, a cat with a racing strip." He leans over to get a better look, "Here kitty, kitty, here kitty, kitty."

Jake yells, "Ok I know for a fact we saw a whole segment on the animal channel about skunks........Stop Theo!!"

He's too late. The skunk sprayed Theo all in the face. He falls back on the ground and yells, "Oh my God, it's in my eyes, nose and mouth."

LEE KOHN

Two hours later, Jake is pulling him with a twenty-foot piece of vine. Theo yells, "I think I can see now."

Jake drops his end, turns around with a piece of cloth stuffed in each nostril and says, "Told you your vision would come back."

Theo spots the car and yells, "Thank you God."

Before loading the car, Jake says, "We need to go into town and start asking some questions."

"Screw you! I'm going back to the motel; take some valium and several shots of that whiskey you brought and wash this smell off."

"It won't work."

"The hell you say, if I drink enough, it will."

"That's not what I'm talking about. That skunk smell, won't wash off."

"Now what the hell are you talking about?"

"Skunk juice won't wash off; you have to let it wear off."

"How long does it take to wear off?"

"About two or three days."

"I'm gonna sleep that long in the safety of a damn comfortable bed. I will see you at lunch three days from now."

"The hell you say. You're not going to stink up the motel room. I might have to let you ride in the trunk. I bet that crazy old lady knows how to get the smell off."

"She's not licking it off, I can grant you that."

"You hold your face out the window."

Minutes later they came driving up to old lady Harper's shack with Theo still hanging his head out the window.

Theo glances across the yard and sees so many cats running around; it looked like Grand Central Station for felines. The old lady was rocking away on the porch.

Theo shakes his head back and forth, "That crazy woman hasn't moved from that spot since yesterday."

Jake rubs his chin with his index and thumb and responds, "Yeah, but I bet that crazy bitch knows how to get skunk juice off."

"I think I can take a shower at the motel and do the same damn thing."

They exit the car and walk across the yard.

Jake yells, "Mrs. Harper, it's Lieutenant O'Malley again!"

She yells back, "You bring that negro back with you!?"

68

"Yes, I did, and I need to see if you know how to get skunk juice off."

"Is he gonna rape me!?"

Theo throws his hands up, "You freakin wish!"

Jake snickers, "No sugar, I had a long talk with him, and he says that he has changed his ways!"

Theo gives him a look, "I am not believing this crap."

Jake, with a grin, "Shut up, I'm just humoring the old bitch." He yells as they walked up on the porch, "We just need to get the smell off of him!"

"Lye Lax, tomato juice and vinegar should take care of it. I have a big washing pan outside. We'll fill it with creek water if he can stand the cold."

Theo gives Jake a look, "I'm calling Donna to come get me. I have had enough."

"Just try it. I'll pick you up at lunch and we'll start questioning some folks."

"You're really gonna leave me here with her?"

"It's just for two hours. You'll be back to normal in no time."

"After last night, I will never be normal again, and after lunch, I'm going home. I think I can just wash my face myself."

CHAPTER 10

They're sitting at a local dinner on the main street that runs through the center of town not saying a word to each other.

Jake is quietly slumped over the table with coffee in one hand and the homicide folders in the other. He just sits there staring at the crime scene photos. Theo is so angry he's steaming from the ears. Jake says without taking his eyes off the report, "You know I can feel that angry stare. It wasn't that bad."

"Screw you. I smell like a salad or a douche bag."

"Smells better than skunk juice."

"I'm still debating that one. That horny old woman poured that ice cold water over my head, and I almost went into cardiac arrest. My nipples could have cut a diamond in haft. For somebody that hates blacks she sure took pride in washing me. She kept pretending to slip and touch my man tool, and I kept explaining to her that I wasn't sprayed that far down."

"You should be grateful that anyone would touch your man tool." Jake turns the folders around and asks, "You notice anything about these photographs?"

"Yep, everybody in 'em is dead."

"Look closely. The killer went to a lot of trouble to make them look comfortable. None of the bodies have been lying there long enough to start decomposing. Did you notice on the date the doctor placed the killings?"

"Not really."

"All three were killed on a full moon like I jokingly mentioned to Ray."

"Just tell me what you're trying to say and stop beating around the bush."

"In each case, an anonymous caller called from a payphone and gave the police the exact location of the bodies. This report says the same dispatcher took all three calls and she stated it sounded like the same person all three times."

"So?"

"So, I'm pretty sure the killer called it in so the bodies would be found before any animals got to them. He cared about his victims or he's bragging. It's going to be a local and a local these girls trusted enough to get in a vehicle with or he's baiting them."

"Where do we go from here?"

"You take the car, go to the courthouse and get a list of all the registered voters in the county, and we'll start from there."

"What if the killer doesn't vote?"

"The killer votes, trust me on this."

"I say the monster who paid me a visit last night is the killer. The three victims were all found a thousand feet from the road. It must be him."

"Listen to yourself. A monster doesn't use a phone or burn clothes up. What you saw last night was a figment of your imagination planted in that head of yours by a bunch of country bumpkins who are so bored out of their gourd that they make stories up to amuse themselves."

"I know what I saw last night and ain't nothing going to change my mind about it."

"You used the word 'ain't' in a sentence."

"Let me get this straight. First, three cops called me names and tried to shoot me over banana creampuffs; a crazy, ugly-ass old lady tries to clean my tonsils with a snuff covered tongue; a monster standing ten feet tall, no hair, no ears, pinkish-colored skin, glowing eyes and with green fangs attempts to kill me while I'm taking a dump."

Jake starts to say something when Theo holds his finger up, "I'm not through yet. A four-hundred-pound black bear tried to eat my lips off; a six-foot rattlesnake took a nap between my legs and a cat with a racing stripe sprayed me in the face with some toxic shit and I took a vinegar bath in ice water, and all you can say is my grammars bad? Hey Jake, check this grammar out......fuck you!"

"Not just your grammar, but you distort everything that has happened to you over the last twenty-four hours."

"How in the hell can anyone distort the chain of events that I just described to you!?"

"Okay, listen and listen closely. It was only two cops who tried to shoot you, not three, and it was over three banana creampuffs, not one. Old lady Harper wasn't quick enough to get her tongue in your mouth, the so-called monster that I never saw was most likely a shadow of a pine tree being cast from my lighter that you have managed to keep, playing tricks on your imagination; the bear was just a young cub around two hundred pounds, not four hundred; it was a four-foot rattlesnake, not six, and skunk juice isn't toxic. And did you hear me when I said 'isn't' not 'ain't toxic."

"What about the ice-cold bath with Ms. Harper washing my penis?"

"Now I have to agree with you on that, that was just all wrong."

"I've noticed something about you, smartass that I've never thought about until now."

"And what's that?"

"You are hell with those numbers. I mean you caught every word I said. I bet those numbers would sound a lot different if all that shit happened to you! And another thing, big shot."

Jake quickly interrupts, "Go ahead, unload. Release all that built up anger."

"How am I supposed to check past records on that many people?"

"There's ten people live in the county, so just for now, check only males between the ages of twenty-one and seventy."

"There's several thousand in this county, but thanks for narrowing that down for me. Anything else you want me to do?"

"Yeah Theo, when you get the names, call Donna and have her come get you. Go back to our office and run the names on our database. I don't want anyone up here to know what we are doing."

"You mean that? I can go back?"

"Yeah, I can handle this myself."

"You could have told me that when I packed in Mobile. Are you doing this because you feel sorry for me?"

"Nope, I'm doing it because I'm pretty sure the computers up here run off diesel power. Get packing, I'm going to walk around a little, take in the sites and ask some questions. Then I'm going to see our Sheriff Ray and the city council and ask them some questions."

"If I leave, who's going to back you up?"

"I am my own backup. I want you back here in five days with all that info.

Theo looks up and says in a loud voice, "Thank you God!!"

Hours later, after leaving Theo at the motel, Jake is strolling down the sidewalk checking out some of the old historical buildings when he stops by a barber's shop with a large front-glassed window and a barber's pole rotating next to the door. He steps inside and finds ten older men sitting around in the chairs against the wall talking about the weather and their crops. There was a young thin man wearing a deputy's uniform playing checkers with a large man in overalls. The Deputy is sporting eyebrows that seem to start at one ear and travel across the forehead to the other without a break.

The deputy had a look of anger, caused by two evil eyes with the whites showing all around the pupils. Nobody was sitting in the barber's chairs. A man in his late fifties wearing a white coat stood and said, "Can I help you stranger?"

"I need a trim over the ears and around the back of the neck. Leave my ponytail as it is."

"Well, have a seat in one of them there chairs." He points to one of the four empty chairs. Jake takes a seat and with a smile says, "Nice little town y'all have up here."

The barber, "We like it."

Everybody just stared at him as the barber wrapped a large striped cloth over his shoulders and around his neck and pinned it very tight. So tight that he turns to the barber, "You're cutting off my air supply, do you mind?"

The barber, sporting a full head of gray hair asks, "You wanna shave?"

"Like I want a stranger holding a straight razor to my throat."

The barber, "What brings you to Fairmont?"

Jake replies, "The beaches." Not understanding, everyone just stared.

The deputy yells across the room, "We don't have any damn beaches around here, just corn, pecan orchards and soybean fields."

Jake grins, "I know, that was the joke, but I knew when I said it, it was way over y'all's head."

The deputy snarls and gives him a look, "That was a piss-poor joke stranger."

Jake lets out a snicker, "Yeah, I figured there wasn't a lot of humor up here. I have another that's gonna change those sourpuss expressions on your faces. This white man walks into a store that sells sex toys and says, 'I would like to buy a blow-up sex doll please'. The clerk asks, 'male or female?' The man gives him a funny look and says, 'Female, of course.' The clerk asks, 'white or black?' the man says, 'white, naturally.' The clerk asks, 'Christian or Muslim?' The man asks, 'what has religion got to do with it?' The clerk answers, 'Well, the Muslim blows itself up.''

No one says a word. The deputy stands and walks over to where Jake was sitting, "Don't understand whatcha mean by all that."

Jake laughs, "Easy enough. It means you don't have to blow the doll up because it's Muslim; it blows itself up. You know, the Muslims always blowing themselves up and..." He looks around the room, "What, you people don't get news on the radio up here?"

The deputy asks, "Whatta mean 'you people'?"

Jake, with a grin, "You sound like my partner, but now that you have managed to piss me off, I meant, you people, as in you dumb ass redneck people who live up here."

"I don't like you stranger; you talk funny."

"Then I must talk like you look. If I knew y'all were that stupid up here I wouldn't have used any words over four letters. Now, do I need a freakin translator?"

The deputy places his hand on the walnut grips of his 357 and says, "You have worn out your welcome here boy."

Jake loses his smile. "You pull that pistol … boy … you better use it."

"Oh, don't you worry, if I pull it, I'll use it."

Jake smiles again, "Look, maybe we got off on the wrong foot here. I'm Jake O'Malley and I would like to ask some questions about the three girls y'all found murdered."

Everyone's faces went blank.

The deputy asks, "Whatta you know about the murders stranger?"

"I'm not a stranger anymore. I just said my name was Jake O'Malley and I know that the girls were young, pretty, honor-roll students and were found naked in your so-called haunted forest."

"Now, how would a stranger know that unless he was involved?"

"I am involved. Look cowboy, you don't understand, I'm a…"

The deputy interrupts, "I don't know who you are, or where you're from, but I'll tell you what you just became …. my number one suspect."

Jake laughs, "Talking to you is a lot like talking to a retarded ass spider monkey."

The young deputy pulls his pistol and points it between Jake's eyes. "Let's walk right out that door and over to my police unit. The sheriff's gonna wanna have a word with you."

Jake shakes his head, "Look asshole, if you don't put that away, I'm gonna throw you through the plate glass window."

"You ain't throwing anybody anywhere. Now move your ass boy."

Jake smiles, "Okay, whatever you say."

Seconds later, the deputy goes flying through the front glass window and onto the sidewalk. Jake walks outside with the officer's pistol in hand and snatches the striped cloth from around his neck. He turns to the crowd that had smiles across their faces and throws the pistol on the sidewalk.

74

He leans over the officer lying on the sidewalk, "If I find out that you caused that barber to gap my hair, I will find you and shove corn and soybean so far up your rectum you'll think your ass is a vegetable garden."

The deputy looks up at him from the concrete sidewalk, "That hurt you sons-a-bitch!"

Jake reaches out a hand to help him up. The young deputy shied away, "I don't need any help from you."

Jake nods, "You better take my hand, moron, no sense in you standing on your own when I'm just gonna knock your ass back down for calling me a sons-a-bitch. I'm Lieutenant Jake O'Malley asshole."

The deputy looks up at Jake, "What kind of police officer has a ponytail?"

"The kind that likes it."

An hour later he walks into city hall and is chewing on a short piece of unlit cigar. He walks up to the familiar old gray-haired woman sitting behind the desk and with that Jake grin says, "I'm here to see the town council."

"Well, you're in luck."

"And why is that?"

"They're having a meeting with the sheriff about some matters surrounding you and that 'negro' partner of yours."

"Look lady, he has a name. How would you like me to refer to you as that nagging old bitch? Now if you'll show me to the meeting hall."

"Did you see the no smoking sign as you came in the door?" "Sure did, and if you weren't so damn blind with bitterness, you would have noticed my cigar isn't lit. A little loophole in the no smoking ban I found in my spare time. You see, if it's not lit, well, that's a whole new program. The sign should have read, 'NO TOBACCO PRODUCT ALLOWED INSIDE BUILDING.'"

"That's very funny; third door on your right."

"You better be careful woman; a house may fall on your ass." He walked down the hallway and pulled his coat off and laid it on a chair just outside the room and was only wearing black slacks, a black Tshirt with his gun in his shoulder holster. He enters and discovers a large room filled to its capacity. Six council members, three men and three women are sitting behind a large oval table. The sheriff and the deputy who he put through the window are sitting to the left of the council members. He starts to take a seat when he notices a man in his fifties sitting in a wheelchair behind the table, waving for him to walk to the front.

He slowly makes his way down the aisle to the table and takes a chair on the opposite end to where the sheriff was sitting. The man wheels around the table and stops, "You must be Lieutenant O'Malley."

"Yep, did the shoulder holster give me away?"

"I'm Rodger Stillwell, the Mayor."

"You did it!!"

"Pardon me."

"I'm sorry; habit I guess."

"Can I continue?"

"It's your town."

"Can you tell us what happened this morning?"

"Sure, it all happened when I listened to a scarecrow and followed this yellow-brick road and…" He sees frozen faces on everyone and says, "What…y'all never saw the movie?"

The mayor chuckles a little, "I was talking about the incident that happened this morning."

Jake stares around the room and then says, "Well, I went into the barbershop over on main street to get a little trim over the ears, thinking I was in a friendly little town environment. I started to ask some simple questions when your deputy over there pulled a gun on me and…etc, etc. I threw his ass through the front window after forewarning him not to pull said gun in question. Total misunderstanding and I'll be glad to pay for the plate glass window."

"We're talking about the rape of old lady Harper."

Jake puzzled, "I'm sorry, what did you just say?"

"Old lady Harper filed a rape charge against your partner at eleven o'clock this morning."

"I'm sorry again, what did you just say?"

The sheriff stands, "You heard the man; he said old lady Harper filed a rape charge against your 'niggra' partner."

Jake pops back, "Call him that one more time and I'll put you through a glass window, and I'll throw you by the balls! Now somebody explain to me what's going on around here."

The mayor has the sheriff sit back down with a hand jester.

"Lieutenant, as I was trying to say, Thelma Harper came in a short while ago and filed a rape charge against your partner. She said he made her wash his private parts before dragging her into the bedroom and raping her for over two hours."

Jake is totally taken by surprise and glances around the room then asks, "Well I'll be a bear's left nut! Are you sure about that?"

The mayor continues, "Old lady Harper came here to the Sheriff's Office and signed a warrant out on one Sergeant Theodore Williams. She swore to an affidavit that he forced himself upon her and had sexual intercourse against her will."

Jake starts to laugh but could see that everyone was serious. "Y'all serious?"

"She's taking it serious."

Jake snaps back, "Are we talking about the same crazy old lady who lives out on route seven? And are we talking about the same Theodore Williams that I know for a fact wouldn't sexually assault anyone, especially her? I can show y'all several well-digested banana creampuffs on the ground at the end of her porch to prove it."

The mayor takes a piece of paper from the table, reads a few lines before pulling his glasses off, "I have her sworn written statement right here in my hand."

Jake quickly stands, "I don't give a fat rat's ass what you have in your hand; there's been a mistake. If anyone raped anybody it was the other way around. I can already see that we are going to have an interference in the investigation. My partner would not have taken a trip up here to help y'all, and then for some unknown reason rape a crazy, ugly ass old white lady."

The mayor continues, "She states in her affidavit she can identify Sgt. Williams..." He hesitates. "Your partner's private parts."

Jake gets into a laugh and responds, "She should be able too, because she washed it until it was as white as a piece of chalk. I can identify it also. It's about five inches long which, by the way, is a little short for a black man, and its black, but that doesn't mean he raped me. Y'all do know she's a mental case and blind right?"

The sheriff stands, "She can see images or blurs."

Jake responds, "So she was the one who took the pictures of the victims and that's a lot more than you're going to be able to see if you keep pushing me asshole. Now you say she can I.D. a man's penis from an image or a blur. Well, I guess y'all have an airtight case, you freakin idiots."

Mayor Stillwell smiles, "I can see you have a good sense of humor Lieutenant O'Malley."

"That's fixing to change real quick! .... Call me Jake."

Mayor Stillwell nods, "You can call me Rodger. I think we can put all this behind us and get on with matters at hand."

The sheriff stands and yells, "You can't do that! Ms. Harper filed a legitimate complaint against that nig'...uh...black man and it must be taken seriously."

Jake fires back, "You almost made a major boo boo.!"

Rodger turns to Sheriff Ray and gives him a stare, "Sit down, Ray, we have more important things to deal with than an old lady that would molest a rooster if she could catch it." He turns back to Jake and with a smile, "I must apologize for our sheriff's lack of corporation. We're a close-knit community and these horrible murders have us all feeling a little uneasy. I would also like to apologize for Deputy Miller's rude behavior an hour ago."

Jake nods, "That's alright mayor. I work better when there's a lot of controversy."

"Please call me Rodger."

"Okay Rodger."

"Jake, I believe I speak for the entire county when I say we're very grateful for your help and we appreciate the Mobile Police Department sending their finest. These murders have hit my wife and daughter very hard. You see, the girls belonged to the Fairmont High School Soccer team and my wife is the coach. She's on the verge of a nervous breakdown as we speak."

Jake glances around the room at all the blank faces, "My approach to crime is a little unorthodox, but I assure you that nothing in this world will take priority over finding the, excuse my language, the bastard that murdered these girls."

The sheriff stands, "Is that right? What were your priorities when you camped out in the woods last night?"

Jakes responded, "Now how did you know about that?"

"I heard it from the hardware store when your partner bought some camping supplies."

"Huh, and I thought that maybe you followed us. How about that...well anyway, I was convincing my partner and myself that this stupid-ass legend of a Dragon that you people have created in your mines, called a Dragon, was just a bad smell or just a way to keep us out of the woods."

Mumbling from everyone took over the large room.

Jake raises his hand, "Hold that thought and I'll explain. I don't believe in such shit. And let me tell you why. I've been hunting murdering monsters for many years and not once did any of them ever turn out to be a creature other than a perverted, greedy low life, piss-poor example of a pathetic human life form. So please excuse me if I don't take that monster and ghost shit too serious."

Rodger wheels back around the table to the center, "Say what you may, but most of the people in this county believe this Dragon exists. I'm not one of them, O'Malley, so whatever you need; please don't hesitate to ask for it."

Jake clears his throat, "I think everybody is guilty, but eliminated you when I saw the wheelchair. And now that you brought that up, my partner wanted me to bring up the money subject, not that it has any bearing on finding your killer."

"If you find the killer or killers, the council has approved a reward of two hundred thousand dollars from our general funds."

Jake says, "Well, with that in mind, I would like to talk to a few people starting with your wife, and I would also like to bring old lady Harper in for a formal question session without anyone in the room."

Rodger nods in agreement, "You can have supper at my house tonight, and ask my wife your questions then. I'll have Ray bring old lady Harper in for questioning in the morning. Is that all?"

"For now." Jake stands, looks over at the sheriff and his deputy and gives them a wink before walking from the room."

CHAPTER 11

That evening, Jake wearing blue jeans, his coat over his T-shirt and gun in a light brown shoulder holster, turns onto Landcaster Street in an up-scale neighborhood and then pulls up in front of the large beautiful two-story southern style home with its tall white pillars traveling up past the second story before tying into the roof. The yard was manicured to perfection. He walks up the concrete walkway past the roses and gardenias and makes his way up the steps before ringing the doorbell.

The door opens, and to his surprise, standing there in front of him, is the most beautiful and intriguing petite blonde he had ever seen. She's wearing a short sundress that exposes her perfectly shaped, well-toned and tanned legs. Her make-up is to perfection and her eyes as blue as the sky. Jake felt a little out of place wearing his black t-shirt and sporting his black cowboy boots.

The woman smiles, "You must be the great Lieutenant O'Malley I have heard so much about."

"Well, I'm not sure about all that, but you can call me Jake."

She holds out her smooth, delicate righthand, "I'm Sherry Stillwell, Rodger's wife."

Jake, not taking his eyes off her bright and beautiful blue eyes responds, "It's good to meet you. I wasn't expecting his wife to be so alluring. I figure up here in this neck of the woods you would have been a fat, freckle face woman wearing coveralls with a stem of hay in her mouth and playing a banjo."

"Well thank you, I can see my husband left out a few details of his own. He failed to mention how handsome you are; Italian?"

"Half; the rest is Irish. I'm scared to dig any deeper than that and I believe your decedents are French and German."

"Wow, how did you know?"

"You have that French look about you."

"My husband said you were very charismatic, but I see you're also highly intelligent."

"Not really, I've always had this gift for guessing things. I would say you're thirty-six years of age, one hundred and twelve pounds, you stand five-five without shoes, and you were born in the month of March."

"Oh my God, you're right!"

"I know… I'm always right or maybe not. That's the only defect I have, that and I have a left eye that blinks uncontrollable from time to time when I get really pissed. Pardon my language."

A man's voice came from the den that is partially hidden by the mahogany door, "Okay Jake, you just keep your hands to yourself, she's spoken for." He laughs at himself, "Don't just let him stand in the doorway Sherry, ask the man inside."

Sherry with a smile from ear to ear, "I'm sorry, will you please come in? I was so dazzled; I forgot my manners." Jake steps in and she turns and walks toward the kitchen snickering, "I'll go check on the dinner, our cook is a little slow, but she prepares a meal fit for the queen of England." Jake just stares at her perfect round rearend as she disappears through the double doors.

Rodger asks him to step into the den. "Can I fix you a drink before dinner?"

"Does a monkey have a hairy little…?" Jake catches himself, "Sorry, I'm working on my language. It comes with the job."

"That's quite alright." He wheels behind the bar, traveling up a foot high ramp, and removes a bottle of old Brandy from a lower shelf. He pours Jake half a glass and says, "You strike me as a man who says exactly what's on his mind. I wish more people were that honest."

"Yeah, it has gotten me into more trouble than I can count. I spend more time in the chief's office than he does, but I'm working on that also." He scans the large, impressive den with its deer and wild boar heads mounted on all four walls and says, "Looks like I'm in the wrong line of work. I guess being a mayor sure pays off."

"You guessed wrong, it doesn't pay the power bill for this house. It's the sawmill I own that supplies the material for every new home built within a hundred miles of here and then some. The county's growing in leaps and bounds. People are selling off farmland like crazy and putting up subdivisions, which, means more new houses and lots more material."

"It also means less food for people to eat."

"How's law enforcement?"

"It sucks most of the time, but there's no shortage of crime."

"You're right; I guess that explains why you're here."

Jake sets the glass down on the bar, "Let me ask you a question Rodger while you're pouring me another glass."

"Shoot." He pours another drink as Jake wiggles his index finger indicating he needed the glass full this time.

"How come me? I mean there are a dozen law enforcement agencies close enough to throw a rock and hit, and, they have good homicide detectives. Again, how come me?"

"There's not a police department in this state that doesn't know your name. I called a few of them and your name just kept popping up. They say you're a man who shows no partiality, doesn't mind stepping on toes and a genius when it comes to little details. When I saw how you handled Sheriff Ray today at the meeting and heard what you did to Deputy Miller, I knew I had the right man."

"Yeah, and that's my good side. I like a good challenge ever so often."

About this time Sherry and the cook stepped from the kitchen and started setting the table. Sherry in her soft, sweet voice asks, "Honey, will you call Casey to dinner?"

Jake gives him a look. Rodger smiles, "That's my daughter. She's the team leader and their goalie." He wheels to the bottom of the staircase and shouts, "Casey, come to dinner! We have a guest! And wear some clothes!" He turns to Jake, "She's quiet a lady in her own right. Take your coat off and make yourself at home."

One hour and twelve drinks later Jake is feeling no pain as he sits across from Sherry and Casey. Casey, being an eighteen-year-old brunette who obvious inherited her looks from her mother. He occasionally wipes his mouth with a napkin before taking another drink. Rodger was leaning back in his wheelchair at the end of the long table patting his stomach after gouging himself. "Wow that's a very large gun you have there."

"Yeah, I can never have enough firepower. It's a seven inch 45 1911 converted to a 460 Rowland. It pushes a 250-grain full metal jacketed bullet close to a 44 magnum's velocity and muzzle energy."

"Well Jake, what'd ya think of the food?"

Jake, with a slight slur in his voice, answers, "Fantastic; never had better."

Casey, smiles at him and then blurts out, "You think you can find out who killed my three friends?"

Jake answers, "If I can't solve a homicide, it's because I got drunk and didn't show up at the crime scene. I meant that if I can't solve a homicide, it's death by natural causes."

Sherry frowns, "These crimes have devastated the entire community. You would expect something like this in a big city...but here, everyone knows everybody's business."

Jake nods, "Not everybody. Someone out there is not who they say they are."

She continues, "I know you've only been here a short time, but do you have any leads or ideas?"

"I have a few, but I think our crazy lady out on route seven knows more than she lets on."

Rodger laughs, "Old lady Harper. You've got to be kidding."

"I never kid when I'm drinking. I've learned over the years that there's a little truth in every lie, and a little lie in every truth and even a crazy old lady can give you info if you just listen close."

"That old lady has been crazy ever since she killed her husband."

Jake takes another drink, "So the story she told was true? Point proven. Sounds like she was a little off her rocker before she killed her husband, or she wouldn't have killed him in the first place."

"Yep, I was just a young man of twenty-six when it happened. It caused a lot of excitement for this county. It was our so-called 'trial of the century. That was before the accident. Then I met this fine lady and now I have a daughter."

Jake turns his attention to Sherry and asks, "How long have you coached the girls' soccer team?"

"For the last ten years. You see, I played soccer for Fairmont High myself before going to the University of Alabama and majoring in Physical Education."

Rodger interrupts, "My wife's being modest. She wasn't just any soccer player; she led the team to three state titles and was voted MVP four years running."

Jake gives her a look as he struggles to keep his exposure, "Wow! I'm impressed."

She blushes, "It wasn't that big of a deal."

Rodger blurts out, "Touch it, Jake!"

Jake quickly turns, "Pardon me!"

Go around there Sherry and show him your leg muscles." Sherry responds, "Stop it Rodger, you're embarrassing me. Jake doesn't wanna feel my leg."

Rodger fires back, "She has the strongest legs I've ever seen ...come on Sherry, show him." She stands and walks around the table and stops next to where Jake is sitting. She gives him a sexy look and raises her dress almost to her panties exposing her quads.

"They're not that strong anymore." She says.

Jake just stared at the perfectly shaped legs and could feel an erection coming on.

Rodger yells again, "Go ahead, touch it!"

Jake reaches over and gently places his hand on her warm upper thigh.

Rodger asks, "Well whatta you think? Is it hard as a rock or what?"

Jake in a low voice, "It is now."

Roger, not hearing him asks, "What was that?"

"It's very nice; very nice indeed. It must have taken a lot of working out to get 'em that hard and toned."

Rodger smiles with pride, "You won't find better hams on a prize-winning hog."

Jake, still feeling the warm touch of her fine quad responds in a low mumbled voice, "Sure makes me wanna eat more pork."

Rodger laughed but didn't catch on to what he said. "If she was to wrap those legs around you; she could crush you."

Jake mumbles again, "What a way to die."

Rodger turns his head, "I'm sorry Jake, I must be losing my hearing; what did you say?"

He reluctantly pulls his hand away as Sherry drops her dress and walks back around to her chair and takes a seat. "Nothing Mayor, I was thinking to myself." Jake tries to change the subject and turns to Rodger, "I don't mean to be rude or out of place, but can I ask you how long you've been wheelchair bound?"

"I was driving home from the Mill out on highway 26 many years ago when a drunk driver swerved over in my lane. He walked away without a scratch, but as you can see, I didn't fare as well."

"Sorry to hear that."

"That's okay, I've got to where I can handle this chair pretty damn good, and I always have a seat at soccer games. That was years before I got married."

Sherry breaks into the conversation, "So Jake, are you married?"

"I'm separated for now. My wife is in Dothan trying to get her head straight. I have no idea where that's going. Not the first time she's done that."

Sherry smiles, "I'm sorry to hear that. You must get lonely in your line of work."

"My partner keeps my mind plenty occupied. It's like taking care of a three-hundred-pound silver back gorilla who spends all his time trying to figure out what all in the world is edible."

"Sounds like you two have a good relationship, but he can hardly take the place of a woman."

"I'm not sure about that, he seems to have that nagging crap now to an art form, but I still can't talk him into wearing a pink thong."

Sherry laughs and continues, "We sure hope you can catch this sick pervert." Then a smile takes over. She covers her mouth and then says, "Wow, I haven't been able to smile or laugh for some time now."

Jake responds, "Oh, I'll find the sick pervert. Nobody can commit a crime without leaving a calling card behind. You and your players have a practice routine?"

"We practice three days a week all summer."

"You ever notice anything unusual at practices?"

"Like what?"

"Like someone watching from a distance; someone that fits in with their surroundings. Like maybe a grounds keeper or a school employee, a mail man who stares for ten minutes before placing the mail in the box."

She thinks for a second or two before answering, "No. It's got to be an outsider. There just isn't anyone around here that could do such an awful thing."

"Somebody can and did. There's just no way a stranger could lurk around here and not be noticed."

Rodger interrupts, "You're right, we would have noticed a stranger around here. I've been thinking; maybe there is a connection between the woods and the murders. Everyone is convinced there's a Dragon that lives in there."

"Dragon my ass… pardon my language. You said earlier today that you didn't believe in the monster theory no more than I do."

"Maybe not a monster, but all legends have a certain amount of truth to them."

"Well, my partner and I spent the night out there and we didn't find anything but a bear, snake and skunk, so I'm not going to waste my time chasing ghost." Suddenly, without warning, Jake feels a foot slide up his thigh into his crotch and the toes were massaging his penis. He freezes for a second and glances across the table at the faces of the two beautiful women, not knowing which one had their foot there. Both are staring at him with smiles and lust in their eyes.

Sherry, "Rodger is right that is a very big gun you carry."

Casey, "It sure is …. the biggest I ever felt … I mean seen."

He smiles and turns to Rodger, "Well I guess I need to head back to the motel and turn in for the night. I need to get started early in the morning. I have a hard… hard road ahead of me."

Rodger's cellphone rings and he says before answering it, "I'll hear of no such thing, Jake. My home is your home. You can stay here in one of our guestrooms until you fine this animal."

"I have imposed on your good family enough."

Sherry smiles and winks at him as Rodger wheels into the den to take the phone call.

She licks her lips, "You'll like staying here. It's a very nice guestroom and we have everything you may need, and I do mean everything. Please, stay with us." The foot dances around his crotch as more pressure is applied.

Casey jumps in the conversation, "With that killer running loose, I would feel ….and I mean feel a lot safer if you stayed here with us. Please Jake."

Jake takes another big drink and says, "I really need to go, but I need to sit for a few more minutes for reasons I won't go into right now …"

Sherry giggles and interrupts, "Then it's settled. I'll go make sure the room is ready." When she stood, the circus act between his legs ended and a few seconds after Sherry goes up the stairs a foot returns to continue the message. He starts sweating knowing it was Casey. So, with a grin, he asks, "Casey, how old did you say you were?"

"Old enough."

Jake stands, "I think I need another drink."

About this time Rodger comes back into the room passing Jake who was heading for the bar in the den, "You okay? You look a little uncomfortable."

"I need another drink before I go back to the motel and get my things."

"Drink all you want; I have to go take care of some town business."

Jake pours another drink and downs it all in one swig…

CHAPTER 12

Later that night, Jake was lying in bed in the beautiful guestroom, sniffing the sweet aroma of potpourri and feeling the cool clean sheets against his body. The air conditioner made the whole house a little too cool for him, not knowing it was about to heat up. He was also thinking about the chain of events that are unfolding in front of him. Did Theo really see something in the woods last night? Knowing he was almost child-like in many ways. Why does the sheriff feel so strongly about the so-called myth that makes its home in the woods, or is there another reason he wants to keep people out of the timberlands? The thought of Casey massaging his crotch under the table gave him reason to worry. Suddenly, he hears a squeaking noise from the door hinges as it slowly eased open, allowing a small amount of light to protrude from the bathroom in the hallway traveling across the floor and into his face.

There standing in the doorway is a well-proportioned silhouette of a woman. The light shined right through what appeared to be a very thin T-shirt. He could make out her perfect breast and well-rounded rearend as the luscious figure unpinned her hair and shook her head allowing it to fall past her shoulders. She stepped into the room, slowly closing the door behind her, shutting out what little light he had to identify her with. He felt an uncontrollable erection coming on. That thing had no conscience whatsoever and stood straight up, giving off signals like active sonar pinging away at the target in the dark deep ocean. She takes a seat on the edge of the bed and runs her hand under the sheets like a snake crawling through the branches of a tree, making its way toward a small unsuspecting squirrel perched on a twig. But this wasn't a squirrel it was after. Her hand found his hard shaft that is now pushing the sheets up, making it look like someone had pitched a small puptent in the center of the bed. The warm hand gently made long strokes causing him to take a deep breath. The hand gripped tighter around his hard member as it made a twisting motion with every downward stroke. He decides to test his theory and make sure it wasn't the daughter, so he grabs her by the wrist and pulls her hand away.

A soft and easy-sounding voice filled the room.

"Wow, what a gift. Don't stop me, I need this."

He was very relieved and excited to hear that it was Sherry's voice, but it didn't change the fact that she was a married woman. He did have a standing rule since he first caught his mother humping the ugly little insurance salesman, and he also never got over his first wife leaving him for a lawyer. He didn't want any man to go through the pain he went through, especially a handicapped man who had given him a comfortable place to lay his head and allowed him to break bread with his family.

Jake says, "I know this is a stupid question, but why are you doing this?"

The soft voice with a nervous break between the words, "Do I need a reason?"

"I know I have a reason, but it would make me feel better if you had one."

"I'm lonely. I'm attracted to you and my husband can't perform sex. I have a lot of toys, but none bigger or warmer than yours."

Jake, in an uneasy voice; "All good reasons, but there's other ways to pleasure a woman you know. Why, I have you know I can please a woman if I was paralyzed from the neck down."

Still stroking him, she says as she massages it to perfection, "I bet you can. A woman my age has certain needs and you're the first man I've met who looks like he can fill those sufficiently."

"That sounds like a very good reason also, but what if he comes in here?"

"He won't be back home for hours."

"I just don't feel right about this."

"Look, this won't take more than twenty minutes or so. I haven't had sex in years."

"Well, your enthusiasm has me turned on; I'll be lucky to last half that long."

"I know we just met today, but if it makes you feel any better, I did hesitate in the hallway, having second thoughts before deciding to come in here. However, after placing my hand on that thing, I knew I made the right decision. I got so turned on when you placed your hand on my thigh at dinner a tingle went down my spine."

He goes into deep thought for a few seconds and then says, "I can't do it."

She jerks the sheet back and quickly covers it with her mouth, going all the way down without a gag, grunt or choke. His mind made a complete turnaround. He went out of control as her warm mouth reminded him that he hadn't had sex in three weeks, five days, twelve hours and…and…oh hell, who gives a hoot how many minutes. He grabs the top of her head and forces her down even deeper. Now he has had a lot of oral sex performed on him over the last forty years, but this was a first-place trophy winner for sure. She straddled his body in a sixty-nine position, placing her strong thighs and wetness in his face. Instinct took over and he went at it like Theo at a free all meat buffet.

She lasted only a few minutes, beating him by only six seconds. She didn't even come up for air.

Minutes later they both just lay side by side as he pondered over the horrible feelings that were running through his mind. He turns his head, "You won't be upset if I don't kiss you after all that, will ya?"

"I'm okay with that… for now."

He turns his thoughts to Ann. Ann knows that he can only go for just so long before the urge takes over and this woman being a ten from top to bottom made matters only worse or better, depending on how you looked at it.

She reaches over and places her hand gently on his cheek, "Jake!"

"Yeah?"

"I'm ready again."

"I haven't recuperated from the first round."

"Crawl between my legs and shove that thing inside me. Make it hard and fast. I like it rough."

"I'm not sure I can go again with all these uncomfortable emotions running through my head."

"I'll talk dirty, and you can bite my nipples really hard if you like."

"Ok in the mood again." A split-second later he's stroking her hard and fast as she whispered in his ear, "Stick me deeper, treat me like a whore, spank my ass, hurt me. I'm so wet and you're so big… "

He places his hand over her mouth and says in a low voice, "Stop with the dirty talk, you're gonna make me pop too quick." Silence took over the room except for a mild squeak from the bed every time he made a stroke. Her moaning and groaning in pleasure were driving him into a frenzy. He stops for a second and says, "Okay, you can talk now."

She whispers in his ear, "Do anything you want, and I want it hard. Make it hurt."

He lifts his head, "Are you serious or is that just more dirty talk?"

"I'm serious; I don't wanna be able to walk straight for a freaking week. It has been so long. My insides are burning with lust." He can't stand it anymore and flips her over for round three. As he strokes her hard, he looks up and notices the door cracked open and someone looking inside. He stops for a second.

Sherry, "Don't stop I'm almost there."

Before he could say anything, the door closed.

Ten minutes later she kisses him on the forehead and quietly gets out of bed. She opens the door, peeks down the hallway and steps from the room. He places his hands behind his head and catches his breath before saying in a loud mumble, "Cripple my ass, that woman can bring the dead back to life." He sits up, placing his feet on the floor, walks to the door and opens it, peeking down the hallway and seeing nobody, he returns to bed and slips into an off and on sleep mode. He lays there wondering who was watching him through the crack in the door. Could have been the only other one in the house. Now that's good detective work.

The next morning, he awakens to the sweet-smelling aroma of frying bacon. He drags himself from the bed and after slipping into his jeans makes his way to the bathroom to take a shower. He stood in front of the mirror over the sink for a few minutes thinking hard about last night.

He mumbles to himself, "I sure wish Doc was here." He steps into the shower and makes an adjustment to the spout. The hot water sure felt good. Two minutes later the door flies open, and someone comes in and starts using the toilet. He didn't move a muscle. Surely, they could hear the shower running and know that someone's behind the curtain. For some reason he remembered a movie and in a low whisper, "Don't pay no attention to what's behind the curtain." He reaches over and slowly and slightly pulls the shower curtain back and before he could get it pulled back far enough to see, a hand flew in the other end and slapped him lightly on the left butt cheek. He sticks his head out and sees Casey standing there.

She winks, "Nice ass. You better hurry, Mama's fixing hotcakes and bacon."

He loses all expressions on his face.

Minutes later, he makes his way down the stairway wearing denim and a black t-shirt, adjusting his shoulder holster as he went. Rodger was sitting at the end of the table sipping on a cup of coffee and reading the morning newspaper.

With a smile he asks, "You have a good night sleep, Jake?"

"Like a bear in hibernation."

"Have some coffee. Sherry's fixing hotcakes this morning. She's in good spirits this morning for some reason."

Jake, feeling very uncomfortable, takes a chair and pours a cup of coffee from the pot that's resting on a silver tray in the center of the table. Sherry quickly barges through the kitchen door carrying in one hand a plate loaded with hot smoking pancakes and a plate of bacon in the other. She was wearing a short denim skirt, tight white blouse and had a bright glow about her and reached over and gave Rodger a kiss on the forehead before setting the trays down. He gives her a light pat on her butt, "You sure are in a good mood."

"Easy on the booty honey, it's a little sore this morning." Giving Jake a wink she continues, "I think I slept in an odd position last night and I tried every position."

Jake spits his coffee across the table."

She laughs, "You okay Jake?"

"Sorry about that; hot coffee went down the wrong pipe."

About this time Casey comes running down the stairway and into the dining room wearing shorts and a pullover tank top. She pulls out a chair and takes a seat. She grabs up a glass of orange juice and downs the whole glass, then wipes her mouth with a napkin and gives him a wink also.

Jake takes another sip of hot brew when Sherry asks Casey, "What's wrong honey, you didn't sleep well last night?"

"I couldn't fall asleep, so I stayed up haft the night watching a late show and listening to all the bed squeaking."

Jake spits his coffee across the table again and quickly blurts out, "I couldn't get comfortable in a strange bed, so I tossed and turned all night."

Casey, "I bet you did."

Rodger asks, "You're sure are having a lot of trouble keeping your coffee down this morning Jake. Let it cool down a little, I know how you officers are when it comes to your coffee and donuts." He laughs.

Sherry interrupts by clapping her hands together and says, "I feel a lot better today. I think we can start back training."

Casey jumps up with excitement and says as she runs for the front door, "Great, I'll go tell the team."

Rodger laughs at the funny papers and shakes his head, "So Jake, what's on your agenda today?"

"I'm going to call my partner and find out how he's doing on his project. Then, I'm going to the Sheriff's Office and have a word with our horny old lady Harper."

Sherry walks over and stands behind Rodger and licks her lips at Jake before asking, "I'm gonna fix a shrimp casserole for lunch. If you have time, stop by and have some?"

Jake gives her a look and turns to Rodger, "You going to break for lunch today, Mayor?"

"I'm gonna be tied up all day, so I think I'll just grab a sandwich. You should think hard about Sherry's shrimp casserole though, it's the best that will ever pass your lips."

Jake thinks to himself, '*I'm not sure about her casserole, but I know her pudding's great.*' He nods, "I bet it is Mayor. I'll think about it. Well, I better get going." He stands and takes one more sip of coffee and says, "That was good coffee; sorry about spitting most of it across the table."

With a wink and smile Sherry says, "That's okay, I'm sure it was way too hot for you."

"Yeah, way too hot."

After leaving the Stillwell's residence, he's driving down the road and decides to give Theo a call. He opens his cell and starts punching in numbers. The phone rings several times when Theo picks up on the other end.

"*Hello.*"

"Hey Theo, how's it going?"

"*Not good Jake; not good at all.*"

"Why, what's wrong?"

"*It must be that time of the month.*"

"Those assholes called about your big screen TV payment again?"

"*I'm talking about Donna's time of the month.*"

"How come you say that?"

"*She's bitching up a storm and driving me crazy.*"

"Yeah, that's very important and all, but I need to know what you found with the list of names. You come up with anything?"

"*Do you have any idea how many male voters there are in that county? There must be five thousand names on that list. I'm still in the 'A's.*"

"Did you narrow it down to males between twenty-one and seventy?"

"*Still a lotta names. How's it going up there?*"

"Well let me think. Since you left, I managed to throw a deputy's ass through a barbershop window, moved in with the mayor, screwed his wife in every position possible while her good-looking daughter watched from the door … oh yeah, old lady Harper accused you of raping her."

"*Get out of here; you've got to be kidding me?*"

"It's true, the sheriff actually wanted to arrest your black ass."

"*Screw that. I'm talking about the sex with the mayor's wife.*"

"I feel really bad about it."

"*That's a first; were you drunk?*"

"I had a few drinks; that's all."

"*Then you're covered under the 'drunk and stupid' clause.*"

"Last night his wife did stuff to me that only happens in those porn movies Ann threw out. Hey … get this; his daughter slapped me on the ass as I was taking a shower. That's creepy. The wife even forced me to perform anal sex."

Theo drops the phone … a long pause and then he's back, "*I bet she didn't have to hold a gun to your head; you sorry bastard you!*"

"It was a confusing night. Yesterday evening the wife placed her foot under the table and massaged my crotch for me right in front of her husband, then she gets up and the daughter took over where she left off and she's only eighteen."

The phone drops again … a long pause and then Theo returns, "*You son-of-a-bitch you!*"

"I'm dead serious. It seems like everywhere I go women throw that shit at me like crazy."

"*You poor baby. I wish my life was a third as exciting as yours. Maybe I need to come back up there and help, you know, back you up.*"

"Yesterday you couldn't wait to get out of here."

Theo mumbles in a low voice, "*Yesterday my mother in-law wasn't staying with us for a week. I need to get out of here and fast.*"

Jake not understanding Theo's low whisper, asks, "What did you say?"

"*I can't say it too loud; they're in the other room.*" Jake hears a sound of nagging in the background.

Theo comes back in a loud voice, "*Get me out of here Jake!! I would rather camp out, French kiss that black bear, screw a rattlesnake and put a skunk's ass to my face and use the spray as a facial than listen to this shit.*"

"You just take care of those names for me. I'll take care of this shit up here. I'm heading back to pay old lady Harper another visit."

"Good for you and tell that crazy bitch to kiss my ass, and I wouldn't rape her if Beyonce was shoved up her rectum."

"I'm sure she will be thrilled to hear that."

"Whatever you do, don't get close enough for her to grab your ears."

"I'll keep that in mind. Bye for now." No sooner did he close the phone did it started ringing again. He opens the phone, "Hello."

"This is Sheriff Ray. I need you over here at old lady Harper's place."

"What a coincidence, I was just discussing her with my partner."

"You mean discussing her with her rapist?"

"Man, what is your deal? You know my partner didn't rape that old bag."

"Why would she make up something like that?"

"I have an idea, maybe it's because she's screwed up in the head or just lonely and needs the attention or maybe it's just wishful thinking, but I need her at the station to ask some questions."

"That's going to be a little hard to do."

"I already know she's hard of hearing and blind as a bat."

"Well, you can add another problem to that list of elements. She's dead."

"I'll be there in ten minutes, don't touch anything!"

A little later he comes driving up to the old shack and sees two police units and a red and white ambulance parked out front. Two men were loading a body covered with a white sheet that he assumed was old lady Harper's.

He walks over, "Hold your tater tots dudes I wanna examine that body." He pulls the sheet back, stares for a few minutes, examines her head, arms, wrist, hands and feet and then turns and walks up the steps and into the main living room of the shack. He glances around the room before seeing the sheriff standing in the kitchen doorway with his back to him and Deputy Miller sitting on the edge of the kitchen table. Ray turns around and sees him walking through the door. "Well, looks like your questions are going to be a little too late."

Jake scans the room, "What happen?"

"She committed suicide. It was just a matter of time."

"Let's pretend I haven't a clue, and ask, how'd she do it?"

Deputy Miller, with a grin, "What business is that of yours, dude? You're working on the other murders; this one belongs to us. We don't need outside help on every case in the county. We're not that stupid!"

Jake snickers. "Don't sale yourself short asshole."

He turns to Ray and gives him a look. Ray hesitates for a second before replying, "She slit her wrist while sitting at the kitchen table this morning if you must know." Jake walks around the room glancing over at the stove and sink counter.

Ray walks over, "Look, she just got up this morning, cooked herself a bowl of oatmeal, got depressed and lonely and cut her wrist. We all saw it coming."

Jake laughs, "Yeah, everybody but her."

Miller laughs, "Maybe she was so upset because that 'niggra' partner of yours raped her; she just went and cut her wrists."

Jake walks over, leans close to his face and gives him a look then asks, "How would you like me to throw your ass through another window moron? Don't you ever call my best friend that again; at least not in front of me." He turns back to Ray, "Now let me get this straight, you say old lady Harper prepared herself a bowl of oatmeal this morning, sat down at the table and then just decided to cut her own wrist."

Ray smiles, "That's about the size of it."

"And how long ago did this happen?"

"Whatta mean how long ago?"

"I mean give me a time frame. Was it an hour ago, or two hours ago etc, etc, etc?"

"I'm not sure, but I would guess about two hours ago. Look Jake, this is an open and shut case. She was crazy, always spouting off to people in the grocery store about that Dragon."

Jake laughs, "She wasn't so crazy that you wouldn't take a rape report from her." He walks over to the stove and sticks his finger in the pot of oatmeal, walks back over to the table and glances down at the full bowl of oatmeal so dry it felt like hardened concrete. Next to the bowl resting on the table is a large bloody kitchen knife.

"She was killed last night. After checking the body temp with the palm of my hand, and the fact rigor mortis has set in, I'm gonna take an educated guess and say around twenty-two hundred hours or ten o'clock to anyone who didn't make it out of that second grade."

"How do you know that?"

"Well, the doctor will find that out when he checks her body temperature and other shit like that, and again, rigor mortis has set in and going by how dried and hard this oatmeal is; my guess isn't going to be that far off. And I just thought of something else."

"Yeah, what's that?"

"I noticed the other morning when she grabbed my partner by the ears to slap a wet one on him; she used the heel of her palms because she had arthritis bad. So bad she couldn't have held a knife steady enough to make those smooth cuts."

Miller steps closer, "Now how do you know how smooth the cuts are?"

"I checked her out before they loaded her up and this knife tells us a little story as well."

Miller, "Looks like just an ordinary kitchen knife to me."

"Yeah, it would to a stupid-ass redneck with a cantaloupe for a head. But knives are a little specialty of mine." Jake leans over, takes a pair of eyeglasses from his coat pocket, places them on his face and takes a closer look at the knife. "Yep, this isn't her knife."

Ray steps forward and asks, "Now how in the hell do you know that?"

"This knife was made in Germany by a company called Hanshenkle and Sons and comes from a very expensive set of seven. About nine hundred dollars' worth. Now if you look around you can see that her sink is full of cheap knives you can buy anywhere, but no set containing the other knives matching this one. And before you ask, they don't sell the knives separately either. No, she was killed last night by an intruder. Wow, you two morons have really screwed up this crime scene. I think I can tell you where she was standing before the killer whacked her behind the head with a three-foot black iron fireplace poker."

Ray gets angry, "Wait a damn cotton-picking minute. How do you know she was hit from behind with a black iron fire poker?"

"I took a quick glance around the living room when I came in. I saw a black iron ash broom and black iron fire tongs, but no black iron fire poker, which also comes in a set. The poker is lying behind the sofa next to the front door and that gray stringy shit on the end will be hair samples. I bet you two didn't even look to see the wound on the back of her head." Jake points to the table, "You see the small amount of blood on each side of this table where your deputy was resting his ass? That means she was dead before her wrist was cut. If her heart was working when you say she cut her wrist, she would have bled all over this place. I would say she just sat down to eat her a late-night bowl of oatmeal, which explains why the bowl is full, when suddenly she hears a noise, most likely the intruder taking the iron poker from the fireplace. She walked into the living room where he was standing behind the door. She sees him, turns to run back into the kitchen and that's when he whacked her in the back of the head so hard she was killed instantly. I can see blood droppings in the living room a few feet from the kitchen doorway. He dragged her body back in here and propped her back in front of her oatmeal and cut her wrist. Must have been violent when the perpetrator first whacked her."

"Why do you say that?"

"That woman had twenty cats walking around here like they owned the place."

"So?"

"You see any cats hanging around?"

Wait a damn pea-picking second, old lady Harper was deaf, so how could she have heard the intruder taking the fire poker from the fireplace?"

"I was wondering if you caught that. Deaf my ass, she could hear what she wanted to hear. The other morning when I finished talking with her about the timberlands, I said in a normal tone that my partner was black, and she went to throw up. In other words, she heard me."

Ray snickers.

Jake asks, "I say something funny?"

"I have a question that I know you can't answer smartass."

"Then I hope it's better than the last few."

"Why did the killer leave the knife behind? I mean if it's from a set, he wouldn't be stupid enough to leave it at the crime scene."

"I wouldn't say he's as stupid as you two, but that would be an underestimation. He was startled by someone."

"Prove it."

Jake points to the floor, "You see, late last night we had a brief rainstorm and those big muddy prints on the floor leading from the backdoor is a visitor who discovered the body after she was killed."

Ray asks, "How do you know the footprints didn't belong to the killer?"

"Because I know for a fact he wouldn't have come in the back door and walked pass her sitting at the table, then walked into the living room and grabbed said fire poker. But really, I knew because the killer came in the front door and was wearing size seven or seven and a haft shoes. The prints coming in the backdoor belong to someone who wears a size thirteen." Jake glances down at their feet. "You see Ray, you're wearing about a size ten and your dorky deputy there is wearing what looks to be size seven and a haft shoes. The larger prints were made by a boot, but the smaller prints were made by a smooth dress shoe like the kind you wear with a suit or…. uniform."

"That doesn't even make sense."

"Yeah, taking into consideration how you two handled this crime scene, I'm not surprised."

Ray fires back, "You're saying the killer wearing a size seven and a haft came in the front door, took the fire poker, whacked her over the head and then propped her back in her chair and made it look like a suicide? Then someone else wearing a size thirteen startled the intruder causing him to run back out the front door leaving the knife?"

"Wow, I guess they didn't just give you that uniform because it fit."

"Why would this surprise visitor not have called us last night if he walked in after a murder had taken place?"

"Now that's the first question you've ask that has me stumped."

Miller steps closer, "He's full of shit Ray. I say we run this 'niggra lover' out of the county."

Seconds later the deputy went flying out the front window and onto the front porch and into the yard. Back inside Ray shakes his head, "You warned him, so I guess he had that coming."

Jake smiles, "I try to give everyone a fair warning. Now Ray, let me tell you what I don't know about this murder. Motive: now why would someone want to murder an old crazy ass blind woman before I had a chance to question her?"

"Maybe it was just a burglary and when she confronted him, he felt he had to kill her."

"I don't think so. You can look around this shack and tell that there's nothing of value here or…. is there? And the intruder knew that she would be home at that time of night. Where else would an old blind lady go. She doesn't drive anymore and I'm gonna take a wild guess and say the local church brings her groceries to her."

"Okay O'Malley, I'll write it up as a homicide and run a full investigation. You just find out who our serial killer is." Ray walks from the house where his deputy was brushing himself off in the yard.

"Get in the car."

"You're just going to let that asshole throw me through another glass window?"

He stops for a second, "You're right, go back inside and arrest the son-of-a-bitch."

"Are you kidding me, he'll just throw me back through it again. There's two of us, I say we both go in and arrest him."

"Did you see the look in that detective's eyes? He looks like he can handle both of us with confidence and to be honest, I didn't feel like being thrown out that window behind you."

"Maybe you're right."

"Now see, you're not as stupid as you look; now get your ass in the car like I said. We have things to do."

Jake yells from the front door, "I'll take some pictures with my cell and send them to ya!"

Jake steps out on the porch and shakes his head as they drive off. He walks to his car and removes three large clear plastic evidence bags from the trunk, turns and walks back inside where the sheriff and his deputy had left all the evidence lying.

He snickers and says, "So you're gonna write it up as a homicide huh? Yeah, I bet you are." He takes a torn clean dishrag and carefully grabs the knife by the tip of the blade and places it inside one bag and then places a bag over each end of the fire poker. He lays the stuff out on the worn-out old couch and starts checking each room beginning with the bedroom. It was ransacked. Everything in the closet was thrown out on the floor. The mattress was shifted over as if someone was looking for something.

Jake smiles and says aloud, "Now what where you looking for dude? Wait a minute, I'm asking the wrong person. Okay Harper, tell old Jakey-poo what that asshole was looking for? It wasn't money or Jewelry, so what could an old crazy lady like you possess that would be worth killing you over. Let me think."

He walks around the room and then stops and speaks aloud again, "Where would you keep something that was only valuable to you and the perpetrator?" He checks under the mattress and then the drawers in the dresser. The bottom drawer was only pulled partially out. He eases it open and sees worn out panties and then a strong stinking odor hits him right in the face. "Damn woman, you ever clean out that hole of yours?" He holds his nose with one hand and runs his other hand under her granny panties.

"I should have brought my rubber gloves." He continues to dig deeper. "Bingo!" He pulls out a ten-inch dido and then after realizing what it is, throws it across the room. "You horny old bitch, now that was just gross." He looks up and says, "I bet you got a laugh out of that one."

He walks from the room, checks down the hallway before returning to the kitchen. He walks to the sink and washes his hands then slowly scans the room and stops when he sees a large porcelain cookie jar high up on a shelf above the sink. "Huh, too easy, and you would have known that, wouldn't you? So that's where you have it." He takes the large jar down from the top shelf and dumps it out on the corner of the counter. Stale cookies fell everywhere. He investigates the jar and tape to the inside bottom was a small 3X4 inch diary.

"You smart old hag." He places it in his back pocket and walks out the door.

CHAPTER 13

Later that evening, he drives to the Fairmont High soccer stadium and sees the girls practicing on the freshly cut green grass of the field. He scans the area before walking up the steps and into the bleachers. Taking a seat in the second row, he sees Sherry standing on the sideline yelling across the field. He couldn't help but stare at her perfectly shaped legs protruding from her tight gray spandex shorts.

Sherry turns and sees him watching, so she blows her whistle and yells, "You girls take a break!" She walks up to the second row and takes a seat next to him. Not just close, but real close. "Well, hello stud."

He slides over a little, "I see the girls are really working up a sweat."

She slides closer, "Casey told me that she truly believes you can catch this killer. You really made an impression on her."

Jake slides over a few feet further, "I have no idea what there is about me that attracts younger women, but I have had that effect since I was a young lab of thirteen."

She closes the gap between them and places her left hand on his knee, "Yes you do; that Italian skin tone, that controlling demeanor about you and that ponytail drives me crazy. What do you think about last night?"

"Well, I'm gonna have to say that was something else. With that being said, I need to tell you something."

"You can tell me anything. I'm so turned on right now I have the shakes. I have never had a man please me like that, and it has nothing to do with the fact it's been a while. You wanna a blowjob, we can go under the bleachers."

"I can use the blow, but I have a lot on my mind. What I wanted to say was at dinner yesterday evening your daughter had her foot in my crotch under the table and she was watching us through a crack in the door last night."

"Oh, that was my foot."

"It was… then when you got up, she replaced your foot with hers."

"Can't blame her for that. She is at that age now."

"That doesn't upset you?"

"Not really. You wanna hear something erotic?"

"I'm listening."

"Don't say a word about this to anyone. A few years ago, she brought an eighteen-year-old football player over one day at lunch and he kept staring at me with that, 'I want you 'look' in his eyes."

"I can see his point, go on."

"That evening they were practicing in the field next to the girl's playing soccer and he wanted some red cones for something, so I said, "We have some in the girl's storage room, so I took him over there and he closed the door, and he pulls his thing out. I got so turned on I got down on my knees and took care of him. He was nowhere near your size. I was ten years older than him, and I knew he had sex with a few girls, but I lost all control of myself, so after the blowjob I just stood there with it in my hand wanting him inside me and after a few minutes, I pull my shorts down and he bent me over placing my hands on a self and he must have taken me for over an hour. He didn't hold a candlelight to what you had to offer. I never had sex with him again. Casey would never let him do anything more than kiss her. He moved on after graduation and I never heard from him again. I like the way he used me."

Ten minutes later they were in the storage room and after she had given Jake oral sex, he bent her over and went at it like ants on a piece of sugarcane."

Thirty minutes later they're sitting on the bleachers. She slides up against him and places her hand on his thigh.

"Hey, come on, somebody might see us."

"So."

"So that's not a good thing."

"Thanks for last night and today. I see Casey is watching us again. I feel like a new woman after all these years."

"Do you know your ass is hanging out of those shorts?"

"And that's not all, I'm not hurting back there either. I think you broke me in."

"Yeah, but I wouldn't be showing anything off with a killer rapist running loose."

"Did you enjoy last night?"

"Look, I made a mistake by letting things get out of hand last night."

"Then why did you go to the storage room with me?"

"All that sex talk got me in the mood. I'm a married man."

"Where's your wife right now?"

"In Dothan, I told you that already."

"That's right, and what do you think she's doing as we speak?"

"I have no idea."

She leans closer, "We don't have to get married, just have some fun before you leave and go back to Mobile. Just letting you know that anytime you get in the mood just let me know. I can talk as dirty as you like."

He rubs his chin and thinks for a few seconds, "Sounds damn good, but it's beating my conscious to death. It just isn't right."

"Didn't I do everything a man could want last night?"

"Yep, and then some. Look Sherry, you're a beautiful woman and could have an affair with any man in the county. Which brings up another point. So, you haven't had sex since the football player?"

"Nope, not until you showed up."

"How come you waited until I arrived?"

"Because you're the first man that has ever made me wet just by standing there in the doorway. I want you to come to the house for lunch."

"You mean you just want me for lunch? What about Casey?"

"She wants to go eat with her friends at the local pizza hangout. I'll tell you what. If you come for lunch, I promise I won't lay a hand on you."

"Okay, it's a deal. Can I talk with the girls?"

"Sure." She blows the whistle, and the girls take off running toward the bleachers.

When they all get there, he stands and yells loud enough for everyone to hear, "Listen up girls! I have a few questions to ask that might help me catch this sick bastard!" He looks over and sees Casey as she gives him a wink. He swallows and continues, "Any of you girls notice anyone watching you practice or maybe hanging around at the local hangouts?"

They look at each other and one yells, "Just the normal people."

He asks, "Like who?"

Another girl stands and answers, "The regular people. Our friends and guys we know from school. Are you married?"

"Yes, I am. Did any of you see the victims speaking to anyone out of the ordinary?"

They all shook their heads. One girl says, "Marcy said something in the shower room about having sex with an older guy. That was a few weeks before they found her."

He smiles, "Now we're getting somewhere. She wouldn't have by chance said who?"

"She wouldn't say, said it would get her in trouble. She just said he had sex with her, and he would give her money if she would do things for him."

"Did she say how old this guy was?"

"No, she wouldn't give me any details."

He notices all the girls were anxious to talk but a small blond standing in the back. He continues, "You girls ever walk through the woods over there?" The girls wouldn't glance over in that direction.

Casey stands, "None of us ever go in there. There's a Dragon that lives in there."

He snickers, "Now how many of you girls believe that shit?"

They all raised their hands. He just shakes his head, "How many of you believe this Dragon killed your friends?"

They all raised their hands again. He continues, "Any of you ever see this, Dragon?"

One girl answers, "I saw him once."

Jake, with a grin, "What did he look like?"

"He was ten or eleven feet tall and had no hair or ears. His skin was all wrinkled and he had pink spots all over his arms. He had no ears, glowing eyes and long green fangs.

"Okay, you and my partner have been watching the same Sci-fi channel. Did he look like a dragon?"

"No."

"Point proven. What was this creature doing when you saw him?"

"He was going through the dumpster over there." She points to a large green dumpster next to the concession stand.

"So, our Dragon likes half-eaten hotdogs and stale popcorn. Something else my partner has in common with this place."

The girl quickly says, "He was big and horrible looking."

"Did you call the police or tell anybody what you saw?"

"No, I was so scared that he would come after me."

He glances toward the back row and asks, "You, in the rear."

The girl looks up but doesn't make eye contact.

"You don't say much, what's wrong?"

Sherry steps forward and says in a low voice, "That's Amber; she was really close to the three victims."

He nods, "Look, I know how hard this must be, but I need to stop this killer before he strikes again. I can't do this without your help. Your local law enforcement's not doing their job. They act like a bunch of lazy ass chimpanzees on crack and believe me I know. I spend ninety percent of my time trying to get out of work."

They all laugh as he continues, "I'm all alone on this, so if you girls remember anything, anything at all, let me know and don't let anyone talk you into anything that sets you to thinking. I'm gonna give each one of you my card and if you see anyone that doesn't look right, call me and don't go near those woods."

Sherry shakes her head, grabs him by the arm and leads him a few feet away and in a low voice, "Amber took the murders extra hard. She'll come around."

Casey yells, "You wanna go eat with us Jake!?"

"I have another engagement; sorry, maybe tomorrow!"

Sherry steps forward, "Okay girls, I want everyone back here at ten in the morning. We need to really practice our footwork. Now go eat and stay close together and don't talk to any strangers." They all take off for the parking lot. She turns to him, "Well, let's go heat things up."

He gives her a look, "Are you talking about the casserole?"

"I made it with fresh shrimp."

They both start walking toward the parking lot when he asks, "How do y'all get fresh shrimp up here?"

"We own a seafood market out on the edge of town. Rodger brings home fresh shrimp three times a week when they get fresh shipments in from the gulf coast. He loves shrimp." They walk to Jake's car when she says, "I'll ride with you. No since in driving two cars with gas the way it is."

On the way back to the residence she shifted over to the center next to him.

He nods, "Are you crazy?"

"What's wrong?"

"What if someone sees us?"

"You're right; I'll hide my head in your lap. You want lipstick or not?"

"Yes." When she places her head in his lap, he quickly takes her by the shoulder and pulls her up straight then pushes her ever so gently to the other side.

"Girl, I have enough on my mine working this case without you licking me like a horse on a salt block."

"You think I'm ugly, don't you?"

"Right, that's why I have erection blocking the odometer reading."

"Just relax and I'll take care of it."

"No, you won't. You stay right there. You promised that you would keep your hands off me."

"I was going to use my mouth."

"Look, do you want me to find the killer or not?"

A sad expression came over her face, "I want that bastard dead."

"What about justice?"

"Death is justice enough for me."

"You sound like me."

"I never knew how cops could be so heartless at times, but now I fully understand. I haven't slept a good night's sleep in months, then, you came into the picture. I knew you were the answer when I first laid eyes on you. Standing in that doorway with that controlled look in your eyes, like you were going to take care of business and come out without a scratch. A Dragon slayer for sure."

"Oh, I've had my share of scratches. That's why I drink all the time."

She responds, "I never wanted sex that often until you came into the picture."

"Look, the sex you're wanting from me is to fill the hole in your heart that the death of three of your team members has left."

"That's not the hole I need filling."

"I'm not the cure. As a matter of fact, most of the time, I'm the problem."

She wipes the tears from her eyes and in a soft gentle voice says, "It's Rodger; he just doesn't find me attractive anymore and I don't find him attractive either."

"He would have to be dead not to notice you."

"I think I'm in love with you."

"You've known me for two days."

"I can't help it. Rodger hardly knows I exist anymore, then you came into my life. I need it like a drug, before I'm too old to enjoy it."

Jake's phone goes off. He opens it, "Hello, is that right, hold on for one second." He turns to Sherry, "You know a Marie Middleton?"

"Yes, that's a team member."

Jake puts the phone back up to his ear, "Yes and yes." He hangs up.

Sherry, "What was that all about?"

"Said she was just checking to make sure the number on the card was good and was I still married. Where was I? Oh yeah, if it makes you feel any better, I know an old lady who stayed horny until her death, which was today."

"What?"

"Old lady Harper was killed last night."

"Oh my God! You think it's the same person who killed my girls?"

"Could be... Wouldn't matter even if he had given himself up. The police walked all over the crime scene like teenagers at a pep rally and most likely wrote it up as a suicide."

She grunts, "You'll get no help from the law around here. They're always some kind of cover-up with those assholes."

Jake's phone goes off again, "Hello, uh huh yep it's good and yes to that last question.... ok by."

Sherry, "Who was that?"

"A Kimberly something."

"Kimberly Johnson?"

"That's her."

"That's another team member."

"She wanted to make sure the number on the card was good also and then ask me to guess what color her panties are and am I still married. You think you could have a talk with them tomorrow at practice because I think they're gonna blow my phone up."

They arrived at the house and he's sitting at the table waiting for her to heat up the casserole when he yells from the dining room, "You need any help with that?"

A voice yells back, "I believe I do need some help; this thing is hot!"

He stands and walks into the kitchen and there sitting up on the island was Sherry with her legs spread open and wearing nothing but her blouse. Her spandex shorts were lying on the hardwood floor.

"I thought you needed help with the casserole."

"That's not what's too hot. Come here Jake." He hesitates. The voice inside his head told him to back out and back out fast. She spread her legs even further and there it was staring him in the face. Naturally he didn't listen to the voice inside his head and let his erection guide him home.

Seconds later he's stroking her hard and fast. Her hands had a firm grip on his butt cheeks pulling him deeper and deeper when suddenly she lets out a moan as she has an orgasm. A few seconds later he let out a sigh of relief. She closes her eyes, "I love you, Jake."

"No, you don't."

"Yes, I do."

"No, you don't."

"No, you don't."

"Yes, I do."

She giggles, "Good, than it's settled, I love you and you love me. Now let's go crawl in bed and do it again."

He backs away from the island and pulls his pants up. "You tricked me."

"I know, but my insides are on fire. Take me again. Take me to the guestroom and throw me around like a ragdoll."

"Nope, this is wrong, and I've got work to do. I have some leads I'm going to follow up on starting with a little hiking trip."

She jumps off the Island and steps closer, "I wanna whisper something in your ear." She grabs his face, pulls it slightly down, turns it ever so slightly and whispers in his ear.

He quickly steps back, "How do you know about that?"

"My friend Janet said she tried it with the mailman and now he delivers her mail twice a day."

"That's impossible; I've known only two women who could do that without getting hurt and both are dead now."

She smiles, "If she can do it, so can I."

Minutes later, screaming and grunting could be heard coming from the guestroom. He was wrapped all up in the sheets when suddenly, his cellphone went off. He struggles over to the nightstand when Sherry's voice could be heard under the cover, "Let it ring, I'm not finished yet."

"It may be important."

"What's more important than what I'm doing to you?"

"You have me stumped. I can't think of a thing." He answers the phone, "Whoever this is, it better be important."

"*It's me Theo.*"

He hangs up. He turns to her and asks, "Now where were we?"

The phone goes off again. He answers, "What the hell is it, Theo?"

"*I need to get my ass back up there; my mother in-law is driving me nuts.*"

"She's too late. Now if you don't mind, I'm in the middle of an investigation."

"*I'm serious; I need to get out of here.*"

"I'm in the middle of something important right now, can this wait?"

"*I bet you are. I wouldn't be surprised if you're laying up between some blonde's legs right now.*"

"You're close."

"*Look, I would rather lock horns with that creature than deal with the monster down here.*"

"Go to Pat's place and wait for me to call you back."

"*Okay, don't forget me now.*" He hangs up.

She reaches over and pulls him on top and asks, "Who was it?"

"Wrong number."

CHAPTER 14

Later that evening he changes into his black combat pants. He takes a seat on the edge of the bed and slides his black jungle boots on when Sherry steps back in the room and asks, "Where are you going now?"

"I'm going back in the woods. I can think a lot clearer when Theo's not around bitching about shit."

"Let me go with you."

"Are you kidding? What will you tell Rodger?"

"He works so late on Fridays that he won't even know I'm gone. We'll be back before he gets home."

"Look, I'm staying overnight and I'm going to be making fast tracks and I don't have time to stop under every oak tree and have you performed oral sex on me." He hesitates for a second and says, "That doesn't even sound like me talking."

"I won't be in the way, I promise."

"Like you promised to keep your hands off me at lunch? I wanna see if this so-called Dragon exists, and I think better when I'm working alone." He stands, pulls a black t-shirt over his head and straps his large bowie knife to his belt. He then places his 460 Rowland in his shoulder holster and throws it over his head and snaps it around his waist. As he walks out, he grabs three clips from the nightstand and stops at the door. "I'll be back in the morning." ...

As he's driving his cell goes off.

"Hello."

"*Hey Jake, this is Casey, I got your number off the card, and I think I have some information that I overheard from one of the other girls. Can you meet me at the soccer field in ten minutes?*"

"Sure, I'm on my way now."

Ten minutes later, he drives up to the soccer field and doesn't see her. He calls the number back and she answers, "*Hello.*"

"Hey, I'm here and I don't see you."

"*I didn't want anyone to see us speaking. I'm in the storage shed.*"

Jake thinking that was not a good idea, "Come out to the parking lot and we can speak in the car."

"*On my way.*"

Five minutes later he sees her walking across the parking lot wearing a short school uniform skirt. She looked in every direction to make sure no one was watching. When she gets there, she opens the car door sliding into the passenger's side. She takes another gander around and asks, "Can you go up the road a short ways? There's a short dirt road on the left just a few miles from here. I don't want anyone to see us. This information can get me in trouble."

"Schools out, so why are you wearing a short school uniform?"

"I thought you would like it. All men like it."

He drives a short distance when she yells, "That's it right there on the left." He turns up the dirt road and stops when he's out of sight of the highway. "Whatta got for me?"

She gives him a sexy look batting her eyes, but she hesitates. "Anything your heart desires. They say you're a legend in Mobile and the whole town of Fairmont is talking about what you did to Miller. I want my first to be you."

"First what, I'm all ears."

She unbuttons her top two buttons and then pulls her skirt up until her white panties were showing. She slides closer and in a low voice, "You can touch it if you like."

"What!?"

"You can put your fingers in my panties if you like."

"So, you have information for me about the murders or not?"

"I saw what you did to my mother last night and I want you to do me like that. I could tell you have a nice tight ass from the little slap I gave you when you were taking a shower."

"Ok girl this is not going to happen. I have a daughter your age and I'm feeling very uncomfortable right now."

"I shaved it smooth as a baby's butt for you. I have thought about it, and I want you to take my virginity. I can give you a blow to get you started. I put my hair in pigtails just so you can pull me as deep has you like. I don't have large breast, but you can still put your lips on them."

"Okay I know you're getting to that age, but do you know how old I am?"

"Age has nothing to do with what I want."

"You have any idea what this can do to my investigation. You can have any boy you want."

"It's not a boy I want. I get the jitters every time I'm near you. I'm on the pill so you can have all you want." She undoes her blouse even more.

"Button that up."

"You think I'm ugly?"

"Where have I heard that before? Not even close, and if I was thirty years younger, I would take you up on the offer.

She reaches under her dress and with both hands pulls her panties off, throws them up on the dash and then leans back and spreads her legs open and shows him everything.

Jake breaks out in a sweat, then opens the door and steps out of the vehicle. She opens her door and walks around the car and leans over the fender.

"Do me right here on the hood. I won't scream."

"If you like me that much, you wouldn't put me in this position."

She turns her head around and lifts her skirt up pass her perfect rear end, "If it's positions you like, take it this way, and you can be as rough as you like."

"Get in the car, I'm taking you back to the school now!"

She walks around and gets back in the car. He takes a seat behind the wheel and starts the car. She reaches up and grabs her panties from the dash, "I'll go back, but will you do me one favor?"

"What's that?"

"Kiss me."

"Nope!"

She places her panties in his lap, "Will you keep them and think it over? Please."

"I will think it over if you will put them back on."

"You do know that after you take care of mama tonight, you can sneak into my bedroom."

"You are going to get me thrown out of this county."

"I'm of legal age so you will not be breaking the law."

"What you need is a good spanking for even contemplating such shit."

"You are so right. I want you to spank my bare ass so hard."

He places the vehicle in gear and backs out and drives to the school. She pulls her skirt up and slowly puts her panties on leaving her skirt up."

"Pull your skirt down, now."

She pulls her skirt down, "You'll come around when the time comes. You are all that the girls talked about at the pizza hangout." He stops at the school where her mother's car is parked.

"Go home Casey."

She steps from the car and leans over through the window, "What if I tell Rodger and my mama about this? I can say you talked me into the car and took me to the woods and screwed me so hard."

"Well, that's a good way to get me thrown off the case, and I know you don't want that. Goodbye."

An hour later he's leaning back in the car at the edge of the woods reading from old lady Harper's weathered torn diary. Because she had trouble with her eyes and writing skills, he could hardly make out the words.

He starts reading, '*Today my son went to see the woman who lives in the woods. I told him to leave her alone, but he wouldn't listen. He's hardheaded and I know he's up to no good. I hope he will come to his senses.*' He comes to a part that was illegible. He flips past a few pages and reads on, "*The child from his seed was wild as a bear and showed no signs of getting better. My son tied the boy to the bedposts and poured kerosene around the outside of the shack.*'

"So, the mother didn't burn the boy after all."

He reads on, '*After burning the boy, my son realized that he didn't want her anymore. He choked the grieving woman to death.*' He was unable to make out the rest. He places a black ballcap on and steps from the vehicle. As he checks his flashlight to see if it is working properly, a brown police unit drives up next to him. It was Sheriff Ray.

He steps from the vehicle, "Where do ya think you're going now?"

"I think I'm going to put the Dragon myth to an end once and for all. I'm going to see who's out there."

He starts to walk off when Ray steps in his path, "I can't let you do it. That's all we need is a police officer from out of town lost or killed out there."

Jake asks, "You own this property?"

"It's state land."

"Then you better get outta my way before I dislocate every vertebrae you have."

"Look, there's nothing out there! You're just gonna stomp around those woods and end up getting caught by darkness. You'll get lost for sure, and I don't have the manpower to waste searching for you."

"I found my way out of the jungles of Vietnam far thicker than this shit; I guess I can find my way out of here. Unlike you people up here, I know North from South, and East from West. You sure work hard at keeping people out of these woods. Are you hiding something in there?"

"Not at all. Get yourself killed, see if I care." Ray walks back to his car, jumps in and spins off. Jake lets out a snicker, turns and disappears into the forest.

An hour later he's trailing through the thick woods, pondering, not over the homicides, but now and then he would ask himself how he allowed himself to get involved with another woman and that thing with Casey caused queasiness.

Missing dead branches and stepping flat on the leaves so not to make a lot of noise, he comes to a rest near a brook, bends down and takes a drink. He then splashes water on his face and leans against a large maple tree. "Okay Jake, you're in love with Ann, and Sherry needs to be told that."

He nods his head, putting all that in the back of his mind and with a smile, "Now think, think only about the homicides. These homicides are turning into a complicated puzzle and like all puzzles, the pieces must fit correctly. Hard to work a puzzle with everybody throwing the pieces around and the box missing. Things are never what they seem to be."

He turns and takes in all his surroundings. The forest is a very peaceful place to relax, if you become part of it and do not take advantage of it. Never take it for granted. If there's something out here, he must keep his senses intact, not allowing anyone or anything to get the jump on him. He knew every noise in the forest, from the deer scratching a river birch with his antlers, to the wind whistling through the pines. He scans the ground for any evidence of a human prowling the thickets.

He sniffs the air but picks up nothing but the odor of sweet honeysuckles growing wild on nearby vines.

He takes off again and after about a mile further, he stops in his tracks, having the feeling that someone or something is watching him. He never believed in the boogie man, because there was nothing in existence that was crueler than mankind. All this reminded him of the recon missions he pulled inside enemy territory back in seventy-two. He was now deep in the forest a long ways from any kind of backup. To hell with that, he's never been in a situation that he couldn't handle.

As he made his way through the thick brush, he noticed something coming into view up ahead. It was a large clearing with an old burned-out shack standing in the center. The partial tin roof was rusted to a burnt orange color and two walls were burned completely down, exposing the inside of what was once somebody's home. A home built on state property. He glances up at the sun as it dropped in the west behind the pines. He knew it would be dark in less than an hour.

He approaches the ruins, climbs a few steps and walks into what was left of a charred living room. There were only a few burnt studs separating the bedroom from the area where he was standing. In the bedroom near the outer wall were four iron bedposts pointing to the sky and supported by two angled bedrails slightly bent from intense heat.

He bent over and picked up hotdog wrappers and some candy bar paper. Whoever this is, must scavenge the dumpsters near the highway and then bring what he finds here.

He steps closer to where the kitchen was. He could only imagine someone trying to survive out here by themselves, making the long trip to the road every day to scrounge for food. He turns and walks down the steps and around the foundation of the shack. He notices a large plastic garbage bag sitting near the edge partially covered by old bricks once used to support the flooring. Moving the bricks from around the bag, he pulls it out from under the floor. He slowly opens the bag and sees that it's full of clothes, but not men's clothes, but girls' school clothing.

He takes a sniff of the clothes, "Clean clothes." Our man has been inside the girl's dressing room. But what the victims had on was burned up. Suddenly he caught a whiff of an odor traveling the waves of air whipping in and out of the timbers. It was the odor of a human being that hadn't had a bath in a long time...

The sun had almost disappeared completely when he quickly decided to set up camp. This was as good a place as any, but before he did, he needed to wash the sweat from his face and eyes. He made his way down to the small flowing brook and bent down near the edge where the water had pooled. As he's reaching down with both hands to cup the water in his palms, he sees his reflection, but not just his; a reflection of a large hideous creature standing behind him holding a large oak limb over his head. The figure of a man stood over seven feet tall and was about to drive the limb into the back of his skull. He quickly dives to the side rolling across the bank. The limb drove hard into the creek splashing water in all directions.

The creature takes another swing, and Jake maneuvers from its path, but not before he can catch the thing in the crotch. That didn't even slow him down. He was stunned. Never has that kick not slowed a man down. The large hideous man is in a rage and made a horrible screaming noise. The smell alone was enough to knock an ordinary man out.

The angry man swung again and again until seizing the opportunity, Jake jumped into the air and drove both feet into his chest knocking him seven or eight feet back. The mighty figure of a man loses the limb and Jake goes for his pistol only to find it missing. Somehow it had managed to fall from its holster and into the creek when he rolled across the muddy ground, dodging the fast swings. He runs to the edge looking for it when, suddenly he spots it partially buried in the mud-covered bank, but before he can retrieve it, he is grabbed by two very large hands as big as dinner plates. They lifted him high in the air and drove him to the ground. The man handled him like a ragdoll with the ass tore out of it.

Jake grunts and then yells, "Ouch! That hurt you son-of-a-bitch!" He tried to catch his breath but when he attempts to pull his Bowie knife from its sheath, he finds it has fallen out also. By now the fierce fight had made its way over near the burned-down shack. He had handled men this size before, but this guy was mental, and his adrenaline is flowing through his veins like a river overflowing its banks. He knew his strength was no match for this man. He felt like he was in an arena with a raging bull.

He quickly realizes if he is to win this battle he will have to cheat. He falls back and finds his hand resting on a broken piece of brick.

"This should do the trick." So, like David and Goliath, he throws it as hard as he can, striking the large out-of-control beast between the eyes. The man falls to his knees, but before he could regain his footing Jake jumped on his back and placed his forearm around his throat and chokes him as hard as he could. The large man gets to his feet and staggers everywhere as Jake held on tight. The large beast of a man backs up and presses him against a pine tree driving the bark through his t-shirt and into the flesh. He banged over and over until Jake didn't think he could take another slam. Finally, the giant falls to the ground and goes into a state of unconsciousness.

An hour later the big man awakens and sees Jake heating a can of beans over a fire. The man sees the fire and jumps quickly back with total fear in his eyes.

Jake, "It's ok dude, it's just a small fire to heat the beans." The large man attempts to get to his feet when Jake pulls his 460 and fires an ear shattering gunshot in the air, "That's far enough. I'm tired of fighting dude. I'm getting too old to play that shit anymore. Now sit back down, nobody is gonna burn you."

The big man rubs the large bloody knot between his eyes and says, "You hurted me."

Jake chuckles, "Well it's not like you threw me on a bed of cotton. That ground is hard, and that damn pine tree hurt my back. I would have killed you if I could have gotten my hands on my gun or knife. You have a name?"

"My Mama call me Bo."

"Well, Bo, before you even ask about your wet clothes, I let you soak in the creek for about twenty minutes. Your body odor was borderline toxic."

Bo asks, "Who you be?"

"I'm Jake, a worn-out police officer from Mobile."

"You come take me to Jail?" Bo asks.

"That depends on where you got those clothes you had hidden under the shack in a garbage bag."

"I found them in a place where the pretty girls leave them, but nobody see me. They smell good, I bring them back here. They pretty."

Jake places his cigar between his lips and looks out into nowhere and says, "I have the same problem with panties."

"What you say?"

"Never mind. Why did you do it Bo? Did you do like Linnie with the girl in *'Mice and Men?'*"

"I don't know who Linnie is, but I didn't take their air away. They were pretty."

"You got a last name?"

"I don't remember."

Jake watches as Bo's eyes stay glued to the can of beans he was holding. "I know you're hungry. You have that look on your face that my partner always has every minute of the day. You want some beans? I brought several cans and a few pieces of beef jerky."

Bo nods with anticipation. Jake takes a rag he had found in the remains of the shack and wraps it around the hot can, "I'm not going to loan you my knife for obvious reasons, so you'll have to dig in with your fingers." Bo grabs the hot can, throws the rag down on the ground, turns the hot can up and downs the whole thing in one gulp.

Jake shakes his head, "Be careful Bo, that's hot." He watches as the man downs the hot beans without even a change in facial expression. "I can see how you can get used to the heat. How long have you been out here Bo?"

"I don't remember."

"I heard your mama tied you to the bedposts and burnt the shack down around you."

Bo yells, "You take back, my mama loved me!!"

"Okay, calm down. It's just what I heard but I know now a man did it...You remember his name?"

"I don't remember things. I think the mean man did."

"What mean man?"

"I don't remember, he was mean, and he did things to me and my Mama."

"Like what kind of things?"

"He would hold her down and stick his thing in her. I tried to stop him, but he beat me bad. One day he was touching her with his thing, and she was hollering for him to stop. He knocked me away. He tied me to the place where I sleep at night and start the fire. I found my mama down a far hill. I buried her but don't remember where. She loved to brush my hair. My mama loved me. She said I had the prettiest hair in the whole wide world. Now my hair all gone. I look bad now, so the pretty girls run away when I get close to them. A bunch of people look long time for me, but I hid. My mama loved me."

He starts to cry and rubs his hands together as Jake just sat there feeling sorry for him.

"I bet she did Bo. My mama never loved me."

"Was she pretty?"

"She was very pretty, but she did some bad things that I could never forgive her for."

"Bad things like the mean man did to me and my mama?"

Jake hesitates for a second or two before going down memory lane. "I guess you could say something like that. Do you remember anything about this mean man?"

"At first, he was nice to my mama and then one day he pushed her down on the floor and hurt her with his thing. Sometimes he would put his thing in her face and make her cough. He would tie me to the chair and make me look at him hurt her. Sometimes when mama went to town to get some food, he would hurt me with his thing. I loved my mama."

Jake loses all expression on his face, gets angry, reaches over and places his hand on the big man's knee, "Bo, if you can help me catch this sick bastard, I'll shove a mulberry limb up his ass and make it hurt really bad."

Bo laughs, "You funny."

"I wasn't trying to be. I think this mean man killed those girls and he's trying to make it look like you did it."

"I wouldn't hurted those girls; I like to watch them from the bushes when they play with the ball. I can't come out because the people will hurt me. They scared of me because I don't have ears no more and all my pretty hair is gone. I can hear things without ears. Why did God make ears?"

"I'm not sure about us Bo, but he gave them to my partner so old ladies would have handles to grab. And for some reason God gave him these real big ones, but he still has trouble listening to me at times. And people are scared of you because they don't really know you."

"I don't wanna go to jail and leave my mama."

Jake leans back, "Hey Bo?"

"Yeah Jock?"

"It's Jake, Bo, not Jock. Did you by chance know an old lady, Thelma Harper?"

"She my gramma. Sometimes she would come see me here and give my mama money and food and clothes for me. My mama loved me. I saw the mean man hit my gramma in the head and took the air away."

Jake slowly turns to him, "You say you saw the man who killed your grandma?"

"Yea, but he ran away, but I know it was him."

"So, you didn't see his face?"

"I just know it was him."

"Bo, is the mean man your daddy?"

"Gramma say he did a bad thing to my mama and made me come out of her tummy. He called me stupid, and mama would hit him and then he hurt her over and over. I was little, now I'm big and strong and when I see the mean man again, I will take his air away for what he did to my mama and my gramma."

Jake mumbles, "You'll have to beat me to him…that rotten ass child-molesting, raping, murdering pile of shit."

"You say a bunch of bad words."

"Sorry, I thought I whispered that. You know Bo, catching a child molester is my specialty…You speak English well. If you've lived out here for so long, how did you learn to talk?"

"My mama show me how to read and write a little. The mean man burned my books gramma gave me. And when it gets cold, I hide and hear the hunters talk. They say bad words too. Sometimes, I scare the animals off so they can't hurted them."

"I'll tell you what Bo, in the morning you can go back with me, and I'll find you a nice place to stay."

"I don't go back. The people will hurt me. They call me stupid."

"Nobody's gonna hurt you as long as old Jock's hanging around…Come closer and I'll tell you a secret."

Bo leans over and Jake says in a low voice, "Don't repeat this but I heard through the grapevine I'm crazy too."

"What is crazy?"

"One step above retarded."

"I wanna stay with my mama. I can watch over her now. I'm big and strong. I can pick up that log over there and it's really heavy. I can pick it up over my head."

"You're not bad when it comes to picking detectives up over your head either. You need to be real careful Bo; people fear what they don't understand." Jake places his hands behind his head and leans back, "You ever heard of a Sheriff Ray? He's the man who wears a uniform and a tan cowboy hat."

"I see him with other people going into the woods. They funny. They all have shinny stars on them and sometimes they dress up like ghost."

"Is that right…are they hunting?"

"No, they just go to the hills and stay a long time. I touch their trucks."

"You don't know why they go up there?"

"They go see the Dragon. He smells bad…bader than me. Sometimes I smell him at dark and, and sometimes fire comes out of his mouth."

"Wow, I thought it was your odor they called Dragon's Breath. Which way do they go when they disappear into the woods?"

"I never follow them. They will hurt me bad."

"Okay Bo, you listen to me and listen close. I'm going to ask you a question and I want you to think hard. You can take as long as you like before you answer. Is the Sheriff and the mean man the same person?"

"He's a bad man. The man who hurt my mama was mean and he hurted those girls and take their air away."

"Okay Bo, I'm getting nowhere here... You say the Sheriff is a bad man, but not the mean man?"

"I don't know. My head hurted. You make me think hard."

"You can't tell me what the mean man looks like?"

"I don't remember things."

"I bet you could if you saw him again."

"My mama loved..."

Jake interrupts, "I know Bo, ya mama loved you."

"Did you love my mama?" Bo fires back.

"I didn't know your mama, but she sounds like she was a good mother." Jake closes one eye and says, "Get some sleep Bo, we'll go to town in the morning, and we can sit down and have a long conversation."

Minutes pass when Bo asks, "Mr. Jock?"

"Yeah Bo?"

"How you sleep with one eye open?"

"It's a habit I learned a long time ago in a war. I can't take the chance of you hitting me with a tree limb while I sleep."

"I wouldn't do again; you my friend now."

"You sure would have saved me a lot of back pain if you had figured that out sooner." He throws a piece of beef jerky in Bo's lap, "Chew on that Bo, it's not ribs, but it sure beats the hell out of dumpster food..."

CHAPTER 15

Jake wakes up just before sunrise to a cool morning chill and dense fog. He turns and finds Bo gone and his knife's missing too. He places his hand on his throat to make sure he wasn't cut and bleeding from asshole to elbow, then checks for his 460 to make sure it was still snugly in its holster. He kicks some dirt on the smoldering ash and yells, "Bo!!"

There's no answer. He yells again, "Bo!! If you can hear me, bring back my knife. It was given to me by a very good-looking woman at my promotion party!!"

He was very surprised the man didn't slit his throat. A few years back, he could have heard a paperclip drop in his sleep. Old age was creeping up on him and he didn't like it.

He makes the journey back to the highway only to find that his car has four flat tires. He walks a few yards to the road and tries to hitch a ride, but when people saw him wearing a shoulder holster and dressed like he was going on some covert night mission, they sped off leaving him to kick a beer can, to pass the time as he walked back toward town.

A few miles down the road an old farmer, driving an old rusted out black pickup, stops and gives him a ride. The door almost fell off when he opened it, and the muffler must have been completely missing. He jumps up in the truck only to discover a large pit bull staring him in the face. He glances down and sees the dog's balls hung ten inches and looked like it had baseballs shoved into the sack.

The old farmer laughs, "He won't bite, but he might hump your shoulder."

Jake grins, "With balls like that, I might let 'em."

The farmer grinds the gears and shifts down before taking off, "Sorry, it's old like me."

"That's okay, if I didn't know better, I would arrest you for stealing my truck. I have one back in Mobile just like it."

The farmer smiles, "I see you're carrying a piece."

"I'm a police officer; I don't take a bath without it. It's the only thing I can sleep with and not have to buy dinner first."

"I hear ya... You're that lieutenant they brought in to solve those murders."

"Yep."

"The whole town is talking about you."

"Any of it good?"

"They say you threw Miller through Al's barbershop. If that's true, it's good."

"Actually, I threw him through that one and old lady Harper's front window the other morning."

"Well, I be damned. I bet that was a sight for sore eyes; I hate I missed that. I've been waiting for twenty years for someone to have enough guts to do it. Little smartass has written me ten tickets over the past few years. He was a little mean shit when he was a kid too. He would get his kicks by pouring lighter fluid on cats and dogs and stick a match to 'em so he could watch 'em run around on fire."

"Well... Mr...."

"The name's Fred, Fred Stringer."

"Well Fred, the name is Jake, and the target was a little blurry, but the wind was just right, and the projectile was ugly but aerodynamic, so I said, 'what the hell', then out the window he went."

"I'm not sure what you just said, but that bully had it coming. I'm surprised Ray didn't put ya in jail for doing that to his cousin."

"I would have just thrown him out a window, too."

Fred laughs, "I can take one look at you and can tell you would have done it. Butch here can tell too. He normally growls and barks at a stranger but hasn't muttered a sound at you."

"I have a way with animals, its people I don't get along with. Can I ask you a question?"

"If it's about the murders, I can't help ya. Only know what the news lady tells me."

"It's not about the murders. I'd like to know what you feed this dog to make his balls so big and hang so low?"

"Wasn't food that caused that; he got 'em hung in a fence after he bit into a wild boar that was more than he could chew."

Two hours later Jake comes walking into the house and is met by Rodger. "Hey Jake, can I have a word or two with you in the den?"

"Whatever I did, it's not true." He follows Rodger's wheelchair until they make it into the den. Rodger rolls behind the bar and fixes two drinks.

"Do you drink this early Jake?"

"You kidding? I could have used it earlier this morning for sure."

Rodger slides the glass over, "I have two things I wanna talk with you about. I've decided to put another twenty thousand dollars of my own money in the can if you can solve these murders and I'll put three deputies under you to help you with anything you might need, at least until your partner comes back."

"Well, my partner will be glad to hear about the money, but if your deputies are anything like your Sheriff and his sidekick, I'll pass. I work better alone."

"Sheriff Henderson is an okay dude; he's just a little embarrassed because he doesn't have a clue how to solve crimes this big."

"He doesn't have a clue on how to wipe his own ass. He wrote up a homicide yesterday as a suicide."

"Oh yeah, I heard about old lady Harper. That's a crying shame; she was crazy but made some of the best damn peach cobbler in the state. She won first place at the county fair last year. Why, I bet there isn't a soul in this here county that hasn't tasted her peach cobbler."

"I'm pretty damn sure that if the people of this fine county knew what I found in the bottom drawer of her bedroom, they'd all have a spitting contest at the next fair."

"Well, she'll be missed, God rest her soul."

Jake takes another drink and has a quick thought, "There is one thing you can do for me."

"Just name it."

"I would like a private radio link to your dispatcher."

"Sure, but why?"

"I want her to inform me directly if there's another homicide. And I mean me and me only. I don't need anyone stepping over the crime scene before I get there and then writing it up as a barking-dog complaint."

"I'll have it brought here in the morning. The second thing I wanted to talk with you about is my wife and daughter."

Jake spits his drink across the bar. "What about your wife and daughter?"

Rodger shakes his head, "You should get that looked at. It could be something like bad acid reflux or maybe worse."

"Look Rodger, I can explain everything."

"Well, that's fine and dandy, but we can talk about your medical problems a little later. My wife and daughter are going to the big square dance tonight that they're having in Cooper's barn out on 32. It's a very big event and I would feel better if you would escort them and watch out for 'em."

Jake felt like a ton of brick had just lifted off his shoulders. "Why can't you take 'em?"

"It's a little hard to square dance in this contraption, besides, I need to work in my office all night on the road commissioner's new plan for the bridge out on highway nine. They keep me busier than a blue-tick puppy with two peters. I've wore out two set of tires on this chair just this year."

"Lucky bastard."

"What?"

"Good thing I don't have two peters, I'd really be in trouble."

"You are one funny dude. Sherry has her heart set on going to this dance and I would feel better if you were with them, especially with this killer still on the loose."

"Well Rodger, I want to thank you for letting me stay here and all, but I need to follow up on a few leads tonight."

"Look Jake, a few hours of dancing won't matter. Please, do this favor for me, there may be a bonus in it for you."

Jake in a low voice, "Yeah, I'm sure there is."

"What'd you say?"

"I said, 'maybe so'."

"Thanks a lot; that takes a load off my mind. I knew I was going to like you the first time I laid eyes on ya. You just had that look, like you take what you want, and do it your way. That's what we need up here. I have complete confidence in your ability to solve these murders."

About this time Sherry comes walking in the door with a large shopping bag. Her face brightened up when she saw Jake standing there.

She gives him a smile, "Oh hey Jake." She walks over behind the bar, leans over and gives Rodger a kiss on the cheek.

Rodger asks, "Well, did you max out the credit card?"

"You silly goose. I bought a new dress and new shoes for the dance tonight." She pulls a short, beautiful green dress out and shows it to them. "Let me try it on for y'all."

Rodger laughs, "I'm late for the stockyard sales, try it on for Jake, he's the one taking you and Casey to the dance." He takes a big drink and rolls to the door leaving Jake there like 'meat for the wolves.'

She runs into the backroom, but yells from the hallway, "Stay right there Jake, I'll be out in one minute."

He walks behind the bar, pours himself a big drink, opens his cellphone and starts punching in numbers. Theo picks up on the other end.

"*You forgot to call me asshole!*"

"Sorry, I got busy."

"*Where the hell have you been? I've been trying to get you all night.*"

"I spent the night with that big-ass Dragon you met two nights ago."

"*Holy crap!! And you're still able to call?*"

"It's a man, Theo, just like I said."

"*Bullshit, that thing was ten feet tall and...*"

Jake interrupts, "He's seven foot tall, not ten and its two rotten green teeth, not fangs."

"*Well excuse the hell out of me. I stand corrected. How about that skin condition, huh? Tell me that couldn't use some lotion.*"

"He was burned, Theo."

"*He was what?*"

"It's the boy who was tied to the bed and burned, but he's not a boy anymore, he's a man, just like you and me. He's a little slow upstairs like someone else I know, but a man still... Oh yeah, he eats like you."

"*Well sounds like you have found a new best friend, so just throw my ass in the garbage can.*"

"Listen to me, you tub of shit, I have bigger problems to worry about. The mayor's wife is trying to wear me out and her daughter tried to seduce me."

"*Again, you poor baby. I'm all broken up about that. I'm having my own affair down here in Mobile with a tube of KY jelly, but I'm thinking of breaking it off because it doesn't stand up to the friction like the label said it would.*"

"Shut up Theo, I don't have but a few minutes. I want you to go to the letter 'H' on that voters list and check how many Harpers there are and check them all on NCIC and ACIC. Let me know if you find anything. Oh yeah, old lady Harper has molested her last cop."

"*What happened, flies ate her?*"

"You can say that."

"You're kidding, right, because I was kidding."

"I'm not kidding; seems somebody didn't like the service she provided."

"I wonder why? Now I feel bad about wishing her dead."

"Look Theo ... " About this time, Sherry comes walking out with a short hip-high thin pink negligee, pink panties, red garter belt, redfish net stockings and black-high heels. Jake drops his phone.

Sherry licks her lips, "You like?"

Theo's voice could be heard yelling on the open cellphone lying on the floor, *"You there? What's going on up there? Jake! Jake! Tell me what's she's wearing ... hold own for a second; I'm going for the KY!!"*

Jake was speechless. "Where's the dress you bought?"

"I bought that for the dance tonight. I bought this for you."

"Look Sherry, somebody could come walking in here any minute."

"Are you saying you want somebody to watch us?"

Theo's voice could be heard again, *"Hell yeah ... me!"* Jake reaches over, takes the phone, closes it and lays it up on the bar.

Sherry walks around the bar and places her hand on his crotch. "That thing wants out. Set it free, sugar, and let sweet Sherry relieve some stress."

"Nope, not this time. I'm standing my ground."

She licks her lips again, "If you won't let it out, I'll open the cage for you." She unzips his pants, reaches in and pulls it out.

"Look, we can't keep doing this." She goes to her knees and disappears behind the bar. She places her mouth over it. He closes his eyes for a minute knowing he was about to explode, when suddenly the door flies open and Rodger wheels to a stop in the doorway yelling, "I almost forgot my paperwork!" He sees the expression on Jake's face, "What's wrong? You look a little pale. I'll make you an appointment with my doctor sometime this week."

Jake couldn't say a word. Sherry could hear her husband, but never took her mouth off him. Rodger wheels over to the table, then suddenly stops and turns, "Look Jake, no matter what the dress looks like, say it looks great and don't let her over-eat. She worries about her weight and is hell to live with the next day."

Jake says, "Too late."

"What?"

"I said, 'okay.'"

Rodger laughs, "You kill me; always got it going on." He wheels out the door.

Jake pulls her up from her knees and says, "Enough, we almost got caught."

She walks around the bar and over to a deer head mounted on the wall. She reaches up and grabs the wide placed antlers, throws an arch in her back, pushes her ass out exposing her well rounded cheeks and shakes it wildly. "Suppers on the table, try my new casserole out." She slaps herself on the ass and pulls her thongs to one side. He can't stand it anymore. He runs around the bar, shoving it so far that she pulls the mounted head off the wall.

She yells, "Oh shit!! I pulled the head off."

"No, you didn't, it's right where it belongs." He starts stroking fast and vigorously with her still holding onto the antlers of the deer head that's now resting on a small rectangle oak table.

"I'm talking about … Oh my God, that … feels … so … great!" (Moaning and groaning take over)."

Thirty minutes later, Jake's adjusting the deer head back on the wall.

"How does that look? And why is this deer head so low on the wall? I'm surprised somebody hasn't walk into that damn thing and put an eye out."

She's standing at the bar, "Looks like it's straight to me. Roger lowered it further than the rest so he can use it for a hat and coat rack."

Jake, "I'm not sure about hats and coats, but it works well for quick sex."

He turns after putting the deer head back on the wall, "I need to tell you something."

"You wanna do it again?"

"Yea, but that's not what I want to talk about. Casey called me yesterday and said she had some info to tell me about the murders. She got in the car and then had me drive down a short dirt path. She said she didn't want anyone to see us talking. When I parked, she pulled her skirt up and ask me to finger her."

"Well, did you?"

"No, I didn't; if I did, I wouldn't be telling you. She pulled her panties off and then offered me a blowjob to get me in the mood. I jumped out of the car, then she got out, walked around and bent over the fender pulling her skirt up, stretching her arms across the hood wanting me to give it to her."

Sherry giggles, "I'm surprised you didn't take it; any other man would have. I have no idea what I'm going to do with that girl. She got that sex drive from me. I am a little jealous though."

"That's all you got to say?"

"She's been sneaking in my room taking my sex toys out and using them since she was fifteen."

"Ok I'm not getting anywhere with this. She also threatened to tell you and Roger I took the sex, if I didn't give it to her. She's out of control."

"She won't tell a soul Jake, she's horny as hell. That's why I put her on the pill. You didn't hurt her feelings, did you?"

"And that's what you're worried about."

"She just tried what I would have tried. She's a grown woman now."

Jake being a little sarcastic, "Well I guess next time she tries that; I will give it to her then. What do you have to say about that?"

"Well, I say, go easy on her at first because she's a virgin, I think, and I know for a fact you will wreak it with that thing you carry around."

"I can't believe how easy you're taking this."

"Mother nature, that's all I can say. Will you help me try on my new dress?"

"Sure, why not?"

"If you think I'm a bad mother, you should bend me over and punish me by spanking me really hard."

"What is it about the spanking stuff, it must run in the family."

CHAPTER 16

Later that evening after he had some tires put on the car, he was driving down Highway 32 with Sherry sitting in the passenger's seat and Casey in the back. Suddenly Sherry's hand crawls toward his thigh. Casey leans forward causing Sherry to quickly jerk her hand back.

Casey asks, "Hey Jake?"

"Yeah?"

"Can I have the first dance with you?"

Sherry intervenes, "Now Casey, he may not like to dance."

He gets a little excited at the thought of dancing and replies, "I love dancing. Why, I have you know, I'm the dance king of the Mobile Police Department. Nobody, and I mean nobody, can keep up with old Jakey-poo. You should see me drunk and on roller skates."

Casey continues, "Well I want the first dance."

"You got it sugar."

They drive up in front of a large metal building and park in an open slot to the side. He scans the full parking lot and then looks the large metal structure over, "It doesn't look like a barn."

Sherry quickly jumps out, runs around to his side of the vehicle and grabs his right hand as he exits the car, "They haven't used a real barn in thirty years, and before this night is over, this place will be crawling with people from three counties." As they start to walk, Casey grabs his left hand.

He smiles, "Wow!! I feel like the head rooster at a hen-pecking convention."

They walked through the front door, and he could see a live band setting up in the corner on a foot-high platform getting ready to play. He shakes his head and turns to Sherry, "Holy cow, a real hoedown, or is it called a shindig up here?"

Casey shouts out, "It's a square dance!"

Thirty minutes later, Casey sees him at the punch bowl and grabs him by the hand as the music starts up and heads for the center of the floor. They make their way around the dance floor with him making all the right moves.

Casey was trying to keep up when she says in a loud voice, "Wow, you dance great!! I can feel your thing pressing against my belly. I should have worn high heels."

He shouts back, "Thank you. Coming from the younger generation, I feel flattered." They continue to dance with other people joining in for a little line dancing. Sherry walks over to the large punchbowl and pours punch into three small plastic cups.

A young beautiful brunette in her thirties wearing short denim hot pants walks over to get a drink and says, "Hey Sherry, check out the Italian dude dancing with your daughter."

"Oh, I have checked him out alright and he's staying at my house."

"You're kidding me?" She steps closer, "So, how is he in bed?"

"Now Janet, what makes you think I would do such a thing?"

"I know if he was staying at my house, I'd kick George right out the front door. Your husband is disabled, and a woman has certain needs."

Sherry snaps back, "Why Janet Singletary, you are one dirty minded girl! You stick with the mailman."

"Oh, come on girlfriend, you mean you're going to stand there and tell me that you have a man who looks like that, and can dance too, staying in your house and you're not letting him hit that?"

"I'm not that kind of woman." She leans over and in a low voice, "He's got a nine inch…"

About this time Casey comes running over pulling him by the hand, "Mama, did you see us dance?"

"I sure did." Sherry grabs him by the hand, winks at Janet and takes off for the dance floor."

Suddenly the door flies open and in comes Deputy Miller with three other ornery dudes. They walk over to the glass punchbowl with bottles of beer in hand.

Miller asks Janet, "I see our new lawman is having a good time when he's supposed to be out looking for the killer."

She gives him a look, "Is he that smart good-looking Lieutenant they brought up from Mobile that everyone's talking about?"

"He doesn't look that smart to me." Miller responds.

She quickly pulls out a tube of lipstick and places a thick red coat on her lips. "He doesn't have to be smart; he has a nine-inch plow handle, and he can frisk me any damn time he wants. Wow!! Big change from all you dumb-ass hicks around here. Y'all dance like you're dodging cow shit. They said he's as rugged as a lumberjack, but I never imagined he looked that good."

Miller, with a smirk on his face, "He's not that tough looking either."

She leans closer, "I'm not going to mention any names, but I heard from everybody in town, he threw a certain deputy through, not one, but two windows."

"You're a real smartass tonight, Janet. Where's George … at home watching TV?"

"Yep, right where that sourpuss should be. I'm glad he's not here. I would like a shot at that man. He can bend me over anytime anywhere. That ponytail is driving me crazy."

Miller looks down at her cheeks hanging out of her short denim hot pants and asks, "You wanna dance?"

"Not with you I don't. I'm waiting for a turn on the floor with that side of beef out there." The music slows down and Sherry steps in close, placing Jake's left knee between her legs.

He steps back and in a very low voice, "Stop that before someone sees us."

"You kidding? Every lucid woman in this place hasn't taken their eyes off you since we walked through that door." She steps even closer, "I can feel it rubbing my leg."

"Yeah, I should have left him back at the house."

A few minutes later Casey comes running out on the floor and with a smile, "Hey mama, let me slow dance with him before the song is over."

Sherry laughs and says, be my guess, I need another drink from that punch bowl anyway." She walks off as Casey steps in closer, grabs his hand and starts dancing. She pulls him even closer, looks up at him and with a very big smile, "You having second thoughts about yesterday? You know if I was a little shorter you could put that thing right in my…."

He interrupts her, "I'm going to stop dancing if you don't cool it down a bit."

"You remember when I told you I peeked in the bedroom the other night and saw you putting it to my mama. I knew then you were the man for me. All that moaning and groaning my mama was doing. I was so turned on that I had to go into my room and play with myself. I saw your, 'you know what', when you took a shower the next morning. Tight ass too."

"You said that already. How old are you again?"

"Eighteen, will be nineteen in five months and I'm a virgin."

"You have already told me that too."

"I want you to break it in for me. I also know my mama took you to the equipment shed. I bet you were a mouth full."

"For a virgin, you sure know your way around."

"My girlfriends and I read a lot of dirty magazines. I want you to teach me everything you can. I know a corn silo not far from here, maybe when my mother gets busy telling all the women about you, we can sneak off. I'm so turned on right now I could explode."

"Wow that sure is a mighty long song. You have me feeling a little uncomfortable.........again."

Sherry walks back out on the floor, "Ok Casey, it's mama's turn."

Casey gives him a wink as she walks off.

Sherry grabs his hand and starts dancing. She leans in close and says in a low voice, "You make me so horny; let's have a few more drinks and take a walk across the field. I know where there's a nice empty silo just waiting for some hot, steamy sex."

"I just heard about that silo just a few minutes ago from Casey."

"I'm not wearing any panties either."

"Well Sherry, thanks to you I now have a silo of my own just waiting to have sex, but we can't leave; Casey is sitting over there waiting for another turn on the dance floor again."

Sherry nods, "I think she has a crush on you."

"Really, I would have never guessed. How can you tell that?"

"A woman can tell when another woman wants a man by the twinkle in her eye."

"My first clue was when she pulled her panties off for me and ask me to finger her. I have a daughter that age."

"That makes no difference to a girl with hormones racing out of control."

Jake, "She's not the only one with their hormones racing out of control."

"My hormones are not out on control, I'm in love."

Jake reaches up and pinches his own cheeks, "My face in going numb, what's in the punch?"

Sherry, with an uneasy expression answers, "I'm so sorry; I forgot to tell you that someone always spikes the punch with homemade moonshine."

"Don't be sorry; pour me another. I've never felt so good after drinking so few."

Hours later he can hardly stand on his own and is watching a large group of women lining up against the wall, when Casey walks over and asks, "Are you gonna be all right Jake?"

"Sure, what the hell are all those women lined up for?"

"They all wanna dance with you."

"Where's your mother?"

"She had to go to the bathroom." He glances around the room with his head bobbing back and forth. Casey tugs on his belt and in a nervous tone says, "I think I'm in love with you."

"Are you old enough to know what love is?"

"I've never felt this way before. My heart is racing like crazy."

"Look Casey, I'm fifty-five years old and you're only eighteen."

"Almost nineteen."

"It would never work. Our kids would look like old people with fine asses."

"I want to have sex with you, right now."

He places his finger against her lips, "Not too loud, people can hear you."

"Will you have sex with me tonight? That empty silo is just waiting for us."

He gets nervous, "That sure is one popular silo." He glances around the room, "It sure is taking your mother a long time, maybe I should go check on her…"

Back in the lady's bathroom, Sherry steps from of a stall and straightens her short green dress. She stops in front of a mirror to check her make-up when she sees Miller standing behind her, with a sinister grin on his face, "Hey Sherry, you sure look good enough to eat in that sexy short dress."

"What the hell are you doing here? Get out right now!!"

"What's wrong baby? You think that worn out old detective can give you what you need."

"He can give me what I need and more. I'm telling you to get your skinny ass out right now or I'll scream."

"Oh, you're gonna scream for sure."

"Look Miller, you've had too much to drink, so get out of here before someone comes walking in."

He staggers closer, "I'll tell you what sweet cheeks, you turn around and lift that dress up and show me that sweet ass of yours and I'll leave."

"I'm not showing you anything. Now get out of my way."

He grabs her by the hair of the head and forces her to except his kiss. He then flips her around and pushes her up over the sink. She tries to turn back around but is unable to break free from him. He pushes her face against the mirror, smearing make-up on the glass, lifts her dress forcefully and unzips his pants. "Wow no panties. Well, this is gonna make it easy, and I know for a fact that cripple bastard isn't doing it for you. I've been thinking about you lying in bed all night not having what a woman needs. I have exactly what you need, and I bet that thing is tight after years of no sex."

She struggles harder to get out of his tight grip, "You're hurting me, now let me go!"

He shoves her tightly against the sink once again, this time rougher than before. "You're going to enjoy this! I can watch the expression on your face in the mirror when I slide this big corn cob up in that juicy hole, and you can watch my face as I enjoy myself. I've been watching you walk all over town for years with those short dresses, just begging for this."

"Stop it, you're hurting me!"

She could feel his small rock-hard penis as it started to slowly press against the crack of her ass. He smiles into the mirror and then closes his eyes as he says, "I'm about to launch a missile in you, whore. Five, four, three, two..."

Another voice, "One, blast off!" Suddenly, a hand grabs him by the hair of the head and pulls him off of her. She steps away as Jake shoves Miller's face against the same mirror sending a vertical crack from top to bottom. Jake looks into the mirror with a grin, "Well whatta ya know Deputy, I can see the expression on your face, and you have that, 'oh shit I've screwed up again' look on it.' Oh yeah, and get this, you can see me as I enjoy what I'm going to do to you."

"Look O'Malley, I was just having some fun that's all. I didn't mean her any harm." He forces his eyes toward Sherry, "Tell 'em Sherry, I was just kidding, I meant you no harm."

Jake shakes Miller's head back and forth, "Don't you even look at her you redneck bastard. Now if I was gay, I'll watch the expression on your face as I shove this watermelon, I have between my legs up that dry hole you have, which is so tight right now I bet you could pinch a railroad spike in half. But I'm not gay, so I guess I will have to settle with throwing your ass out the door."

Miller stutters, "You're too drunk to throw anyone out the door."

Outside the bathroom in the corridor Janet is walking toward the bathroom when suddenly the door comes off the hinges as Miller lands against the opposite wall. Jake grabs Sherry by the hand and leads her out into the main room where he sees Casey.

Janet laughs, "Hey Sherry, I think I wanna spend the night at your house tonight!!" She turns to Miller lying on the floor with his small penis sticking out his jeans, "Again Miller!! What is it about you flying all around a room like a ballon cut loose!?"

Miller, "Help me up."

"You help yourself up asshole! And you are about to lose your pencil!"

As they walk across the dance floor, Jake shouts, "Let's go Casey, it's time to get home."

"Crap, it's still early." She replied.

They walk outside and there standing between them and the car are the three large men who came in with Miller. Jake steers the girls over to the side and then turns back toward the group of men. "Okay assholes, do we go at this one at a time or all at once. I've done it both ways."

One big man steps forward, "When we get through with you, we're gonna put what's left of your ass on a bus back to Mobile."

"Well, you boys might whip my ass, maybe, but after we're through here, I doubt very seriously any of you will be able the put me on a bus. I love sex, but fighting like a bagger turns me on too."

The big man swings and Jake ducts and drives his fist into his ribcage. The man falls to the ground when another runs toward him. Jake takes a foot and drives it into the man's kneecap. His vision is a little blurred from the liquor and he has trouble keeping his balance. They all piled on top of him dragging him to the ground. Jake grabs a calf and bites into it when two others start kicking him in the face and ribs. He's taking a beating and thinks that this may be the first battle he's lost in a long time. He wasn't really feeling the kicks but could tell there was going to be some damage in the morning.

Suddenly a loud ear shattering blast from a shotgun went off. The men stopped kicking and turned around only to find a large dark figure standing with a sawed-off pump shotgun in hand.

A smooth voice in an easy tone could be heard coming from the shadows, "That's my white ass wop cracker brother you assholes are beating on and I'm damn funny about somebody kicking my kinfolk......enough!"

One-man yells, "What business is this of yours, dude?"

The dark figure speaks out, "If he wasn't drunk, I would have just stood here while he whip y'all's ass. Now that sound you just heard is what number two buckshot sounds like hitting the ground. You assholes wanna hear what else Bertha can spit from her mouth?" Jake knew that voice. He rolls over on his back as the men backed off. Sherry and Casey ran over and helped him to his feet. He could barely see for the blood pouring from his head and down over his eyes.

Jake says, "I'm not sure of the voice, but I know that shotgun blast anywhere. It's Big Bertha and the only other man who has access to that gun is my black ass shadow!

Theo steps into the light, smoking a cigar and motions with the short barrel of the pump for the men to step back against a red four-wheel drive truck covered with mud. Theo says, as the cigar shifts to the corner of his mouth, "Now just stand there against that ridiculous monster truck and don't twitch a muscle."

Jake leans against a car fender, "Is that one of my cigars, Theo?"

Theo snickers, "Yeah, I needed a special affect or a prop as the movie people call it."

Jake nods as he wipes the blood from his mouth, "I don't give a shit what you call it, it's still one of my ten-dollar cigars?"

Theo frowns, "I drive all the way up here to save your drunk, miserable ass and all you can do is bitch about a cigar?"

About this time Miller came sneaking up behind Theo. Jake winks a swollen eye and Theo shoves the shock of the gun backwards into Miller's gut. He falls to the ground as Theo steps closer and shoves the barrel in his face, "Say hello to my little friend' redneck?!"

Jake looks over at Sherry and Casey, "He's been looking for the right opportunity to use that line ever since we saw the movie but wasn't sure he wanted to violate any copyright laws."

Theo yells, "Whatta we do with these K.K.K. rejects Jake?"

"Let 'em go; they've had their fun."

Theo nods his head, "Okay boys, you heard the boss, move your asses before I remember what y'all did to me in **Roots**."

They take off running toward their trucks. Miller walks off holding his stomach. "Your black ass is as good as dead!"

Theo turns with Bertha pointed right at his midsection, "What did you call me, you toothless piece of white cornbread?"

Miller looks down at the barrel of Bertha as a lump forms in his throat, "I'm sorry, I meant Sargent Williams."

He staggers off as Theo turns to Jake and the girls, "So, introduce me to these two awesome white roses."

Jake smiles, "Sherry, this is my partner and brother and closest friend, Sergeant Theo Williams. Theo, this is Sherry, the Mayor's wife, and this young lady to my left is her daughter Casey."

Theo holds his hand out, "Jake exaggerates a little, I'm his only friend. And I have already met you, Sherry."

She asks, "You have?"

"I was on the phone earlier today when you…"

Jake interrupts, "Enough said. If you three will help me to the car we can go home before I pass out."

Theo asks, "Home, as in Mobile?"

Jake answers, "We're staying in the guestroom at the mayor's house. You can sleep with me, Theo."

Sherry interrupts as she helps him to the car, "But Jake, you need a room to yourself because…" She looks over at Casey hoping she didn't catch on.

Casey shouts, "Yeah Jake, you need a room to yourself!"

Theo smiles, "I definitely need to see this special room y'all keep talking about."

Jake looks out across the parking lot as Miller staggers off holding his stomach, "I have no idea how that asshole closes a door or window, but I know how he opens them." He turns to Theo and changes the subject, "How did you know we were here?"

"I called the mayor this morning and he told me you were escorting his family to the dance."

"What made you think to bring Big Bertha?"

"Well, I put alcohol, women, and rednecks together in the same place as you, and I came up with drunk, sex or trouble. I brought a condom and Bertha just in case I was wrong. Pretty good detective work huh?"

"Yep, my black knight in shining armor. I really didn't need your help you know."

"Is that right? Well, it looked like they were kicking the shit out of you pretty good there."

"They were getting tired and then I would have had them by the balls. And now that I'm not eating dirt, why are you here? You're supposed to be in Mobile running names … "

"I put Freddy in charge of that. As soon as he finds something out of the ordinary, he'll call me on my cell."

"Freddy?"

"Yep, Freddy."

"You're talking about stuttering Freddy?"

"One in the same."

"It takes him two hours to say ten words."

"What's that got to do with him running the names on that ridiculously long list you gave me. The computer doesn't know he stutters. Do you know how embarrassing it was for the guys to see a fine, hardworking detective like me behind a desk doing a menial task? Anyway, Freddy's a wiz when it comes to computers."

"You dumb-ass Theo; when he finds something, it will take him hours to tell us."

"Well, if this isn't a fine thank you for saving your white ass, maybe he can use a fax machine. It doesn't know he stutters either."

CHAPTER 17

Later that night, he sits on the edge of the bathtub with Sherry doctoring his face. Casey was standing at the doorway when Sherry asks her, "Honey can you go downstairs and get me some Betadine from the other bathroom for these cuts?"

"Sure mama." She turns and walks away and as soon as she goes down the stairs Sherry reaches down and starts rubbing him between his legs.

He pushes her hand away, "Somebody is going to catch us."

"Why would you want Theo to sleep in the bed with you when you can have me?"

"It doesn't look so suspicious. He might snore, but he won't pull on me all night."

Casey returns, "I can't find it mama."

"I'll get it myself." She walks out and down the stairs. No sooner did Sherry leave, did Casey walked into the bathroom, reached down and grabbed him between the legs.

Jake pushes her hand back, "Enough girl! Do you know how hard it is to hide this budge as it is. You two have me hard 24/7?"

"If you hadn't let Theo sleep in your bedroom, I would have sneaked in there and let you have the tightest stuff you have ever had. Pull it out and let me just look at it."

"Look, I need a shower, so I can get some rest. I have a long day tomorrow."

Casey, "I have an idea, why don't you wait until everybody is asleep and I'll take one with you, say about two in the morning. I won't miss a spot." She winks and turns to walk out the door when Sherry enters the bathroom.

Casey starts to close the door, "He said forget all that, he's going to take a shower."

Sherry steps out in the hallway where Casey was standing and smiling, "What were you two talking about while I was gone?"

"Detective stuff."

"Yea, I bet you were. Look, I know you have a crush on him but he's closer to my age."

"I'm going to bed now. I'll see you in the morning mama." Casey avoiding the conversation.

Ten minutes later, he's in the shower when he hears the door open than closed.

In a low voice but just over the sound of the shower he says, "Look Casey you need to give it a break."

Sherry steps into the shower butt naked, "It's not her. Here let me clean that for you." She drops to her knees as the water ran off his body and onto her long blonde hair."

Twenty minutes later she steps from the shower, dries off and puts her robe on and walks from the bathroom. She takes notice of Casey watching from her bedroom door.

Casey, "How was it?"

"I'll be lucky if I don't have lockjaw in the morning…. It was fantastic!" She winks an eye and with a smile she walks to her bedroom."

Minutes later he comes limping into the guestroom. Theo is lying in bed with his hands behind his head grinning from ear to ear.

"You gonna be alright little buddy? What took you so long in the shower?"

He sits on the side of the bed, "What a wild ride my friend. I hurt worse than them damn hemorrhoids you're always bitching about, and it had nothing to do with the fight I had."

"You'll feel better in the morning. I've seen you take worst asswhooping's on more than one occasion."

"First of all, buffalo butt, they didn't whip my ass."

"Yeah, right; then how come you were eating dirt when Big Bertha and I showed up?"

"Look lard-ass, I was just catching my breath when you popped up and ruined what was supposed to be a good exercise session. Have you ever seen me lose a fight?"

"Nope, not until tonight."

Jake stands and takes off his robe that Roger let him use and wearing nothing but boxers he crawls in bed next to Theo.

"Man, it feels good to stretch out and relax."

Theo turns his head toward him, "Man these sheets feel good on my black ass."

"How in the hell can you feel sheets on your ass through your underwear?"

"Who's wearing underwear?"

"Get…out…of…this…bed…right…now!!"

"What the hell for? I always sleep naked."

"Not next to me you don't. Now get some freakin boxers on."

"I don't have any; I wear briefs. My boys need to have a secure place to rest. I can't have my giant man tool flopping from side to side."

"They're going to have a secure place in your throat if you don't put something on."

Theo jumps out of bed, "Fine then, be that way. I don't see how me not wearing underwear has anything to do with you. It's a king size bed."

"I don't want your shit accidentally flopping over on me in the middle of the night, if that's possible. What part of that you do you not understand?"

Theo puts his briefs on and jumps back on the bed so hard it bounced Jake right out on the floor.

Jake peeks over the side of the bed, "Damn you!"

"Sorry." He pulls the sheets up around his chest as Jake crawls back in. He laughs and says, "Sherry told me that they have three guestrooms, so why did you suggest me sleeping with you?"

"She has me screwing all hours of the night and day. I'm not getting any rest. My penis has been fondled, washed, and sucked nonstop since I got here."

"She sure is a fine-looking woman and that daughter of hers is sharp looking too. I've said it once, I'll say it again; you are by far the luckiest bastard I know. How do you do it?"

"You have asked me that every day since I first met you. Again, I have no idea; I guess I'm just a goodlooking man after all. I heard through the grapevine that when I was born the nurses had a fight to see who was going to care for me when I wasn't feeding."

"How does her husband not know she's sneaking in here to have sex?"

"The only time I see him is at mealtimes."

Sherry told me he's at the office catching up on all kinds of shit. So, what time of night does all this take place?"

Jake opens one swollen, sleepy eye and then the other, "What time does what take place?"

"The orgy you've been having since I left."

"What orgy are you talking about?"

"Oh, for crying out loud, didn't you tell me over the phone the mayor's wife was sneaking in here and having sex with you?"

"So?"

"So, what time can we expect her tonight?"

"She's not sneaking in here while you're here."

"Is it because I'm black?"

Jake thinks for a second, "Yes, she does not wanna jump in bed with us because you're black."

"What's the big deal with my color? You jumped in bed with me...and out."

Jake, trying to be funny, "It's okay with me; you're not my first black man."

"Well, I appreciate that. You're not my first white cracker I've been in bed with either."

Jake, with a fake frown says, "That hurts."

Silence takes over when Theo asks, "You gonna give me the details? I would like to get a boner even if I don't get sex."

Jake turns his head, "Ok, it looks like you are not going to get any sleep until I tell you. Two nights ago, after Roger left, she came in here and did everything a woman can possibly do while her daughter watched through a crack in the door. Then she raped me again in the school's equipment shed. Then she rubbed her thigh all over me at the dance until she was wet enough to qualify as a lake, and then her daughter danced with me giving me another erection with the dirty talk, and to top all that, they took turns rubbing my penis in the bathroom while doctoring my head up and not the one on my shoulders."

Theo places his hand over his mouth and says in a loud whisper, "Oh my...."

Jake interrupts, "I'm not finished yet; Sherry, not twenty minutes ago got in the shower and cleaned it with her mouth. I'm surprised I can't see myself reflecting off the head of it. I'm also surprised they both didn't put sleeping pills in your drink so they can come in here at two in the morning and have their way with me while you sleep right next to the action."

"Oh crap!!"

"What's wrong?"

"Sherry fixed me a drink then handed it to Casey to hand to me...before I came up here. Oh crap, they both had the opportunity and the means to commit the crime."

"Well, if that doesn't beat all. No sleep for me tonight. If that doesn't take the cake!"

"Well now I'm hard as marble, what are your thoughts on the homicides?"

"I'm narrowing it down each day."

"You have any particular suspect in mind?"

"I think it's the sheriff or it could even be Deputy Miller. I mean he did try to sexually molest Sherry tonight."

"Could also be this Bo who you spent the night with?"

"It's not him; he doesn't have the brain capacity to pull a murder off."

"Didn't he say he watched the girls from the woods as they practiced?"

"It's not him."

"I say he's just fooling you with that dumb talk."

"Then how come he didn't cut my throat with my knife when he had the chance?"

"I have no idea; that would have been the first thing on my list."

"So fat, yet so funny! Go to bed Theo... Theo... Theo!!" He turns his head and sees him knocked completely out. He hears the door opening and then closes.

The next morning Rodger knocks on the bedroom door. He knocks several more times before slowly opening it. Jake was laying half off the bed and Theo had his leg and arm wrapped around him. Rodger slowly wheels in and leans over whispering in his ear.

"Hey Jake, wake up."

Jake again opens one eye then the other. "Good morning, Rodger. That arm and leg, does it belong to who I think it does?"

"Yes, I believe it does."

Jake yells at the top of his lungs, "Get the hell on your side of the bed Theo!!!"

Theo moans and then opens his eyes. "Oh my God!"

Jake sits up, "What the hell were you thinking crawling on top of me like that!?"

Theo yells back, "What the hell were you thinking crawling under me like that!?"

Jake gets really pissed, "That is your side of the bed, and this is my side of the bed!!"

Rodger breaks in, "I hate to interrupt a lover's spat, but Ray called, and they found another girl. I'll have Doc Turner come by and give a mild sedative to the girls when they wake. I told Ray to rope off the murder scene and not touch a damn thing."

Jake responds, "Yea, I bet he does just that. They find her in the woods?"

"This girl was found under the bleachers."

"Which girl is it?"

"Amber Jennings."

"That's the girl that wouldn't talk the other day."

Rodger shakes his head, "She's not going to speak today either."

Jake turns to Theo, "Get dress Casanova, we have work to do."

Twenty minutes later they drive to the scene and see several police units parked in the parking lot next to an ambulance. Theo gives Jake a look.

Jake asks, "What's on your mind elephant ass?"

"Did you see the mayor row down that stairway? He made it look so easy. How does he get up the stairs?"

"Let me guess, you didn't see that slow moving apparatus attached to the stairwell?"

"I did not, so why does he not use it to go down those stairs?"

"I not sure but it sounds like he's got the going down part to an artform."

Jake steps out and walks past the cars and toward the yellow tape around the south end of the bleachers. Theo is right on his heels. Three officers are standing near the body smoking cigarettes and talking with Sheriff Ray. Ray sees them coming and meets Jake halfway.

Jake, "You guys getting turned on over the naked corpse and throwing cigarette butts on the ground. I sure hope the killer didn't throw his on the ground as he was taking care of business. Let me explain some basic investigating practices. Every time somebody throws a cigarette butt on the ground, every time you take a step, and every time to many damn police officers are standing to close to the body, you contaminate the crime scene."

Ray, being sarcastic, "I guess while you were dancing and fighting last night our killer decided he needed another. I don't know why we need you two up here, my men can screw up that bad."

Jake's left eye starts blinking when Theo steps up and hands him a cigar. "Take this Jake, it will calm you down."

Jake, "Too late for that Theo, but I'll take it anyway." He turns back to Ray, "I didn't come up here to do your damn job asshole! You should have placed a close patrol on the school. I guess your guys were drinking coffee discussing who's gonna have sex with their sisters or aunts, and why are you idiots so adamant about screwing up a crime scene?"

"We didn't touch a thing just like the mayor told me not too."

"Prove it dip wad."

Theo, "Calm down Jake, just pay no attention to him. This girl's death had nothing to do with what happen last night. They're just pissed because they can't solve a jay-walking complaint or whack off without instructions."

Ray, "I guess you would know more about whacking off."

Theo in a loud voice, "Just what the hell does that mean!? And for your information redneck, I have the instructions right here in my wallet. And if I remember correctly, your deputy was at the dance last night, also, and he was starting trouble. Why the hell wasn't he out guarding the freaking streets?"

Jake steps up closer to the Sheriff, "Dancing and drinking makes me concentrate better. I'm narrowing my suspects down a little at a time and you and your deputy's not off the list yet. So, one more smartass remark from you and I will slap your teeth out of that funny shaped empty head of yours. And another thing Mr. Chicken-shit, your deputy tried to rape the mayor's wife last night."

"So what, she wears those dresses up to her ass and boobs pushed up like a hooker. She's just asking for it. Hell, I bet you're even tagging her and her slut for a daughter too."

Jake responds, "Oh my God, you're a physic." He turns to Theo, "Hey Theo, this man's a physic."

Theo nods and in a low mumble, "And it's showtime."

Jake smiles, "It amazes me the way physics can see shit beforehand that ordinary people can't see. Hey Ray, can you see what I'm going to do next?"

The Sheriff laughs, "What's that, get mad and call the mayor?"

Jake slaps him so hard he immediately hits the ground holding his jaw. The other officers attempt to make a move when Theo steps forward with his hand under his coat, "Say the word, Jake. I've just about had enough of this hillbilly mentality shit anyway."

About this time a voice was heard in the background, "Hold it right there Theo, I'll take care of this." They all turn and see the mayor rolling up. He says to the Sheriff in an angry tone, "Get up and go back to the station Ray, I'll take care of you later."

Ray struggles to his feet, "You saw what he just did to me Rodger."

"Yes, I did, and I heard what you said about my wife and daughter. You're lucky I can't stand on my feet, or I would slap you myself, now get outta here, before I let Jake continue whipping that sorry ass of yours!!"

Ray walks off as Jake turns his attention to the body lying under the bottom of the concrete steps leading up to the bleachers. He turns to Theo, "Get your camera from the trunk and start taking photographs. I want clear ones from every angle."

Theo nods and walks back to the car. Roger follows Jake as he walks over and bends down toward the girl. He pulls some rubber gloves from his back pocket, slides them over his hands, and commences to examine the young beautiful naked body particularly the neck area. He lifts her body up slightly and runs his hand across the ground. "She was strangled like the others and there's a fresh needle mark on her left arm also."

Rodger leans closer, "I know this girl, and she would have never used drugs. She was a good girl, kind of quiet and from a good family."

"Somebody gave her the drugs, raped her, strangled her and then threw her body here. And I think I know who called this in."

The mayor says, "How do you know that?"

"Because I think he called the other three in, but puzzled to know what phone and how he knows to use it. He's mentally handicap and I'm not talking about the Ray and Miller…. this time. This man goes by the name of Bo, and he lives about five miles from here in an old burned-out cabin."

"How do you know that?"

"Because I spent the other night with him and that's not all. His grandmother was old lady Harper. He hides in the woods watching the girls practice soccer. I need DNA from every officer in the department, especially from Ray and Miller. I will send them to Mobile for a proper analysis. I'll get the results quicker."

"Okay, what else do you need? Just name it and you got it."

"Our killer is carrying around a small heart-shaped locket."

"How do you know that?"

"Well, it's just a good guess right now, but look right here just above the breast. This girl has been lying out soaking up some sunrays for tanning purposes and a heart shape locket of some kind blocked the sun, causing her to tan everywhere but where it was hanging."

"Maybe she just didn't have it on last night."

"If she didn't remove it before lying out, it meant a lot to her, so she had it on when she was murdered."

Theo walks up and starts taking pictures. Jake points to her upper torso, "Get some close ups of her chest and neck area and take one of that needle mark on her arm." Jake turns to Rodger, "I'll get her blood samples from the coroner or doctor and send them off for testing. That will tell us what kind of drug she was injected with." He starts to walk off when he turns back to Rodger, "Don't tell anyone about the locket. If word gets out, he'll lose it."

A deputy yells across the distance where the dumpster is. "Hey, I found her clothes!!" They walk to the dumpster as the officer is collecting pieces of garment and throwing them out on the ground.

Jake gets pissed and turns to the mayor and Theo, "See what I'm talking about! This asshole touch the clothes with his bare hands and then threw them on the ground contaminating all evidence." He gives the officer an angry stare, "Now that you have screwed up the evidence, you can take them to my car and put them on the backseat!"

Rodger wheels over, "I'm sorry Jake he's new on the job."

"Well, this shows Bo hasn't been through the dumpster yet. Looks like somebody was in a hurry and forgot to burn them."

"Look Jake, it sounds like this Bo dude is your man." Jake scans the soccer field and then the pine thicket. He walks around the edge of the woods and stops at a crop of bushes, glances down, then picks up a candy wrapper. He smells the wrapper then walks from the woods. Rodger and Theo meet him at the edge of the road.

Theo nods, "What's up?"

"Bo didn't kill anybody, but I bet he witnessed the murder last night. We need to find out who was the last person she talked to. I wanna question every girl on the team separately, and I wanna know if she had a boyfriend. See if he was the one who gave her the locket. Theo and I are going to get a bite to eat and then we can all meet at the Sheriff Office. I wanna question everyone there one at a time." He turns to Rodger, "Can you have Sherry round up the rest of the team and bring them there?"

"I sure can; anything else?"

"Not right now. I'll go find Bo this evening and maybe, that's if he was watching last night, I'll have a description on our man."

Rodger has a puzzled look on his face.

Jake asks, "What wrong Rodger?"

"I was just wondering how you know the candy wrapper wasn't left from another time. It could have been there for weeks or months."

Jake snickers, "The ants told me that, they were still crawling over the chocolate residue and before you ask, yes they can pull prints off of paper, but it won't do us any good."

"Why is that?"

"Because I already know Bo's prints are on it. This is where Bo was watching the murder take place."

They all turn as an ambulance attendant yells, "Can we take the body now? It's getting hot out here."

Jake turns to Theo, "You have everything you need?"

"Yeah, I looked the ground over pretty good for the locket, so I guess it's okay to remove her."

Jake yells back at the ambulance attendant, "Go ahead … !!"

CHAPTER 18

Jake sat there at the table cutting an over-cooked porkchop as Theo destroyed two pounds of chopped steak, a large pile of mash potatoes with gravy, a side of collard greens, cream corn and a large triangle piece of cornbread. Jake takes a bite and stares out the window as Theo with his mouth full of mashed potatoes spits some across the table when he asks, "What's wrong Jake? You're not acting like yourself."

"Thanks for the mashed potatoes. Swallow your food before you speak."

"I'm just saying I want the old Jake back."

"I'm no different than I've always been."

"Oh yes you are. An hour ago, you slapped an asshole to the ground, and it took you twice as long to think about it before you acted. And you said you were going to slap his teeth out, but none went airborne."

Jake looks out the window of the cafe and hesitates before saying, "You're right, something has come over me. I would never have gotten involved with a married woman a week ago or maybe, especially a handicapped man's wife, and when I was humping the life out of her, I thought of nothing but Ann. She went at it again last night."

"How did I miss all that action?"

"The sleeping pills. Did you forget that already?"

"Damn pills; I need to start fixing my own drinks. How'd you keep a boner if you were thinking about Ann?"

"You know as well as I do that thing has a mind of its own. And get this, today when I saw Amber's body, I thought of Jackie and for the first time in a lot of years, a murder took on a whole new meaning."

"Quite normal, my friend."

"Not for me it isn't…"

"Face it, you're a human being and subject to its rules. That and the fact we're not getting any younger."

"It's somebody these girls knew and knew well. Somebody they trusted. He's close; I can feel him watching me."

Theo glances around the café at all the people sitting there having lunch, "Stop it, you're giving me the creeps again with that kind of talk. If he's watching you, he's watching me, and I can't have that. You wanna here a joke to cheer you up?"

Jake turns to him, "It better not be the one about the inflatable sex doll you told me about on our way up here?"

"That was a gut-buster and a half. You laugh for ten minutes."

"I was laughing because that girl you where winking at in the other car flipped you off. Seriously, I told that joke the other day and ended up having to throw a heckler out a barbershop window."

"Did you tell it right?"

"I told it like I heard it."

Theo starts eating again then spits corn across the table and in Jake's face as he says, "Why don't you give Ann and Jackie a call. I bet they will be overjoyed to hear from you."

"Thanks for the corn, and they haven't called me once in three weeks."

"Oh my God, you of all men should know how they play their little games. Every woman in the world is as crazy as a shit-house rat. What makes you think Ann and Jackie are any different?"

"Let's change the subject. What should I do about Sherry?"

"What do you mean?"

"I can't keep this up, or can I? She needs to know I will never leave Ann."

"Why don't you use the plan 'B' of the sex code?"

"Plan 'B' of the sex code. I'm not sure I remember that one."

"That's the one where you screwed the shit out of her every freaking chance you get until you leave town, then give her the phone number to animal control and tell her to call you sometime."

"That works?"

"You have changed; of course it works. You remember that girl in Dallas a few years back, before Ann was in the picture?"

"Sherry's not that kind of girl."

"Holy shit; you have fallen for this woman."

"I have feelings for her, that's all. She's different from Ann. Sherry and I have sex without the bitching."

Theo spits collard greens across the table as he says, "Okay Jake, look into my eyes and listen closely, I'm about to repeat something you told me five years ago. All women are alike, especially if you turn 'em upside down."

"Thanks for the collard greens, and I was wrong. Sherry's different."

"Listen to yourself; you always said that when a jet is about to crash, pull the two loops over your head, ejecting your ass out and then you gently float to the ground. Never ride that bitch too long or you will splatter your guts over a cornfield."

"You actually remember all the shit I tell you?"

"Look Jake, before you came along, I had no life."

"You still have no life."

"That's my point exactly. You made me realize I really don't have one."

The waitress walks over and asks, "Separate checks or both on the same ticket?"

Jake replies, "Might as well put 'em on mine. I ate both plates." He pays the girl and they both walk out. Jake lights up his cigar and stares into the sky as the dark clouds travel rapidly out of the northwest. "Looks like rain moving in."

"Good. Maybe it will cool things off a little. Where to now?"

"Sheriff's Office."

Twenty minutes later they come walking into the lobby soaking wet. After seeing the old woman behind the desk he says to Theo, "This has got to be the biggest bitch I have ever met. Talking to her is like getting a tooth pulled without Novocain or a prostate examine with a 35 mm film projector with a zoom lens shove up your ass."

As they approached the desk, Jake could see that the building appeared to be deserted except for the angry ass old lady.

He asks the woman, "What's going on? It must be a holiday like a 'Annual tooth decay celebration."

Theo laughs, "Hey, I got one, maybe it's, 'Preacher off the Moonshine Day, or 'Corncob up the ass Day, or ... "

"Enough Theo." He turns to the old woman.

She nods, "They all met a few hours ago over at old lady Harper's place. They're going in after the skunk that killed those girls. They even borrowed six men from Alexander City's police department."

Theo gives Jake a look, "What guy?"

"The bastards going after Bo."

"But you told the sheriff and mayor he had nothing to do with the murders. You were supposed to go get Bo."

"Ray spotted a way out, a way to solve the homicides and get us out of the way. They're going to pen it on poor Bo."

"What do we do now, they will shoot first and ask questions later. Just from what you told me this Bo is too mentally unstable to go to trial."

"Let's get back to Roger's place and change clothes. I'm not stomping around in the woods in these wet monkey suits."

An hour later, the rain had stopped. They came pulling up next to a long line of patrol cars parked along the road not far from where the bodies were recovered. Jake sees Rodger sitting in his wheelchair facing a camera and anchor woman. Other council members were standing behind him. Across the street was a large crowd of town people.

Jake, "Word really gets out up here. They couldn't have started their search more than a few hours ago. Did you notice the clothes that officer put in our backseat are gone."

Theo looks in the back, "What the hell!"

They walk over to within ear shot of Rodger and listen as he spoke into the camera.

Rodger, "The good people of this county can be relieved that this nightmare is over. Through hard work and excellent police skills, we can now bring this horror to an end. I have been notified by radio, the suspect is in custody and they're on their way out as we speak. It took five officers to bring the suspect down."

The news woman asks, "Mayor…is it true that the suspect has been watching the girls' practice soccer?"

"Yes, and that's all I can say for now. We will have more information after the suspect has been booked and questioned. Thank you very much."

Roger starts to wheel away as the camera crew gathers their equipment, but is met by Jake and Theo.

In a loud tone Jake asks, "What the hell is going on here Rodger!?"

"Sheriff Ray, Miller and some others have apprehended our savage cold-blooded killer."

"It's not him. You have the wrong man. I told you that already. I thought we were all going to meet at the sheriff's office."

"I thought it over and then got to thinking it must be Bo, so I called the meeting off. Sorry I forgot to call you. Look, you said yourself, that Bo had watched the girls from the woods as they practiced. You said he took their clothes. We have the right man."

Jake, "That's not what I said. Bo took some uniforms from the dressing rooms. The clothes the girls had on were burned to cover up any DNA, and I know for a fact Bo didn't take the clothes from the rear seat of my car. Bo would not have enough sense to do that. Listen to me, Rodger. It's all too easy. Our killer is still out there waiting for the opportunity to strike again. It's like a shark's feeding ground around here. You're gonna have people relaxing and thinking that you have the right man."

"Look, I'm sorry I even brought you in on this. You have done a good job, and we appreciate what you did. We could not have made the arrest without you. I will see to it that you and your partner are fully compensated for your time."

"Screw the money, you have the wrong man! Bo is so disfigured that he couldn't get close enough to the girls if he wanted too. Think about something…. Would any girl get in a vehicle with Bo even if he had one or a driver license or take a locket from him even if he had the money to buy one. How would he have gotten them off by themselves? Hunger is what brought him out of the woods in the first place. The man who killed them girls is a regular who knew the girls personally, who the girls trusted like a police officer."

"I disagree with you. It was evil lust that brought that sick perverted animal out."

"Can I come by and at least talk to the man?"

"I'm pretty sure Ray's not going to let that happen. As mayor I can be accused of hampering the investigation. You can stay in the guestroom for one more night and you two can leave in the morning." He rolls toward his van when he suddenly stops and turns, "You boys take it easy and thanks again for all your help. You will be notified when the court proceedings start up in a few months." He rides up on the van ramp and slides inside, then struggles into the driver's seat and drives off.

Jake stares at the crowd as a grieving woman in her late thirties walks over and asks, "Did you know yesterday about this monster watching the girls practice?"

"Yes, I did, but…" She slaps him across the face, catching him with total surprise.

He asks, "What was that for?"

"My daughter, Amber, would be alive today if you had arrested this maniac when you found him." The grieving woman walks off with the help of several other women consoling her when Jake says, "Your daughter's killer is still out there." The woman disappears into the crowd.

Theo shakes his head, "That was totally uncalled for. They're wrong, and too blinded by rage and stupidity to see the truth. I'm not surprised one bit. Everybody up here has done nothing but make this case harder to solve. I say let's go back to Mobile and leave these hicks to feed pigs, grow corn and using their sister's as inbreeding shock."

Jake places his hand on Theo's shoulder, "It's okay, she has a right to unload. I would be the same way if it had been Jackie."

"Well, I guess we need to go pack."

"Why?"

"You heard what the mayor said."

"I'm not going anywhere. We can move back into the motel. I have a killer to catch." They start to walk off when Jake stops and sniffs the air. "You smell that?"

Theo sniffs the air, "It wasn't me."

"Take a deep breath."

"I'm not falling for that. And if it wasn't you, where is that stink coming from?"

"I'm not sure, still trying to put my finger on where I've run into that odor before."

They walk over and take a seat in the car as Jake stares into the crowd of people, "He's in the crowd."

"How do you know?"

"I felt his ass watching us the whole time I was talking to the mayor." Jake flips his cellphone open and punches in some numbers.

Theo asks, "Who are you calling?"

"Freddy; I wanna see if he's found anything yet."

The other end of the phone picks up, *"Hel...hel...hel...hello."* "Hey Freddy, this is Jake, have you found anything new with the list Theo gave you?"

"I, I, I, I'm glad you, you, you called me Jake. I, I, I, found out, that, that, that..."

Jake holds the phone away from his ear and places his hand over the mouthpiece. "I could just kill you, there are twenty people you could have given that list to and you had to give it to stuttering Freddy."

"What's the big deal Jake?"

"I…I…I…I will tell…you…you…you…later asshole." Jake continues, "Hey Freddy, slow down and tell me real slow what you found."

"I…I…I…found out… that… that… that…"

Jake yells, "Okay Freddy, give the damn phone to Jim!!"

Theo, "Have him sing it to you. They say a stuttering man doesn't stutter when he sings."

Silence comes over the phone for a second. Jim gets on the phone and says, ***"Hey…hey…hey Jake, what's… what's…new up there?"***

"Very funny, 'turd for brains.' Get the information from Freddy and call me back before I get pissed and come back down there and give you two assholes a reason to stutter."

Jim asks, ***"Hey Freddy, Jake wants to know what you found out on the list."*** A voice in the background could be heard, ***"I…I…I…was trying to…to…to…tell him. I…I…I…run the name Harper and…and…and…I…"***

Jake gets pissed and yells, "Okay, enough Jim!!! I'm going to hang up and when I call back in an hour you better have that shit of Fred's interpreted. You are literally five hours from getting your balls kicked!" He closes his phone and gives Theo an angry stare.

"I know that look, I'm telling you that Freddy can find more shit in ten minutes than I could have in ten years."

"Great Theo, it only takes him ten years to tell us what he found in ten minutes. For Pete's shake you have played cards with all of us, and the game takes hours because it takes Freddy ten minutes every time he ask for a card. You call him back in an hour and speak to Jim."

Theo smiles, "Where…where…where…to now?"

"Don't push it Theo. Let's go pay a doctor a visit."

"Why, my hemorrhoids took a turn for the better?"

"I…I…I feel a… flare…flare…flare-up coming…coming…on. We're going to find out what doctor treated Bo when he was burned."

"What makes you think he saw a doctor?"

"Those burns would have gotten infected and killed him without proper treatment."

"What if the doctor's no longer living?"

"Then we won't see him, will we?"

They drive off toward town…

156

Back at the Sheriff's office, Ray looks over at Miller, "I need you to take the girls clothes you took from the backseat of O'Malley's car and wipe Bo down with them. Make sure all his DNA is on her clothes or her DNA on his."

"What if that big bastard goes off on me?"

"He's still out cold; then after you do that, make sure he's not able to say a word to anyone. Get Ryan and Carl to help you. Don't make any mistakes this time. That O'Malley is smarter than a bloodhound. Take one of the girl's socks and place it in Bo's pocket."

Miller leans closer, "Why don't you let me shoot that bastard and his black ass partner?"

"That's all we need is a bunch of Federal agents getting involved. And the best reason is that if you miss, he will rip you to pieces. My God what is it about O'Malley you just don't get! The bastard is like grabbing a chainsaw by the wrong end while it's running or trying to finger fuck a damn tiger. Not another word."

CHAPTER 19

They drive into the rear parking lot of Doc Riley's office when suddenly, Theo turns to Jake, "Why don't we just go back to Mobile. They don't want our help."

"I'll tell you why, because four girls and an old lady have been killed, and an innocent man may get the death penalty for being in the wrong place at the wrong time and in the wrong mental state of mine. And the best reason of all, they don't want our help."

"How do you even know this is the right doctor?"

"I don't know, but that skinny-ass old black man back at the gas station says he's been practicing for over fifty years right here in Fairmont."

They walk into the waiting room and up to a young receptionist.

She smiles, "What can I do for you gentlemen today?"

"We would like to see Doc Riley please."

She glances down at an appointment book, "And your name."

"We're not here to see him for medical reasons. We need to ask him some questions."

"I'm sorry sir, but you'll have to make an appointment. I can check your blood pressure right here if that will help."

"I don't think your monitor will go that high." He scans the waiting room and sees it full of old people coughing and making hacking noises. "Yeah, they're in a hurry. Look sweetie, I'm Lieutenant O'Malley and this is Sergeant Williams. We are investigating the soccer girl murders."

"Oh, that was just horrible, but I heard on the news a few minutes ago that they arrested the killer this afternoon."

"We're just doing the final touchups and all; can we speak to him?"

She stands and walks into the backroom. A few seconds later an old gray-haired man sporting a short gray beard and wearing a white smock steps into the waiting room.

"What can I do for you two gentlemen today?"

Jake steps closer, "Can we step in your office for a few minutes Doc?"

They all walk from the lobby and into a small, but clean, office.

"You say you're police officers?"

"Yes sir."

"That's funny. I've treated every police officer in the county for one thing or another and I don't remember ever seeing you two. And I know for a fact we don't have a black officer."

"We're on loan out from Mobile."

"So, how can I help you?"

"Do you remember treating a young boy for severe burns, say, somewhere around twenty-eight years ago?"

"You'll have to be more specific; I've treated a lot of boys for burns over the last twenty-eight years."

"This boy was very large, burned bad; no hair, no ears and no reason to live, yet he still clings to life."

"You're talking about Bo."

"Bingo!!"

"Big boy weighed over 160 pounds at only ten years old. I'll never forget that day. His grandmother brought him in. I thought for sure he wouldn't make it. Burns were over ninety percent of his body. They say he was mentally handicap or something. I never got a chance to speak to him. I gave him antibiotics, wiped him down with ointment and wrapped him up like a mummy."

Jake tilts his head, "Why didn't she take him to a hospital for something as life threatening as that?"

"You have to understand the times and mentally of country folk."

"I can totally relate to that. Do you still have a file on Bo?"

"Don't have anything that goes past twenty-five years. I don't have the storage space."

"You said he was burned over ninety percent of his body. What ten percent was spared?"

"A small portion of his back. Why all the questions about a man that hasn't been seen since that night? I thought he died a long time ago."

"You must not watch the news. They arrested Bo this afternoon for the murder and rape of the four high school girls."

Doc Riley snickers, "Well I be damned."

"Why the snicker Doc; you find something funny about that?"

"Well, I'm not a detective and not sure if he murdered them or not; I'll have to take your word on that, but I do know for a fact he couldn't have raped anybody."

"Now why do you say that?"

"Because Bo has no wee wee."

"What?"

"He has no penis. It was burned down to a little black nub and his balls are gone too."

Theo gets a sick look on his face, "If that was me, I would be pissed at you for treating me in the first place. Without my special tool, I have no reason to live."

Jake shakes his head, "I don't see why you wanna live anyway Theo; that's all you have is a little black baby thumb a half inch long."

"Why do you find the need to say that shit in front of people asshole!?"

Jake leans closer, "You know this for a fact Doc?"

"I treated him, of course I know it for a fact."

"One more question Doc, where would a judge's office be around here?"

"That would be Judge Tyler, but you won't catch him in his office this time of day. You might catch him on the ninth hole at the Fairmount golf range."

Theo, "Let me get this right. This town doesn't have an English class within twenty miles, and they have a golf course?"

Thirty minutes later they drive a golf cart across the green asking each golfer for the where-a-bouts of the Judge. Finally, they drive up to three men with one lining up for a shot. They exit the golf cart and walk over as the man starts to swing.

Jake, in a loud voice, "You're leaning too far back!" The man leans forward and starts to swing when suddenly Jake yells again, "You're shoulders are slouching!" The man straightens his shoulders and starts to swing again when Jake yells, "Wrong stick!" The man strikes the ball and slices it into the tree line.

He turns to him with an angry stare, "Can I help you!?"

"Yes, you can."

"It must not be about golf, because you obviously have never played before."

"This is golf, I thought it was croquet. Actually, we have an act for messing up people's golf games."

Theo laughs and gives the judge a wink, "We do play miniature golf, at least until Jake here gets mad and starts hitting the dinosaurs with his... (Theo does the hand quotes with his fingers) ... stick."

The man steps closer, "Can I ask who I'm speaking with?"

160

"I'm Lieutenant Jake O'Malley and this is my partner, Sergeant Theo Williams."

"And how did you two get past the front gate, especially a black man."

Theo, with a grin, "I told them I was the ball boy."

Jake smiles, "Not me, I just hit the boy in the balls, and he let us through."

"State your business before I have security throw your asses out."

"If your security is anything like the Sheriff's department, I will turn this day into the worse day of their lives. I need a court order to see a prisoner they have locked up at the Sheriff's Office."

"You're talking about Bo. You can speak to him before the arraignment in three days. I'm not giving you two clowns a court order. I'm not even sure you're police officers."

Jake smiles, "That's funny Judge; after that last shot, I didn't think you were a golfer."

"You two gonna leave or do I make the call?"

Jake nods, "I guess you need to make that call and while you're at it you might wanna call a proctologist."

"A proctologist?"

"Yeah, you're gonna need one to remove a seven iron from your ass. I feel the need to bust a dinosaur!"

"Look O'Malley or whatever your name is, I've got two hours to play before it gets dark, and my wife starts calling and bitching about the pool boy not showing up."

"You go right ahead Judge. Theo and I will just work in-between you three, but you might wanna get you some ear plugs and a nose clamp."

"Nose clamp?"

"Yeah, my partner ate a whole plate of Mexican beans before we got here and when he starts farting, look out! Sounds like a freight train coming. I'm sorry, up here it's called a tornado."

"Okay smarty pants, I'll call my secretary and have her stamp my name on a court order. Just leave so I can get on with my game."

Jake turns to Theo, "Save the farts, we might need 'em later." He turns to the Judge, "Oh yeah, you might wanna choke up on your putter a little to give you more control."

The Judge held up his putter and says, "I think I know how to hold my clubs."

"I wasn't talking about your clubs. You might wanna check the pool boy out closer though. I think he's cleaning out the wrong drain."

They walk off with Theo passing gas every step of the way.

Jake says, "Let's go by and talk with the coroner and give asshole's secretary time to type up a court order. And no more beans for you."

Thirty minutes later, they knock on the door of the town's acting coroner several times when suddenly the door opens and a very short man about five three and in his early thirties' yells, "What the hell do y'all want?"

Jake wants to laugh, but manages to hold it in, "We would like to see the doctor who acts as the town coroner sometimes, please."

"You're looking at him."

Theo mumbles, "More like looking down at him."

"What did you say?'

Jake answers, "My partner is complaining about his feet killing him. Can we come in?"

"No assholes, come back tomorrow, I'm busy."

Jake, "Look asshole yourself, an innocent man has been charged with four counts of murder maybe five so if you don't mind."

As the man attempts to slam the door, Jake places his foot between the door jam and the door.

"Look you little smartass, we just wanna ask you some questions that's all."

The man steps back, "You boys aren't Jehovah witnesses, are you?"

Theo laughs, "I've witnessed a lot of shit in my life, half of it in the last three days, but if I had witnessed Jehovah, He would not have put me through that shit."

Jake gives Theo a look, "What does that mean?"

"It was all I could come up with on such short notice."

The doctor shakes his head, "I would like to go home if you two are through."

Jake turns back to the small man, "That plate of butter beans can wait, we're police officers." The short man opens the door, and they step inside.

"We're short-handed around here so you'll have to excuse me if I ask you to cut to the chase."

Theo snickers.

The man asks, "You hear something funny?"

Theo replies, "Yeah, you said short-handed, and I thought that was funny you short and all."

"I guess being short is a lot better than being fat and black."

"Is that right; at least I can see over the counter at the ice cream parlor."

"In your case that's not a good thing, lard ass."

"Why you sawed-off little elf. I bet you don't have any trouble tying your shoes being your arms look like they're growing out your rectum."

"Yeah, fat boy, at least I can see my shoes." Jake crosses his arms and leans against the door jam. Theo continues, "You would think that being a part time coroner you could steal some legs off a cadaver longer than my penis."

"Is that right, now why would I want legs an inch long?"

Theo points to the door, "Because that's a half inch longer than yours. Now would you like to take this outside you munchkin reject?"

"Yes, I would. I think it will be funny wrapping your fat, black ass around an oak tree!"

"Well, good then! I think I will enjoy shoving your head into the yellow-brick road or parking lot pavement, whichever comes first!"

"Is that right...I think I can whip a big monkey's ass!"

"I don't know how you gonna whip it, but you're at the right height to lick it, you ugly-ass Lollipop kid!"

The short man yells, "That did it, you fat-ass gorilla!"

"Oh, did I offend the little circus midget? Well, bring it on, you fire hydrant with damn eyes!"

The little man runs at Theo catching him at the knees and knocking him out the front door and into the parking lot. Jake starts laughing. The short man had his teeth dug into Theo's calf as he gets slung around the parking lot.

"Stop it! I say stop slinging me around I'm getting motion sickness!!"

Theo, "Well you should know better that to eat too much calf!"

Thirty minutes later Theo was sitting in the doctor's office with torn clothes rubbing his calf. The coroner was sitting behind the desk with asphalt burns to his elbows and his smock ripped down the back and he's shaking a tooth that was knocked loose.

Theo gives him a look, "You do know biting a man's leg is cheating?"

"Kneeing a man in the mouth is cheating too."

Theo fires back, "I was aiming for your nuts, you just weren't tall enough."

"That's funny, because I was aiming for your nuts, but you were too tall … and fat."

Theo, "Is that right? So, you're saying you wanna bite dis nuts?"

"Yes I am."

"What!?"

"You heard me."

"If my leg didn't hurt so much, I would limp right back out there in the parking lot and finish what you started. What did you just say?"

"I started? You made fun of my height before I said anything about your weight."

"For your information, I have a thyroid problem."

"Yes, you do. It has food passing by it every five minutes like the busiest truck stop in Alabama."

"At least I don't look like a third grader who needs a shave. Where's your little Star Wars lunch box Dwarf Vader?"

"Up my ass, you fat bitch, you wanna see for yourself?"

They stared at each other for a few seconds as the room went silent, then suddenly, they started laughing. Jake is leaning back in the chair taking a snooze until the loud laughing woke him. He jumps up and glances at the two laughing.

The short man says, "Maybe I can buy your fat-ass a drink before y'all leave town."

Theo catches his breath, "Maybe I can buy your short-ass one."

"It's a deal. They call me Doc Jerry aka the coroner and what can I do for you two?"

Jake answers, "I would like to see the report on the first three girls murdered."

"Can't help you; they're seal in the Sheriff's vault at the station."

"Well, let us see your copies."

"He took them also."

"Why would you let him take those?"

"Duh! He's the Sheriff, that's why."

Jake shakes his head, "You do know that, as the coroner or acting coroner, you're the highest-ranking official in the county and subject to no one."

The man leans forward, "Come again."

"That's right, nobody and I mean nobody can overturn a coroner's decision."

"I didn't know that. I was just a country doctor who accidentally got this job."

Theo interrupts, "Yep, you're the top midget in the county."

Doc gives him an angry look and then continues, "Well, I'll be a buzzard's left nut."

Theo laughs, "You are, but you're the top buzzard's nut around here with the sheriff running a close second."

Jake leans in closer, "I bet if you tried really hard you could remember what was on those reports."

"Maybe I can."

"Were there any needle marks on their arms?"

"Yep, could have been mosquito bites, we have then bigger than a hog standing on his hindlegs."

"Could have been, but it wasn't. What was the official cause of death?"

"Strangulation. There were bruises all around their necks."

"Have you gotten any toxicology reports back?

"I got one, there were traces of a Benzodiazepine drug known as Midazolam in their system. The sheriff has those also."

"Were there any signs of trauma around their vaginas?"

"They were all raped if that's what you're asking. They had rectum damage also. And before you ask, the sheriff has those reports also. He's the one who sees that it goes to a lab in Birmingham."

"What about the girl that was murdered yesterday?"

"They didn't send her to me."

"They just bypass the coroner altogether?"

"Look around you dude, the sheriff runs the show up here."

"What about a D.A. up here."

"There's one in Alexander, but I never spoke to him."

Jake stands, "Thanks for the information and all that free entertainment." They start to walk out the door when Theo turns and says, "I apologize for the short jokes."

"Well, I don't apologize for the fat jokes you giant Milky Way bar." He smiles and Theo smiles back. They head toward the door when the short man yells, "Hey, I'm not sure if this will help y'all, but I found particles of corn dust all under the first three girl's fingernails and in their hair."

"Corn dust?"

"Yeah, but they grow that shit everywhere around here. The dust can be found in any pig, horse, cow trough or chicken pen. It's what's left over after they eat the corn."

Theo asks, "Sweet corn or regular?"

"I didn't taste the shit."

Jake, "Wow their bodies wasn't found anywhere close to a cornfield." They walk out the door with Jake standing there with the sun in his eyes. He places his aviator sunglasses on and takes out a cigar.

Theo asks, "What's on your mind?"

"I was just wondering why the sheriff took all the copies of the coroner's report. The state will want their copies."

CHAPTER 20

Thirty minutes later at the Fairmont funeral home, they're sitting in an office speaking to the mortician.

Mortician, "What can I do for two today? I'm running a special this month, so if you let me set you two up for funerals, you save two thousand dollars."

Jake, "We both have discussed it and I think we're gonna go with the cremation. We will save two thousand dollars by putting the money in our pocket, get good and drunk while smoking cigars in bed and accidently burn Mary Maes whorehouse down about thirty years from now. Have you worked on the girl Amber yet? The one that was murdered yesterday?"

"Not yet."

"I'm Lieutenant O'Malley and this is Sergeant Williams, and we are with the Mobile homicide division. I would like to see her body."

"Why?"

"I'll tell you when we get in there." They stand and Jake sees Theo still sitting.

"Let's go Shadow."

Theo, "Oh hell know, I'm gonna sit right here until you come back."

"You do that."

In the back-room Jake is combing through the girl's hair with a brush and shaking the particles into a clear evidence bag. He then takes out his knife and scrapes under her fingernails over the paper. He turns to the mortician and asks, "Can you look at this through a microscope and tell me what this is?"

"Sure can."

As they walk into the main lobby of the courthouse, Theo asks, "So you're saying it was corn dust?"

"Yep, just what Doc Jerry said about the other victims."

They come walking in the Sheriff's office and walk right past the receptionist leaving her yelling, "You can't just barge up in there!"

They shove the door open, and Jake throws the court order down on the desk in front of Ray. Miller was standing next to the window with a large grin on his face.

With a frown, Sheriff Ray asks, "What's this?"

"It's a court order giving me permission to talk with Bo Harper. And if Miller doesn't wipe that grin off his face, I will do it for him." Miller loses the grin.

Ray, "Bo Harper?"

"Yeah, it seems old lady Harper was his grandmother. Now I wanna talk with him now."

"That's too bad Jake; you should have been here twenty-one minutes ago."

"Hold on, I'm pretty good at that physics shit myself and I can see that you're gonna need some renovations to this office soon. Now why twenty-one minutes ago?"

"Because Bo hung himself twenty minutes ago."

"What?"

"That's right; I guess he couldn't deal the shame of killing those girls. And after you showed me those footprints at old lady Harper's place, I was going to charge him with that murder also."

"Well Theo, I think we spent twenty-one minutes too long at that funeral home." His left eye starts blinking, "I wanna see the body."

"Can't do that, it's all still under investigation."

"You can show me to his cell, or I will shove that court order so far up your ass, you'll shit fancy legal terms for two weeks."

"Okay O'Malley, if you wanna see him go right ahead. Miller, show the Lieutenant to Bo's cell.

They stroll down through the cellblock until they come to where Bo was hanging from the top bar with a belt wrapped around his neck. Jake slowly walks in the cell and stares at Bo's blue lifeless face.

He asks in a sarcastic way, "How long y'all gonna let him hang there?"

Miller walks in behind him, "What's the hurry, he doesn't have any place to go now. Too bad that he done this to himself. I sure would like to have seen the juice put to him. Yeah, he sure had one ugly puss there."

"It would take a bunch of sorry ass people to hang that poor unfortunate man. Why didn't y'all assholes just go out and find some kids with down syndrome and hang then while y'all were in the mood, you homicidal bastards." He looks closer and examines the large body as it hung there. "Yep, you redneck clowns hung him."

Miller fires back, "That's bullshit, he hung himself. The Jailer forgot to take his belt."

Jake gives Miller a look, "First of all, he's wearing coveralls and I wonder how a man with a 44 or 45-inch waist was wearing a 32-inch belt? Now what skinny little bitch do I know wears a 32-inch belt? Where's your belt Miller?"

"I don't wear one under my gun belt."

Jake, "Whatta you think Theo?"

"I'm not a damn bit surprised. These rednecks have been doing this shit to blacks for the past two hundred years. I'm completely taken by surprise that they didn't find a black man and say they thought he was Bo."

Miller fires back, "You can't prove he didn't hang himself."

"I don't have to Miller. Before this week is over, I'm gonna kill me a whole bunch of douchebags, and save the taxpayers of this county a lot of money."

"Are you threatening me O'Malley?"

Jake looks up at Bo's face then turns to Theo, "I just don't have it in me to say it anymore, so will you do me the honors?"

"Sure." Theo turns to Miller, "Let me say this real slow, so you can understand the words I be a saying, it was not a threat, it was a promise … you skinny ass cracker. If you knew the great, short, fused O'Malley that I have known over the last five years, you would know that you will never see your birthday or Christmas again. That's if yo aunt had you in the first place. I think a buzzard laid you and the sun hatched you. Now if I was you and I'm not, because I have a little intelligence about me, I would be on the next bullet train to anywhere but here." He turns to Jake, "Did I cover all bases for you little buddy?"

"Thank you, Theo, I'm gonna rate you at about eight out of ten on accuracy, because you know that Miller here will not make it for another five days." He steps up closer to Miller, "You will be dead before Bo gets buried, that's a promise."

They walk back into the sheriff's office and Jake pulls up a chair. Okay Ray let's cut through the bullshit. There was no need to hang that poor man, but I know why you degenerates did it."

Ray, "Why, Jake?"

"You bunch of idiots thought he might give me a half ass description. He most likely couldn't remember anything anyway. You bunch of badge and gun toting monkeys have been hiding something in those woods for years. Now what is it you're trying to cover up?"

"I don't know what you're talking about."

"Look, you have screwed up these investigations from the beginning, you try too hard to keep everyone out of the state land, you wrote up a homicide as a suicide. You arrested a man you knew had nothing to do with murdering the girls, you took important records from the coroner and now you've killed an innocent man to keep him from telling anyone about what he saw last night. Anybody in their right mind would think you or this skinny ass-wipe standing over there were doing the killings."

"You are so full of shit Jake. We found the girls sock in Bo's pocket."

"You mean one of the two that was put on my backseat?"

"I thought the mayor told you to leave town."

"He did, but this isn't the old west. If it was, I would have shot the shit out of you two ten minutes ago."

"Look Jake, you have me all wrong. I knew Bo lived in the woods; he's been there since he was born. That's why I tried to keep people out. He was too big and retarded and as you can see from the murders, very dangerous. I would have brought him in years ago, but he knew the woods too well and stayed hidden."

"What are the chances of me seeing the autopsy reports on the first two victims you have in the vault?"

"Those records are missing."

"Why am I not surprised to hear that?"

"There are sixteen people who have access to that vault."

"Wow! These serial killings are getting more interesting by the minute. Do you know what I think Ray?"

"What's that O'Malley?"

"I think me, and my partner will go check those woods out a little closer. I believe there are some answers out there somewhere and I'm going to find them. I think we'll look in the area behind Bo's shack and see for ourselves what's in those foothills."

Ray stands, "I wouldn't go digging too deep if I was you, O'Malley. Accidents have a way of happening around here, and I'm talking about accidents that can be hazardous to your health."

"It seems like everything I do is hazardous to my health, Ray. But then I like it that way. I also have a way of causing things that are hazardous to your health, but I don't call them accidents. You two pig turds will be dead before the next full moon which is coming up soon." Jake and Theo stand, turn and storm out the door and to their car…

Driving down the highway thinking in silence.

Jake, "Corn dust in the fingernails and hair. Call Jim and find out what Freddy has found out. Theo pulls his phone out, but before he can push the numbers, Jake's phone rings.

"Hello."

"Hey, Jake, this is Sherry. I heard about the arrest the sheriff made. I gotta see you before you leave for Mobile."

"I'm not leaving just yet; I have some leads I'm working on."

"I just want you to know that Casey and I do not hold you responsible for Amber's death. Things happen."

"Well, no one should hold me responsible because they had the wrong man."

"Had?"

"Yea, they killed poor Bo not long after the arrest."

"Oh my God!" Look Jake, I wanna see you tonight. Meet me at the old silo across the field east from where Cooper's barn dance was at about nine o'clock. Come alone, I have some information for you."

"Is it the same kind info Casey had for me?"

"Maybe, maybe not."

"I can do that, bye." He hangs up the phone.

Theo asks, "Who was that?"

"Sherry wants to meet me at an abandoned silo tonight."

"Sounds like a trap to me."

"Everything sounds like a trap to you. Sherry's the one person in this county I do trust."

"And that's the one you should never trust."

"She's in love with me."

"More reason not to trust her. Is she bringing a friend for me?"

"You can't come, you'll be too busy moving our stuff back to the motel."

"How come the sidekick never, ever gets the sex?"

"I'm not sure Theo, but that's the exact reason why I took the lead position and not the sidekick position in the first place. I'll tell you what; why don't you take the night off and go have a few drinks with your new midget friend Jerry, the so-called coroner?"

Theo being sarcastic, "That's not a bad idea. You go to an abandoned silo, screw your brains out with a beautiful woman, and I'll go hang out with a guy who cuts up dead people. I'm so thrilled, oh boy I can't wait!"

That night at 2049 hrs. Jake drives down a dirt road and sees a large, tall metal silo. Minutes later Sherry comes pulling up in her black BMW convertible. She parks and walks toward him with a blanket in hand.

He asks, "What kind of information do you have for me?"

"I'll tell you when we get to the silo. You bring a flashlight?"

"Sure." He pulls a small silver flashlight from his pocket.

They walk across the field towards the silo standing over a hundred feet high. When they get there, Sherry pulls back a flat of metal to gain entry. Once inside she takes a red ribbon from her hair and hangs it over the flap. Jake could have sworn the silo had an air-conditioned unit attached somewhere outside.

He asks, "What's the deal with this place and why did you hang a ribbon over the flap?"

"It's where everyone for a generation has come to make out. The ribbon lets anyone else with the same idea, know that the silo's occupied."

"Whatever happened to the backseat of a car?"

"You feel that cool breeze flowing from the top? That's why. At night the air funnels down from holes in the top and by the time it gets to the bottom, it's cool as can be."

With his flashlight he scans the large open area and sees several bales of hay against the wall. Sherry lays the blanket out and pulls her jeans off. He's still looking around at the dusty space and could see piles of old mildewed corn all around the edges. He turns around only to find her stepping from her pants and wearing a black lacy thong partially covered by her blouse.

"I thought you had some information for me?"

"Nope, like Casey, I just need sex really bad."

"That's it? We could have done that in the field. It doesn't have corn dust everywhere."

She smiles and takes him by the hand and shoves him on the blanket cushioned by the hay. She sits on top of him and says, "I want you to give me all you got."

"Whatta, you mean?"

"I want you to slap me real hard on the ass, pull my hair and bite me all over and then I'm gonna slide on top of you and ride you hard." She leans over and bites his nipple through his black T-shirt.

"Ouch!! What the hell, that hurt."

"I thought you liked it rough."

"Not when I'm on the receiving end."

A few minutes later she bent over as he slaps her ass causing it to turn a shade of red. She looks over her shoulder, "Harder Jake, harder!" The slaps could be heard echoing throughout the silo. "Pull my hair!"

She reaches down and grabs him, finding him soft as a melted candy bar.

"What's wrong, don't you want me?"

"I'm not sure why it's soft, it's never happened to me before. I guess I have a lot on my mind with what happened to Bo, or it might be taking a rest; you have been working it like a beaver building a dam here lately."

She giggles, "I know how to make it hard." She jumps up straddling him with her perfect legs and rubs up against him.

A few minutes later he takes her by the waist and throws her on the blanket.

"Okay, enough playing, you want it hard and fast, you got it!" He throws her legs up high in the air and she yells, "Ouch!!"

"You said you wanted it rough, so I aim to please."

"I'm not talking about that. There's something digging in my back."

"I can promise you one thing, it's nothing like what I'm about to dig in your front."

"I'm serious; something is stabbing me in the back." He reaches under her and finds a chain with a red heart-shaped locket attached to it. He sits back and shines the light on it.

"It's a locket."

"Huh! Somebody must have left it in here when they were making out." She lies back down on her back and places her legs high up in the air. He stands and stares at the locket.

Sherry with her legs still in the air, "I'm waiting lover boy." She sees him concentrating on the locket. "What's wrong?"

"This locket is the right size and shape."

"Size and shape for what?"

"Amber was wearing a locket shaped just like this one, the night she was killed, and if this was hers, the killer was here."

"Lots of girls come up here. It could belong to any one of them."

"But it doesn't, it belongs to Amber." He bends down and runs his finger across the floor picking up corn dust." She was here. I was wrong the other day. She was raped and killed here and placed at the end of the bleachers under the stairway and not in the woods. Somebody wanted me to be on the scene of a fresh body. He's playing games with me. He wanted me to see her, but why?" He thinks for a second and then snaps his fingers, "So I wouldn't leave town when I was told to leave. Three girls killed on a full moon, but amber was killed one week before another full moon. He has something planned for the next full moon which is Saturday."

"He who?"

"Our killer was here and we're right down the road from the school and the woods where Bo lived."

"But Rodger said Bo was at the scene of the crime. He watched the girls from the woods. It's him. That locket could have belonged to anyone. Lots of couples come up here."

"The girls were raped Sherry."

"So, what, that animal raped them before he strangled them. He got what he deserved."

In a loud voice, he yells, "Unlike me, Bo had no penis!!"

"What? How do you know that?"

"Somebody raped Bo when he was small child about eight or so and then tied him to a bed and set the shack on fire where his penis was burned off. He didn't have enough to make penetration."

"You need to tell Ray and Rodger that Jake! An innocent man hung himself for nothing."

"Oh, shit, Ray and Miller hung that man to keep him from giving me any more information!"

"What are you saying?"

"We still have a killer on the loose just as I thought. And by the looks of it, I'm on a timeline."

"Oh my God!"

"They tasered the man until he couldn't move and then hung him by a belt from the bars of his cell with the help of a few others."

"Are you sure?"

"Yep, pretty much. When did you learn about this silo?"

"When I was seventeen, all the boys would bring me here and try to get me drunk hoping to get a piece of ass. And if it makes you feel any better, only a few got it. Even Casey was conceived in this silo."

"Roger was crippled in an accident; how did he get you pregnant?"

"Roger's not the father of Casey. She doesn't belong to him. Casey's father was killed in a boating accident on the river before she was born. Rodger never even adopted her."

"Get your clothes on."

"Why? You haven't pleasured me yet."

"The mood has passed."

"I can talk dirty if you want."

He turns to her, "So can I! You have no idea what's going on here. Four of your players were brought up here, raped and strangled right here on this very spot then thrown out in the woods to make it look like Bo did it. He's still out there looking for another girl. He's going after another one of your team members, it could even be Casey."

"I guess I wasn't thinking. I've just never been so much in love before. Whatta, we do from here."

"You do nothing. I'm going hunting and I want you to go home and tell Rodger to keep an eye on you and Casey and make sure you let the other parents know to keep an eye on the girls. Give no other information to anyone and I mean no one about why we were here or what we found. Now get your pants on, I need to call Theo." Jake takes out his cell and attempts to call him but gets no signal. "Huh, I get no bars, must be this round metal silo. That's okay; I think I know how to find him."

CHAPTER 21

At a local lounge Theo was sitting on a stool at the bar telling Jerry stories of him and Jake. They had already downed seven or eight beers a piece and were feeling no pain. Jerry is laughing so hard he almost fell off the stool.

"You mean to tell me that he actually pissed in the mayor's coffee cup?"

"Yep, twenty-four hours after sleeping with his wife. Jake takes no shit from no one. When he was a kid, he chased the paperboy down and shoved the morning news up his ass for hitting the family dog with the Sunday addition."

"He's some dude."

"Yeah, my Jake is 'one of a kind.' That's not all, by some freak of nature he's hung like a black man."

"Really, so, you're black, are you hung?"

"You damn straight I am. Back in my neighborhood I was known as the black stallion." Theo almost falls off the stool but catches the lip of the bar to steady himself. "When I was born, the doctor wanted to cut it off because he thought it was a third leg. I'm lucky I pissed out of it before he got the chance."

"Wow!! Can I see it?"

"What?"

"Nothing; have another drink, I wanna show you something that's gonna blow your mind." He winks at the bartender.

Theo takes a big drink, "You know something Jerry? I really like you and for a midget, you fight damn well."

"Oh, I can do a lot of things well."

Ten minutes later Jerry makes a toast, "Here's to our new-found relationship!" They clink the bottles of beer together and emptied them with one swallow.

Theo laughs, "Wow I have never seen anyone shove the bottle that far in his mouth. To each their own."

Jerry smiles and reaches over and grabs Theo by the crotch. Theo with head bobbing says, "Hey, what's going on there!?"

"I'm sorry big boy, I dropped a pretzel."

Theo laughs, "Well be more careful, that wasn't your pretzel you grabbed. I'm saving my pretzel in case we run up on some horny country girls."

Jerry laughs again, "We don't need any girls; we have each other."

"What?"

"Nothing; drink up, I have a surprise for you."

"Yeah, what may that be?"

"A cow with five legs."

"Wow, I gotta see that."

"It's in a pasture about five miles down the road from here."

Theo downs a whole beer with one swallow and yells, "Let's go, I'm loaded for bear."

Minutes later Jerry's driving the car down Highway 31, when suddenly he turns to Theo, "Hey Theo, pull your pants down."

Theo, feeling no pain, but still thinking straight, "What!"

"Pull your pants down and moon some people as we pass 'em. That will be funny as hell."

Theo starts laughing, "Why not?" He pulls his pants down and sticks his butt out the passenger's window.

Jerry looks over at Theo's penis, "Smaller than I thought, but still worth some fun."

Theo, "What?"

"Nothing."

Every time they passed a vehicle Theo would yell, "Hey rednecks, you wanna see what the dark side of the moon looks like!?"

Jerry is laughing so hard he was about to cry. An elderly man and woman drive up next to them in an old seventy-four Chevy pickup in mint condition and sees Theo's rearend hanging out. The woman covers her mouth as her husband says, "That looks like a negro's butt, honey!"

As Jerry drives on, Theo takes a seat and says, "Boy Jerry, I haven't had this much fun since Jake hid a baby gator in the Chief's backseat twenty-four hours after sleeping with his wife or was it when we got drunk, went to the zoo and tried to teach checkers to an orangutan twenty-four hours after sleeping with his wife!"

Ten minutes later and five miles outside of town they are sitting in the car just off the road next to a barbed wire fence around a cow pasture with scattered pecan trees sipping hot beer.

Theo, with his head still bobbing back and forth asks, "So, where's that five-legged cow you spoke of? Wait a minute; I know what's going on here!"

Jerry gives him a look, "You do?"

"You have some Daisy Duke girls with those short shorts crammed all up their ass coming to meet us. Let me guess; they're going to do all kinds of shit to my corn cob."

"Not girls Theo, just me."

"Just you, I don't get it. There's not going to be enough for me?"

"Oh, you are going to have so much pleasure. Let's get out of the car and walk a few hundred yards over there under that pecan tree. I wanna show you that five-legged cow."

"What if there's a bull out there, because I know for a fact them damn things will hurt you. And for no particular reason, they hate my guts."

"There's no bull. I come out here almost every night. I just wanna show you something that I think you will like."

"Okay, but when are those girls gonna show?"

"After tonight, you won't ever fool with a woman again."

"You must be going to shoot me in the back of the head, because anything short of death won't work."

Jerry looks out across the moonlit field, "Beautiful night for a blow."

Theo was busy checking out the pasture when he turns to Jerry, "You got that shit right!!"

They exit the vehicle and jump the fence with Theo catching his crotch on the barbwire.

"Wow! If I wasn't so drunk, that would have hurt!"

Jerry laughs, "You must have balls as hard as pecans. Do you know I can crack two pecans in my mouth and get the pecan out of the shell with my tongue?"

"Now that's talent, if you were a woman, you'd be worth a fortune." Theo responded.

They walk out under the pecan tree when suddenly Jerry comes to a stop.

Theo asks, "So, are these girls going to be pretty or is it going to be an ugly toothless fest? Don't get me wrong, I'm not picky, but I do draw a line with some women. Just joking, I don't draw a line with any."

Jerry drops to his knees and tries to unzip Theo's pants. Theo steps back and yells, "What the hell is wrong with you!?"

"I'm gonna relieve all that pressure built up inside you. Let me taste that big black monster."

"If you think for one minute, you're gonna warm me up for those girls…. You are wrong. Are you queer or something?"

"Queer for you, now just pull that black thang out and leave the rest to me."

Theo steps back in shock and yells again, "Oh my God!! I think I'm gonna be sick!!"

Jerry rolls his eyes up at Theo and with a big smile, "It's no big deal, Theo, I'll give you my special."

Theo was speechless then takes two steps back, "Special my ass! I thought we were meeting girls out here. I'm straight, you sawed-off little fagot!"

"What's wrong, you didn't know I was gay? I grabbed your crotch back at the bar."

"You said you dropped a pretzel."

"I lied."

"You're a queer!? Oh my god. I can't believe I fell for this! Thank God Jake isn't around to see this shit!"

Jerry takes a few steps on his knees and says, "Calm down Theo, you'll like the way I do it."

"I don't care if you can suck a groundhog from his hole, you're not touching this… I can't believe I just drove out to 'God knows where,' only to be hit on by a queer!"

"It's LGBTQ."

"Yes Latin, for queer, fag, rump ranger, etc. etc. Call it anything you like; it all means the same damn thing, you sick son-of-a-bitch!" Suddenly headlights from every direction lit up their faces as pickup trucks came flying across the field. Theo just stands there as ten men wearing white sheets step out and point their pistols and rifles at them. Jerry looks around in shock and slowly stands on his feet.

Theo shakes his head, "Well, this is awkward."

Jerry nods, "Just keep cool, they're just going to try and scare us."

Theo grits his teeth at him, "Bullshit! They pass that scared shit already; these guys mean business and you know it rump ranger. They're not wearing sheets to give their sister's something to wash."

Jake walks into the lounge and up to the bar.

The bartender, "What can I get for you?"

Jake takes a stool, "Nothing; let me ask you a question. Have you seen a black man bigger than a milk truck and a short guy about the height of these stools?"

"You must be talking about Jerry and his new lover. They left a while ago heading to a pasture to see a five-legged cow."

"Lover? Wait a minute, y'all have a cow with five legs? Hell, I gotta see that for myself."

"Nope, Jerry uses that line to get men to go to the pasture so he can pleasure them as in blow them. I go out there sometimes with Jerry. He's really good at it."

"You think you could give me the directions to this pasture you speak of?"

"Sure can."

Back in the pasture mumbling is heard in the crowd as the leader, wearing a red sheet with a white cross on the front and a red hood over his head steps forward.

"Well, I'll be damn, what a lucky night. We done run up on two queers and one's a nig#&%."

Theo starts to sober up a little with fear running down his spine. "Hold on dudes, there's been a misunderstanding."

"Yeah, boy and you made it. Get the ropes boys and make one thick. We have a double-header tonight."

Theo reaches for his pistol that was supposed to be in his holster and remembers he left it in the car back at the bar like Jake always told him to when they went drinking. Funny being Jake always has one in a bar.

"Hold on guys, I'm not queer, I'm a police officer. I'm a sergeant with the Mobile Police Department."

They all start laughing as the leader steps up in his face, "We saw this short ass fagot on his knees and you standing there waiting to get a blow! I bet you just couldn't wait for your turn."

"Look dude, I had no idea what he was going to do. I thought he was bringing me out here to meet some women or a cow with five legs!"

The leader steps closer, "You say you was gonna meet some white women out here?"

"Nope, now I remember, it was definitely a cow with five legs. Yeah, that's what I meant."

One of the men walks a few yards and removes two ropes from the bed of his pickup truck. He walks back as two others tie Theo's hands together and then Jerry's. They drag them over to the pecan tree and throw the ropes over a five-inch limb.

The leader walks over to Theo while two others place the ropes around their necks.

"You ass wranglers got any last words?"

One man tightens the rope up around Theo's neck. Theo grunts, "Do you have to pull it so tight asshole? Wait a minute; I was kidding about that asshole crack I just made."

The leader chuckles, "I'm going to enjoy this spook."

"The name is Theo, Sergeant Theodore Williams! Get it right man!"

They all start laughing again when Theo gets really pissed, "Okay, you're all under arrest, now if you untie me, I'll talk with the judge and maybe he'll go easy on your asses. Now just to show you I have no hard feelings, y'all can hang the short ass queer."

Jerry quickly turns, "Thanks a lot, Theo."

"That's what you get for tricking me into this shit in the first place. I didn't know when you said you had something that was going to blow my mind; that you were actually talking about blowing mine."

They pull the slack out of the ropes when Theo changes gears, "Look, I don't think I'm even black. My Mama was Creole, and my father was Irish. I even have hemorrhoids shaped like a four-leaf clover."

Jerry turns to him, "I bet you are magically delicious."

Theo slowly turns to him, "Are seriously going with that?" Theo turns back to the man in the red sheet, "You all can go ahead and pull him up if you want, but as I was saying, I voted Republican. I got a hard on when they bombed Iraq. Is any of this stuff turning you boys on? I laugh so hard when they kicked the shit out of Rodney King…. I mean he had that shit coming to him, right?"

Jerry smiles, "You got a hard on during Desert Storm? Let me see."

Theo yells, "Shut the hell up, you wiener sucking homo!"

They all laugh again.

Theo scans the men standing in their white sheets and says, "Does it make any difference that I'm a Crimson Tide fan?"

"Nope."

"So, you're all Florida Gator fans, huh…Okay guys, this is just medieval behavior. They haven't used hanging in years. I thought y'all dragged their asses behind a truck these days using a chain and if you don't have a chain, I'll wait right here while y'all go purchase one."

The leader laughs, "Ropes and pecan trees are cheaper than gas and begging won't help you yard ape."

"Begging is not in my nature, but if you're gonna hang me, hang me because I'm black, not because I'm queer."

Jerry yells, "Don't give them the satisfaction Theo. We're queer, we're here and we're proud!!"

Theo yells, "You're proud; I'm embarrassed! How can I get that in your head? I'm not queer you homo asshole, so again, shut the hell up!! We wouldn't be in this predicament if you had told me up front you were queer and that cow with five legs didn't exists. I'd still be at the bar drinking by myself!!" He turns back to the crowd, "Look dudes, I have a reputation to uphold, and I don't mind dying for being black, but I be damned if I'm gonna hang for being a queer and I demand that to be stricken from the records."

"You're just stalling boy. You are in no position to demand anything. Hang 'em dudes!"

"Wait a cotton-picking minute! What's your damn hurry!? Y'all got another hanging scheduled later tonight!?"

They start to pull the ropes when Theo yells, "Okay! Okay! Can I at least say a prayer? I would like to say something to my Maker, if you crackers don't mind."

"Okay spook, say your prayers."

"Hey, enough with the spook shit!" Theo looks up into the sky and says, "Dear Lord, I was hoping this day would hold off for…" He turns to the man beside him, "Would you loosen the rope a little? I would like my last words to be clearer if you don't mind. After all, I am speaking to the Lord, not that anyone of you would know Him." They loosen the rope a little. "Thank you…as I was saying, I was hoping this day would have been later and not sooner, but I guess these assholes are not going according to Your schedule. I was going to ask that You forgive them for they know not what they do…but!! These white bread cracker, son-of-a-bitches know exactly what they're doing! So, I hope you find it in Your heart to strike them dead with a mighty bolt of lightning and send them straight to hell. I hope you fry their asses good and…"

"That's enough!!"

"Wait a freaking minute, I wasn't through. I still need to read the Gospel of Luke to you, after all it is the longest book in the New Testament."

"Sorry, we don't have a bible with us."

"Well cut me loose, I saw one on the nightstand back at the motel room."

"That's not gonna happen."

"Well, that's okay then, I memorized it all by heart."

"Nice try queer."

"Look guys, what do I have to do to prove to you I'm not a queer? I know, why don't you guys let me help you hang the queer."

Jerry, "I can't believe you want to see me hanged."

"That will teach you to drag me out here under false pretenses."

The man in red, "Stalling ain't gonna help."

"Well, at least un-tie my hands and take this rope from around my neck so I can kneel down and pray."

"Untie him boys, I'm a God-fearing man myself."

Theo, "Yea right."

They untied him and as he starts to go down on his knees he mumbles, "God fearing man my ass."

The leader asks, "What did you say?"

Theo points out across the field, "I said, 'look over there a black, queer, Jew!!" They all turn and glance to the side when Theo suddenly jumps up and takes off running through the field as fast as he could. The leader yells. "Three of y'all get in your truck and catch that fat black bastard for me."

Theo's running through the darkness as fast as he could and yelling at the top of his lungs, "Oh God! Oh God! Stepped in cow shit! Oh God! Oh God! Feet don't fail me now! Oh God! Oh God!"

A few minutes later the truck came pulling back up with Theo in the bed of the truck gasping for every breath of air. They tied his hands and put the rope back around his neck. Theo shakes his head, "That did it, untie me right now and I will whip all five of y'all with my....(He catches his breath)... bare hands."

The man laughs, "There are ten of us."

Theo scans the crowd, "I stand corrected. I was going to let the short faggot take care of the other five."

Jerry yells, "Hey! Don't bring me into this."

Theo slowly turns his head toward him, "Did you just say, 'don't bring you into this?' You wiener licker!"

"Look Theo, I'm sorry and I wish I had it to do all over again."

"Why would you wanna go through this shit again!?"

"I'm talking about, if I had it to do all over again, I would have just given you a blow in the parking lot back at the club."

"The hell you say. What is it about women you don't like?"

"I was born this way."

"Bullshit! Nobody comes out of the womb queer."

"Hey! I told you already. I take offense to that word."

"Well, you should have thought about that before you brought me out here in the middle of nowhere for a pecker-pumping session."

The leader yells, "Okay boys, hang 'em!!"

Theo yells back, "You boys have taken this shit too far! What kind of men are you? You're running around like kids pretending to be ghosts. This is not exactly adult behavior."

"Did you say, 'you boys? Hang their asses!"

Theo yells, "Did I say boys? I meant to say men, yeah, that's what I meant. Look when I get scared, I say stupid things. I'm very sorry."

Two men stretch the ropes tight pulling their feet off the ground. Theo felt the weight of his body pulling the rope tight around his neck.

He tries to yell, "Jake!" The rope tightens shutting their air supply off and Theo starts to choke, when suddenly three loud ear-splitting blasts from a shotgun cut the limb almost in half causing it to break over, allowing them to fall to the ground. The crowd of white sheets turns and finds a dark shadow standing there holding a shotgun.

A voice cuts the darkness like a knife through butter. "Hold it right there assholes."

One in a white sheet steps forward, "Who are you?"

"I'm the owner of that black ass y'all are about to hang."

"You own the short white queer too?"

"Nope, that one belongs to the county."

The man says as he raises his pistol, "They're queers' dude."

Jake steps forward with a cigar in his mouth and points Big Bertha waist high. I have four more rounds and you might miss with those rifles and pistols, but I'll cut five of you right in half. Now drop the guns or I'll turn those white sheets blood red except you with the red one; I'll just make yours wet."

They all drop their guns with one stepping even closer.

"Look man, these two were sucking each other off. We caught 'em red handed. The short guy was on his knees unzipping the pants of the fat one."

Jake frowns and turns to Theo and Jerry, seeing Theo as he shrugs his shoulders.

Jake turns back to the leader; "I've seen Theo eat about everything in the book, but never a dick. Now I can't speak for the short bastard, but Theo's only crime is being horny, drunk and misjudging his drinking companions. Cut 'em loose before my left eye starts twitching."

They cut both loose.

Theo walks over to Jake, "I prayed for deliverer, and He sent you and Bertha. Now that's what I call connections! Now shoot the bastards, they almost hung me!"

"If I had been five seconds later, your neck would have been long enough to eat the leaves from the top of that pecan tree. When we get back to the motel, I wanna hear this whole story or maybe not." He turns to the men in the white sheets and says, "Pull the sheets off bitches."

They hesitate for a second causing Jake to throw another loud shattering round in the ground. They start to take them off when several decide to take off running in different directions. Jake cuts another round loose striking the man wearing the red sheet in the ass with a few pellets. That didn't slow him down one bit. Jake turns his attention back to the last two and pops off three more rounds." He pulls six rounds from his pocket and loads faster than a hummingbird flaps his wings. The two men just froze there in place. They quickly take off their clothes.

Jake starts laughing. "Looks like you two need to be hung." He turns to Theo, "Maybe they're girls, Theo."

"I don't give a shit what they are! If I was holding Big Bertha, they'd all look like that pecan limb you blew in half."

Jake yells at the two naked men, "Take off running now!!" They start to pick up their guns and clothes when Jake yells, "Leave the guns, clothes and vehicles and start for the woods!!" They take off running. Jake fires an unnerving shot over their heads, and they pick up speed until they disappear into the thickets.

Theo places his hands on Jake's back, "What took you so long? I almost had to open a can of whoop-ass on the whole bunch. How did you know I was here anyway?"

"A bartender told me. Seems Jerry here gets men drunk and then talks them into coming out here to see a cow with five legs. Cuming, that's funny" Jake hands Theo his 9mm and three clips, "Here Theo, go relieve some of that anger steaming through your veins and stop crying."

Theo wipes his eyes, smiles, walks over to the trucks and cuts loose. He's laughing like a mad man in-between shots. He goes into a shooting frenzy. "Call me a queer will ya!" He fires three more rounds. "Call me a niggra will ya!" He fires three more. "Call me a spook will ya!" Suddenly he fires a round into Jake's rear door.

Jake yells, "Not my car stupid!"

Theo yells back, "Sorry, I got caught up in the moment!"

Jerry walks over to Jake as he watches Theo shoot the trucks up. "Thanks, for saving our lives."

"You better step away from me Jerry. I'm a homophobia and unlike Theo there, I will shoot your balls off. Now, I'm not sure, but if I was you, I wouldn't be standing here when Theo gets through, because if my guess is right, he will save that last bullet for you." Jerry takes off running back to his car…

CHAPTER 22

They drive back to the motel in silence with Jake occasionally snickering. Suddenly Theo yells, "Okay smartass, get it out of your system!"

"I have no idea what you're talking about." He snickers some more.

"You know very well what I'm talking about. I didn't know he was gay."

"Why did you think he was taking you to a cow pasture five miles down the road when there was another one two miles from the bar?"

"I thought he was going to show me a freakshow or have some country girls meet us out there."

"And a freakshow it was. I was pissed, shocked, flabbergasted and embarrassed all at the same time."

"Look, in my defense, I had downed about twelve beers. I didn't have a clue until he dropped to his knees."

"Didn't you tell me he grabbed your crotch at the bar? That would have let the cat out of the bag for me and a palm upside his gay melon size head."

"How long am I going to have to hear about this crap?"

"How long have I had to listen to that alligator shit?"

"I just wanna know why we didn't arrest the whole bunch?"

"I'll tell you why. I didn't wanna have to listen to my partner testify in a court of law to why he was in the middle of nowhere with a homosexual man on his knees. And I know for a fact those sheet wearing assholes would have all walked out of that courtroom. Hell, I'm pretty sure the judge was in that bunch. Yea an all-white jury from Hick town, are going to convict white guys for trying to scare two queers and one being black. And I wouldn't mention that you thought you were going to meet some daisy duke white girls for sex We're not in Kansas anymore Toto."

"All I know is, that if you hadn't showed up with Bertha when you did, I would have the neck of a giraffe right now."

"Well, it would have stretched that dwarf to normal. Now changing the subject, what did you find out from Freddy?"

"He came up with five Harpers, all five deceased. Three, Thelma Harper, Bo Harper, Robert Harper haven't been removed from the voter's registry for obvious reasons being Thelma and Bo were killed in the last few days. Robert Harper has been dead for years but has not been removed from the register."

"How did he come up with Bo Harper? I can't see him as a registered voter… …"

"Thelma must have registered him when he turned nineteen. She must have wanted him to have a last name. What puzzles me is why Robert Harper was still on the list."

"Dead my ass!"

"And listen to this and you will understand why I gave the job to Freddy, aka 'stuttering fool'. Bo was born April 23, 1969. There was a rape charge against this Robert Harper in July of 76, but the charges were drop for unknown reasons. No photos on anybody."

"How did Freddy get all that?"

"Don't ask questions, just listen. The victim of the rape was Carrie Walker, Bo's mother. She went missing in March 77. Guess who filed the missing report?"

"Bo's Grandmother Thelma."

"Good guess."

"Now what we need to know is when Robert died."

"Freddy said after twenty minutes of ear-throbbing stuttering, Robert was born April the fifth in 51 and died in 79. That would make him 57 today if he was alive. I check with the county courthouse and find no records of a Robert Harper other than the voter's registration, ever existing and all files on Bo and his mother were missing also."

"If all the records are missing, how did Freddy get it?"

"The names popped up on ACIC out of Montgomery. You owe Fred an apology."

"Sounds like someone has removed all traces of himself from around here."

"It would have to be somebody with access to the records."

"Like our Sheriff Ray, after all he's been sheriff of this county for over twenty-eight years according to the mayor. He is also in his mid-fifties which eliminates our Deputy Miller."

Theo, "I don't know, seems awfully thin to me. How do you know there is any relationship between the girl's murders and Thelma's murder? The only connection you have is her grandson had watched the girls play ball."

Jake pulls the Diary and locket from his pants pocket and hands it to him, "Thelma was killed for this, and the Locket was found in an abandoned corn silo earlier tonight. Apparently, it got snatched off during the rape and our killer was so turned on that he fails to get it when he took the victim out in the woods to strangled her."

"This could belong to any girl."

"That's what Sherry said, but you remember when Jerry said he found corn dust under the victim's fingernails and in their hair?"

"Yes, I do. That was before he almost got me hanged."

"Well, this silo has that shit everywhere."

"What were you doing in an abandoned silo as if I didn't know?"

"I was going to have the wildest sex ever and I didn't have to find a pecan tree to do it under."

"See! That's exactly what I was talking about. You gotta let that shit go. If the guys back in Mobile find out about that, they will rag me until I die. I don't need anything else against me. You have had sex nonstop since you got here; I on the other hand have been stung by a jellyfish, pissed on, had two guns pulled … …."

Jake interrupts, "Ok already with the list of shit that has happen to you."

"I'm just saying here lately, I'm everybody's big black piñata."

"I'm not going to say a word. I'm as embarrassed as you are. After all, it was my fault for letting a wild horny black man loose in an all-white neighborhood in the first place. Now what lesson did you learn from all that?"

"I learned not all rednecks are Republicans and Alabama fans."

"And what else?"

"Never trust anybody."

"What else?"

"A three-hundred-pound black man can't out-run a truck load of Klansmen no matter how scared he is. I didn't know until we got under the pecan tree that Jerry was a homosexual trapped in a midget's body."

Jake points to his nose, "You need to have a nose for 'em. I can tell by the way they hold a cigarette or by the way they put their lips around a bottle of beer. They shove the nipple too far in their mouths"

"Wow!! You got that shit down to an art form."

"That's right, that's why I was out trying to do the wild thing in a silo tonight with a real woman and not standing under a pecan tree about to get a blow. Why was he on his knees anyway? You're 6' 4" and he's 5' 3 or 4, he's perfect height for blowing in a standing position."

"Not another word about that. Now I wanna ask you a question. How do you do it? Everywhere we go; women throw that shit at you like you're Prince Charming."

"Ok, let me tell you for the twentieth time, I don't know; it boggles my mind sometimes. It seems the worse I treat 'em the better the sex. And get this, I have had sex in the backseat of cars, front seat of buses, hammocks, on the beach, in the water, in the bathroom, I even had sex on an airplane, and every other place you can imagine. There were only a few places I've never had sex and that was in a corn silo or under a pecan tree, and I almost did that. Half the fun is doing it in a strange place."

"How about an eleva…"

"Been there, done that! Bent that woman over and had her pushing every button in that damn thing. You should have seen the expressions on those people's face when that door opened. I even did my first-grade teacher in the school hallway."

"Ah ha! I caught you in a lie Jake. There's no way you could have had sex in the first grade."

"I didn't say I was in the first grade; it was at my eight-grade banquet. I stepped out in the hallway to get a breath of fresh air and there was my first-grade teacher wearing a short skirt and bending over a water fountain. We walked down the hallway and into the broom closet. I gave her a lesson alright and it had nothing to do with Crayons and Elmer's glue or a pecan tree."

Theo shakes his head in disgust. "My first-grade teacher had a mustache that made her look like a three-hundred-pound Groucho Marx and even she wouldn't have anything to do with me. I was a virgin until I turned 18, and my father had to pay this ugly prostitute to get that done. I whacked off to every dirty magazine ever published. Donna's the first woman who's ever really like me and now I can't get any of that because she went all ghetto on me before I left…. I mean look at me Jake, I was propositioned by a queer tonight and I even managed to screw that up."

"You try too hard. If it makes you happy, I strike out all the time, you're just not around to see me take the plunge."

"You're just saying that to make me feel better. You've been in Fairmont for less than a week and how many times have you had sex? Two, three…"

"Seven times."

"See what I'm talking about! I made a list one time of all the shit that has happen to me since I've known you and I ran out of ink and only one line covered my sex life. Listen Jake, let me tell you a very short story, I was so horny in my late teens, that I went to a petting zoo, and I let a female camel spit right in my face!"

"Well, that's a poor ass excuse for a story."

"Let me finish. She spit in my face, and I got a boner and just stood there and let her spit again!"

"That's almost as bad as my sheep story. You're just tired Theo, we'll get plenty of sleep when we get back to the motel and start a whole new day in the morning."

"If it's like the last six, days, I'll pass."

CHAPTER 23

They meet the mayor at a local breakfast house and sat down to talk when a petite waitress walks over with pen in hand and asked Jake, "All one ticket or separate?"

Before Jake could answer, Rodger interrupts, "Put it all on me Sara."

She gives Jake a smile and ask, "What would you like sir?"

"I would like a sausage-egg sandwich and a cup of coffee."

She turns to Theo, "And you sir?"

"I would like three eggs over easy, grits, three sausage patties not link, two waffles, a small slice of ham, coffee, a large glass of cold chocolate milk and a shit load of bacon."

"And you Mayor?" She asks.

"I would like just a cup of coffee please."

Jake leans forward, "I'll bet you'll wait a few minutes in the future before volunteering to pay for breakfast again."

Rodger laughs, "Let him eat all he wants, he deserves it."

Jake notices him in pain and leans slightly forward. "You okay Rodger?"

"Yeah, this damn wheelchair gives my ass hell sometimes. I think it's time for a thicker cushion." He continues by changing the subject, "I just wanna apologize for the way I acted at the news conference. I guess Bo saved everybody a lot of time and money by hanging himself. It's all for the better. He had a lot of mental issues."

"First of all, Rodger, he didn't hang himself. Like I've said all along, Bo wasn't our man. He didn't deserve to die like that. If you don't mind later after this case is solved, I would like to find out where his mama is buried and have her removed and buried next to Bo."

"I will arrange it as soon as you find out where she's buried. Look Jake, I know you would like to have been the one who solves these murders, but that's not important. The killings are over, and this county can go back to its dreary existence."

"Dreary yes, over no."

"What are you talking about?"

"Tell 'em Theo."

Theo takes a sip of coffee and says, "It wasn't Bo because Bo had no wee, wee, no man tool, no one-eyed wonder worm, no pecker, no penis, no heat seeking missile, no wang...."

"Okay Theo, he gets it." Jake turns back to Rodger, "And that's not all." He pulls the locket from his pocket.

Rodger is puzzled, "What's that?"

"It's a locket Amber Jennings had on the night she was murdered."

"Where did you find that?"

"Ten miles from where Bo's shack is. Bo could not have walked that far without being seen. It wasn't Bo."

"Okay, if not Bo, then who? And whatta we do from here?"

"We check with all the jewelry stores within a twenty-mile radius to find out if anyone remembers the person who bought this locket. There's a chance someone will remember selling it. I talked with Amber's mother and after explaining to her it wasn't Bo, she told me she noticed the locket around Amber's neck about ten days ago. I questioned her boyfriend, and he didn't buy it."

Rodger asks, "Do you have an idea who it could be?"

"I believe our sheriff is the man doing the killings."

"That's impossible. I've known Ray since high school, and he's been a good sheriff for a lotta years. I know he's not the reddest apple on the tree, but murder? You have the wrong man."

"Look Rodger, he's been fouling up the investigations all along. The crime scenes were treated shabby, and evidence tampered with, all records on the homicides and the reports on Thelma and Bo Harper are missing. Records the sheriff had in his office. He's the man we're looking for or the worse record keeping clerk in the world. He keeps people out of those woods like he's hiding something, and I don't give a shit what anybody else says, the sheriff and Miller hanged Bo. When I can prove that I'm gonna arrest them and I know for sure they will put up a struggle and I'll have to kill them both, so, if I was you, I would pull some new applications out for a deputy and start a campaign for the election for a new sheriff. If you went to school with him, that would make an interesting conversation at your next reunion."

Theo interrupts, "Not to mention he has that crooked eye. Jake's never that far off Mayor. He starts at the top and works his way down and trust me on this, he doesn't get far before solving the case."

Rodger shakes his head, "I've known him for years and other than roughing a few criminals up, he has an impeccable record. He's married with three daughters who he has put through college and is well-liked by everyone in the county."

Theo raises his hand, "We don't like him, and nobody around here likes Miller at all."

Jake makes a snorting sound before saying, "I know a man who owns a Pit bull with balls that hang ten inches that hates Miller's guts."

Rodger nods, "Okay, Miller isn't the most popular person around; I'll give you that, but Ray's not like that."

Jake hesitates for a second, "I picked up some bad vibes from Ray when I first met him. Ray and Miller are the only two people that are not real glad to see us."

"I damaged a little pride when we ask for outside help, Jake."

Jake leans forward, "Listen to this; back in the late sixties Bo's mother was raped many times before she was killed, that same woman conceived a child by that man around 69 or 70. He continued raping her and then started in on the boy around the age of eight. The woman was strangled and buried around the shack somewhere. Now old lady Harper had a son who would be in his mid to late fifties. You see, mental disease runs in the family. Old lady Harper was mental, I believe her son is mental and her grandson was mental, so I think your sheriff is crazy as a wood rat hooked on amphetamines. Old lady Harper was Ray's mother."

"I can't accept all that, Jake. Ray has never showed any signs of a mental problem, and I knew his mother. He came from a good family."

"I've seen signs of a mental problem since I first spoke to him. Where does his mother live?"

"She lived in Alexander City until her death twenty years ago."

"Theo and I are going into the woods today and we're going to go into the lower foothills and find out where that odor is coming from, and you can bet one thing Rodger."

"What's that?"

"It's not going to be Dragon we find. I think I know what that smell is."

Roger shakes his head, "What can I do to help?"

"Just sit back and wait. This show hasn't even started yet."

"I feel helpless. I wanna do something... Hey!! I can check on that locket and chain for you. I'm off today and it would make me feel like I'm contributing something to the case."

Jake turns to Theo and shrugs his shoulders, "Why not. It would save us some time." He hands the locket over to Rodger and the waitress brings them their breakfast.

Rodger lays a fifty-dollar bill down on the table and says, "The county fair starts tomorrow, so if we can keep this thing under wraps for now, people can enjoy themselves. Maybe you and Theo can come check it out. They have a greased pig chasing contest, a pie eating contest and lots of rides. Everyone will be there. It will give you a chance to look over the citizens of this fine county."

Jake, "I would like to see Theo in the pie-eating contest... It's a sure-fire way to make a few hundred dollars in the betting arena. Watching Theo eating in a pie eating contest is like running a thoroughbred in a donkey race. We'll be there."

Rodger starts to roll off when suddenly he spins the chair around and with a smile, "Hey Theo."

"Yeah Mayor?"

"Every year we have a large man dress up as Coco the bear and entertain the children for a few hours at the fair. For reasons I won't go into right now, everybody has refused to do it this year. You are as big as a bear, and I bet the suit will fit you. Whatta, ya say, can you help us out?"

"Well although I have had a bad experience with a bear here lately... I'll do it for the sweet children. Hell, I thought I was going to be wearing a bear suit the other night in my tent."

Later that evening they're walking down a trail passing Bo's shack. They walk several miles when they stop for a rest. Theo, who's sweating like crazy says, "About damn time, my feet are killing me. How much further?"

"Just another mile and we can turn around. I figured I would have found something by now."

Theo pulls his Tide cap off and wipes the sweat from his brow. Did you fart?"

"No, I didn't Theo; I'll let you know when I do."

"Well, somebody did, it stinks to high heaven."

Jake sniffs the air, "You're right, I do smell something and it's coming out of the west."

"What are you, part Indian?"

"For God's sake, the wind is coming out of the west, carrying that odor with it. That means we walk west until we find the source." He walks off with Theo trying to catch up.

An hour later they walk through a pine thicket and find a small gate with a 'NO TRESSPASSING,' sign on it. Jake slowly turns to Theo, "Bingo!!"

Theo waves his hand in front of his face, "Wow!! Smells like a cross between shit and more shit."

"Yea more like rotten eggs and cat urine.... Meth!!"

Finding a padlock on the gate, he climbs over. Theo hesitates.

"What are you waiting for?"

"I'm respecting somebody's wishes. The sign clearly says, 'NO TRESSPASSING."

"Get your fat ass over this gate." Theo climbs over and follows him down a narrow path until they come to a twenty-foot bluff. They crawl their way up to the top and to their surprise; there are rows and rows of makeshift buildings down in a valley stretching for acres.

Theo's mouth drops open, "Holy crap, there must be ten acres of meth labs. Damn big operation."

"Yea, now I know why they wanna keep everybody out of these woods. So, this is the source of the odor. I knew that odor was familiar."

"How do you know so much about the odor?"

"I worked narcotics before I met you. Been a long time so the odor didn't ring a bell until now. That shit smells different at every meth lab. Those smokestacks over to the right?"

Theo glances over, "Yeah, what about em?"

"That's where the odor is coming from."

"Okay, I have two very important questions. One, shouldn't there be armed men guarding this place?"

"They don't need any guards. They control who goes into these woods and we're so far from the highway, somebody would have to be looking for this place like we were to find it. The Sheriff could control all of that, which makes him crooked as a snake and still our number one suspect."

Theo nods, "So, he deals in meth and rapes and murders as a part time job. Whatta, we do from here?"

"We go check those shacks out. Pull your gun just in case the chef's in."

"I have a better idea. Why don't I watch the front door from here and you go check it out. If I see anyone, I will yell out a whooo, whooo sound."

Jake smiles as he slowly turns to him, "I bet they have naked foreign girls cooking banana creampuffs down to extract the sugar and mixing it with the drugs. I've heard they do that."

"Get outta here... You're just jerking my chain."

"How often am I wrong?"

"Okay, I'm in. Now let's go confiscate that shit before it's all cooked down."

Minutes later they make their way around to the rear window of one of the structures. Jake tries to look in, but the window is too high.

"Get down on all fours Theo. I'll stand on your back."

He gets down on all fours and Jake hops up on top. "Damn you, can't you just step up? My back's not a freaking trampoline and what's with the cowboy boots?"

"Sorry."

Theo grunts from the weight of Jake's body and asks, "You see any naked girls or packages with banana writing across them?"

"Not yet."

"Well hurry up, your heels are digging in my back."

"Hold on... I see something." Jake jumps back to the ground and in a low voice, "I see three beautiful naked Latino girls with perfect breast and ten cases of extra thick banana creampuffs."

Theo in a low voice, "What the hell are we waiting for? Let's knock the front door in."

Seconds later Jake kicks in the front door. Theo quickly jumps in front with the pistol drawn. He scans the empty room and then turns to Jake, "I don't see any naked girls or banana creampuffs."

"I know; I'm not wrong often, but I do lie from time to time. I can't believe you fell for that. Didn't my story sound too good to be true? I could have just said there's a five-legged cow in here." They walk around stove after stove with pots cooking on low.

Theo, "You know what pisses me off?"

"Work?"

"Yes, but get this, I leave a pot of chili on the stove cooking and go check the mail and almost burn the place down, but these assholes leave fifty pots cooking and leave it for days without burning one single pot. Theo takes a sniff, "That shit smells bad."

Jake takes a sniff, "Smells like those egg farts you're always blowing out your ass. I guess we should have worn mask."

"They must have a large propane tank nearby. I say let's blow this place up."

"That will put my rapist and murderer on the run and I wanna solve those. It's about the victims. I really don't give a shit if the whole county is on meth. It's not like they have any teeth to lose." Jake opens a cabinet and finds a large quantity of over-the-counter cold medicine.

Theo snickers, "Wow! Somebody must keep the freaking flu."

"Flu my ass."

Theo slowly makes his way around the room and then suddenly stops and asks, "How come there's no one here? I mean this is a big operation. Why would they leave it unattended? They must let this stuff cook during the day and come in here at night to mix it."

"I have no idea, Theo; I've never cooked the shit."

"Whatta, we do from here?"

"Whatta, we do from here, whatta we do from here, you sound like a broken record. I say we keep quiet about this visit and say we found nothing if anyone ask."

"You can bet Ray already knows we're looking into these woods again."

"He doesn't have to know we found anything. If he asks, we tell him we found nothing. Let's get out of here before someone does show or we damage our lungs."

Thirty minutes later they both are lying under an oak tree feeling woozy.

Jake, "We stayed in there too long. Let's get going."

As they walk through the woods on their way back, Theo stops to rest and leans against an oak tree. Suddenly an earth-shattering rifle shot is heard in the distance and a chunk of oak few in ten different directions. They jump to the ground.

"You okay Theo?"

"That almost took my head off!"

Jake looked close at Theo and could see a piece missing from his ear. "Crap Theo, you are not going to believe this."

"If it has anything to do with me shitting on myself, I bet I will!"

"Somebody shot a piece of your ear off."

Theo reached for his ear and felt the jagged mess that was once his ear lobe. Blood covered his hand. "Son-of-a-bitch, they shot my ear off!! I guess I can add this to my list of misfortunes!"

"It's just nicked, stop crying like a baby, it doesn't look that bad."

Jake crawls over to the base of a large pine. Theo stays flat on the ground with his pistol in hand. "Who do you think it is?"

"How the hell would I know? Either he meant to kill you and made a lousy shot, or he meant to scare us and he's an expert marksman."

Jake turns on his back and stares at Theo.

Theo asks, "What's the plan?"

"That was a bolt action 30/06 and taking into consideration the time I first heard the shot and the time it hit the tree or ear whichever, I will say that shot was made at about two hundred yards. That will place him near that tree line across the clearing to our left."

"If you know that much, why don't you tell me his freaking name and address!"

Jake turns over on his belly and peeks around the tree. "He's gone."

"How do you know that smart guy?"

"You're telling me you can't hear that four-wheeler riding off to the east?"

"I'm sorry, maybe I could hear better if my freaking ear was still attached to my head and not spattered on that oak tree!" Jake stands and starts walking across the clearing.

Theo, in a low voice, "Where the hell are you going? He could still be out there."

"I said he was gone, now let's go." Jake walks across the clearing for about two hundred yards and stops at a rotted tree stump. Theo follows, holding his right palm over his ear. Jake checks the ground around the stump and picks up an empty shell casing. He tosses it over to Theo. "30/06 just like I said, still warm." He bends down and checks out the footprints around the base of the stump. "You see those two prints?

"What about 'em?"

"Looks like a girl's footprint…size seven. I bet they belong to Miller."

"Oh my God, Jake! You're good, but you're not that good."

"Miller left those same small prints at old lady Harper's residence. He has those little girl's feet, and these prints were made by smooth shoes just like Miller uses when in uniform. You know something?"

Theo, "Not much."

"I need to repeat myself all the time to you. So, let's get back to the motel room and dress that ear up. We have a big day tomorrow."

"Why, what's happening tomorrow?"

"We have that County Fair to go to and you have a date with Coco the bear."

"I was thinking, and I think I should back out of that whole idea."

"What, and disappoint the sweet children, as you called them?"

"I have a bad feeling about it."

"Now what could possible go wrong in a bear suit while entertaining children?"

"I could have a heatstroke.... I don't know, but I have a bad feeling that's sending chills up my spine. I remember something the mayor said, something about nobody wanting to do it for reasons he wouldn't mention. "Light bulb!"

"Then why the hell did you volunteer for it?"

"Sounded like the right thing to do at the time. I thought it might show these rednecks I'm one of the good old boys."

"Yeah, and if frogs had wings to fly, they wouldn't bump their little green asses when they jump ... "

"You know something Jake, I was thinking about how you knew that was a 30/06 and the distance thing out, and every other thing you figure out in our past investigations, and I bet you could have investigated what exactly happen to the Titanic in detail."

"I doubt that, but if I had been in charge of that ship, it would have never sunk."

"How so?"

"I wouldn't have listened to that ass who wanted to break a speed record in the first place. I would have slowed that bitch down to five knots and enjoyed the sex and booze with all three classes of people. That's why I never listen to supervisors. If I'm assigned to a homicide, I'm in charge or I don't work it."

CHAPTER 24

The next morning, they're having coffee at a local dinner.

Jake glances at Theo's ear, "Does not look that bad. Just a little band aid and you're as good as new. If it doesn't grow back, I'll clip the other off when we get drunk again."

Jake's cellphone goes off. He doesn't answer and keeps sipping his coffee as if he heard nothing. It stops for a few minutes and goes off again.

Theo gets aggravated, "You gonna get that?"

"It's Sherry; she's been calling all morning."

"She just wants some more of Jakey-poo's donkey wang."

"She's about to wear my donkey wang out. I've never met a woman in my life who wanted sex that much."

"For the one hundredth time, oh, poor baby…you finally meet a woman who thinks about sex as much as you and you pretend to be dumbfounded."

"I'm married and so is she. It's not right and I feel bad about the whole affair."

"Well, that didn't stop you from tagging it seven times already."

"I'm gonna put a stop to it right now." He opens his cell and dials her number, and she picks up. "Hey Sherry."

"*Jake! Where have you been? I've been trying to call you since last night.*"

"I know. I've been busy with work."

"*I've heard. Rodger said you think you're on to something.*"

"I have a few leads, but what I wanna talk to you about is us. I think we need to…"

She interrupts, "*That's what I wanted to talk to you about. I've been reading in some magazines, and I think I've found a few new techniques on oral sex. You take this cherry and cool whip and…*" He smiles and gives Theo a look. She continues, "*I can't wait until we meet again.*"

"How about after the fair this evening?"

"*Sounds great, I'll see you in an hour at the fairgrounds.*" She hangs up. Jake closes the phone and sips his coffee.

Theo, with a smartass grin, "I thought you were going to break it off?"

"Oh, I'm gonna break it off alright. I'm gonna break it off in her mou…"

Theo breaks in, "Tis, tis, tis, you poor weak individual you."

"I will tell her after tonight. She wants to try a new kind of blowjob she read about in a magazine, and it has something to do with fruit and cool whip."

"You've already used every fruit and vegetable in existence."

"I know that, but she doesn't."

"I can't even look at a cucumber at the market anymore."

"That's so funny I spend an hour in the vegetable and fruit section just trying to figure what I can do with them. I'm surprised I haven't turned every woman into a vegan. The potato throws me off. I can't seem to come up with anything to do with a potato."

"Oh, for God's sake, I'm just now getting into the old way and you're moving into the advanced stage already. If this just doesn't beat all. If it were raining whores, I'd wash down the drain with a homo and you swim around in a pool of shit and come out smelling like wet beaver. You make me sick."

"You just worry about your 'Coco the bear' routine."

"Oh yeah, I've been thinking about that, and I think I'm gonna start off with a little foot shuffle to some rap music and ease into a few twists and turns to warm things up a little. That should dazzle the shit out of the little rednecks."

"Rap music up here. You're gonna get yourself killed. You're the only black guy I know who can't dance."

Theo's cellphone goes off. He opens it and it's Donna.

"Hello."

"*Hey Sweetie, how are y'all doing?*"

"Not good, but Jake's doing everything and everybody. I'm just waiting for another encounter with mother nature as usual."

"*Well, I have good news.*"

"Your freaking mother passed away."

"*Don't be a smartass, you sound like Jake, I'm pregnant.*"

Theo stares into space and then drops the phone on the table. Jake reaches over and takes the phone, "Hey Donna, Theo's in shock right now, so tell me what's going on."

"*I'm pregnant.*"

"Who's the father?"

"*This is where Theo gets those smartass remarks. Theo's the father.*"

Jake holds the phone away from his mouth, "You're in luck Theo, either your milk will be free for the next eighteen years or your mail will be hand-delivered." He places the phone back to his ear.

She yells, "*I heard that, Jake!*"

"It can't be his, his penis is too short, and your muffin is too big."

"*You're the one who made my muffin that big!*"

"Sorry, if you could only see Theo's face right now, you would see the humor in what I said. I'll have him call you back as soon as his ass lets go of the chair." He closed the phone.

Theo mumbles, "I'm going to be a father...I'm going to be a freaking father!"

Jake laughs, "Or maybe I'm going to be a father. Who really knows these days?"

"Holy crap...I'm going to be a father. What am I going to do?"

"Don't ask me, I'm still trying to digest the first Theo."

"I'm lost, whatta I do?"

"I'll tell you what we're gonna do. We're going to have a few drinks to celebrate the burnt bun in the oven, and then we're gonna get to the fair, so you can dress up like 'Coco the bear', and make a complete fool out of yourself..."

Later they're sitting at a table in the middle of an upscale restaurant and lounge. Jake downs a glass of Scotch. Theo's drinking white Russians and staring into space.

Jake snickers, "Relax, it's no big deal. You'll make a great father. They say those silver back gorillas tend to their young more than the mother which means you'll be feeding, rocking and changing shit filled diapers for a long time. That's so funny, being you having that uncontrollable gag reflex. You are going to throw up all over that baby's belly."

"I don't know Jake, raising kids these days is a tough nut to crack."

"I have a cousin who has seven kids, and he does very well."

"What cousin?"

"My cousin Randy."

"Randy with the screwed-up face?"

"That's him. His face wasn't always like that. When he was about ten years old, he tried to stick his dick in a Shetland ponies' ass and the damn thing kicked him with both barrels. Obviously, the pony didn't think he look that good in the first place."

"I say he had that coming."

"I agree with you, but what I'm trying to get across is he still raised all those children and kept his sanity."

"I can't believe he was able to find a woman who would marry him with his face all smashed in."

"He sued the insurance company for the pony farm and got over a million dollars. His wife doesn't even know he has a face."

"He was raping the pony… how did he win that lawsuit?"

"The pony can't very well give any testimony. Most likely told the jurors he was pissing in a stable and the pony backed up to it."

"Life's funny, but I'm still sad about the thought of raising a kid."

"I have something that will cheer you up." Jake pulls a packaged condom from his back pocket, tears it open, places his lips to the opening and inflates it. He makes a few twists and turns and then presents it to Theo.

Theo takes it in hand, examines it from end to end, gives him a funny look, "What the hell is it supposed to be?"

"I was going to say that will be about the color and size of your newborn, if my mailman theory is correct, but it's really a sea turtle."

"It looks like an inflated condom tied at both ends."

"I didn't say it was a perfect sea turtle, but a sea turtle it is."

Theo, feeling the effects of the white Russians says, "Let me try it."

Jake reaches into his pocket, brings out another condom and hands it to him. Theo places his lips on the open end and inflates it, but before he could twist and turn it into a funny animal; it slips from his hand, and with graceful fluttering, it flew across the room, landing at another table in a plate of spaghetti where a young couple were having a romantic dinner.

Jake starts laughing so hard he almost fell from his chair. "What kind of animal was that supposed to be Theo, a wounded bird?"

"Cut the shit Jake, how come that condom wasn't in a package like yours?"

"I tried it on at the drug store to make sure it fit."

"You better be kidding; I had my lips on that damn thing."

"Let's just say I lied for all moral purposes and leave it at that. Now let's get to the fair before we're too drunk to drive."

CHAPTER 25

Hours later they show up at the fairgrounds. Miller is working the main gate and sees them staggering up, he says, "I thought you two were supposed to leave town."

Jake, "We were, but didn't asshole. Theo, Theo here is going to have a baby."

"Yea a baby m… …"

Jake swaying back and forth places his finger against Millers lips, "Shissss, I wouldn't say that if I was you." Jake gives him a drunken smile, "I will literally create a freakshow for this fair with what's left of your a..a..ass."

"You two drunks are not welcome here, it's a local thing."

"Well, well if we can't come in, you'll have to be coco the bear and I don't see that happening with both of your legs broken and my foot up your ass, you low life murdering son of a bitch!"

Miller steps to the side. As they walk off Theo with his hand on Jake's shoulder for stability looks back and with a smile, "And he'll do it too!"

They walk through the gate and see Sherry and Casey waiting just inside with excited anticipation. They stagger over with Theo holding onto Jake's belt loop for support and with a blank look on his face.

Sherry starts laughing, "What happened to you two?"

Jake grunts, "Well we're on our way to being drunk… again… when we got thrown out of a restaurant for exploring the animal kingdom made from condoms. We were celebrating. Theo just found out two hours ago that he's going to have a little baby Coco cub."

"Congratulations, Theo. Are you going to be alright?"

"Just, just point me to my air-conditioned cage."

Casey grabs Jake by the arm and with a wink, "I wanna ride everything." She winks again.

Sherry winks, "And I wanna ride everything too."

Jake shakes his head, "Well let's get us some black coffee and get Theo over to where he's supposed to be, and we'll get this thing started."

An hour later and a little more sober, they all walk over to a large cage up on a platform with a curtain covering the front of the cage with small openings at each end for children to come in and out. Rodger was sitting there waiting when he saw them approaching. When they get there, Jake places his hands on Rodger's shoulder for support and says, "Okay Mayor, I believe I brought Coco's guts with me."

"I'm glad you made it; the children are lining up out front. It's the biggest crowd we've ever had." He looks over the two of them and asks, "Are you two drunk?"

Jake snickers, "Damn near it."

Rodger continues, "Later on I need to talk with you about that locket. I think I have a description of the one who bought it."

"Good because I wanna hear it."

Casey pulls on Jake's arm. "Come on before the lines get too long."

Rodger gives him a wink and mumbles, "I'm so glad it's you instead of me."

Sherry grabs him by the other arm, and they drag him off into the crowd.

Theo starts laughing.

Rodger asks, "What's so funny?"

"Jake has an inner-ear problem. Any motion other than sex, holding a cigar or picking up a mixed drink makes him sick as a dog."

"Well, he must have that charm down pat because the girls sure have taken a liking to him."

"It's not his charm Mayor, it's his big…" About this time a man walks over with a large, dark brown bear costume in his arms and drops it at Theo's feet. "Good luck dude, you're gonna need it."

Theo turns to Rodger, "What did he mean by that?"

"Nothing. Just having some fun with you, that's all. The last guy just didn't get along with children." The mayor rolls his wheelchair over to Theo and helps him into the suit as he staggers about.

Rodger, "You gonna be, okay?"

"Yeah, I just found out I'm going to be a father."

"Well congratulations. This fulfilling little job should let you know what's in store for your future." The mayor pulls the zipper up in back and then hands the head to Theo.

"Okay Theo, you just look through the mouth and you'll be all right. Mack over there has a little blower he sticks through the flap in the lower back to cool you off if you get too hot."

Theo, wearing the large cumbersome outfit, struggles into the cage as the announcer yells over the P.A. system, "*Okay children, get ready for the world's smartest, funniest, and most loveable bear!! Ladies and gentlemen, here from the grizzly country of Montana, for one appearance only, is Coco the bear!!*" The curtain opens and to Theo's surprise there are thirty to forty kids lined up to talk with him.

Across the fairgrounds Jake, Sherry and Casey were making their way to the roller coaster. He stops as the girls walk to a roller car. He leans toward the man controlling the ride and hands him a twenty.

The man asks, "What's this for?"

Jake still feeling the effects of the liquor answers, "I want you to take it real slow and easy dude."

"But I don't have any control over…"

Jake interrupts, "Real slow and easy, like I said."

They sat down as the crossbar closed and the coaster slowly made its way to the top. Jake nods and gives the man a thumbs up.

The coaster peeks at the top and Casey yells, "Throw your arms up Jake."

"I like 'em right where they are, tightly wrapped around this bar." The coaster takes off like a rocket and he yells as it flies down the coaster, "Stop the ride… Oh shit!! Stop this damn ride!! Oh Shit!! Stop this fuc&#$* ride!!"

The great Grizzly bear, Coco, was taking the children one at a time. A little girl walks up and jumps up in Theo's lap, "Hey Coco, I want a tricycle and a Barbie doll and a pair of roller skates and…"

Theo interrupts, "I'm a grizzly bear little girl, not Santa Clause. I eat reindeer. What is your name?"

"Shelly."

"Well Shelly, it just so happens I have the connections you need." He gives the mother, who is standing to the left, outside the cage, a thumbs up. "So, I'll see what I can do…. Next!"

A very large chunky boy jumps up onto Theo's lap.

Theo yells, "Ouch!" In a low voice, "Hey kid, watch the bear nuts."

The boy asks, "Can you give wishes?"

"No, but I might be able to get you a case of slim-fast." The boy gives him a look as his mother grabs him by the hand, "Let's go Bobby, I have never been so insulted in my life." Seconds later a ten-year-old boy walks up wearing a sleeveless white t-shirt and chewing stuff jumps up in Theo's lap, "You're not real."

"Now what makes you say that scooter pooter?"

"Because real bears can't talk. My daddy shoots bear all the time and they never talked."

"Oh well, that's because he doesn't have his ducks in a row, he needs to talk first then shoot."

"I can see your eyes in your mouth."

"I can see a vison of my foot up your little ass too! How else am I supposed to breathe and see your little yellow teeth? Now move along you little jerk, so believers can get a turn. I see what I can do about getting you a toothbrush."

"My old man says you're just a stupid man in a bear suit."

"Then why the hell did you get in the damn line in the first place, smartass?"

"Because I wanted to see the fake bear for myself."

"Well, now you've seen him, so get your little redneck ass off my lap and out of the cage before I forget I'm a nice, friendly bear."

"I'm gonna tell my old man you said some dirty words."

"Well, you go right ahead and do that monkey-boy...Next!!"

The boy spits snuff on Theo's fur. "What do you think of that Coco?"

"Why you little nasty shit!"

The spoiled kid yells as he walks off, "I'm gonna go get some more snuff and tell my dad what you said and then he's gonna come back and hold you down while I kick you in the nuts!"

"Hey, while you're at it, tell your old man about your own damn vocabulary...Next!"

The boy runs off as a little girl steps up eating a corndog.

"Hello sweet thing and what can Coco do for you today?"

"You funny."

"Yes, I am. That's my job. That looks like a delicious-looking corndog you have there. Is that mustard dripping from the end?"

"Yep, you wanna bite?" She pulls her arm back and rams the corndog as hard as she can into Coco's mouth striking Theo in the right eye.

Theo yells, "What the Fuc----!!" He falls from the chair trying to get the corndog out, but the large bearpaws prevented him from reaching in. He's rolling on the floor screaming, "Oh my God, I'm blind! I'm blind!"

Knowing she had hurt Coco bad; the little girl takes off screaming.

The coaster comes to a stop with Jake holding his hand over his mouth. He slowly steps off and leans over the rail and throws up. He takes a handkerchief from his back pocket, wipes his mouth and looks up with his left eye blinking and then staggers over to the carny.

"What part of 'slow and easy' did you not understand, you stupid asshole? Give me back my twenty."

The nervous operator says, as he's reaching in his pocket for the twenty, "I tried to tell you buddy, a roller coaster only has one speed and that's whatever gravity allows it to be."

"I'm going around the back to throw up and when I get back, your Sir Isaac Newton, scientific little ass best not be here."

After the exhilarating ride on the fast roller coaster and throwing up, Jake is totally exhausted, sobered and drained to a large degree. He looks at the girls and gives them a big, nasty frown.

"How about we go to the shooting gallery, I know for a fact I can do that without getting sick."

Minutes later he's shooting metal ducks moving across the rear of the gallery.

He yells, "One supervisor!" ping "Two supervisors!" ping "Three supervisors!" ping "Four super.... ... "

Sherry interrupts, "Why do you call the ducks, 'supervisors?"

"I'm not sure but it makes my aim a lot better."

They walk down through the main fairway with girls carrying arm loads of stuff animals.

Jake, "We need to get over there and check on Coco."

They started in that direction.

Minutes later they return to Coco's cage.

Jake stops when he sees the empty cage. He turns to a man standing there holding a small blower motor and asks, "Where's the mighty Coco?"

"He's around back recuperating. I tried to talk him into going to the first aid station, but he flipped me off."

They walked around to the back of the cage and saw Theo lying in the dirt in a fetal position. Not far from him is another man lying in a fetal position.

Jake takes a knee, "Looks like Custer's last stand. What the hell happened to you Coco?"

Theo, still wearing the suit and head gear says in a broken voice, "Pull…this… damn… head off."

"Won't that hurt?"

"I'm…talking about…this stupid ass…bear head. And be careful, there's a corndog stuck in my eye."

Jake slowly and gently pulls the head off and sees Theo's swollen bloodshot eye and a half-eaten corndog resting on his forehead. "Holy crap, Coco, your eye's all messed-up. What made you think you could eat a corndog with that bear head on?"

"A seven-year-old girl tried to feed Coco and as you can see; his freaking mouth is where my eyes just happen to be. A design flaw, if I ever saw one. Then a little ten-year-old redneck-bastard chewing tobacco kicked me in the nuts."

Jake takes a sniff, "What's that putrid smell?"

"A six-year-old threw up cotton candy all over me. Help me up so I can get this hot-ass bear suit off before I drown in my own sweat."

"Shit, Coco, you look awful."

"Enough with the Coco shit! Unzip me."

Sherry yells, "I'll go get some ice for that eye."

Jake, "What in the hell happened to that guy over there on the ground?"

Theo sits up and answers, "That's the little bastard's old man, and as you can see, Coco don't play that shit. I mauled his ass good and kicked him in the nuts with my big-furry ass foot. This is what happens when you marry your ugly ass sister which by the way made that boy's mama, his freaking aunt and his daddy his uncle. That will teach the bastard to mess with his gene pool."

"This suit should have had enough padding to protect the crotch area. Someone should have told you to get one of those athletic crotch-holders!!"

"You would think. For some unknown reason the manufacturer of this damn suit didn't foresee this shit happening. They left that area without padding so I could take a piss, which I did on that guy's face over there. I also have a few words for the mayor."

"Damn Theo, we have had it rough the last few days."

"What's this 'we' shit? You have a rat in your pocket? I wanna go home to my wife."

"You did that, and you couldn't take your mother in-law."

"I hate that bitch with a passion, but she hasn't poked me in the eye with a corndog loaded down with mustard or kicked me in the nuts yet."

"Just a few more days, we're getting close, and I have that feeling that we're going to have to kill some people."

"It's about damn time, and for your information, I would like to kill about thirty right now. Another day like today and I'll have to kill from a hospital with a patch over my right eye and a scope in front of the other. I'll get those bastards from the hospital window with a rifle."

Jake helps him to his feet and as they start to walk off, Jake asks, "You wanna enter the greased-pig-chasing contest?

"Yea! Now I know what I haven't experienced yet. A pig dragging my blind ass, torn ear, and sore nuts around a pig shit filled area."

"It will be small piglets I think...you sure?"

"Only if they greased him with barbecue sauce and cover his ass with honey."

CHAPTER 26

They knock several times before Rodger opens the door. He greets them with a smile, "Glad you could make it Jake; y'all step inside and I'll fix you a drink." He sees Theo holding an ice pack over his eye, "What happened to you?"

"You know damn very well what happened to me Mayor! The kids in this county should be locked up in maximum security prison or used as shark bait, that's if they don't shove a corndog in its eye or kick it in the nuts."

With that, they step in, follow Rodger into the den and take a seat on the stools in front of the bar.

He pours the drinks, "I want to apologize to you, Theo, for that whole Coco mess. I figured it would have gone better this year."

Theo grits his teeth, "Screw those little bastards. What you need is a freaking lion tamer with an electric cattle prod. And fill my glass to the top!"

Rodger finishes pouring his drink and suddenly notices the mounted deer head slightly cocked on the wall. "Wonder how that got messed up? That woman kills me, it's been ten years since I shot that thing, and she still can't stand it being in the den. You would think she would at least straighten it up when she walks pass. You like hunting Jake?"

"I like hunting humans. I don't mount their heads though; makes the room look trashy. Uh, like I want those faces staring at me."

Rodger pours another drink from a bottle of fine scotch, "In the article written in the Police Gazette, they say you're a decorated soldier of the Vietnam War. I guess you saw a lot of killing. That would turn anyone off to it."

"Actually, I've killed a lot of men in the war and quite a few since then. I just don't have any reason to kill animals. I shot a deer once and never got over it. Poor bastard just laid there gasping for air. I missed his heart and hit his lungs. He drowned in his own blood."

"Well Jake, the deer are over-populating like crazy."

"And that's another thing, is it over-population or is it just people turning the woods into shopping centers and subdivisions. Who's the asshole who counts how many deer there is anyway, because I've got to know how he does that shit." He turns to Theo, "Whatta you think?"

Theo was standing there looking the other way, staring out the window. "Hey Theo, are you okay?"

He turns as he wipes a tear from his one good eye, "I can't talk right now."

"What the hell's wrong with you?"

"When you were telling that awful story, I thought of Bambi's mama, and it just broke my heart."

Jake nods and then turns back to Rodger, "His heart is as big as his ass." Jake takes a drink, "You said you had something for me."

"I have some good news and some bad news."

"I think I'll go with the good news first this time. After a few more drinks I can handle the bad news."

Rodger nods before saying, "A salesperson at *'Jewels for You,'* in Alexander City said she thinks she remembers who bought the locket. The description fits Ray, but she's not sure. Apparently, it's a popular piece, very expensive and it's sold at most Jewelry stores. Where did you say you found it?"

"I'm not ready to say right now. It's a little too premature."

"You can trust me, I'm on your side."

"I know that, but I need to tie up some loose ends first. Where's the locket?"

"That's the bad news. I stopped to pick up some cigars to kind of make amends for not believing you about Bo, and somebody broke into my van and took it. I was being followed by a sheriff's unit, but he never got close enough for me to see who it was."

"You bought me cigars?"

"Three hundred dollars' worth."

"Wow! It's a good thing, because Coco here smoked my last one the other night."

Theo butts in, "Okay, enough with the Coco shit, and I only smoked one freaking cigar!"

Rodger continues, "Did you hear me? I think I was being followed by Ray, and I think he's the one who broke into my van and stole the locket."

"Hold that thought for a second Rodger." He turns back to Theo, "You know how I am about my cigars. You could have used a toothpick or pencil and got the same effect."

Theo fires back, "Bitch, bitch, bitch. I'll buy you a replacement."

"You'll forget; you always do."

"Not with you reminding me every five-freaking minutes I won't."

Rodger takes a drink and shakes his head, "Look Jake, can we discuss the cigars later? We need to talk with the Judge about getting a warrant for Ray's arrest and you can serve it."

"You're not going to get an arrest warrant, and I thought you were sure about Ray not being a suspect."

"Too much is falling into place. And why can't we get a warrant?"

"We don't have the locket anymore, and you said the saleslady thinks she remembers him. You can't get an arrest warrant for murder on what somebody thinks, and I have no DNA to link him to the crime scenes."

"So whatta we do from here?"

"We might have enough to get a search warrant. If we can find the locket in his residence, we can hold him for receiving stolen property until we get some harder evidence. But that locket being a popular piece might put us in a position to prove it's the same locket. That's if he still has it. Wonder how he knew you had the locket."

"I told him by accident over a cup of coffee."

"This is why I never show my hand until I see the last card."

"So, you think Ray was having an affair with all four girls and bought them jewelry."

"The parents of the first two victims told me that the girls had acquired gifts they could not explain. The locket was the first piece that's left a trail. Our killer is slipping up."

"Look Jake, I discussed it with Sherry, and we want you and Theo to move back in until this case is solved."

"I can't do that Rodger, for some reason I sleep better at the motel. And another thing; I think Miller shot Coco's ear lobe off this morning."

"I was wondering about his ear. You see Miller, do it?"

"Not really, but I did find some small tracks next to some four-wheeler ruts that could be his. And that's not all; Theo and I found a damn large meth lab set up about a mile past Bo's shack."

"Meth? Well, hell, let's go raid the place."

"Nobody was there, and I think all this is tied into the murders somehow. I wanna wait, but you can't say anything to anyone. I don't want anybody knowing we found the stuff."

"Again, whatta we do from here?"

"Theo and I are going back to the meth labs and take some photographs and samples. I need you to get the judge to issue us a search warrant for Ray's house. We won't need one to check his car; that belongs to the good people of this county and whatever you do don't let Ray know about the search ahead of time. If you see him before the search is made, talk about your sore ass, anything, but nothing about the warrant or the locket."

"I can do that. Call me when you get the pictures, and we'll go in the morning and meet over at Ray's place."

"Thanks Roger, you've been the only help we've had since we got here."

Theo, "I have been in them damn woods so much I could qualify for squatter's rights. I'm starting to know those woods better than I know this den."

They all downed their drinks and walked out the door.

CHAPTER 27

Early the next morning back at the motel room, Jake's lying on the bed in deep thought when Theo comes strolling from the bathroom, wrapped in a towel with a bloodshot eye and is gently drying his wounded ear.

"Hey Jake?"

Jake tilts his head, "Yeah walrus butt?"

"Do you think a plastic surgeon can fix my ear?"

"I would be more worried about having one fix that nose first."

"I'm being serious."

"You can hardly tell a piece is missing."

"You think Donna's gonna freak out when she sees it?"

"She didn't freak out when she first saw that short penis of yours. Look Theo, your ears were already slightly too large."

"I said be serious!"

"I am being serious; now stop worrying about that damn ear."

Theo could see Jake was still upset over the Meth lab being destroyed. "We should have taken a camera the first time around."

Jake places his hands behind his head, "I didn't think they knew we had found it. How did they know we were going back to take pictures? Only three people knew we were going back; me, you and Rodger."

"What about the guy who shot my ear."

Jake slowly turns his head and responds, "That's right. They must have thought we had found it and were expecting us to return. I think Ray and Miller are dealing some big-time shit, which means Ray is doping up his victims, raping and then killing them and Miller is helping him for a taste of the girls."

Theo takes a seat on the edge of the bed, "The drugs don't match up." He changes the subject. "Can I ask you something personal that's been on my mind for some time?"

"Go ahead, as long as it's not about your ear."

"Besides Ann and your ex-wife, have you ever been in love? I mean really, truly in love."

Jake ponders over the question for a few minutes and then replies, "Let me think... I fell in love with every female teacher I had, except Ms. Flowers who would pop my hand with a damn wooden ruler, but even then, I was turned on. That's when I discovered I like spanking asses. But the first time I was truly in love was in the sixth grade with a beauty named Susan Griffin."

"Tell me about her. I've never been in love before Donna came along."

"It was six months before turning twelve, about mid-way in March. She sat next to me in class for seven hours a day, five days a week. She was, by far, the shyest, sweetest, and prettiest girl I have laid my eyes on. My heart pounded like Indian war drums every time I looked into her eyes that were blue as a clear midday sky. She always had this smell about her that drove me crazy. I was oblivious to every other girl in the classroom, well not all oblivious. There were a few more that turned me on, but Susan was the one. It was the early sixties, and she always wore them short skirts that showed off the best set of legs I had ever seen on a twelve-year-old and the prettiest flower-covered blouses I had ever seen. She had long dark flowing hair that looked like waves of silk when the wind would blow in through the school windows. We didn't have air-conditioner in those days."

"Did she have big breasts?"

"Back then girls didn't have big breasts like they do now."

"Did you ever have sex with her?"

"You don't think about sex when you're in love for the first time. You just walk around all day with a lump in your throat and a strange feeling in your gut."

"I thought about sex when I fell in love with Donna."

"Me and Susan would meet every day on the school playground during play period. I would save my nickels and dimes I earned from doing chores for people in the neighborhood on the weekends, so I could buy her a rose from a vender on the corner three blocks from a portable. I would give it to her every time we met under this old oak tree near the old wooden bleachers. Her lips had a natural luscious shape to 'em. I just knew this girl was for me. I wanted to spend the rest of my life with her. There wasn't a minute past by that I didn't think of her."

"What happened?"

"One day I waited under the oak tree for thirty minutes, holding that damn rose and when she didn't show, I went looking for her." He goes silent for a few minutes as his smile turns to a frown.

Theo says, "And?"

"I peeked behind the equipment shed and found her kissing Doofus Davis, a chubby kid that sat across the room and always farted and picked his nose. I gave him that nickname. I caught her trading long, wet kisses for chocolate bars. My heart felt like it was being ripped from my chest by a mountain lion and I had a burning flame in my gut that was being chopped up in a blender. It was the first time I ever cried in the open and the last. It seems she had a sweet tooth for chocolate like someone else I know."

"That's one sad ass story."

"Yeah, it was. All she had to do was tell me the roses weren't doing it for her."

"What did you do after that?"

"I lost it. I put my fist in between two rows of fat in the back of Doofus's neck and he fell to the ground like a large sack of potatoes." Jake pauses for a second, "Potatoes, potatoes…"

Theo, "Potatoes?"

Jake comes to his senses, "Sorry, for a second there I thought I had an idea for potatoes… Well, where was I? Oh yea, then I pulled his pants down and his brown-stained briefs and took the candy bar from her hand and shoved it between the cheeks of his ass. Look just like he was taking a shit. Susan never spoke to me again. She went to the banquet with that fat hoe!! No offense meant, Theo. I think she had a fat fetish."

"None taken. Then what happened?"

"I was suspended for five days, but my stepfather knew how hurt I was, so he neglected to tear my little ass up."

"I'm sorry about that, I really am."

"Don't be, it had a happy ending."

"How so?"

"I saw her on a domestic about ten years ago, over near the poverty-stricken boondocks. She weighed over two hundred pounds and had seven kids by Doofus who was lazy, unemployed and living off food stamps. Seems she should have taken the roses instead of trading kisses for candy bars. Roses don't have any calories. She recognized me but I pretended to not recognize her. The house was filthy and there were dirty diapers lying in every corner. Her legs look like two white columns at the Lincoln Memorial made from cellulite, and her breast look like two very large hairy oblong coconuts."

"Crap!! I bet that was a relief."

"That's an understatement. I've never even heard of hair growing on a woman's breast before. But, if you really wanna hear something that will blow your mind; I was sexually molested by my seventh grade teacher, Ms. Cromwell. She was a fox dude. She had a space between her desk, and she sat me right in front so I could pay my respects to her panties. I have a long list of other teachers that did that. That's when I discovered what an erection was. She would make excuses to keep me after class and she would take me to the coatroom and pull my pants down and perform oral sex on me and she would place my hand between her legs and have me rub her until she had an orgasm. My hand would smell like cucumber and bananas, but don't ask, I was so young and naive I had no idea how she got that up in there."

"What a sick pervert. She was a disgusting child molester."

"See what I'm talking about Theo, a normal man would have given me a thumbs up, but you see it as a perversion. It was a dream come true for a thirteen-year-old boy who wacked off in front of barbie dolls."

A small rise comes protruding up under Theo's towel. "She was molesting a child. You should have brought it to the attention of the authorities, and they could have arrested her."

"Do I look that stupid to you? You couldn't have dragged that info out of me with ten wild horses. That attitude is why you never had sex when you were a kid. It did take my mind off Susan though."

"Shit, my six-grade teacher looked like a cow with buck teeth. If I remember from past conversations, you have had sex with every female teacher you have ever had."

"Yes, yes, I have. I went to a class reunion when I was twenty-six and Mrs. Cromwell gave me more sex. She still looks better than Susan and she was in her early sixties."

"Get out of here!!"

"Yep, I lost all respect for women after Susan and gained a whole lot of respect for the educational system."

"Your adolescent life was so exciting. I was picked on by every kid in the hood and girls as well; I don't even wanna go there. One day I walked by the girls dressing room and the door was cracked open and I got a glimpse of a cheerleader wearing just her panties."

Jake snickers, "Wow! Better than nothing. Did it give you a little black boner?'

"I wet my pants, Jake."

"Shit, what grade were you in?"

"I wasn't in school. That was four years ago when I did a police report on a locker break-in at the Mobile Junior College."

"I worry about you. My younger days were not all a bed of roses. It's not easy going through life with a larger than normal penis."

"Stop it before you get me to crying over your sad childhood."

"I'm telling the truth. It's a horrible curse going through life humping, humping, humping, stroking, stroking, stroking, choking, choking and...."

"Okay, I get it! I would trade with you in a heartbeat."

"Look Theo, I caught my Mama screwing an insurance salesman, my father was killed by another police officer; I caught the crabs from Mrs. Longmire, my wife left me for a lawyer, I was stabbed by an old drunk lady with a knitting quill, drove a car into the river, I was shot by some S.W.A.T. officers and the list goes on and on and on."

Theo stands and slowly turns, "How did that crab thing go?"

"I shaved around my, again, larger than normal penis and they move on. For some reason they don't do well without the jungle."

"Let's go back to Mobile Jake. I'm home sick and my mother-in-law should be gone by now. Let 'em keep their two hundred thousand dollars. We don't need the money this bad."

"It's never been about the money; I have a thing for child killers. I want this bastard bad. This case is like a Rubik's cube. You keep turning until the colors match. Sometimes you think you have it, but then, you find you're three blocks off."

"The guy who came up with that shit should have his ass turned inside out. I could never figure those damn things out."

"I still can't do a hula hoop, and if it makes you feel any better Theo, I could never do a Rubik's cube either."

"I just wanna go home. I have a bad feeling about this case."

"With what has happened to you over the last few days, I can see why, but with that being said, you have a bad feeling about every case. We can figure this out. I can feel this murderer. He's close and why didn't you just stay in Mobile when I sent you back."

"I thought you were having orgies up here and one more day with Donna's mother and you would have had another murder to solve."

About this time Jake's cell goes off. He flips it open and says, "Hello."

"*Hey Jake, I got the search warrant. You and Theo meet me at 5673 Brown's Ferry Road. It's out on 31 about six miles.*"

"We'll be there." Jake closes his phone, "Get dressed Theo; we have work to do."

220

CHAPTER 28

They're leaning against their car with Rodger sitting next to them in his wheelchair as several deputies went through Ray's upscale house. Ray walks from the porch and gives Jake a dirty look.

"How come you're not in there searching my home; letting someone else do your dirty work?"

Jake with a grin, "Why waste my time, they won't find anything anyway."

"If you knew that, why did you go through the trouble for a search warrant?"

"Because you pissed me off about what you did to Bo. I see you managed to burn your factory up this morning."

"You can't prove I had anything to do with those Meth labs. Why don't you go back to Mobile where you belong?"

"That's what my partner was asking not more than an hour ago, but I like it up here and I'm getting close to solving these murders. And how did you know I was talking about meth?"

"I heard you talking about it, that's how."

"I never said anything around you. Yeah Ray, I'm getting close to solving these homicides, I can feel the fear floating through the air like one of Theo's farts."

"You're no closer than you were five days ago. I still think it was Bo."

"You wanna bet?"

"I've been sheriff a long time and I might be guilty of not being a good one, but I'm not a killer." He turns to Rodger, "I can't believe you allowed this to happen; we've been friends a lotta years."

"I have a responsibility to this town, Ray, just like you. If it was my house, I would expect you to do your job."

"Yeah, but it's not your house, its mine and I take offense to this intrusion."

Jake turns and gets back in the car with Theo. "Intrusion? Wow Ray did make out of the three grade." Ray stomps off in anger.

Rodger wheels over as Jake rolls his window down.

"What now? They didn't find the locket."

"I kind of figured they wouldn't. I'm gonna wait and see what happens, but you make sure y'all keep a close eye on the soccer girls or any other female teenager for that matter."

"Look Jake, Sherry's having a pre-season tournament tonight at five o'clock. We're playing Alexander City High. There will be five or six thousand people here. Sherry thinks it will help the other girls get over the trauma. It will be a good time to look the crowd over. I bet that sick bastard will be there also, looking over the menu."

"We'll be there." Jake nods and drives off…

Jake's cruising along when Theo asks, "I know this is redundant, but what's on your mind now?"

"Where do I start?" About this time his cell goes off. Before he can answer, Theo says, "You know who is horny again." Jake places the speaker on and answers, "Hello."

A deep garbled voice comes back, *"Hello Jake."*

"Hello … and may I ask who the hell this is?"

"I'm the Dragon you're looking for … Dragon slayer."

"That still doesn't answer my question. Can you be more specific? Can you give me a name or an address or can you just meet me somewhere and I'll kill you if it's not a lot of trouble for ya?"

"Kill me? I doubt that very seriously. I've been breathing down your neck ever since you got here. You're a very unorthodox cop. I knew when you came to Fairmont that this was going to be fun."

"Stop it, you're making me blush."

"You do know I'm going after another, and you don't have a clue to who I am."

"I've narrowed it down to an ugly-ass white male who can't get laid in a free whorehouse if he had a thousand dollars in his pocket. You're in your mid to late fifties and you have a lot of knowledge about police investigations which, rules out the sheriff… or does it? Oh yeah, and I know your last name … Mr. Harper."

"Wow, you are good, but you're way off."

"I also know you killed your mother, but you didn't find the diary you were looking for, Ray…"

"That blind bitch was never a mother to me."

"That's obvious from the way you turned out."

"So, you found the diary. I bet you couldn't even read the damn thing. The bitch was blind, and her penmanship was bad to begin with."

"I couldn't read all of it. I knew she didn't kill herself. You thought you were smart, but you left calling cards all over the crime scene."

"I can't wait to spread the legs out on the next young girl and give it to her while I strangle the life from her warm naked body."

"What a coincidence, I can't wait until I get to do the same thing to you. Except I won't spread your legs or strip you naked."

Theo, "Why didn't you just say strangled in the first place?"

Back on the phone, *"Even if you could catch me, I'm insane. The courts wouldn't convict me O'Malley."*

"Wait just one minute; I need to ask my partner something." Jake turns the phone sideways, "Hey Theo, do we have to go to court on these killings?"

Theo hesitates and then replies, "I thought you would just kill the bastard and let it go at that. That's what I always liked about you. We may have to sit through some boring ass Internal Affairs hearings, but never court."

Jake turns the phone back to his lips and says to the caller on the other end, "Nope, we're not going to court, I'm just going to kill you."

"I was very impressed with you figuring out the locket and all. Where did you find it?"

"Wouldn't you like to know?"

"Let me ask you something; do you strangle the mayor's wife when you're stroking that thing? There's a sense of freedom about getting off as their life slowly fades away."

"I don't know about strangling her, but I defiantly have that choking thing down to an art form."

"Are you going to the game tonight?"

"Why yes I am, are you?"

"I wouldn't miss it for the world. I wonder which of the girls is going to be next. I know; maybe the mayor's daughter will be next. She has nice legs and a well-rounded ass and certainly pretty enough. Are you humping that also?"

"It was tempting, but I draw the line at eighteen or maybe not."

"I don't draw a line at all Jake; the younger the better."

"I heard you like little boys too."

"It's okay, but the young healthy girls are more fun. They put up a better fight until I drug 'em."

"I bet you won't think it's fun when I get my hands on you."

Theo raises an eyebrow, "His voice sounds like he has a cold."

Jake turns the phone slightly, "Sounds like Ray talking through a toilet paper roll." Jake puts the phone back to his lips, "I'm sorry, my partner wanted to know what sorry ass crazy son-of-a-bitch I was talking to, please continue."

"*Yea I heard. I sure like the way young girls smell, young and innocent.*"

"I have an idea, why don't we cut right through the next killing and meet somewhere. We can swap sex stories until you're dead, which should take about three seconds considering my age and all."

The killer laughs, "*You'll do nothing; I know every move you two make. Oh yes, congratulations Theo on being a soon-to-be-father of a baby monkey. I must be getting old also. I missed that nappy head by a quarter of an inch with my 30/06.*"

Jake tilts the phone again and says, "He says congratulations Theo on the soon to be baby monkey."

"I can hear just fine. Tell him thanks and I hope to see his ass real soon."

Jake snickers and says on the phone, "Theo says thanks."

"*I can hear his ass just fine too. This is so cool. I'm going toe to toe with the great legendary Jake O'Malley. I'm so glad you chose to come up here to our neck of the woods. I knew the locals couldn't give me a run for my money.*"

"Wow!! I'm flattered. So, you know me from the past, huh?"

"*I've known about you for years. I liked what you did to the S.W.A.T team a while back, and then what you did to Ace, and his bunch was just awesome. I was a little surprised when you let the vigilante go. I especially liked what you did with that evangelist last year. That gave me an erection.*"

"Well, we do have something in common."

"*I tell you what, because I'm a little disappointed at how the investigation is going, I will give you a clue.*"

"Well, it's about damn time; I was about to get bored and hang up."

"*You ready for this?*"

"Oh shit, will you get on with it?"

"*Black is wet and runs wild when it rains, black is smart and hides when she sangs. Now to ....*"

Jake interrupts him, "Hold on for a second." He turns to Theo, "Get your pad and pen out encase I forget any of this."

"As I was saying, 'Black is wet and runs wild when it rains, black is smart and hides when she sangs. Now to beat me at this game, you'll have to find my real name. She can see things, but you'll have to find her before I do my thing."

"That was beautiful, but it didn't rhyme that well, and I don't think 'sang' is an actual word. I mean 'sing' is a word, and 'sung' is a word, but I doubt 'sang' is one."

Theo shakes his head as Jake gives his little English lesson.

The killer continues, *"I've watched you close ever since you got here. I'm even watching you as we speak."* They look in every direction. *"I'm so excited about when we have our final meeting. I mean, it can go either way. You think after I kill you, they will write songs and stories about the legendary Jake O'Malley?"*

Jake turns back to Theo, "What do you think Theo? You think after I'm dead and gone, they'll write songs and stories about me?"

"I'm working on a title for the song right now. I like, 'Kicking nuts, drinking beer and humping women'. It has a country twang sound."

Jake goes back to talking on the phone, "We just wrote another country song. Hey pervert, if you have a beef with me, why the girls?"

"I knew you had a thing for child killers. Hey, that just gave me an idea. Why don't I find a ten-year-old and rape her good, then I can burn her little body up so you can't find where I jacked off on her. Whatta, you think about that super cop?"

"Like you did to Bo? Real sloppy work all around."

"You're so right Jake; I'll stick to the teenagers for now. Bo was a bastard child. I raped his mama a hundred times before she had that retard."

"Yeah, that mental disability gene must come from your side of the family."

"You're a very humorous man... Oh yes, I almost forgot, how's that daughter of yours doing? She's about the right age for a good rape."

"Now you've done gone and pissed me off good, but I don't think you can find her."

"I don't have to; she's coming up with Ann."

"What!!"

"Ann and Jackie are on their way up here from Dothan. I can't wait to meet your daughter. I bet that if I could get the mayor's daughter together with your daughter, I could make one watch as I screw the other and then

slowly strangle them. Who will be first? I hate making these decisions. I wonder what Ann will think about all the sex you're having with the mayor's wife?"

Jake grits his teeth and says in a very low, soft voice, "I can feel you, and I will have your ass in three days. Mark that on your calendar."

"That's Saturday night. I can't make it; I will be busy screwing two young luscious girls. I need to go now; maybe we can make it on Friday night... so is Friday night a date?"

"Maybe sooner." The caller hangs up. He turns to Theo, "This guy knows me. He also knows Ann and Jackie."

"I heard that....wonder how he knows them."

Jake checks his phone and sees the caller I.D. was blocked.

Then suddenly his phone goes off again. He flips it open and says, "Hello, you son-of-a-bitch, I believe I heard you the first time... asshole!"

"Well thanks a lot Jake. Jackie and I are on our way up. We need to talk."

"Sorry, I thought you were somebody else."

"No, it's me. How come you haven't called?"

"Why haven't you called me? You're the one who decided you needed some time."

"I've just been thinking things over, and I know now I can't live without you."

"Took you about three weeks to figure that out?"

"I just wanted to wait and let things simmer on the stove a little until I got my head straight."

"I think you let it simmer too long, you almost burnt it. Look Ann, I need a woman who will stick by me regardless of how much money I have."

"I'm sorry Jake, it's just that I've never had anything growing up and the money made me see the other side of life. When you lost it, well so did I. Can you forgive me?"

"I never held it against you. I love you."

"I love you too."

"Listen Ann don't take this wrong, but I'm in the middle of an investigation and I need my mind clear from anything else right now. I need you and Jackie to go back to Mobile. I will have two officers watch the apartment."

"Is that so? Well, why did Theo call and leave a message on my phone saying you wanted us to come up there? He said you were in trouble and needed us."

Jake turns to Theo and asks, "Did you call Ann?"

"Why the hell would I call her, she's not giving me any sex."

"Listen Ann, it's a trap, I need you to take Jackie back to Mobile and wait for me there."

"Are you hiding something from me?"

"I'm hiding a whole bunch of shit from you, but I can send the pictures of four teenage bodies to help you with your decision to come up here."

"I don't know, but I can always tell in your voice when you're guilty of something."

"I'm guilty of something every time I take a breath of fresh air...no, I'm serious Ann, take Jackie back to Mobile, I'll be home in four days."

"Look, we can discuss this when I get there. Love you." She hangs up.

"Stubborn-ass woman is coming anyway."

Theo asks, "That SOB say anything that can help us find his ass. I know how you can pick up little details. And from what this poem says, this guy should be the one writing country songs."

"The voice is the same voice on the 911 tapes. He's talking through an empty toilet paper roll...oh yeah, read that back to me."

Theo reads his pad, "Black is wet and runs wild when it rains, black is smart and hides when she sangs. Now to beat me at this game, you'll have to find my real name. She can see things, but you'll have to find her before I do my thing." Theo snickers, "You're right, that sucks. We can eliminate any poets being our suspect."

"We'll work on it after the game tonight. We're going to be looking for a white male, about fifty-eight, well-educated and he'll be a well-known member of society."

Theo nods, "Which brings us back to the sheriff."

"Can't be him. I said the guy we're looking for will be well-educated, like maybe a teacher from Fairmont High. That would keep him in the loop with the girls and they would trust him. I need a list of all the male teachers."

Theo replies, "What is it with you and these lists? I thought we decided it's the sheriff."

"He's still on top; I just like to look at other options."

Theo shakes his head, "I'll have them before the game. You know I was thinking..."

"Did you hurt yourself?"

"No, but when you said it must be someone the girls trusted, I was thinking …. What about the local pastor?"

"I checked and he's eighty-years-old. And about that list, I mean for you to get them, not turn it over to Freddy."

CHAPTER 29

Later that night at the game, Jake is scanning the crowd from an upper stairway. Theo walks up behind him and passes him a list of the male teachers.

"I circled seven names that fit our boy. They all have clean records. Six are married with children and one is a widower. None are directly related to the soccer team in any way, shape or form other than they teach at the same school and they're all here at the game and sitting up there near the announcer's box with the other teachers."

"Good work, Theo. Now I want you to go downstairs and watch the bathrooms and concession stand."

"Will do boss." Theo starts to walk off, when suddenly he stops, turns and asks, "You have a twenty?"

"What the hell for?'

"I need a coke."

"Whatta ya need a twenty for? Damn expensive coke if you ask me."

"I need it to wash down the hotdogs and skittles."

Jake pulls out his wallet and hands him a twenty. "Look Theo don't get down there and get caught up eating and watching soccer mom's asses. You have a job to do."

"I'm on top of it, stop worrying."

"You just keep an eye on those teachers. If they get something to eat or go to the bathroom, I want you on top of it."

"What good does it do me to be downstairs? The killer knows me, and I stick out like an aardvark at an ant's convention."

"We can let him know we're looking. Maybe he'll slip up or something." Theo turns and walks downstairs.

Thirty minutes later Jake walks down to the sideline. Sherry walks over and says, "The girls are doing great."

"Better than I am." Jake replied.

"You are so tense; after the game you wanna go have some fun? I'm wearing fire red panties with little white hearts and lace trim."

"Look Sherry, I don't wanna upset you, but I talked with our man this evening and I think he's after Casey and my daughter."

"Shit!!........Wait a minute, your daughter isn't even here."

"That's another thing, my wife and daughter will be here before this game is over."

"You gonna tell her about us?"

Jake loses all expression on his face, "Du, do I look that stupid?"

"But I thought you loved me."

"I care about you, but as you already know, I'm married."

"Then why did you make love to me all those times?"

"I didn't make love, I was just having sex...the best sex I've ever had, but still just sex. I never once thought of leaving my wife."

"So, you used me for your sexual pleasure."

"What the hell are you talking about? You seduced me."

"I did things for you that I've never done for a man before."

"And I appreciate all the enthusiasm, but it was you making all the aggressive moves."

"I noticed you never pushed me away."

"I knew this was going to happen! My head upstairs said back out the door and the little head downstairs said dive in with both feet. You know you have a body built just the way I like 'em, but I have a family."

"You used me. I was going to ask Rodger for a divorce this weekend and move in with you."

"Yeah, I'm sure Ann will love that, and where exactly will you move into? I won't have a place to go either."

"I have lots of money in the bank. We can go wherever you wanna go."

"I know where I'm going if you say anything about us, straight to the intensive care unit. Ann can shoot better than Theo which isn't saying much but enough to know she can cripple me."

"You can divorce her. She left you over money. I don't care if you are poor." She crosses her arms and stares out across the field. "I put up with no sex for a lot of years. Now I've had nine and I'm not letting it go, so you can tell your sweet Ann about us, or I will tell her myself."

"Listen to what I'm saying, if you tell her, there will be no us. And this is the very reason why I try to avoid sexual relationships with married women."

"Then you should have never let it get this far."

"You're the one that massaged me under the table with your foot and you're the one that came into the guestroom and seduced me, you're the one that made me knock the mounted deer head off the wall and it was you who dropped to your knees every time I came into a room and again, it was you who took me to the silo and attempted to treat me like a five-dollar Filipino whore."

"You're turning me on, meet me at haft time under the bleachers and I'll lick your balls."

"Are you right about those panties?"

"Yep, just for you."

"Okay!"

Theo is standing near the concession stand eating his fourth hotdog wearing his black slacks with a black T-shirt and sporting his gun and badge on his belt. He has ketchup and mustard dripping down the front when suddenly he sees a large suspect looking in all directions and then stepping into the girl's bathroom. He wraps the paper around the ketchup-dripping hotdog and shoves it in his front pants pocket and walks over to the entrance of the bathroom. He looks around making sure no one was watching and slips inside. He finds nobody, so he strolls over to the small toilet cubicles and looks under one, seeing the suspect's pants around his ankles. Theo pulls his gun, "Okay dude, cut it short and step out here right now!"

The subject flushes and pulls the pants up. He jiggles the latch as Theo steps back and points the gun right at the center of the door. It opens and the subject freezes.

Theo smiles, "You have a lot of explaining to do asshole, starting with, why the hell are you in the girl's bathroom?"

"I always used the girl's bathroom. I'm a woman you jackass!"

Theo starts laughing, "Nice try dude, but I'm not falling for it. No woman is that ugly."

"I'm a woman, smartass!!"

"Prove it."

She drops her pants and Theo steps back and in a loud voice, "Pull 'em up, pull 'em up!!"

She yells, "I told you I was a woman!"

"I'm not sure about the woman stuff, but I know damn well your kin to a black bear I personally know!" She pulls her pants up and storms out the main door.

Theo grabs his stomach, "I think I'm gonna be sick." About this time a voice comes from a few feet away.

"What brings you in here, Theo?"

Theo turns and finds Jerry, the coroner standing there. "Are you having second thoughts about us?"

"Hell no, I was just leaving."

"Look Theo, I think that if you just let loose of your true inner feelings, you'll find that what I have to offer you will bring the greatest satisfaction to your sexual needs."

"Look Smurf butt, you almost got us killed the other night. Now listen and listen well; I love women, always have and always will."

Using his whole short body, he shoves Theo back into the cubicle and down on the toilet and looks up into his eyes.

Theo yells, "Look faggot, I'm not gay, and will never ever be gay, so back off or I will put a bullet hole between your eyes! And I think you smashed my damn hotdog."

Jerry stands there for a second and with a smile drops to his knees, "I'm in love with you, all I wanna do is pleasure you! Pull that Alabama black snake out and let me have a go at it!"

"I don't wanna to be pleasured by you!! You people need to go back in that closet."

Jerry starts grabbing at Theo's zipper when suddenly the cubicle door flies open, and Jake is standing there staring at Theo with Jerry on his knees.

Jake grins, "You explained to me the first time Theo, and it was a little shaky, but I don't think I even wanna hear this story."

Theo yells, "It's not what you think! The bastard's in love with me. He won't take no for an answer! I'm a good-looking black man, so I can see why the persistence. I just followed a man or woman in here because she or he looked suspicious. This penis sucking asshole just won't give up."

Jerry stands with a smile, "Okay, I'm sorry. I just thought we had a chance."

Theo yells, "A freaking chance at what!! I'm not gay, how many times do I have to explain that to you!? I'm a three-hundred-pound cat chasing machine!"

"My heart is broken; I just want you to know that."

"Well excuse me for not getting all torn up inside."

Jerry turns to Jake and asks, "How about you... you wanna have some fun? Theo here said you have a nine-inch penis."

Jake's grin turns to a frown, "You had not known Theo here for more than a few days and already two timing the poor unfortunate bastard, and it upsets me that you two even had a conversation about my pleasure tool, now unlike my big mouth, hotdog-eating partner who is a very kind and understanding man and knowing, I'm not the type to beg someone to get out of my face, I will rip your damn tongue out of that midget head of yours and flush it down the shitter! I will write a novel with a title in seven words, *"THE WORST OVERESTMATED DECISSION A MAN CAN MAKE!"* So, you better leave Theo alone. I know for a fact that if he wanted a real man, it would be me! Now you have two seconds to get lost."

Jerry runs out of the bathroom as Jake turns back to Theo.

Theo counts on his fingers, "That's eight words."

Jake gives him a disappointed look, "This is what happens when you spend more time doing math than letting that teacher molest you. Right now, I'm embarrassed to the highest degree, dumbfounded to no limit and...."

Theo interrupts, "I get it already and don't even go there."

Jake shakes his head, "What is it with the homos these days? Truckers, coroners and maybe even a black cop are just running amuck. It's getting where a man can't even go to the bathroom without one hitting up on him."

"I know Jake, it's getting ridiculous."

"I was talking about me. You seem to fit right in."

"I said, don't say it; I was just doing my job like you told me to."

"I don't remember telling you to hide in the girl's bathroom with a homo."

"I freakin give up; maybe I should just gag the man to death and get it over with."

"I don't think you could gag a fly with that thing of yours, but enough about your homosexual tendencies, I have bigger fish to fry. Sherry wants a divorce."

"That's impossible, you two aren't even married."

"I'm talking about her wanting a divorce from Rodger, moron."

"Well, let her go for it, dude. We can't worry about everybody else's troubled marriages; we have enough of our own problems... I think that bastard squished my hotdog."

"Okay Theo, those bio-engineered hotdogs have eaten your brain cells up. She's in love with me and wants to get a divorce so she can marry me."

"That's funny, she can't marry you; you're already married."

You village idiot, that's my point exactly!! She wants to tell Ann about us."

Theo, with a puzzled look on his face, "Shit! What about us?"

"Not us, as in you and me, us, as in me and her."

"Well, that's stupid. This is what you get for throwing nine inches of oil drilling equipment around like it was a party favor."

"Tell me you are not saying that after being caught in a bathroom with a gay man. Is it my fault the Lord seen fit to giving me the gift?'

"It's not His fault you're passing it around like shots of whiskey at a biker's party."

"Is that right?"

"Yep, He gave you a gift and you mis-used it, like Samson did with all that hair."

"Well, I haven't thrown it around in the girl's bathroom with a peter cleaner for a mouth, like someone else I know." Jake shakes his head and rolls his eyes back.

"What about the time you had sex with the ticket girl at the bus terminal … in the girl's bathroom?"

"I forgot all about that, but she was over five feet tall and straight. Trust me, straight as an arrow."

"Okay, let's drop it and worry about things at hand."

They walk out as Sherry comes running up screaming, "She's missing Jake! She's missing!"

"Who?"

"Casey! She went to the locker room at halftime and now she's missing. He's got her; he's got my baby!!"

"I told you not to leave any of the girls alone for any reason. Now don't panic!" He turns to Theo, "Have them seal off all the gates. Call the parking-lot officers and make sure no vehicle leaves the lot without checking it." Jake looks over and sees a red 4X4 burning rubber as it flew through the parking lot.

"That's him Theo, get to the car!!"

"How do ya know it's him?"

"Because I can feel the bastard, now get to the car." They took off running to the car as the truck turned in one row and out the other making its way out on the main drag. Jake jumps behind the wheel as Theo struggles to get in the moving vehicle. They make their way out on the main road and Theo places a flashing blue light on top. Jake takes the radio and yells, "Operator, have units block Route 7 at the county line."

"*That's negative; all units are working the game.*"

"Then notify the State Troopers and have them block it off."

"*10-4.*"

Theo yells, "They'll never get there fast enough." Jake says nothing as he increases his speed to over a hundred miles an hour.

Theo reaches over, pulls his seat belt across his wide girth and struggles for several seconds trying to snap it. Jake does the same.

"Slow down a little Jake, we're not even sure it's him. I'm having Deja vu. No wait a minute.... I watched that movie, *'Bullitt'* night before last."

"It's him Theo, it's him. I can feel that slimy bastard crawling up my spine." They can see the truck's tail lights as they slowly close the distance between them. Suddenly, the red truck turns off the road and takes off through a pasture tearing down a wooden gate. Jake quickly gets in behind him.

Theo yells, "Watch the pecan tree! Watch the pecan tree!"

"Shut up, I see it!"

"Watch the hump! Watch the hump!"

"Shut up, I see it!" The unmarked unit goes air born and bottoms out when it hits the ground. Theo is holding on for dear life.

"Watch the bush! Watch the bush!"

"Shut up, I see it!"

"Okay Jake, you're going to get us killed."

"Shut up, I see it!"

"What?"

The truck spins around as Jake tries to cut him off.

Theo yells, "Watch the water trough! Watch the water trough! Watch the...!"

"Shut up Theo, I see it!"

The truck spins around again and passes them going the other way. Jake spins back around slinging dirt and grass high in the air. The truck makes another sharp turn and flips over.

Jake yells, "We got that son-of-a-bitch!" About this time three cows ran out in front of them.

Theo yells, "Watch the cows! Watch the cows!!"

Jake turns, avoiding the cows and glanced off a pecan tree causing the car to flip over the water trough and lands on a large bush.

Theo, sitting upside down turns to Jake, "Hey, got milk?"

"Very funny, Theo."

"I plainly said, 'watch the cows.'"

"You wanna drive?"

"You saw the tree, the bush, and the hump, but failed to see three seven hundred pound black and white spotted cows. You managed to hit everything I mentioned. Hey, did any have five legs?'"

"I didn't have time to count them, and the other shit wasn't running around the pasture like crazy." Jake's cell goes off. He struggled to find it on his belt, but it had fallen on the headboard of the car. He undoes his seat beat and falls to the roof finding his cellphone. He flips it open and yells, "Hello!!"

"*We found her Jake; she was in the restroom.*"

They glance over at the truck and see three young, intoxicated teenagers limping off into the woods.

Theo gives him an angry stare, "So you can feel it huh?"

Jake reaches over and undoes Theo's seatbelt allowing him to fall hard against the roof.

"Damn you, that hurt! I always wondered if a seatbelt would hold me up in an upside-down position."

Jake smiles and starts laughing. Theo couldn't help but laugh too.

"We sure can get into some kind of shit, that's all I can say."

"There's never a dull moment with O'Malley and his trusted Shadow."

The cell goes off again. Jake struggles to open it and answers, "Hello!"

"*You're not even warm Jake. If you could see you two right now, upside down in that smash cruiser. This is so funny. I'm really enjoying this. See you tomorrow.*"

Thirty minutes later as they walk down the road towards the stadium, a farmer eases up to them in his old rusted out truck, "Hey Jake… you boys need a ride?"

Jake, "We sure do." He opens the door and there sitting next to the farmer was his Pitbull.

Theo, "I think I'll ride in the back."

One hour later they step from a farmer's truck at the game.

Theo, "You were not lying about that dogs nuts."

Jake, "The chief was a little upset when I ask him to send another cruiser up here."

"He gets so upset over the little things. What's the big deal?"

"It wasn't about the unit. He was upset that I called in the middle of him and his wife having sex. Seems he doesn't get it but three times in a year."

"That's his fault. Have you ever stopped and really taken a good look at that mug of his? There should be an ongoing investigation to why she married him in the first place."

They slowed down a little when there standing at the gate, they noticed Ann and Jackie speaking with Sherry.

"Oh my God, my goose is cooked! The outhouse has fallen! The fish jumped from the frying pan....Oh hell forget it Theo. She's gonna kill me for sure. How in the hell did they recognize each other? They've never even met before!"

Theo shakes his head, "They have mind powers we're just beginning to understand."

Theo starts to walk away when Jake catches him by the arm, "Just where the hell do you think you're going?"

"Look, I can face gators, monsters, bears, snakes, bad guys, queers, Klansmen, and even a little girl with a corn dog, but I'm not going to be around when Ann explodes."

"The hell you say, all this is your fault in the first place."

"And how in the hell did you come up with that!? You act like I held a gun to your head and made you have sex with Sherry."

"Hey, that may just work. I can tell her I had no intention of having sex with that ugly woman until you got drunk and put a gun to my head."

"No way anyone in their right mind could convince Ann, that Sherry is ugly." Theo looks closer at the girls carrying on a conversation, "You know what I'm thinking?"

"How much my funeral gonna cost?" Jake replied.

"I was just wondering what it would take to get those two in the motel room and record them eating each other."

"You know what I was thinking while you were planting that image in my brain?"

"What?"

"How am I going to enjoy that with two swollen eyes and a bullet in my ass?"

Theo shakes his head, "I guess I could walk you through it as it unfolds. I never wanted to come up here! You know something Jake; that nine inches you have gets us into more trouble than we get into ourselves. Why don't you just let me cut five inches off and get it over with?"

"And be like you?"

"No; you didn't just say that? I can cut it off, but I can't make it black!"

Jake takes a deep breath, "Let's go and face the music." As they walk over, Ann takes off running and meets them halfway. She gives him a big hug, with him closing his eyes expecting the worst.

"I missed you so much. I will never leave you again, Jake."

Jackie wasn't far behind her. She grabs him around the neck and gives him a big hug.

"Sorry Daddy, I should have known better."

Jake looks across the way as Sherry gives him a wink.

Jake winks back and says, "Let's get back to the motel."

Ann says, "I was just talking with the mayor's wife, and she said we can stay in their guestroom and Jackie can sleep with Casey, their daughter."

Jake gives Sherry a sarcastic smile as she just grins back.

Theo shakes his head, leans over towards Jake and in a low voice, "Ann better fix her own drinks, but this will make it easier to get them to have girl on girl." He turns back to the girls, "I think I'll ride over with you guys, but I'm staying at the motel." He leans back over towards Jake and in a low voice, "You call me if there is even a hint of girl on girl."

CHAPTER 30

Jake carries the luggage upstairs as Theo and Rodger wait in the den. The girls are walking ahead of him as they make their way up to the guestroom. Sherry opens the door and stands to the side as Ann steps in and ganders over the room.

With a smile, "It's beautiful. Your whole house is beautiful." She gives Jake a look and continues, "I was supposed to have a house by now but had to change plans because somebody…I won't mention any names, lost all our money."

Jake just frowns as he felt her jab to the gut.

Sherry walks over and pounces upon the bed, "Yeah, there's a lot of fond memories in this room." She gives Jake a wink as Ann looks around at the beautiful pink shades of flowered wallpaper, the antique oak dresser, matching lamp stands and the hardwood floors.

Sherry pats the bed with her hand, wanting Ann to have a seat next to her. She gives him an awkward stare, "Just feel this mattress Ann, you can bounce on this all night if you get my drift." She glances up at him and with a smile, "Why don't you set that luggage down, go to the den and have a drink with the boys. I wanna have some girls talk with Ann. You can put Jackie's luggage in Casey's room. She will get a kick out of having a sleepover."

Jake's mine wanders for a few seconds as he sets the luggage down and in the back of his mind, '*Sherry reaches over and starts kissing Ann on the mouth and works her way to her breast. Ann places her fingers between Sherry's legs and then leans her back on the bed and goes south with her tongue…*'

Ann, "Jake! Jake! Will you give us a few to have girl talk?"

Jake, with a sarcastic grin, "Maybe I wanna hear the girl talk."

Ann stands and pushes him out the door, "See you at supper." She closes the door. Jake leans over and places his ear next to the keyhole. After not hearing anything through the thick door, he turns and walks downstairs and into the Den where he catches Theo telling Rodger about all his misfortunes over the last few days. He pulls out a stool and joins them in a drink.

239

Rodger laughs, "What's wrong Jake, the girls lock you out?"

"Yeah, something like that. By the way, what does this girl talk mean anyway?"

Theo takes another drink and replies, "The real name for it is 'plotting.'"

Roger, "Plotting?"

"Yeah, that's where they close the door and come up with a plot on how to cut your balls off and make it look like an accident. And then the conversation will turn to buying shoes."

Jake gives Theo an evil stare, "I could kill you for planting those visons in my head."

"What visions?"

"The alternative to her shooting me!"

Rodger laughs as he places his glass on the bar, "I thought it was shopping tips. My wife is a professional at that shit. If they ever put shopping in the Olympics, I'm going to enter Sherry; she's a shoo-in for the gold."

Jake, in a low voice, "That's not all she's a shoe in for."

Rodger, "I'm sorry, what did you say?"

Jake, "Nothing, going over things in my mind." He walks over to the bar grabs a bottle and pours himself another full glass of Bourbon and then walks back over to the foot of the stairway, looks up the stairs and wonders what Sherry is telling Ann. He just knew any minute Ann was going to knock the door off the hinges and run down the stairs and cut his throat with a pair of scissors.

Rodger shakes his head and laughs with Theo. "Relax Jake; come tell me about the chase through the cow pasture."

Jake walks back over to the bar, "It was just three drunk boys who thought we were chasing them for something else."

"I'll have a deputy bring over a spare marked unit for you two in the morning. It will do until Mobile sends one up. Theo was telling me about this riddle the killer gave you over the phone. Can you make heads or tails from it?"

Jake downs the whole glass and gives Theo a look.

"What did I do now?"

"You run your mouth too much."

"The mayor's okay, he thinks he can help us with it." Rodger pushes a piece of paper across the bar with the riddle written on it, "I'm pretty good at this stuff. I play a lot of mystery games with Casey on her laptop."

Jake sets his empty glass down on the bar and nods, "Okay, let's see what you come up with."

Rodger moves his wheelchair closer, "Okay, I figured he's talking about a black woman who lives near the river. When it rains heavily up north, the Tallapoosa River runs wild and flows way over its banks just northwest of here turning the area for miles into a swamp. Then a week later it's back to normal. It stormed a few days ago, so the river is high right now."

Jake turns the piece of paper around and looks it over. "How do you know he's talking about a black woman?"

"Because he refers to black female when it says, 'Black is smart and hides when she sangs.' Look Jake, I know an old black woman who lives up the river in a Negro community. People around here just refer to her as Granny and they say you can hear her sing from her shack for miles and she can see things that no one else can."

Jake shakes his head, "What they mean, is she's as crazy as a rabid bat."

"Yep, pretty much!"

Theo interrupts, "She can't be any crazier than old lady Harper."

Jake leans over the bar resting on his elbows. "What else do you see Rodger?"

Rodger places his finger on the piece of paper, "This killer says Granny knows his name."

"I already know his real name; it's Harper. Like I said, he was Thelma Harper's son."

"I think he's telling us she knows the name he goes by. And you need to talk with her before he kills again."

Theo puts his thinking cap on and blurts out, "I think this damn riddle is nothing more than a bowl of crap soup. He's leading us on a wild goose chase or he's setting up a trap."

Jake glances over at him, "Why do you think that, Theo?"

"Because if it's not a wild goose chase, it means you'll have to go up on that river in a canoe and find this crazy-ass bitch who's into all that voodoo shit, which means I'll have to go as your backup. And that also means I'm back on water and you'll wanna go at night because that's when you always wanna go. I'm not comfortable in the woods or swamps. Snakes are everywhere."

Jake gives Rodger a look, "I bet someone will let us use their boat with a nice cabin and lots of food."

Theo nods, "I know what you are trying to do, and it won't work."

Hours later Jake is sitting in the rear of a canoe paddling, switching from side to side and occasionally placing it in the water at the rear for rudder control. Theo' is in the bow with a flashlight in one hand and his pistol in the other looking in every direction.

Jake snickers, "We could go a lot faster if you would lay that shit down and grab a paddle."

"I bet Roger is watching Ann and Sherry eat each other as we speak."

"It wouldn't do him any good… he's dead from the waist down."

"I'm scare to death and still getting a boner, so don't shoot that fantasy down."

Jake, "It's peaceful out here at night. It's almost a full moon, but I can see rain clouds moving in."

"Hey, screw you, where's that damn big boat full of food? And I'm not putting the flashlight and gun down. I saw this movie where this monster comes out of the lagoon and kills the shit out of everyone? And for some unknown reason the hero never has a gun close by or a flashlight. Yea, that monster had big lips, and gills, and had a hard-on for the leading actress. I swear the name is right on the tip of my tongue."

"That describes you to a tee, and the name of the film was, '*The Creature from the Black Lagoon.*' Now stop working yourself into a frenzy."

"I don't care; if he sticks his fish head out of the water, I will pepper his ass with jacketed hollow points and turn him into sushi. I do have a question though; how do you know which way to go? I can't see a thing."

"I don't. Rodger said he thinks she lives up a small tributary on the right five miles from where we launched."

"Next question, how can you see a tributary in the dark?"

"I see better at night, that's if you'll stop blinding me with that damn flashlight! You gonna give us away. Now turn it off and let your eyes get focused in the dark."

"Hey Jake, you remember that movie where these four guys went in a canoe on a fishing trip in redneck country, and one was raped by this hillbilly?"

"*Deliverance.*"

"What?"

"The damn name of the film is '*Deliverance*', and it was Ned Beatty who got raped in the ass. But you don't have to worry about that, they can't find your black ass in the dark. You bring that movie up every time we get near water."

"It was awful; they made that poor guy squeal like a pig."

"I'm gonna make you squeal like a pig if you don't turn that damn flashlight off."

Theo turns the flashlight off and mumbles to himself.

Minutes pass when Theo whispers, "psst, psst."

"What now?"

"I think we missed the turn. We've gone a lot more than five miles. Maybe the bitch moved or died. Rodger did say he was a kid when he last seen her."

"I think you're right. I think it's a few miles back. It will be easy; we don't have to fight the current."

"I say we keep going and don't stop until we're back at the boat ramp."

Jake turns the canoe around using the paddle as a rudder.

Not a word is spoken for about twenty minutes, when Theo asks, "What are you thinking about? You haven't said a word since we turned around."

"I was just wondering what Sherry's telling Ann right about now."

"Most likely telling her how you bowed her legs up behind those ears and turned that thing into a head of lettuce or, or they're talking each other into eating their heads of lettuce."

"I should have never let it get this far, Theo."

"I'm the one who has all the bad luck. In your case, they both are most likely sitting up this very moment, wondering how to talk you into a threesome."

A smile comes over Jake's face, "I never even thought of that. That would be awesome. Two beautiful women, pleasuring me in every way."

Theo laughs, "If I know Ann, and I think I do, she will shoot your balls off the minute you get back. End of story."

Jake frowns, "Well you just turned that fine vision into a horror tale." Jake looks to the right and then the left and suddenly yells, "There it is Theo, there's the creek."

"I thought he said it was on the right side."

"We're going back the other way now. The left side is the right side. It was only the right side and not the left side when we were traveling north up the river."

"Okay, now I'm lost."

They cut the canoe to the left and slowly made their way up the creek fighting the swift current.

Theo scans the boggy creek beds in every direction and says, "It's spooky as hell up in here. You remember that movie, '*The Swamp* Thing?'"

"Can't you ever watch anything that's not a horror flick. Try some reruns of, '*I love Lucy*, damn, you do this every time."

About this time, it started to sprinkle.

Theo throws his hands up, "Well if this ain't a fine howdy do. Where's that damn poncho when you need it."

Jake whispers, "Keep it down, I think I see some kind of light up ahead." He runs the canoe up on the bank and jumps out causing it to flip over. Theo falls in the dark murky water and yells, "I'm drowning Jake, I'm drowning!!"

Jake places his finger over his lips, "You loud-mouth pompous ass. Stand up, the water's only a few feet deep."

Theo stands and finds the water is knee deep. "Daji Vu."

"Daji Vu?"

"You remember all that rain and mud when you talked me into sneaking up on Ace at that old factory?"

"Oh crap, here we go again."

Theo steps from the creek and follows Jake as he makes his way through the thick underbrush. They ease through the bald cypress trees getting ever-so-close to the light when Jake suddenly stops and says, "I think it's a campfire."

Theo, in a loud whisper, "My socks are soaking wet; you know how I hate that feeling…Maybe I can dry my clothes by the fire, that's if they're not busy trying to make me squeal like a pig …. The rain won't get too heavy for a while. Move over a little, I have a stick poking me in the back."

Jake turns around and sees a large black man pressing a single barrel shotgun in Theo's back.

"It's not a stick."

Theo slowly turns around and sees the white teeth of the smiling black man. "Well so much for stealth. I guess I did yell, 'I was drowning' too loud." Jake, "You think?"

The large black man pushes the barrel deeper into his back, "Keep moving white boys."

They start walking when Theo looks over his shoulder, "You do know I'm not white, right brother?"

The man, in a deep voice, "Why yo ass calls me yo brother, we kinfolk?"

244

Theo replies, "Maybe, but that's what we call each other in the city."

"Yous saying my mama was a street hoe?"

"I wasn't saying that at all, I was trying to…"

The man interrupts, "I says, keeps yo white asses moving." They ease into a campsite where two black males are sitting around several moonshine stills mixing corn mesh in a large pot.

Jake snickers, "Looks like we've run up on a moonshine operation."

Being sarcastic, Theo responds, "You think?"

The man with the gun says, "Pull up a log white boys and have a seat." Another black man frisks them down and find Jake's 460 Rowland in a shoulder holster under his light wind breaker.

"Damn!! Just looks at du size of this here bitch!! Dis cracker came to do some business." He checks Theo and finds his 9mm Glock stuck in the small of his back.

"Well, dis cracker didn't. He bes carrying a plastic gun."

Jake, "I told you Theo about that plastic toy. You spend a fortune on clothes and then buy the cheapest gun they sale, and it's the one damn thing your freaking life depends on. Wow, you are an embarrassment."

A black man turns to one who's sitting on a log and says, "Both des crackers packing guns, Jerome."

Jerome shakes his head, "What be brings yo two white cracker asses up here in our neck of du woods?"

Theo nods, "Why you keep calling me a white boy, I'm black. Are you freaking blind asshole?" Jerome stands and walks over to and slaps Theo across the face as Jake lunges forward in anger, but another man aims a shotgun at him causing him to set back down. Theo places his finger on his lips and wipes the blood that had trickled down his chin from his upper lip. He gets pissed and turns to Jake, "No he didn't."

"Oh, yes he did."

"That was totally uncalled for. I sure wish I had Big Bertha right now. Are my lips swelling Jake?"

"How can anyone tell. They already look like catfish lips."

Jerome steps closer and takes a knee in front of them, "You boys gots to be the law. Who be told yo asses abouts dis place?"

Jake stares into the man's eyes and responds, "Yeah, we're police officers, but we don't give a shit about your rotgut-making tin pots. We have bigger fish to fry. You don't even rank in the top one hundred, asshole, unless you slap Theo again. That'll move you up that damn ladder with me."

Jerome starts laughing out loud, almost like a mad man. Theo starts laughing too.

Jake quickly turns to Theo, "What are you laughing about?"

"I'm not sure. I was just laughing with him. I thought the joke was on your white ass."

Suddenly Jerome stops laughing. "Yo Chester; tie der hands and den bring mees that there tin pot over here."

Chester ties Jake's hands behind him and then Theo's. He then walks over and picks up a large pot with a lid on it and hands it to Jerome.

Theo smiles, "I sure hope that's chicken and dumplings. I love chicken and dumplings better than a dog loves dragging his ass on a rug."

Jake gives him a look, "I don't think you can eat what's in that pot."

Jerome leans closer to Theo and slowly removes the lid. "Yous ever sees a pissed-off cottonmouth white boy?"

"For the one hundredth time, I'm not a white boy! I'm a damn Kalruba tribe warrior from east Africa and if you can't see that, you must be from the Pee Wee tribe of west Africa... By the way, is cottonmouth anything like cotton candy?"

Jake shakes his head, "You stupid ass Theo, a cottonmouth is a moccasin snake."

Theo jumps back as a large man standing behind him grabs his arms and forces him forward. Jerome slowly and carefully reaches into the pot and grabs the snake by the tail and pulls it out. The dark colored snake was a little less than four feet long and as big around as Theo's forearm.

Theo yells, "Hold on man, I don't like snakes!! Jesus, that's a big ass mean ugly thing!"

Jerome slides his hand down the large snake's body until he is holding its head and uses his thumb to force its mouth open. The fangs are over an inch long. He pushes it closer to him. The expression on Theo's face is an expression of total fear and he couldn't move a muscle. Tears started pouring down his face.

Jerome laughs again, "I's be gets da truth from yo asses one ways or anuther."

Jerome holds the snake's fangs several inches from Theo's nose. Jake could see the tears running down Theo's cheeks and his busted lip quivering.

Jake, "Okay asshole, that's enough. My partner has a thing about snakes and if you cause him to have a heart attack, I'll have to kill each, and every one of y'all. And I be means what I say. We're telling you the truth. We're cops investigating murders, and Theo is black, check his damn license if you don't believe me."

Jerome turns to Jake, "So du badass cracker wants to play?"

Jake snarls, "Yeah, I wants to play; cut these damn ropes loose and I'll play."

To Theo's relief, Jerome turns and takes the snake and pushes its head within an inch of Jake's nose.

Jake, in a low voice, "Bring it closer you black bastard and I will bite its head off. I'm more scared of those nasty-ass hands of yours than the snake."

Jerome gives him a look and could see that there was no fear in his eyes. "Yous one crazy ass white boy. Do yous knows dats one strike from one of dese cans kill a man?"

"Well, I'm not sure if it will kill a man, but it can make you hurt yourself trying to get away from it. Now if you boys are tired of letting the snake do your dirty work, cut me loose and I'll show you some shit that will ruin your freaking miserable lives!"

Theo whispers, "Easy Jake, these guys ain't refined."

"Neither am I!! Shut up Theo! I don't give a shit about these backwoods' pieces of shit, and the words is 'are not', Theo, not 'ain't.'"

"What is it about you and the grammar lessons? You do that every time. They're gonna kill us. I'm sure they'll spell our names right on our headstones."

"If they were going to kill us, they would have already done it by now. They're just trying to scare us, that's all."

"Well, they're doing a damn fine job of scaring the hell out of me."

Jerome turns to Theo, "Yous ain't black, cause yous talks like yous white man."

Jake answers before Theo had a chance, "That's because unlike you ignorant shits, he went to college and learn how to spell and speak clear, you uneducated jackasses! We're looking for an old black woman they call Granny."

They all step back.

Jerome asks, "Whats da hell y'all's ass wants with crazy-ass Granny?"

Jake looks up, "It's not any of your damn business what I want with her, but if you must know, I was hoping she could help me solve some murders."

"Yous talking about da white girls dey be a finding?"

"That's the ones; and they say swamp monkeys can't be taught!"

"I guess yous ass up here trying to pins it ons one of us niggras."

Jake smiles, "Maybe another day smartass; the guy I'm looking for is white and uses far stronger shit than that poison you're brewing."

"So yous must bes the Dragon slayer dey be talking abouts."

Jake, as he was making headway with the rope binding his wrist, "Maybe."

Jerome steps closer with the snake, "Wells dragon slayer, Granny ain'ts here, so I's guess it's time for yo ass to die."

Jake grunts and then says, "Thank God, I don't think I could stand another second of listening to your arrogant shit."

He holds the snake closer when Jake raises his leg and kicks it from the man's hands, causing the snake to land in Theo's lap.

Theo screams, "Oh shit! Oh shit! Damn you Jake, damn you to hell!!" He starts jumping all over the place and kicking his feet in a panic.

Jake quickly jumps up and takes the small piece of rope used to tie his hands and forces it around Jerome's neck. The others point their guns at him, but Jake pulls the rope tighter, "Drop the damn guns or I'll cut his air supply off real quick."

They hesitate when suddenly he tightens the rope cutting his air off. "I said drop the guns now you 'rejects from a damn cheap Tarzan movie."

Theo catches his breath knowing he had kicked the snake a good distance, "You're talking about the Tarzan with Ron Ely, because I know for a fact Johnny Weissmuller was the best Tarzan."

"Not now Theo!" He pulls the rope tighter.

They drop their guns to the ground. Jake loosens his grip and yells at Theo, who was looking around for the snake, "Get our guns Theo, the snake's gone."

Theo kicks Jake's 460 over to him but scans the ground for any signs of the snake. Jake picks up his pistol and pushes Jerome to the ground. He straddles him and sticks the barrel of his pistol in one nostril and asks, "How would you like me to blow the snot from that wide ass nose of yours? This gun will clear any sinus problems you may have, permanently. Now where can we locate this Granny?"

"I ain't telling yo ass nuttin."

Jake pulls the hammer back and with a smile covers his face with the palm of his hand, "Step back Theo, eyeballs and teeth are about to go airborne in every direction. Now before I pull this trigger let me say, this isn't a snake, and you can't suck a bullet out of your brain, but it will get the job done a lot faster. Say good-bye to this miserable existence you call a life."

About this time a broken voice was heard in the background, "Lets him go white boy, I bees the one you looken fer."

Jake slowly turns and sees an old black woman standing there with a cane in her hand. Jake places his pistol back in its shoulder holster.

An hour later they're sitting at a large, old wooden cable spool used for a table and the rain starts to pour again and can be heard beating out a rhythm on the leaking tin roof of the rundown shack. The old woman with a wrinkle, weathered face is thumping on a wooden box with guitar strings attached and stretching across a small opening and singing an old folk song.

Minutes later she stops and with a smile asks, "Whats y'all think so fer white boys?"

Jake slowly turns to Theo and answers, "Sounded like you should be in Nashville cutting records to me granny; what do you think Theo?"

"Sounded like a crazy-ass old black woman screaming like a squealing hog about to be de-nuted to me."

Jake slaps him on the knee and winks his eye, "You mean it sounded just like Celine Dion...right Theo."

"Are you kidding? That sounded like shit."

Jake slaps him on the knee again. Theo rubs his knee and says, "Okay, okay; it sounded like an angel....with a nasty cold."

Granny starts laughing, "Dat's okay white boys, to each theirs own. I be fix y'all crackers a cup of hot tea."

"I am a black man Granny."

Jake, "This here is Sergeant Williams and I'm Lieutenant..."

She interrupts him as she makes her way across the room, "I know whos yous bees....you the Dragon Slayer!"

Minutes later Granny comes back with two tin cups of freshly brewed tea. She took small steps, and they didn't think she would never make it back to the spool.

Jake smiles, "Thanks for the tea, Granny."

She takes a seat at the table, "Whats ya two white boys wants with me?"

Theo interrupts, "Why does everybody up here think I'm white?"

Granny laughs, "It bes abouts da white girls the Dragon be killing ain't it?"

Jake takes a sip and sets his cup down, "You know who he is Granny?" Before she could answer, Jake squints his face and says, "Shit that tea needs some sugar."

"He's be Harper's son."

"I know that much; do you know what name he goes by?"

"I haves to talks with da spirits to finds dat out. It will cost yo white asses twenty dollars."

Jake takes out a twenty as Theo shakes his head, "Okay, here comes the crystal ball shit."

The old black woman shouts, "Don'ts disrespects du spirits white boy!!" She takes the twenty from the table, stands and walks over to a shelf as fast as her old, hunched back would allow her and removes a rusty coffee can from the lower self before returning to the table.

Jake asks, "How old are you Granny?"

"I'm bes a hundreds ands one."

Theo in a loud voice, "Well I'm not sure you have the info we're looking for, but I bet it was a sad day for you when Lincoln was shot."

Jake gives him a look as the old woman empties a dozen or more chicken bones out on the table.

Jake laughs, "Hey Theo, looks like you've been here before."

Theo does a fake laugh and responds, "Very funny, I'll get you a banana for that one…No seriously I could use some chicken right about now. Do you have any bones with meat on 'em Granny?"

"Silence!!" The old woman yelled at the top of her lungs, then her voice returns to a normal tone. "Da spirits bes very strong on dis one…I be sees a man standing alone withs a sword in his hand…His mouth spouts bad words likes a fire from a blazing furnace, hes be hung like a donkey and spares no pudding …….."

Theo interrupts, "This is easy; that has to be you, Jake."

"Silence!!" The woman shouted again. "I be sees a mighty red Dragon withs foul breath, standing on his hind feets and hes be devours everything in fronts of him."

This time Jake interrupts, "You're right Theo, this is easy. She's talking about you now."

Again, she shouts, "Silence!!"

They jump back a little. Theo frowns, "Sure is a snappy little minx, isn't she?"

Jake holds his finger up indicating for Theo to let her finish.

She continues, "I sees wheels rolling, feets walking and I sees a Dragon dats crawls on his belly, but cans stand."

Jake says, "Finally some info of value. Is it a car or truck? What kind? What color?"

"I just bes sees wheels dats keeps rolling and rolling … wait! … I sees da red Dragon and he stands on two powerful loins. I sees the Dragon slayer with his shadow. The shadow is wounded in du legs, and the Dragon sprays his breath in yo back. She looks over towards Jake, "It bes yo back, … ." She slides her stool back, "You surely bes the Dragon slayer!"

Jake, getting aggravated says, "Okay, he parks the vehicle and he's standing. Where is he going Granny? Where has he been? Who the hell is he? I need a damn name."

Theo, "How much info you think chicken bones can give? You want them to solve this case for us too?"

"He seeks yo ass Jake O'Malley. He takes du innocence from the white girls and strangles du life from 'em for sins of the flesh, but it's yos white ass he seeks."

"Yeah, that's fine and dandy, I seek him too, but I need a name, Granny; the name he uses."

Theo interrupts, "Hey Granny, if chicken bones can tell you all that; I bet turkey bones won't shut up." Theo laughs at himself.

She leans closer and stares deeply into the pile of bones as They lean closer trying hard to see what she was seeing.

She smiles, "Da name you seek is … "

Suddenly without warning, Theo sneezes and bones flew from the table in all directions.

Theo, "Sorry about that!"

The old woman being sarcastic says, "Now I's be sees nuthin but chicken bones scattered on my damn floor." She slowly looks up and gives Theo an angry stare. Jake does the same.

"What, I couldn't help it. I said I was sorry."

"Way to go snot-slinger. How about covering those two tunnels with your hand next time." Jake turns to the old woman and asks, "Can we do this again?"

"The spirits be left and wills not returns. The fat white boy be insulted the spirits."

Jake turns to Theo, "You heard that lard ass, not only have you managed to piss me off, but you have also insulted the spirits too. Good going Theo."

Theo gets angry, "I didn't interrupt anything. It was nothing but a bunch of old chicken bones and this old woman is full of voodoo crap, and I think I'm catching pneumonia."

The old woman grits the only four teeth she has and says, "Leave here now before I's puts a curse on yo fat ass white boy."

"I said it once, I'll say it five freakin times; I am not white, and I don't need any chicken bones to prove it!"

Jake stands, "You're too late Granny; Theo has already been cursed with a very small penis."

Theo frowns, "Why in the hell do you see fit to tell everybody about my penis, again!"

The old woman grabs Jake by the arm, "You must protects du ones around you Dragon slayer! Dis dragon wills not rest until he kills yo ass. Dig deep in yo past and yous remember the Dragon in a faraway land."

Theo, "Everybody wants a piece of old Jake. He'll have to stand in line Granny."

"Dis Dragon stands in no line and bes waits fer no one."

Theo shakes his head, "I'll see you later Granny, if by chance I see the funny rubber coated wagon I'll send it this way."

The old woman reaches for her cane when Jake pushes him out the door.

They walk out on the porch and look out into the rain filled night.

Jake nods, "What a wasted trip."

Theo sneezes again, "That old woman is crazy. She just screwed us out of twenty dollars. That was just old chicken bones left over from last week's supper. With that twenty we could have bought a whole bucket of fried chicken."

"Just a few more minutes and she would have told us the name."

"You of all people, don't believe that voodoo shit for one minute."

"That's true. I thought she knew his name and was using the bones to make a little money. Did you notice she called me by my full name?"

"So what?"

"I never told her my full name. She only heard you call me Jake."

"Well, if you really think she knows the killer's name, let's go back inside and kick her old, wrinkled ass like there wasn't a tomorrow. You know, beat it out of her."

"You mean you would really kick the shit out of a hundred and one-year old woman?"

"You damn right I would; I'm just about tired of these old women taking advantage of me. Now I say, let's paddle our asses back to town, get some dry clothes on and get me something for this cold I've caught. And if you see fit, you can buy me some chicken and I'll save the bones for you so you can sit up all night listening to them tell you how I ate the meat off of 'em."

"You wanna wait until it slacks off a little?"

"We're already soaking wet and the faster we get out of here the better I'll feel."

CHAPTER 31

Back in the pharmacy department of a local grocery store, they're walking casually down the medicine aisle dripping water everywhere and checking out all the assorted treatments and brand names for colds. Jake places his glasses over his eyes and starts reading some bottles.

"Hey Theo, here's one that works on sore throats… Sherry could use that one… and it also says here that it treats nasty, green mucus pouring from big-ass noses."

Theo snatches the plastic container from his hands and with a smirk, "That'll do smartass; now let's get over to the banana creampuff aisle, I'm starving."

A few minutes later they pass a large tray of chicken surrounded by Plexi-glass.

Theo, "Wait a minute Jake, you hear that!!? You wanna say anything to these chicken legs before we leave?"

Minutes later they're slowly strolling down the bread aisle looking over the cupcakes and other pastry items when an old man riding a motorized shopping cart runs over Theo's foot.

Theo yells, "What the F---!?"

The old man yells, "Well, get your fat black ass out of my way, you're blocking the aisle!"

Theo yells back, "Go around old man."

"The only way I can get by that big ass of yours is spout wings and fly over the top."

"Look grandpa, spout wings if you must, but you're pushing the weight thing a little too far."

The old man attempts to squeeze between Theo and the bottom shelf causing Theo to press tightly against the bread.

The old man really gets angry, "Look boy, I'm trying to get to the coffee and you're standing in the way."

Theo gives Jake a look. Jake shrugs his shoulders as Theo turns back around, "You call me a boy one more time and I'll shove that cart up your ancient ass, you old racist geezer."

The old man grabs his cane from the buggy and shakes it wildly, "I'll show you who's a geezer."

"Okay old man, drop the cane or you won't be needing that coffee in the morning, because you won't be seeing morning."

The old man snaps back, "I fought in WW II and killed twenty Japs with my bare hands, so one fat niggra boy won't be a problem."

Theo fires back, "You're mistaken you old fart, it was WW I and if you don't drop that cane, I'm gonna hook it around that shriveled up neck of yours and drag your ass over to the produce section and show you what I can do with an ear of corn. It's late, why aren't you in bed?"

A crowd starts gathering as Jake grabs him by the arm, "Look Theo, they have the extra-thick creampuffs."

"Did you hear what this old man called me? And he just threatened my life with a cane."

"What is it about old people and you. Mrs. Harper, Granny and now an old-world two war vet. How's he going to kill you, he can't even walk? I kind of like the old man, serving our country and I got a boner when he said he killed twenty Japs with his bare hands."

"So what, my granddaddy served in the army during the war, before he was thrown out."

"Why was your granddaddy thrown out?"

"He ate everything in the mess hall and then got caught putting it to a white girl who just happened to be the commanding officer's daughter. Apparently, they frown on both."

"I have a lot of respect for that old man."

"Well damn-it Jake, those old folk homes should have a curfew of some kind."

"One day you'll be there and sooner than you think now that you're married."

Theo, "He acted like you twenty years from now."

"Let's get those creampuffs, so we can get back and change out of these wet clothes."

Ten minutes later they're standing in line behind some customers. The cart is full of creampuffs and one bottle of decongestant.

Jake snickers, "You sure you have enough?"

"You think I should get some more?"

"You already have enough to last you two weeks."

Theo responds, "You kidding, this is just for tonight. These extra thick ones are hard to find and when you do, you need to take full advantage of an opportunity."

Jake shakes his head, "I've said it once, I'll say it twice; the thick ones are the same as the thin ones, they just say they're thicker to fool dumbasses like you into buying more."

Jake turns around in line and sees an obese, middle aged, white woman wearing tight grey spandex, with her fat belly overlapping a dirty white t-shirt with food stains down the front, and purple curlers stuck in her filthy bleached out hair. Her make-up is thicker than a bowl of grits and her breasts were hanging down to her navel. She had a strong body odor about her and has two small children with her, one five-year-old boy and a seven-year-old girl. Jake just stared at the unattractive woman with amazement.

She sees him staring, "What the hell are you looking at asshole?"

Jake turns to Theo and asks, "Should I tell her?"

"I was two seconds from whipping an old cripple war veteran's ass; I guess you're entitled to a turn."

Jake turns back around and with a smile says, "I was going to say, I'm looking at an ugliest hippo in the world, but it can't be, they take a bath once in a while, but that sure is nice twins you have there."

The unattractive woman frowns and in an angry tone, "You stupid ass, what makes you think they're twins? There's two years difference and they look nothing alike."

Jake replies, "For reasons I just mentioned, I can't picture anyone screwing you twice." The clerk busted out laughing…

Thirty minutes later they entered Stillwell's residence still a little wet from the canoe trip. Ann, Sherry and Rodger are sitting in the den having a drink. Jake could hear Casey and Jackie upstairs playing music. Theo is shivering and takes a seat in a brown leather recliner holding his bag of creampuffs secure in his arms. Jake makes his way over to the bar when Rodger asks, "Well, y'all find her?"

"Yep!"

"Well, how'd it go? Did she give you the name?"

Jake takes a drink from a shot glass, turns and replies, "Wasted trip. The bitch talks to chicken bones."

"Maybe I was wrong about the riddle. Has the bastard called you back?"

"Nope, not yet. I'm beginning to think Theo was right; he sent us on a wild goose chase. That damn riddle doesn't make any sense to me. The only facts I learned is she's wet, crazy, black, and sangs when it rains, that's if you can call that shit singing."

Theo sneezes and says, "I think I have pneumonia."

Ann politely says, "Well I have some good news that should brighten up the conversation."

Jake takes another drink, "Please do; I could use some good news after paddling my ass off in a rainstorm half the night....by myself."

As he turns the drink up, Ann says, "I'm pregnant." Jake spits his drink across the bar.

"You and Donna drinking from the same fountain?"

Rodger laughs, "We have got to get a doctor to look at that spiting thing you can't control, Jake."

Jake slowly turns to Ann, "You sure about that?"

"Yeah, I'm three months."

Jake, with a blank expression on his face says, "So that explains the pooch. I thought you were just eating a lot of chocolate."

Ann gets pissed, "I'm not showing yet, smartass."

"Sorry about that." Jake turns and sees Theo frozen in time. He turns back to her and says, "So, when did you find this out?"

"I actually found out three weeks ago, but I wanted to wait until I saw you again to surprise you." She turns to Rodger then back to Jake and says, "The Mayor here was telling me that the city council approved a reward of two hundred thousand dollars if you can solve these murders and he's going to kick in an extra twenty grand himself."

"So?"

"So that will provide a good home for our new addition to the family."

"You do know half of that goes to Theo, don't you?"

"Theo!!... You're going to give him half the money for walking around scratching his ass and eating everything that doesn't move."

Theo yells, "Sometimes I can eat stuff moving, but thanks a lot Ann, I'm sitting right here you know."

Jake gets pissed, "If you knew what he's been through the last week, you would give him all of it."

"Well, I've been through a lot the past few weeks myself Jake."

Theo interrupts, "Is that right? Huh, have a sit and let me ask you a few questions about the horror of the unprovoked disasters I have undertaken over the last week and tell me if you need a damn valium when I'm finished. Have you been stung by a jellyfish, pissed on by my best friend, almost shot by two cops for asking about banana creampuffs, kissed by a ninety-year-old, horny bitch…in the mouth? Have you come face to face with a ten-foot-tall creature, and I'm not talking about my mother in-law, licked by a wild black bear, in the mouth? Have you spent the night with a rattlesnake near your crotch? Sprayed by a kitty cat with racing stripes…in the mouth? Charged with the rape after said old lady fondled you, had your ear shot off, a heatstroke from being dressed in a fur bear costume in a hundred degree heat wave, with nothing but a flap in the ass to cool you off? Stabbed in the eye with a corndog covered with mustard? Kicked in the nuts by a snuff-chewing ten-year-old asshole? Threw up on? Slapped in the mouth by a brother, had a damn poison snake shoved up your nose, almost hung with a queer by the KKK, for wanting you to stick your you know what…in his mouth? Your feet run over by a black-hating war veteran? And are you going to die because all your bodily fluids are leaking from your nose… down in your mouth, and did you just have your best friend's wife throw you under the bus? I didn't think so."

The room went silent as everyone just stared at him. Theo catches his breath, "And I assure you; I have only touched the top of the iceberg."

Rodger snickers, "Damn, I think you deserve an extra hundred thousand."

Jake turns back to Ann and asks, "Do we have a due date?"

Minutes later Casey and Jackie come running down the stairs toward the front door.

Rodger yells, "Just where do you two think you're going?"

Casey blurts out, "To the video store!"

"You have any idea what time it is?"

Casey, with a disappointed look on her face, "We're bored and wanna rent some DVD's."

Rodger fires back, "We have a killer running loose and I'm not taking any chances."

Sherry interrupts, "It's just a mile down the road Rodger."

"A lot can happen in one-mile, right Jake?"

"After listening to Theo, a lot can happen in just a few feet around here. Rodger's right. Theo can drive y'all up there."

Theo interrupts, "Yeah, that'll work!! A black man riding around with two young, pretty, white girls... that should go over really well up here! I don't need to add that shit to my list of misfortunes."

Ann jumps into the conversation, "There are two of them.

He gives the girls a look.

Jackie smiles, "Please Jake."

"Okay but speak to no one and make sure you lock your doors. If you're gone for more than thirty minutes, I'm going to come looking for you."

Jackie yells, "Thanks we'll be right back."

Casey grabbed her mother's keys and ran out the door.

Rodger asks, "You think that was wise, Jake?"

"They'll be alright. My girl Jackie can fight like a crocodile and she's smart when it comes to talking to strangers. She has a lot of her old daddy in her."

Theo, "Like we need a video store clerk kicked in the nuts."

Five minutes later the girls pulled up to the video store and ran inside. Casey quickly starts thumbing through a stack of DVDs as Jackie checks out the ones on the wall.

Casey turns to her, "You wanna grab a few dirty movies?"

Suddenly a voice can be heard behind her.

"Hey Casey."

She's startled and turns around quickly only to find Sheriff Ray standing there with a styrofoam cup of coffee in his hand.

"Crap Mr. Henderson, you scared the shit out of me."

"Sorry, but isn't it a little dangerous for you to be out this late?"

"It's okay; I'm with a friend."

"How are your folks doing?"

"Fine, they're just sitting around having a few drinks."

Jackie walks over, "I found one we might like."

Ray smiles, "Who's your pretty little friend Casey?"

"This is Jackie; Jake's daughter."

He nods, "Quite a looker, isn't she?"

Jackie sees him looking her over from top to bottom and says, "Why don't you take a damn picture dude, it last longer."

Ray laughs, "I can see the similarities between her and Jake."

Casey interrupts, "Well, I guess we need to go now."

Ray reaches out and lightly grabs her by the arm, "What's your hurry?"

Casey replies, "With this killer running loose, we need to get back home."

"Bo is dead, ain't nobody gonna hurt you as long as I'm around. You girls wanna take a ride in the patrol car?"

Jackie shakes her head back and forth, "I've seen the inside of a police car before. Let me know when you get a Lamborghini. Like Casey said, we're in a hurry to get back home."

"I bet you girls never saw a cow with five legs before. Ned Brown has one in his field just a few miles from here."

Jackie grabs Casey by the arm and pulls her a short distance. "If I wanna see a freakshow, I'll go watch Uncle Theo eat ten pounds of banana creampuffs."

Ray laughs, "You say that niggra can put away some food huh?"

"If you call him that in front of my dad, he'll kick your teeth out."

Ray frowns, "Smartass like your father. What makes you think I won't kick his teeth out?"

"I've seen my father in action, and he doesn't play, and I really don't think your belly will allow you to kick that high."

They turn and walk to the counter and pay the clerk then walk out the door leaving Ray standing there watching through the front plate glass window fluming mad. When they get into the car Casey says, "You sure pissed him off."

Jackie responds, "That guy was giving me the creeps. He was looking at us like he wanted to rape us."

"Sheriff Ray…he's okay; I've known him all my life. He's been Sheriff around here for decades."

"I don't care how long he's been Sheriff, he's a pervert."

Casey, "Why do ya say that?"

"The whole time he was speaking, he was glancing at our ass and licking his lips."

"Like how?"

"He looked over us like Theo looks over a free buffet while watching porn."

"I think you're wrong about him."

"Again, I saw him checking our asses out when we walked to the counter."

"All guys do that. I like it. It lets you know you're packing all the right equipment."

They pull out of the parking lot as Ray watches them leave when suddenly Casey pulls down a short dirt road a few blocks away and stops under an old oak tree.

Jackie asks, "Why are we stopping here?"

"I have a twelve pack of beer iced down in the trunk, you wanna get a buzz? I took it from the refrigerator and put it in the ice chest while they were all in the den."

Jackie glances through the windshield at an almost full moon and then glances into the woods, "You don't know my father; if we're two seconds late, he'll be looking for us."

Casey giggles, "I'll get the beer. You stay put; I wanna ask you a few questions about your daddy." She opens the door and then the trunk. A few seconds later she jumps back in the car with a small red cooler, sets it in the center between them, opens the top and takes out two canned beers.

Jackie looks out her window again, "Spooky out here."

"It always looks spooky out here. I come out here occasionally when I wanna get some action."

"What kind of action?"

"You know, make out stuff."

"You've had sex?"

"Not sex, I just let them play with it. Don't you?"

Jackie takes a sip of beer and replies, "Not yet. I told my father one time I had sex a bunch."

"Did he get mad?"

"Are you kidding me, my ass is still shaped like the toe of a cowboy boot. I shit leather for a week after that. I don't think it was what I said, but how I said it."

They laughed at each other and took a few more sips. Jackie turns and checks outside the windows again.

Casey snickers, "Relax, we'll get back in plenty of time. Well?"

"Well, what?"

"Well, tell me about Jake; you think I have a shot at it?"

Jackie has a shocked look on her face and for a few seconds couldn't say a word, then replies, "Please, do you mind? That's gross."

"I wonder what sex is like with him. He looks like he knows all the tricks."

"Can we talk about something else? I feel a little awkward talking about my father. You do know he's in his mid-fifties, right?"

"That doesn't matter these days. I think he's hot."

"Let's change the subject to something else. Maybe we should go back to the store and sit under the lights."

"You kidding me? If we get caught with beer, my mother and stepdad will kill me."

Jackie keeps looking over her shoulder, "So, you were friends with the girls who were murdered?"

"We all played soccer together. I really miss them. My mama is taking it a lot harder than me. So, you think your dad likes younger women."

"Okay Casey, you're really creeping me out with this obsession with my father."

Casey, "I'm in love with him."

"I think I've heard enough; I think we should get back to your house."

"I saw my mother sneaking from the guestroom one night wearing a sexy night gown and she was all sweaty and walked like she had been riding a horse all day."

"You couldn't have seen that; my father would never do that to Ann. He has this thing about married women."

"He sure does. I thought they separated for three weeks."

"They do that all the time. My father is devoted to his marriage."

"I saw what I saw. My mama has been depressed for years. And now that four members of her team have been murdered...I'm surprise she hasn't gone bonkers. But since she's met Jake, she has that glow about her again. My mama was the hottest thing in school. Not many men can turn that down. She likes wearing short dresses to tease the locals."

"That can't be good."

"My mama says, 'why have all those goods if you can't show 'em off."

A sad look comes over Jackie's face. She slowly turns to Casey, "You can never tell anyone about this. If Ann finds out, she'll leave him, and I do not wanna see him go through that again."

"I won't say a word, I promise."

Jackie quickly turns and looks out the back window. "What was that?"

"What was what?"

"I heard something."

"It was just a possum or an armadillo. They come out at night and scrounge for food."

"Are you sure that's what I heard?"

"Have another drink, that'll relax you. You're just a little jumpy."

Jackie hears another noise, "Okay, I guess you didn't hear that either?"

"I heard it. I'm telling you it's just wild animals stirring up the underbrush."

"I don't like this; I feel something wrong. Believe me; I inherited that from my father."

Casey reaches for the key in the ignition, "Okay, we'll go. I can sneak the beer in the window when everyone goes to sleep." She attempts to start the car, and nothing happens. She tries again to no avail. "That's funny, this has never happened before." She starts to panic, "Whatta we do, I left my cell at the house?"

Jackie replies, "Yeah, mine too, but calm down, we'll just walk back to the main road and then to the video store. I'll call Jake from there."

"We can't do that; he'll tell my mother."

"Jake will surprise you; he's cool about some things. He won't say a word. He'll just use the situation to teach us a lesson about the 'does' and 'don'ts.'" They step from the car and start walking.

Suddenly, Casey sees a shadow move between two large trees off to the right. She yell's, "Who's out there!?"

Jackie grabs her by the arm and starts pulling her, "Let's go now Casey!!"

They hear a branch break and Casey yells again, "Okay, whoever you are, show yourself. Mike, is that you!!?"

Jackie stops in her tracks, "Let's get back to the car!" They started running back and as they ran; they could hear loud footsteps running in the woods. They jump back in the car and lock the doors.

Jackie asks, "Do you have any weapons in the car like a knife or a baseball bat?"

Casey is now in panic mole, "I don't think so!"

Jackie looks around for anything that could be used as a weapon. As she's looks over in the backseat, she notices the rear window on the driver's side is down six to seven inches.

She yells, "Oh shit... turn the key on and close the rear window."

"I can't; the battery's dead!"

"There should be enough juice to close it."

Casey starts crying, "I don't understand... I... I..."

Jackie reaches over and turns the key on, then reaches across Casey's lap to push the window button. It went down all the way before Jackie realized she had pushed the button the wrong way. She quickly corrects herself, but before the window could close, a large arm flies in through the opening. The window jams the arm at the elbow. A loud scream is heard. Jackie grabs Casey and pulls her out the passenger's door. They take off running through the dark woods catching low branches in their face every few feet, when suddenly they run into a solid object and fall to the ground. They scream when they see a dark figure standing over them.

A voice is heard, "What part of 'hurry up and get back' did y'all not understand?"

Jake moves from the shadow into the moonlight.

Jackie yells, "Thank God, I've never been so glad to see you! We heard noises and the battery was dead, then we could hear somebody running through the woods and then somebody tried to get in the car. His arm is trapped in the back window!!"

"I know, it's Theo. I heard him scream like a bitch. We went looking for y'all when you became five minutes late and I figured what was up, so we decided to scare y'all and teach y'all a lesson. Let's go see if Theo has an arm left."

Back at the car Theo is yelling in pain trying to get his arm out when suddenly he hears a large branch break in the woods.

"Hey Jake, is that you? I think my arm is broken! Hey, Jake!!" He looked deep into the darkness and saw nothing. He pulls his pistol with his left hand and yells, "Okay Jake, again, not funny!" Still, he heard noises, but could see nothing. Suddenly he sees a wide shadow moving toward him, "Okay asshole, enough is enough!!" He fired five loud, explosive shots into the woods and then a loud voice could be heard.

"Damn you Theo, you almost shot us!" Jake comes walking out of the woods with the girls hanging tightly on his arms. He tells Jackie to let the window down.

Theo pulls his arm out and says, "Damn you Jake, how come you can't answer me when I yelled, 'Jake, is that you?'"

Jackie, in a low voice says as she walks around to help Theo, "Sorry, we thought you were the killer."

Jake gives him a funny look, "Good damn thing you're a bad shot."

Back in the driveway Jake is sitting in the driver's seat with Theo sitting on the passenger's side holding his arm. The girls were in the backseat.

Jake looks into the rearview mirror, "Okay girls, you stopped at the video store and left your lights on. When you came out, the battery was dead. Do not change the story in any shape or form." He throws two pieces of gum over in the backseat, "Chew that before you say goodnight to your moms and leave the dirty DVDs and beer with us." The girls open the door and walk to the house.

He turns to Theo, "You gonna be alright?"

"Yep, we sure scared the hell out of them though."

Jake gives him a grin, "Okay, what did we learn?"

Theo starts laughing as he reaches down and takes two cold beers from the floorboard. He hands one to Jake and they pop open the tab and take a drink.

Theo places his left arm on Jake's shoulder and replies, "Not a damn thing, not a damn thing at all. This cold beer sure hits the spot."

Minutes later they're leaning back in the seats sipping their beers when Theo asks, "What do you think happens after we die?"

"Well, after the body starts to decompose you start to stink really bad, then you…"

"I'm talking about when you die. Do you go straight to Heaven, or do you just sleep until He calls you up there?"

"I'll let you know after Sherry tells Ann about what's been going on up here." About this time Jake's phone goes off. He flips it open and says, "Hello."

"*Hello Jake, did you enjoy your trip up the river?*"

"Why yes, we did. Dark, quiet and soothing to the soul."

"*Did the old black bitch give you my real name?*"

"Theo blew that info on the floor with one mighty sneeze."

"*She really did know my real name. You blew it Jake.*"

"Well maybe Theo and I will take another trip up there tomorrow and get it from her."

Theo mumbles, "Like hell you say, you couldn't get me back on that river if it was flowing with whores."

Jake shakes his head and says into the phone, "I'm listening, go on."

"*You can't get the name out of her now.*"

"And why is that?"

"*Because I killed her ten minutes after you two left her shack. Her body is floating down river as we speak. I enjoyed killing that black bitch.*"

"Man, are you just doing this for fun?"

"Yes, I guess I am. You know something? That Casey and Jackie really have nice asses."

"I have an idea, why don't you tell us who you are, and I will put you out of your misery."

"Not yet; tomorrow night we can meet and discuss the way you will die."

"I already know how Theo and I are going to die."

"And how's that?"

"We both are gonna have a heart attack walking down the steps of a whorehouse with an empty bottle of Viagra and Scotch at the ripe old age of ninety-nine. Theo and I have already discussed it and that's how we gonna die."

"I don't think so; we need a death fitting a legend and his shadow. I know you're a smart guy, but you're thinking too hard. I'm watching you and that fat ass right now."

Jake scans the area and laughs.

Theo asks, "What so funny?"

"This guy just called you a fat ass."

"Asks him to tell us something we don't know."

Jake goes back to talking on the phone, "I have an idea, why don't you show yourself now and I'll show you how you're gonna die."

"All in good time. That Sherry sure likes sex. Is it any good?"

"I've had some loose stuff, tight stuff, trimmed stuff, and untrimmed stuff that smells, stuff that didn't, but never any bad stuff. As the old saying goes, 'the worst I've ever had was fan-foo-footastic'...How about you?"

"I have watched the mayor's wife walk around town just asking for it. When the mayor goes out, I watch her from the window trying on clothes. She nothing compared to the last four I had. They were awesome. Let me ask you something Jake...have you ever had two young girls at the same time?"

Jake holds the phone away from his mouth, "Hey Theo, the killer wants to know if I've ever had two girls at once."

Theo laughs as he takes a sip and asks, "What country is he from? Of course you have, does a cat have a furry little ass. Obviously, he doesn't know the great Jake O'Malley too well. I know for a fact you have had three at the same time on several occasions."

Jake places the phone back to his mouth, "Yep!! Been there, done that. I even had a t-shirt made commemorating the event."

"I'm going to rape two at the same time soon Jake. Will it be Ann and Sherry or Casey and Jackie?"

Jake gets pissed, "Look you spineless asshole, I can sense you and before tomorrow night is over you will be in little pieces."

"I don't think so ... Hey, ask Theo how's his arm feeling? I would have hung that fat ass and that queer the other night if you hadn't showed up when you did. I have two pieces of lead shot in my ass because of you."

"Stop it Dude, you'll have me busting out in tears in a minute. If I had known, that was you, I would have killed you then for sure."

"Bye Jake, see you tomorrow night." He hangs up as Jake closes his phone. Theo could see the look on his face.

"What's wrong little buddy?"

"We had him and let him get away. He's the Grand Dragon of the local KKK. It was him wearing the red sheet and hood the other night when you and your boyfriend almost got hanged. I had Big Bertha aimed right at his gut and let him get away."

"We had him my ass, I told you to shoot 'em, but nooo, we had to settle for shooting their trucks. You still think it could be our sheriff?"

"Yep; there's nothing that has happen to eliminate him and that's not all, he just said he's been watching Sherry walk all over town in those short dresses just begging for it."

"Everybody knows that."

"Those are the very words Ray use the other day on the fourth crime scene. Also verbatim."

Jake stares out the windshield with a blank expression on his face.

Theo takes another sip, "What?"

"Ann and Jackie popping up here sure did throw a wrench in the gears and now I'm going to be a father again. Life's just one big do over."

"I know what you mean partner. Hey, our kids are going to be the same age when they go to college. Maybe they'll be born on the same day."

Jake, pondering over the murders, then changes the subject and says, "You know, it's a funny thing about this case. Every clue points to Ray and Miller."

Theo nods, "We know they're crooked and that's enough for me. I say those two are the ones we need to focus on."

"Too easy."

"Whatta mean by that?"

"You can bet they killed Bo, but under normal circumstances I would say if it looked like a pig, smelled like a pig and squealed like a pig, it must be a pig. Then on the other hand I screwed a woman one time who squeal like a pig, smelled like a pig and even looked like a pig, but the next morning after I sobered up, it was just a hooker who had all the similarities of one. Still felt good though."

"You think that's funny; I slept with a hooker one time, and she looked like a hooker, smelled like a hooker and even squealed like a hooker, but I woke up next to an actual pig from my aunt's farm... still felt good though. What's your point?"

"They murdered Bo, but they didn't murder those girls. I need more evidence."

"I wish you would make up your mind. Who then?"

"I'm thinking."

Suddenly Casey and Jackie return to the car in their pajamas. Jake rolls down the window, "I thought you two would be in bed by now."

Jackie responds, "We forgot to tell you something."

Jake, "If it's about the beer, you're too late, Theo and I finished the last one off already."

"It's not about the beer." She hesitates for a few seconds and turns to Casey, "Tell 'em."

Casey steps forward, "While we were in the video store, Sheriff Ray asks if we wanted to take a ride in his police car."

"And?"

"He wanted to take us to a pasture and show us a cow with five legs."

Theo interrupts, "Don't go if you don't wanna be sucked or hanged."

Jake turns and gives him that look. Theo blurts out, "What?"

"Watch what you say. I might have to see this cow myself. I can't believe it wasn't at the fair."

"I'm not going back to that pasture unless Bertha goes with us. That bitch has saved our asses a bunch and I think I'm in love with her."

Jake turns back to Casey, "Anything else?"

Jackie interrupts, "It wasn't what he said that made me nervous, it was the way he looked at us. Like a fox in the chicken pen. Like Uncle Theo on the pastry isle at the store, like Ann when she finds a pair of shoes on sale. He really gave me the creeps."

Jake smiles and turns to Theo, "Well, I think we just got more." He turns back to the girls, "You two go to bed and I'll take care of Sheriff Ray."

The girls return to the house then Jake turns to Theo, "Let's go check on our sheriff and see what he's up to."

Theo, "That Casey looks like her mother …. fine off her ass!"

"You pervert!"

"She's almost nineteen and I've notice you looking."

"Damn Theo, we gotta draw a line somewhere."

"I have been with you for five years and I haven't found that line yet."

Jake starts the car and backs out of the driveway.

CHAPTER 32

They pull up to the sheriff's residence and step from the car. As they approach the house and up the front steps, Theo scans the structure, "Just look at the size of this house; it's good to be sheriff."

Jake knocks on the door. Minutes past and he knocks again. A few more minutes pass when a soft voice could be heard coming from inside, "It's late, who is it?"

Jake replies, "It's Lieutenant O'Malley and Sergeant Williams." The porch light came on and she opens the door and stands there with a short, see through night grown on.

Jake smiles, "Mrs. Henderson, I'm sorry to bother you this late, but we work with the Mobile Police Department and would like to have a word with Ray."

"He's not here. Didn't you do enough today when you searched our home?'

"I apologize for that but right now we're just tying up some loose ends. When do you expect him back?"

"If he's where I think he is, he won't be back until about two or three in the morning."

"Where do you think he's at?"

"I'd say he's at Jane's Beer Palace out on 52 drinking with that little bastard Miller. Why do you wanna talk with my husband?"

"Look Mrs. Henderson, we're just trying to find out who killed the four high school girls. Can we step inside for a second and ask just a few questions?"

She steps back allowing them to step in. As she walks to the kitchen she says, "I thought it was that crazy man, Bo. I'll fix y'all some coffee."

As she walks towards the kitchen Theo turns to Jake, "I can see right through her night grown. She has no panties on."

Jake, "I need to ask her to put a robe on."

"Now don't be hasty, she's a grown woman and can make those decisions for herself."

"Good detective work."

Twenty minutes later they're sitting in the den sipping coffee. Theo sees a large confederate flag hanging on the wall.

Mrs. Henderson asks, "Does it bother you, Sergeant."

Theo takes another sip of coffee and replies, "No, I always thought it was a pretty flag."

"My husband hates blacks. A matter a fact, you're the first to ever set foot in this house."

Jake asks, "Does that unset you Mrs. Henderson?"

"Nope, some of my best friends are black. But he doesn't allow them inside the house. You need to understand how my husband was brought up."

Theo interrupts, "I completely understand. I was brought up thinking all whites were racist, but I learned from Jake here that everyone is racist to a certain extent. It's when you take it too far that it becomes a problem. I'm black and can't do a thing about it. I have about as much chance of changing my color as I do losing weight. I don't dwell on crap like that."

Jake changes the subject, "Mrs. Henderson, would it offend you if I ask, does your husband fool around on you?"

"Sure he does, he's been seeing a young twenty-seven-year-old whore who lives in a trailer park not far from here. It's been going on for years. I think he first started seeing her ten years ago when she was seventeen. About ten years after we got married."

With that, Jake looks over at Theo with a funny look.

She continues, "I've learned to live with it. We just stay together for the kids, but they're almost grown now."

Theo shakes his head, "It's a crying-ass shame people can't be more loyal to their spouses." He turns to Jake and winks an eye.

Jake swallows and continues, "You say he has an eye for the young girls?"

"Don't all men?" She looks Jake over and pulls her grown up exposing more thigh, "Let me ask you a question Lieutenant, are you married?"

"Yes I am."

"Well, that's makes no difference these days. Why don't you let your partner sit here on the couch and sip his coffee and we can continue the questions in the kitchen. Won't take more than twenty minutes."

Jake looks over at Theo, "See, I have no idea why."

She then changes the subject, "I know where you're going with this, and I can assure you Ray didn't kill those girls. We have three teenage daughters, and they mean the world to him."

Jake looks around the room and then asks, "Mrs. Henderson, do you two sleep together in the same bed?"

"No, he sleeps in the extra bedroom, so he doesn't wake me up when he comes in late." She spreads her legs out. Theo spits coffee out and says, "Sorry."

Jake continues, "Would you mind if we look around that room? You can say no, and we'll leave."

"They searched that room the other day, but you can do anything you wish O'Malley."

"Well, most of the officers work for him and could have missed something."

"Go ahead, but don't let him find out; he'll kill me for sure."

She shows them to the room, and they start checking around. Theo turns and sees her rubbing herself as she stares at Jake looking in the closet.

Jake, sliding clothes to one side, "Ray doesn't have a red sheet or long red robe does he?"

She continues rubbing herself, "I'm not sure, I never go through his things."

Jake feels around the closet when he suddenly steps to one side and hears a squeaking noise. He reaches down in the closet and pulls the carpet back and discovers a small piece of rope coming from the wooden floor with a knot tied into it. He pulls a small section of the floor up and discovers a stack of large brown envelopes. He opens one and then another and another and finds they are all filled with pornographic pictures of young girls around the age of twelve and up. Then as he looks through the pictures, he comes across the photos of the victims naked and lying at the crime scene. He turns to Mrs. Henderson and shows her the pictures.

"You recognize any of these girls?"

She covers her mouth in shock, "No, he must have gotten them off the internet or something. I know most of the girls in this county. I had no idea he like them so young."

"Some of these pictures are of the four victims."

"He took the pictures of the girls while investigating the crimes."

"Not the last girl; Theo here took those."

She starts crying and says with a sniffle, "Please don't tell anyone. If our daughters find out about this, it will destroy them."

Jake gives her a look as Theo checks out the bookshelves.

"Mrs. Henderson, you knew about these photographs, didn't you?"

She hesitates and then turns away, "Not all of them. How did you know?"

"I can read faces. You looked shocked, but not that shocked."

"Yes, I found them when I was vacuuming in here, but he doesn't know. I only look at a few then couldn't look no more."

"Your husband's a pedophile which brings us back to the murders. He has botched the investigations from the start and tampered with evidence and even wrote up the murder of old lady Harper as a suicide. Did you know he had a meth lab in the forest a few miles further from where the girls were discovered? He and his deputy were brewing the stuff. You know as well as I do you can't afford a house this size on sheriff's pay."

She takes a seat on the edge of the bed, "I can't believe he would kill those girls."

Jake takes a seat next to her and places his hand on her shoulder, "I'm going to arrest him Mrs. Henderson for the murder of those girls."

She slowly turns to him, "That will destroy our family."

"Yes, it will, just like he destroyed four other families. I'm sorry, but there's no other way. You are very attractive women and life goes on."

"I'm so upset, you think you can sit here while your partner waits in the car. I have more info to tell you in private." She reaches over and grabs his hand and places it up her grown and on her enter thigh.

Theo is shocked and says, "Maybe I can wait in the car." He walks over and opens the curtains.

Jake quickly stands, "I would like that very much, but I will not jeopardize this case any further. Let's go Theo we have work to do."

Thirty minutes later they pulled up in front of Jane's Beer Palace. Parked over to the side were two marked county units.

Theo, "I thought Ray's wife was going to rape you right there in front of me. She was fingering herself the whole time you were looking in that closet. I could have watched from outside to window… … for investigative purposes."

Jake shakes his head, "If I wasn't married and not working a case involving her husband I would have wreaked the shit out of it."

A few minutes later they enter the club and discover Ray and Miller sitting at a table drinking with two underage girls. Jake walks over with Theo right behind him.

Ray sees him walking over to their table and in a loud voice, "Well look what the damn dogs dragged in!"

Jake smiles, "We need to talk Ray."

"I'm sorry Jake, but there aren't any more chairs at this table."

"Sure, there is, these sixteen-year-old girls were just leaving." The two young girls could see the serious look in Jake's eyes, stood and left the table. Miller starts to stand when Jake places his hand on his shoulder and forces him back down in the chair.

"You just stay put Miller; I might need to throw something out a window."

Miller snaps back, "You can't make me stay."

Jake smiles as he and Theo take the two now-empty chairs. Not taking his eyes off Ray, he says to Miller, "You might wanna take your hands off that pistol grip. If you don't I'm gonna get pissed and shoot your balls off with a 460 Rowland under the table."

Miller places both hands on the table.

Ray snickers, "What's on that mind of yours?"

"I'm here to arrest you and Miller for seven counts of murder. All of them, the four girls, old lady Harper, Bo, and Granny who should be floating up anytime now. You just made too many mistakes. At first, I didn't think you were smart enough to pull it off but overseeing the investigations made it easy. You stole the locket from the mayor's car. I mean you handed all this shit to me on a silver platter. You could have sunk a ship with the clues you left."

"That is the most ridiculous thing I've ever heard."

"I had a talk with your wife Ray, and you have no alibi for where you were at the time of all the murders except one. I'm sure Miller took care of old lady Harper for you."

"This is outrageous! You have no proof I killed anybody. What motive would I have?"

"Sex."

"I can get sex anywhere and anytime. I even have a twenty-seven-year-old lined up waiting for me right now in a trailer park just down the road from here. It's not against the law to screw a twenty-seven-year-old."

"Not young enough Ray. I've seen the photos hidden under the floor in your closet."

Ray gets angry, "You've been in my house!?"

"Yep!"

"You had no search warrant to do that again."

"Didn't need one, your wife gave us permission this time."

"She had no right to do that."

"Wrong again, Ray."

"So, what; you found pictures of little girls, that doesn't prove I kill anyone."

"You killed them alright. After your phone call the other day you know, the one where you gave me that stupid riddle. I could tell you were talking through an empty toilet paper roll. I had some friends of mine check, and you'll never guess where the cell tower your signal bounce off was. But you don't have to guess, do ya Ray? You know exactly where that tower is. It sits right in the middle between City Hall and your residence."

"My God Jake, hundreds of people use that tower."

"It was your cell that pinged, just like the call you made an hour ago."

"I hate to break this to you, but I lost my cellphone three days ago. I have a new phone and new number."

"You still have your old phone; you just got a new one to throw me off. It won't work. You're a sick pervert and a murderer to boot."

Miller jumps in the conversation, "You Jackass; you have nothing. You're bluffing, and you don't have anything on me. I didn't kill old lady Harper."

"Actually, I do. Your little footprints gave you away. You see Miller, Ray had you kill old lady Harper, because he was at the station that night. That gave him an alibi. He couldn't bring himself around to killing his own mother, so he had you do it. You couldn't find the diary that he sent you for, because you never looked in the most obvious place. Yeah, old Ray here was Bo's father. Bo was born from a woman he raped two to three times a week many years ago when he was a young, perverted lad. He even raped the boy in the ass. Bo told me so. The meth lab is why he tried to keep everyone out of those woods and is why you and him tasered Bo and then hung him with your belt. Bo didn't wear a belt. I bet that if I force Ray here stand and pull his pants down, I would find two holes in his ass where I shot him the other night when y'all were trying to hang Theo here. He's not a member of the KKK." Jake turns to Ray, "He's the Grand fucking Dragon! You two have your hands in all kinds of shit. I could go on all night, but I'm getting tired. I'm going to take you two in and lock y'all up in your own jail."

Ray, "Look Jake, we're a lot alike."

"In what way? I like my women of breeding age and I've never killed any innocent person in my life."

Ray gets a lump in his throat, "Listen to yourself, you're crazy. Okay, I was involved in the meth lab and I'm a member of the KKK, and I like the pictures of the young girls, but I never killed anyone. You're making a big mistake I tell you."

Jake stands and shoves his chair back. "You and Miller wanna walk out or make me handcuff y'all and drag your asses out?"

Ray gets more pissed, "Listen to me, if you arrest me and I go to trial, it will tear my daughter's lives apart. I can't let you do that."

"I hate it, but you brought this on yourself. You two have crossed that line and not once, but many times like a jump rope."

Ray leans back in the chair. "You're one smart cop; I see why the mayor brought you in on this, but you over-estimated me and underestimated the real killer. Mrs. Harper was not my mother and Bo was not my son. I killed Bo because he was bringing too much attention to the drug factory, but I didn't kill Mrs. Harper, Granny or those girls. You have the wrong man. I'm not the Dragon you seek."

"It makes no difference if you kill once, or six times, murder is murder to me. Now stand up and turn around."

"I can't let you do this. My wife and daughters would have to sit in court every day and listen to the prosecutor tear me apart."

"That part I hate because I feel for your family. You should have thought of that before you started your killing spree." Ray, with tears forming in his eyes, glances around the room at all the empty faces glued to him. He reaches down and pulls his pistol out. Jake quickly pulls his as did Theo. Miller didn't move an inch. Everyone in the bar takes a step back.

Jake yells, "The bullet from this gun will send you out in the parking lot. Drop it now!!"

"I'm sorry Jake; I can't drag my family through this." He places the barrel of his revolver in his mouth and pulls the trigger blowing the back of his head into the crowd.

The room went silent as Jake slowly walked around, undoes Ray's belt, flips the body over and jerks his pants down. Theo slowly walks over and sees no wounds on Ray's rear end.

Jake looks up and says in a low, easy voice, "Then, on the other hand, I could have been wrong with some of that synopsis. He confessed to Bo though, I got that going for me."

Jake's cell goes off.

Theo frowns, "I bet I know who that is."

Jake flips his cell open, "Hello."

"Wow Jake, you really took care of old Ray there. You were so far off. You won't believe this, but I'm staring at four frighten women right now. Which one should I rape first? You better hurry, I'm getting horny."

"Look, it's me you want, not them. Just tell me where you want to meet, and we can end this."

"I'll tell you what; I'll reframe from raping your women as long as you two meet me tomorrow night."

"Name the time and place asshole."

"Now don't be rude, I'm having trouble resisting the temptation here. Did you know that your daughter has a tattoo of a rose on the cheek of her ass? I must go now. I have to administer a small amount of drug to each one. I don't want anyone trying to escape. I will call you tomorrow night say around 2100 hours."

"I'll be waiting you son-of-a-bitch and if you harm any of those girls I will…"
The caller hangs up…

Jake turns around and asks Theo, "Where'd Miller go."

"I don't know; he was standing here a few seconds ago."

"Damn you, you let him get away."

"Crap, I just saw a man blow his brains all over the place. I was too stunned to keep up."

"Let's get back to the house."

Theo, "Ray's house?"

"Get your mind off sex. The killer said he had the girls."

"That impossible. We hadn't been gone that long. He's bluffing."

"I'm not taking any chances. I'll drive and you try to call the girls on their cells."

CHAPTER 33

They drive back to the residence as fast as they could. Theo is holding on for dear life as Jake is doing well over a hundred.

"Easy Jake, the girls are most-likely just fine. This guy hasn't had time to kidnap four women. He's just trying to get us off track."

"This guy's good, he hasn't had a problem pointing us in the wrong direction since we got here. Try and raise them on their cells again."

"They're sleeping; I'm telling you this guy is trying to get us all worked up."

"He's past that point. Try calling Rodger."

Theo shakes his head, "I can't believe the sheriff blew his brains out right there in front of everybody. I guess that makes his wife single now." He punches in the number, but Rodger doesn't answer.

"Rodger doesn't answer either."

"Too bad Miller got away; I bet he knew who the Dragon is."

They fly up in front of Stillwell's residence, jump out and find the front door left wide open. At the bottom of the stairs lying on the floor was Rodger and next to him is his wheelchair flipped over on its side. They quickly ran over to help him up and back into his wheelchair. He had a large purple knot on his head.

"He hit me over the head and pushed me down the stairs. He's got the girls."

"Did you see his face?"

"No, I heard a noise and when I checked in the girl's room, he had a rag of some kind over Casey's face and Jackie lying on the floor. I think he used chloroform on them. I wheeled over and we struggled into the hallway where he hit me on the head with the base of a lamp and then pushed me down the staircase. He must have already rounded up Sherry and Ann. He put them in my van. His face was covered with a ski mask."

"Damn, how did he get inside the house?"

"I think the girls left it unlocked. I'm sorry I couldn't stop him."

Jake gets frustrated, scans the room and asks, "You hurt bad?"

"I'll be hurting in the morning that's for sure. Whatta we do now? This guy could be raping them as we speak."

"He doesn't want sex yet; he took them because he's after me."

"Why the hell does this guy want you?"

"I'm not sure; I've pissed so many people off that it could be anyone."

Theo interrupts, "He's not lying about that, and that ain't all Mayor… Sheriff Ray blew his brains out all over Jane's Bar Palace."

Rodger, with a shocked expression on his face, "Why the hell would he do that?"

Theo shakes his head, "Jake blabbered until old Ray couldn't stand it anymore. He's not the first person he's done that too."

Roger gives Jake a look. Jake shrugs his shoulders, "What can I say, I aim to please. The guy was a pervert. He had kiddy porn buried under his closet floor and I'm real funny about that shit."

Roger asks, "Whatta we do from here?"

"We try and get some rest; tomorrow's going to be a busy day and a full moon tomorrow night."

None were able to get any sleep that night for worrying about the girls.

Early the next morning Jake's driving down the road pondering over questions but getting no answers. Theo is in deep thought when he suddenly turns to him, "I can't stand the suspense, where do we start looking?"

"I have no idea. I made some phone calls this morning that's gonna change things in our favor."

"What kind of things?"

"I'll tell you later." They drive by the old cemetery and see Amber's funeral taking place. Jake pulls through the main gate and drives around a short curve. The beautiful grassy meadow with scattered grave markers is crowded with several hundred people. Jake parks and steps out. Theo steps out and gives him a look, "Why are we stopping here? We should be looking for the girls."

"Sometimes a killer will attend the funeral of a victim. You take one side and I'll take the other."

"What are we looking for?"

"Just scan the crowd as you make your way through. You'll feel this guy when you spot him. He should be the one not taking Amber's death too hard."

Jake starts walking up the west side behind the crowd as they hold graveside services. Theo makes his way up the east side.

Jake is checking out every male he saw. The hair on the back of his neck was standing up. He could feel the killer staring at him.

He whispers to himself, "Okay think. If Ray didn't kill the girls, it must be Miller, but that asshole isn't smart enough or old enough to be the man I'm looking for, and why would he want me dead other than I threw him through a few windows. He murdered old lady Harper for sure… Think, think." He walks in and out of the crowd of people checking out their faces. Who could it be? He walks further, turning ever-so-often, and looking at the rows and rows of old grave markers when suddenly he stops, and takes a few steps back. There staring him in the face, is a headstone with a name written across the front. The name jumped out and grabbed him like someone had his nuts in a vise.

"Well, I'll be a son-of-a-bitch!! I see you now asshole!!" He checks the date of birth, October the 12th 1951. He turns and heads back to the car. Theo makes his way out from the crowd toward the spot where they had parked.

Theo, "They all just look like a bunch of grieving people to me." He could see that look on Jake's face, "Holy shit!! You just figured it out, didn't you?"

"I didn't, a small piece of marble just hit me in the ass. I know who the bastard is, and the Dragon was breathing down our necks the whole time."

"Who is it?"

"Not now Theo, I need to check on a few things first. Let's get back to the house."

That afternoon Jake is going through Rodger's closet, throwing shit everywhere. Theo just watches with amazement. "I can help you look for it if you'll tell me what the hell you're looking for. I think the mayor's going to be pissed when he comes home and finds out you've been throwing his shit around."

Jake suddenly stops and stares at some muddy dress shoes in the closet, then slowly stands and turns to the nightstand and sees a picture of ten young soldiers standing next to a UH-1 helicopter. He walks over and takes it in hand and then slowly turns to Theo, "This is going to knock your socks off. I know his real name."

"Okay, now tell me what you know."

"Our killer is Troy Seymour."

"What? Who the hell is Troy Seymour!?"

"He was in the Ranger battalion with me in Vietnam. I knew I had seen that face before, years had changed him. He remembered me though."

"I don't get it."

"Back in the summer of 72 my platoon had chased a bunch of Vietcong gorillas into a hamlet north of Saigon. So, we started our sweep and checked every hut, then we realized they had somehow slipped out on us. As the platoon started to move on, I checked this last hut at the very rear of the village and found a man and woman with their throats cut and Troy standing over a strangled and raped 12-year-old village girl. He just stood there with his bloody dick hanging out and was laughing like a mad man over what he had just done."

"What did you do?"

"Stupid question... I beat the shit out of him and turned him over to the military police. He only got a few years in a military mental institution though. They say that the war brought it on, but I had a feeling he was a sick bastard by the way he would look at the little Vietnamese girls. All the prostitutes he paid in Saigon were around fourteen or fifteen."

"I'm lost, what has that got to do with anything and how did Troy Seymour's picture get in here?" Theo takes the picture from Jake's hand, looks close at it and asks, "Which one is you?"

"I'm the one at the far right scratching my nuts. Who's been looking over our shoulder the whole time? Who knew every move we made? Who brought us up here in the first place? Now I know what Granny was talking about. Wheels go round and round, the Dragon stands on two powerful loins... I can't believe I was that stupid."

"Right now, I can believe I was that stupid. I haven't a clue to what you're talking about."

"Look at the picture and tell me who that is standing to the far left."

"Never seen him before."

"Our killer is the damn Mayor, Theo!! Rodger Stillwell, A.K.A, Robert Harper, A.K.A, Troy Seymour!"

"Okay Jake, I hate to burst your bubble, but the mayor is a cripple, and I think it would be a little hard to rape and strangle girls from a wheelchair."

"Is that right? Well, in his closet is a pair of muddy dress shoes size seven and a half, and a 30/06 rifle with your ear written all over it. Troy Seymour was born in Andalusia in 1951 to one Thelma Seymour, who changed her name to Thelma Harper and moved here to Fairmont, when in 1973, they released Troy back into the public. He changed his name to Robert Harper and somewhere down the line changed it to Rodger Stillwell. That's why there's no record of Robert Harper at the courthouse. The asshole's been plotting his revenge against me all these years. I'll bet you anything, that's what Fre...Fred...Fred, Freddy was trying to tell me all along. He just didn't have any idea how important the shit was. The headstone at the cemetery had a name on it. You wanna guest what name that be? Rodger Stillwell. He used a name that nobody would check. That means he raped Bo's mother in 74 and Bo was conceived in 75 which means he was raped, then tied to the bed and burned at six years old."

Theo nods and asks, "Sick son of a bitch! Is there anyone out there who's not trying to kill you? I got a question; how did anybody up here not remember Rodger Stillwell?"

"Too old, too stupid. You would have had to be looking for the headstone to fine it."

"When did all this come to you?"

"Dude, I need to go over everything three times to get you to understand. I accidentally came across the headstone with the name Rodger Stillwell on it. He was the same age as Troy. He had to change his name again after his failed attempt to burn Bo up. He thought he had killed Bo, but that didn't happen. When he found out he was still alive, and walking the woods, well, you know the rest of that story."

"No, I don't. I'm more confused now than ever. You know very well I got sent to homicide by accident or they wanted to punish you for screwing some head honcho's wife. You're saying this Troy changed his name to Robert Harper when he moved here and then changed it again when Bo survived the shack burning down?"

"Yep."

"Well, why didn't he go back and kill Bo when he found out he screwed up?"

"Because Bo stayed hidden in the woods. He would venture over to Thelma's place from time to time. And when Thelma got older and crazier, Bo found himself scrounging through dumpsters near the soccer field for food. He didn't witness the last girl's murder like I thought, but Troy didn't know that. The other three victims Bo just came across while making another journey to the dumpster. When Troy thought Bo could I.D. him, he had Ray and Miller find him and they hung him in a jail cell to keep him from saying anything. Troy called in and gave the locations of the bodies. The faster they found them the quicker he could get me up here."

"Then why didn't they kill him in the woods during the search?"

"Too many people in on the search. That's why all the stories were made up about the creature in the first place. It was to keep people from wandering around in the woods looking for the boy and finding the drug operation. The sheriff was right, he didn't kill those girls, but he worked for the man who did."

"I can't believe you badgered the sheriff until he shot himself."

"He killed Bo, that's good enough for me!"

"This Seymour dude went through all this just to get to you?" Theo just shakes his head.

Jake nods his head in an up and down motion, "Yeah, he could have saved himself a whole lotta trouble by taking a five-hour drive to Mobile and shooting me while I was drunk at Pat's place."

"Still a lot of unanswered questions. So, you're saying the mayor can walk? Well, he sure had me fooled."

"He had everyone fool, even his wife. He wasn't having sex with his wife because he was a cripple; it was because he was getting it from her team. He was always helping Sherry out with the girls. And you can bet he has two pellet holes in his ass. I should have seen his legs were the wrong size for a man who hasn't walk in years. And he mentions his ass was hurting from sitting in the wheelchair for too long the other day after I shot him running into the woods."

"So, he was faking all these years. You should be flattered with this one."

"I am Theo. I bet if we checked with the county courthouse, we would find a lot of missing teenagers over the years. You see, he was buying the girls lockets and other shit to keep them quiet and when he tired of them, he would drug them up so he could rape them without leaving a trace of evidence. He would use them until he got bored and then strangle them knowing he could use the murders to get me up here. The other girls never had a clue who the other one was seeing. The one he was screwing at the time kept quiet as long as he gave her money and jewelry."

"Wait a minute; when did he complain about his ass hurting?"

"You remember the other day at lunch, when Rodger kept leaning to one side and said his ass hurt from sitting in the chair too long?"

"That's right. Shit!! This means he's the Grand Dragon of the local KKK. Now I know why he lined me up to play Coco."

"I just told you that."

"But if he was having sex with the girls why rape them?"

"He actually didn't rape them just drug them so he could have rough sex and then let his men rape them."

"Well, I'll be a monkey's uncle."

"I'm sure you are."

"So that bastard only pretended to like me?"

"He deserves an Oscar, no doubt about it. Hell, he even had me fool and I served in the Rangers with him. He was wearing contacts to change the color of his eyes. He left out of here the first night to go check on some bridge stuff. What kind of Mayor tends to business late at night leaving his good-looking wife in the same house with a handsome well-hung Italian? And get this, last night he said the perpetrator took his van."

"What's funny about that?"

"How would he have known that if he was knocked unconscious when the man left?"

"The kind that leads a bunch of idiots in white sheets and kills young girls."

"That's not all Theo, come walk with me." They walk down the stairs and into the kitchen.

Theo scans the room and asks, "What are we looking for now?"

Jake walks over to the countertop and stares at a set of expensive knives, "Yep, I was right; six knives with number seven missing. Out in the trunk of the car wrapped in an evidence bag is the seventh knife to this set. That's the knife he used to kill Thelma, when she refused to tell him where the diary was. He thought she would turn it over to us and we would know his identity. But the writing was so bad I couldn't make heads or tails from it anyway."

"But he wouldn't have known that because he never read the diary, right?"

"Right."

"I thought you were sure Miller killed old lady Harper."

"Are you even listening to me? Rodger killed her. They have the same shoe size, and I was wishful thinking. We can't let him know we're on to him. If he finds out we know his identity before tonight, he'll never tell us where the girls are. He will kill them. He must have been the one who took Ray's cellphone which explains the cell tower tracking info."

"I was just thinking, he raised Casey most of her life. You think he would hurt her?"

"Troy Seymour would rape and kill your goldfish, so I know he will rape and kill her at the drop of a hat."

"I don't have goldfish."

"I know that I was rambling on at the mouth. Let's put all this stuff in perspective and ride around for a while and wait for his phone call."

"What makes you think he'll call you?"

"Because he wants us to find him. He's been planning his revenge all these years."

"So, who shot my ear off."

"Troy, and he was trying to kill you, but he was slightly off. Most likely because you were stumbling all over the place."

"I thought Miller shot my ear off."

"Holy cow Theo, my head is racing around trying to put all this shit together and I'm worried about the girls! I bet that if we check in his garage, we will find a four-wheeler. He knew a short cut the Granny's place."

"That rotten asshole."

CHAPTER 34

Later that afternoon Jake pulls up to the curb in front of Fairmont Guns and Ammo store located on Main Street downtown. Theo glances over and asks, "Why are we stopping here?"

"I wanna get you a shotgun."

"Why? I have my Glock."

"We're going up against a mad man and the Klan. I want you to have some firepower not a plastic toy. You can't miss with buckshot."

"We got Big Bertha."

"Arg, she be with me tonight lad, fer sure."

"Ok, is that pirate talk or Irish?"

"Can go either way. Most pirates were of Irish or English decent. We have men running around everywhere who wants us dead and that's what you ask."

"It's just been lingering in my mind for a while."

They step inside the business and see the walls covered with various rifles and shotguns. Right off the bat, Theo sees a cheap nickel plated 12-gauge pump action shotgun. "Hey, I want this one."

"That piece of shit will jam on the first round."

"It looks better than Old Bertha."

"What is it about blacks and shiny shit? And watch your mouth, Bertha has saved you more than once."

"Tell Bertha I'm sorry, but shiny shit shows class."

"It shows you have no taste. Now let's pick out a Remington 870 or Model 12 Winchester."

"I like this one! Now if I'm going to break my shoulder, let me look good doing it."

"Okay idiot, whatever you say."

They walk to the counter and an old man sporting a gray beard meets them and asks, "How can I help you two gentlemen today?"

Jake replies, "We want that nickel-plated piece of shit of a shotgun you have displayed over there in that glass cabinet and one shell."

Theo frowns, "One shell. I'm gonna need two or three boxes."

Jake nods, "One shell is all that shinny piece of shit will fire before falling apart."

The old man laughs, "You're wrong dude, that gun is one of our bestselling models."

Theo smiles, "See Jake, and he sells 'em for a living."

Jake shakes his head, "He's in the business to sell guns, not save you money, but okay, we'll take that gun and two boxes of three-inch number one buckshot and one box of two and three-quarter double ought. I'm gonna enjoy this." Jake counts out some money and throws it on the counter.

Around fourteen hundred hours they're sitting in an old pickup truck parked under an oak tree with a barbed-wire fence between the vehicle and a large field near a four-way stop. Theo is running his hand up and down the sawed-off barrel of his new toy.

Jake is leaning back in the seat chewing a cigar and thinking with his eyes closed. Theo's making moaning noises when Jake says, without opening his eyes, "Will you stop stroking the thing; you sound like you're playing with yourself."

"She's beautiful. I can even see my reflection in the receiver."

"Whoopie-freaking-do and so can the KKK."

Theo starts shoving shells into the bottom. "Where did you get this truck, it has no air-conditioner."

"I borrowed it from the old man with the dog that has nuts as big as baseballs. You saw them, were not those balls the biggest you've ever seen? We won't tip anybody off if we're not in an unmark unit."

"Second question; why are we waiting here?"

"I'm waiting for the phone call from Rodger."

"You mean Troy?"

"Whatever, now shut up, I'm worried about the girls. I mean we ate with him, we drank with him, we ...."

Theo interrupts, "You slept with his wife and damn near drank every bottle of Scotch and Bourdon he had, and he had a shit load of it."

"Yea and now I don't feel so guilty about that."

"You said he wouldn't hurt them until we showed."

"He might rape 'em."

"Man, I can't stand this waiting shit; I say we start looking now."

"Where, where do we start looking?"

"I'm not sure, but anything is better than just sitting here. I'm going to take a piss behind that pecan tree and if you don't mind, I'll take my shinny baby with me, just encase the Klan shows up. Seems like every incident in the county takes place under a pecan tree."

He steps out and walks over to the fence. He stretches two strands of barbed-wire apart and tries to slip through. Jake snickers as he hears him tearing his pants on the fence. Theo finally makes it on the other side and walks behind a pecan tree and leans his shotgun against the base of the trunk.

Jake turns and lays his head on the edge of the door thinking about how bad he had done Ann.

Back behind the tree, Theo is drawing pictures in a fire ant bed next to the trunk with his urine.

He mumbled, "That's right, how does it feel to have someone piss on your home you rotten little bastards?" He finishes with a shake and turns around zipping up at the same time and suddenly freezes when he sees a two-thousand-pound white Brahma bull standing about ten feet in front of him.

He mumbles again, "Nice cow, just taking a piss, that's all." He starts to ease to the side when the bull snorts snot everywhere and strikes the ground with his right hoof. He slowly reaches over and grabs his shotgun and eases it up to eye level and points it in that direction. The bull snorts again then takes off toward him. He fires the gun, but it explodes in his face.

Hearing the shot, Jake quickly jumps from the truck and runs over to the fence. He could see Theo running all over the field with the bull right behind him. He watches Theo as he runs in circles with his face covered with gunpowder. He was temporarily blinded and had no way of knowing which direction he was going.

Jake yells, "Run this way, Theo!"

Theo yells back, "Which way is that!?"

"Run toward my voice!" He turns and runs in Jake's direction with the bull right behind him.

He could see that Theo was approaching the fence and yells, "Go back, go back!! You're going to hit the ... !!" It was too late. He struck the barbwire fence and bounced back on the ground.

Jake quickly grabs a fence post and jumps the barbed wire. The bull, seeing Theo crawling on the ground, no longer a threat, turns his attention to Jake ...

An hour later, they're resting on a limb in a pecan tree.

288

"Stop shaking the limb, pecan trees have very brittle limbs. How's your eyes?" Jake asks.

"Good enough I can see that bull still eating grass down there."

"He damn near gotcha. So much for your new shinny toy, huh."

"Do you have to be right about every freaking thing?"

"I know guns better than knives.... Yep, pretty much." Jake ganders down at the ant bed and can see where Theo had drawn a picture with his piss. "What's that supposed to be?"

"What?"

"You drew a picture in that ant bed, what's it supposed to be?"

"It's my name."

"Doesn't look like your name."

"Yes it does, see the 'T'?"

"What's that on the end?"

"That's an 'O'."

"That sure is one screwed up 'O'."

"I was running out of crayons okay, you happy now?"

"If you had made your 'T' smaller I believe you could have..."

Theo interrupts, "Enough already about my Van Gogh, how do we get down from here?"

"The same way we got up here."

"I'm talking about the bull, what about the bull?" Theo shakes his head and takes a gander up across the field and sees a five-legged cow from a distance. "Oh my God, Jake!! I see a five-legged cow!"

Jake looks across the field and sees nothing.

"Your eyes still have gunpowder in them."

"I swear it was just standing across the field."

About this time Jake's cell goes off. The bull hears the ring and takes off. He struggles to get it off his belt and holding on to the limb at the same time.

Theo yells, "He's leaving!!"

"I can see that, shut up while I take this call... Hello."

"*How are you feeling Jake?*"

"Not bad if you think hanging in a pecan tree with a blinded, fat, negro is okay."

"*You think you're up to the task?*"

"Can't wait."

LEE KOHN

"Listen close then. There's a clearing near Bo's old burned-out shack. In that clearing will be two large crosses and they're surrounded by a lot of armed Klansmen."

"So, what; let them have their cross burnings. What's that have to do with the girls?"

"That's the good part... at the foot of one cross will be your good-looking wife Ann tied to the base. At the foot of the other will be your good-looking lover, Sherry. Now they won't start the fires until you get there, but you still need to take on a bunch of my finest. This is so much fun. I've been waiting for this day a long time."

"What about Jackie and Casey?"

"You'll figure that out when the time comes, but it won't do you any good if you can't save Ann and Sherry."

"Oh, I can save 'em and I have a little advantage over you now."

"How so?"

"I know who you are now."

"You don't have a clue."

"Yes, I do."

"Who am I then?"

"I'm not going to say right now."

"You're bluffing."

"Not this time."

"Be there at 2100 hours, and I will be watching, so don't come early or bring any friends, except Theo. I wanna see that fat ass dead."

"Well, he'll be glad to hear that."

"If you only knew how funny you two look hanging in that tree."

Jake scans his surroundings but sees no one.

"Where are you now? I can't see you."

"Oh, I'm here, I can see Theo picking his nose."

Jake turns and finds Theo digging deep into his nostrils with his index finger, then turns his attention across the road, but sees nothing. The phone hangs up."

Theo stops picking, "I guess that was him, right?"

"I think he was watching us from across the road. He saw you digging boogers from your nose."

"For your information, I was digging gunpowder from it. And how's he doing that?"

290

"Troy was pretty good at that kind of shit back in Nam."

"Why did you tell him you knew who he was?"

"I just wanted to take things up a notch. He didn't believe me anyway. He did say he wanted to see fat ass dead."

"What fat ass?"

"He was talking about you."

"Now that was totally uncalled for. What's he got against me anyway?"

"He's the Grand Dragon, Theo; think about it. Now let's get down from here and clean that face of yours up."

Theo, "When all this is over, can we go back and shove those shinny gun parts up that old man's ass?"

"Oh no, we're going back there right now."

CHAPTER 35

They fly up to the curb in front of Fairmont Guns and Ammo. The place is crowded with customers walking up and down the aisles checking out assorted sporting goods. They make their way up to the checkout with Theo throwing a large heavy paper bag up on the counter.

A young clerk steps up and asks, "Can I help you?"

Theo blurts out, "You damn right you can! Look in that bag and then tell me what you see and where we can find that old, gray bearded bastard who sold me this damn piece of shit."

The young man looks in the bag, "We can't take that back sir, you've damaged it."

"We bought the damn thing not more than two hours ago and it almost got me killed by a bull."

The clerk smiles, "They don't even have a season for bulls."

"Tell that to the bull. I want my money back."

"I'm sorry sir, but all sales are final."

Jake interrupts, "Let me handle this."

Theo places his hand on Jake's chest, "Not this time." He leans toward the clerk and in a low angry tone, "Look into my eyes cracker and tell be what you see."

The man leans in even closer and looks him right in the eyes, "Wow! You must have gotten cayenne pepper in your eyes or watched somebody welding."

"Wrong on both counts' asshole! They look like this because your damn shotgun blew up in my black ass face. Sorry for the bad language, but as you can see, I'm not in the best of moods. Now, go get the other son-of-a-bitch salesman that waited on us in the first place before I rip this place apart, using your ass as a battering ram, and I've not even touched on the lawsuit yet. When my lawyer gets through with this place, I will rename it Theo's Guns and Ammo and guess who the second son of a bitch I'm gonna fire!?"

The young clerk quickly walks off. Theo turns to Jake, "How did I handle that?"

"You've learned so much over the last few years young Shit-talker. It's like a father watching his son take his first steps. You have managed to purge yourself

292

of all the impurities of life's inadequacies and escape the forces of the dark side, and I'm very proud of you. With that being said, I have let you in on every deal I have ever made over the last five years good or bad, and now you have left me out of being part owner of the most lucrative business in a county where everybody and their grandma buys a gun."

"You are right, it will be called Theo and Jake's Guns and Ammo."

"You mean Jake and Theo's Guns and Ammo."

"It was my face, so I had it right the first time."

"Really, after I told you exactly what was going to happen."

An hour later Theo is sitting on the passenger's side feeding shells into the bottom of an old model 12 Winchester sawed-off pump.

"Where to now? I'm in the mood for killing."

"In two hours, we start hiking to Bo's old shack; that will give us a few hours to get there."

"Not the woods again and at dark."

"We can take a bus."

"Now you're speaking my language."

"Look, this is no game. He's going to have a dozen Klansmen waiting for us, so when the action starts, show no mercy. And be careful, Ann and Sherry will be tied to the bottom of the two crosses."

"Where are Jackie and Casey?"

"I don't know yet. He said it would come to me."

"So, he won't be there huh?"

"I guess not, at least not for the first round." Jake reaches down to the floor and pulls out a rifle with scope.

Theo is impressed. "Wow! What's that for?"

"It's Rodger's 30/06 and I think it's going to come in handy when we get to Bo's place."

"You mean Troy's 30/06. So, you're not taking Big Bertha?"

"Oh, she's going to be draped over the other shoulder."

"Then why the hell did we go through the trouble of buying that piece of shit back there, not to mention I almost got blinded for life and gored by a bull. I could have just used Bertha."

"What puzzles me is why a bull with a hundred cows to breed would even give a shit about two foul mouth cops in the first place, and I don't like other people using Bertha. It's like loaning your wife to a stranger."

"I'm not a stranger and you didn't seem to mind me using it when those rednecks had you pinned down on the ground at the barn dance."

"I told you they didn't have me pinned down; I was just getting my second wind."

"Bullshit!!" Theo lays his head over against the door window, "I think I'm gonna take a little nap. I need to conserve all my energy for tonight, so I can kick some KKK ass."

"Like you did the other night in the field with Jerry?"

"Ha ha." With that Theo closes his eyes, falls into a light sleep and dreams.

Theo sits at his desk in his seventh-grade class, staring at the menacing three-hundred-pound teacher with her black mustache stretching across her face like a giant caterpillar had crawled under her nose. With patience, he waits for her to grade his essay on the fundamentals of democracy. She reads and reads and then glances up with a smile and politely says, "This is by far the best essay I've ever read, Theo. This essay will earn you yet another 'A'. He grins and then glances around the room seeing several white boys with the sunlight glancing off their skinned heads as the sun's rays pierce the schoolhouse windows. His smile turns to a frown as one of the boys leans toward him, "Think you're smart, huh fat ass? You just wait until after class. Me and the boys here have a little surprise for you and it ain't no 'A'."

Theo swallows hard and tries to act like he isn't scared, but deep inside he's praying that the class will never end or at least, not until dark. That will give him a running chance. He scans the classroom and notices Motisha Albright sitting at her desk staring at him. She's a black petite, beautiful girl with deep brown eyes and skin smooth as silk and that light brown complexion was giving him an erection. He smiles back as she gives him a wink and licks her lips. Then he notices a young boy sitting behind her with a serious look on his face, but this white kid seemed a little different than all the others. He had thick dark hair slicked back like some little Italian mafia godfather and he was sitting there staring at him also and he's thumping his pencil on the top of the desk like he's bored out of his gourd. It was bad enough having every skin-head bully wanting to kick your fat ass, but to have the Italian Mafia after you too … that's just too much for one chunky black kid to have to deal with.

Suddenly the bell rings and Theo, without hesitation, quickly jumps from his desk causing his over-lapping belly to wedge him in. He carried the desk ten feet before finally breaking free and took off running like a white tail deer on the first day of hunting season. He hits the door so hard it almost came off the hinges. His shoes tap out a quick steady rhythm on the cold tile floors of the hallway echoing like someone tap dancing in the Grand Canyon. It seemed like his feet were moving but his body was frozen in time and going nowhere. He checks behind him only to find the six white boys galloping down the corridor toward him like a pack of hungry Hyenas. He takes a sharp turn into the bathroom and takes aim for a small-flipped opened window seven feet off the floor. Placing one foot up on a sink and the other on top of a urinal, he struggles to get up high enough to grab on to the window seal. Pulling himself up, he forces his head and upper torso through the small opening only to get wedged tightly. He knew that this was most likely his last day on earth and felt the hands of his enemy grabbing at his feet and pulling him down into the lion's den. They drag him over to a toilet in one of the many stalls lined up along the bathroom wall and attempt to make him plead for mercy.

As they kick and punch him in the gut he can hear the leader screaming, "You black bastard. Beg for mercy before we shove that nappy head of yours in the shitter."

Then suddenly a deep voice could be heard a few feet away, "Don't you dare give them the satisfaction of seeing you beg for mercy, Theo."

The leader turned and stepped from the stall, "Mind your own business Jake, this fat-ass belongs to us."

"You gotta a bill of sale or did I miss the free-fat ass sign when I came in this morning?"

"I'm telling you Jake; this bastard's ass belongs to us."

Jake steps forward, "Well since someone's giving ass away, I might as well take my share."

The big boy smiles, "Now that's what I'm talking about. Come on in here and get you a few good licks on this big black ass."

"I wasn't talking about his ass." He reaches out and grabs the boy by the shirt and throws him up against the wall before putting his knee in the groan.

Out in the hallway a large crowd of kids gathered at the doorway. Motisha walks through the crowd and asks, "What's going on in there?"

One short blonde-haired boy answers, "Bubba and his skinheads chased Theo up in the bathroom and I think they're pounding the crap out of him. Sounds like they're wreaking the place."

She pushes a few to the side to gain entry to the bathroom and when she makes it in, she finds Jake and Theo standing over the skinheads who were lying around the floor holding their crotches. She slowly walks over to Theo and says, "My hero." Then gently kisses him on the lips.

Theo smiles, "It was nothing baby girl, I was just walking by and seen these guys whipping on Jake and figured it was time to open a can of good old whoop-ass on 'em."

Jake frowns and interrupts, "What the fuc..!?"

Theo breaks in and says, "No reason to thank me, Jake. I just couldn't stand by and let you get your ass kicked." He winks several times at him before walking off with the girl. Theo's voice can be heard in the distance, "I almost lost complete control in there. Something you didn't need to see sugar." She reaches over and gives Theo a big juicy kiss...

Theo wakes up and yawns before stretching his arms back over his head. He turns and sees Jake staring with a blank look on his face.

"What?"

"I've been sitting here watching you sleep, and it was very disturbing."

"I was just napping."

"At first your legs were moving like you were running, but you weren't going anywhere. Then your head started bobbing back and forth like someone was punching you, then you laid your head over and kissed the window...Huh! What the hell were you dreaming about?"

"I was back in the seventh grade and these bad asses were beating you up in the bathroom when I suddenly stormed in and whipped their asses...why the hell were you watching me nap? That's just creepy!"

"Watching you nap was by far the best entertainment I have seen since the bear incident. You do know that I could not have been with you in school. I'm almost twenty years older than you. I was a grown man when you were climbing out of the crib and up the curtains making chimpanzee sounds and trying to find a bundle of bananas."

"It was just a dream."

"Yeah, I could see that. I have an idea, why don't you go back to Donna until this thing is over."

"I'm not believing you just said that."

"I just don't want you to get hurt that's all."

"We've been working together for over five years now; we've put a lot of bad guys in jail and the cemetery, and we've had more hangovers together than any two people alive and you want me to go home? I don't think so, Wop!!"

"This isn't paintball Theo; I'm just saying that you've already been through a lot and this guy we're after is the leader of the Klan."

"So?"

"So, he wants to kill me, but he wants to kill you twice."

"The Klan don't scare me." A silence comes over the cab of the truck when Theo turns to him, "Hey Jake."

"Yeah?"

"Being that you're my best friend and all, I was thinking of naming my son after you. How does, 'Jake Theo Williams' sound to ya?"

"Like a company that makes housepaint."

"I'm serious."

"I don't like it."

"Have you come up with a name for your boy yet?"

"Damn Theo, I just found out twenty-four hours ago I was going to be a father again, but I was thinking I would name him Jake O'Malley Jr."

Theo gets angry, "How'll about something like Theodore Williams O'Malley?"

"I wouldn't put a boy through that shit."

"Thanks a lot. Hey, what if you have a girl?"

"I'll call her Mrs. Jake O'Malley Jr."

"Changing the subject ... if I don't make it this time, I want you to know I've had a blast working with you."

Jake smiles and turns to him, "Yep, it's been one hell of a ride, Theo ... You know what really gets me by the ass on this case?"

"Sherry's hands?"

"Other than that, this will be the third time Ann has gotten into a situation like this. I mean Ace kidnapped her; Bob the preacher kidnapped her and Jackie, and now Troy has taken them. I spend all my time trying to rescue them."

"Yeah, what's the deal with that?"

"I don't know. They just show up at the worst possible times. It's like it's in the script and the writer doesn't wanna change it."

Theo leans closer, "I have an idea, why don't we stake out that clearing now and surprise the S.O.B.s when they show up? Instead of them waiting for us, we can wait for them."

"For two reasons Theo. One reason is, if they spot us in broad daylight, they'll kill the girls."

"I didn't say go stomping up there like a herd of elephants. I was talking about using stealth. We can wear that camouflage hunting shit like hunters do; find us a good observation point and shoot the bastards when they show up. What was reason number two?"

"I need to give our backup some time to get up here and get situated."

"What kind of help? How come you're keeping me in the dark?"

"In case you get caught; I don't want you to give them any info."

"Wild horses couldn't get anything out of me. They could beat me, cut on me, or drive wooden splinters under my fingernails and I wouldn't say a word."

"You are a lying ass dog. All they have to do is shove a snake in your face and you will squeal like a bitch."

"Touché."

CHAPTER 36

Jake is dressed in black combat pants with a black t-shirt and Theo is wearing the same. They ease down the trail as darkness prevails upon them. Theo stops and leans against a tree taking deep breaths of fresh, clean air, "How much further?"

"Another mile or so … Now is a good time for us to get off the beaten path and take to the woods."

"Oh my God, Jake! It's bad enough to walk this path in the dark. You wanna make it harder and take to the woods?"

"It's the best way. They might have the trail booby-trapped."

Theo shakes his head and catches his second wind, "Bullshit, I say stick to the trail." He starts to walk when suddenly Jake jumps him from behind and knocks him to the ground throwing him forward a few feet.

"That hurt, what the hell are you thinking? I'm not in the mood if that's where you're going with this."

"Don't move an inch."

"Why?"

Jake reaches into his pocket, removes a lighter and lights it up. One inch in front of Theo's nose is a wire stretched across the path.

Jake crawls forward until he's lying parallel to Theo.

"That's why."

Theo snickers, "So those bastards were going to trip us?"

"No, they were trying to blow us up."

"With a piece of wire? Shit, I'll just slip right under it." He reaches out and starts to grab the wire when Jake grabs his wrist, "Listen stupid ass; at each end of this wire is a claymore mine, and if you touch it, you will send thousands of pieces of fragmentation in every direction."

Theo swallows hard, "You mean that silly putty or playdough stuff?"

"That's C-4; a claymore is a shape charge, most likely tied to the trunk of two trees. You trip the wire, and it pulls a pin causing them to go bang and 'end of road' for us. That's why I wanted us to leave the trail. Where were you when they had that class?"

"Recuperating from a hemorrhoid operation. How did you even see this wire?"

"I've been looking for it for the last mile. I expected Troy to set up some booby-traps to keep us on our toes. Good thing it's a full moon uh."

"And when were you going to tell me all this?"

"I took the lead, so it wasn't necessary to make you any more nervous than you already were and then you took the lead and here we are."

"Well, I feel a lot better now knowing that the woods are full of explosives. What else do I need to expect?"

"Expect anything. Troy is sharp at building traps. He could have a pit dugout with bungee stakes sticking straight up from the bottom, or a swinging death pendulum that looks like a big-ass sandspur."

"A what!!?"

"Never mind just stay behind me."

Jake starts to step off the trail when Theo stands and says in a low voice, "I say we step over the wire and continue on, now that I know what to look for." He steps over the wire, and as he places his foot on the ground, they hear a loud click. He freezes, "Tell me I just popped a blood vessel in my ass."

"Don't move a muscle, you just stepped on a bouncing Betty."

Theo, moving nothing but his lips ask, "What's the bitch doing out here in the middle of nowhere?"

"A bouncing Betty is a mine, and I'm not talking about the mimicking mime you see on TV. As soon as you step off it, it will take to the air about waist high and explode."

Theo starts shaking and whispers, "Whatta I do? I've seen this shit in movies before and no one can get off without triggering it."

"There's always a way. Don't move until I get back."

"Wait a damn minute, where are you going?"

"I need to find a heavy log."

"Just check my pants; I believe I just produced a few." Jake walks off leaving him standing there. Theo slowly turns his head and sees that Jake had disappeared in the woods. Five minutes pass when suddenly he returns with a large lighter stump in his hands.

Theo sweating and in tears, "What's the plan?"

"I'm gonna slide my knife very carefully in between the sole of your boot and the trigger. I'm gonna keep pressure on the trigger and you lift your foot. Then you place the stump on the knife blade. That will keep pressure on Betty."

"Sounds way too risky to me. I say I take off running."

"You wouldn't get five feet."

"Obviously you haven't seen me running scared before."

"You tried to out-run a truck loaded with Klansmen and got caught. You will be dead in one second. Now, do as I say." Jake lies down in front of him and slides the knife under his boot, between the trigger and boot, keeping pressure on it.

"Now slowly lift your foot off."

Theo slowly lifts his foot. He walks over to a tree and leans against it, "Jesus, that was close."

Jake whispers with anger in his voice, "Shut up and place the stump on the knife and hope its heavy enough."

Theo places the stump on the knife, allowing Jake to slide his knife out. It worked perfectly. Jake stands and grabs Theo by the arm, "Let's go, and from now on you stay right behind me."

They walk from the trail with Theo so close his belly's rubbing Jake's belt. "Not that close."

CHAPTER 37

About an hour later, they're lying on their stomachs behind a large pine log surrounded by a crop of bushes. Jake, using a pair of binoculars, peeks over the top.

Theo, "You know everything in these woods looks like a snake." He peeks over the log, "You see anything?"

"Yep, I see two crosses on each side of a bond fire not far from Bo's shack."

"How many men can you see?"

Jake starts counting and says in a low voice, "Depends if there's one man under every sheet. I would say about ten."

Theo asks, "What happen to the dozen?"

"I guess he lied."

"He promised a dozen."

"He actually said a bunch. Don't look a gift-horse in the mouth."

"What the hell does that mean?"

"You know, it's when you look into a horse's mouth to see how old he is, when someone is giving it to you." He sees the expression on Theo's face, "Forget it, it's way over your head." He took a closer look and could see the light from the large bonfire casting a glow on Ann and Sherry's faces. "Damn!!"

"What now?" Theo blurts out in a loud whisper.

"They've got Ann tied to the bottom of one cross on her knees and Sherry tied to the other on her knees. Both are pretty good at it. Other than that, they look okay."

"Well, if they kill both, your dilemma on which one to choose will be solved. Are they looking over at each other with lust in their eyes?"

"I hope they don't hurt them, then I gotta go back to spanking Donna's ass. And stop putting that vision in my head, if I get a boner, it will ruin any chance of sneaking up on them."

Theo peeks over the top, "We need another plan, I can't have you over the house every day and night spanking my wife. You see any sign of Jackie and Casey?"

Jake, still looking through the binoculars, answers back in a whisper, "No, Troy must have them at a different location. His so-called backup plan." He looks at his watch, "We have ten more minutes before they expect us; hand me the rifle."

Theo reaches over and grabs the rifle and hands it to him. Theo grunts, "You can't take them all out with a rifle, as soon as you hit the first man, they will scatter like roaches when you turn the light on."

"I was a sniper in Nam, I might get three."

Theo, "I'm gonna work myself around behind them."

"Good idea, but not directly behind them encase I miss."

Theo takes off through the woods working himself around to the backside of the bonfire. Ten minutes later he peeked from around a tree and could see the backsides of Ann and Sherry.

Two minutes later a man wearing a sheet walks over to where the crosses are and yells, "Hey Jake!! I know you're out there!"

Jake recognizes Miller's voice. He opens the bolt on the rife and places five 30/06 rounds down in the magazine and shoves the bolt forward placing a round in the chamber.

The voice yells out again, "Come on, don't keep us waiting. I'll tell you what; I'll let one girl go if you'll send out the spook!"

Jake takes a glance through the scope. The heatwaves from the large bonfire are causing some distortion, making it difficult for him to line up the crosshairs. He slides the scope off and lines up the open sights.

Miller yells out again, "Come on Jake, you're just prolonging the inevitable! Troy is waiting for you at another location, but I disagree with him; you'll never make it past me and the boys! He said you had skill, but other than throwing someone through a door or window, I don't see it!" He walks over to Ann and grabs her by the hair of the head stretching her head back, "I soaked the crosses with Kerosene, and you've got three seconds before I light this cross, and you watch her burn! I'm waiting Mr. Legend-my-ass! One, two, three!" Suddenly, a shot is heard, and the bullet strikes the white sheet between the eyes. Miller stands there for a second before dropping to the ground. The other men cut loose, filling the woods with lead. Jake hunkers down behind the log as chips of wood fly in every direction. Theo takes advantage of the commotion and crawls out from the woods up to the back of the crosses, dragging his shotgun with him. He unties Ann and then Sherry. Ann in tears, says, "He's got Jackie and Casey, Theo!"

"We already know that. Did he say where he was taking them?"

Ann answers, "I never heard him say."

Sherry interrupts, "The killer was Rodger all along, as hard as it is to believe, it's Rodger. He can walk!"

Theo fires back, "We know that too; now let's crawl-the-hell out of here before they look this way." It was too late. Two men run over and start firing toward them when suddenly Theo takes three rounds in the upper thigh.

Theo grabs his bullet filled leg and yells, "Granny was right after all!!"

Ann and Sherry try to drag him into the woods, but two men run over and took aim with their fully automatic assault rifles.

One smiles and says, "This is for shooting my truck up darkie." Before he could pull the trigger, another round pops off striking him in the back of the head. Jake got another and then the sound of choppers could be heard batting the air into submission over the treetops.

Theo laughs, "I think that's Jake's backup plan asshole!"

The man looked into the sky and could see two Blackhawk helicopters with ATF written across the sides; blowing grass, leaves, and fire ambers into the air as they land.

As everyone looks into the sky one turns to Theo, "They're too late to save your ass spook." He looks down, and in Theo's hand, is his shotgun aimed at them.

"I don't think so Casper." He lets off one round striking him in the mid-section blowing him back several feet. Men in sheets run in every direction as ATF officers jump from the choppers in black tactical uniforms. Jake throws the rifle down and runs across the clearing to where Theo and the girls are.

"Y'all okay?"

Theo snickers, "My legs are shot up; do I look okay?"

"You'll live Coco; you'll live. Ann, you and Sherry tear that dead ass Klansman sheet up and tie a tourniquet around Theo's thigh."

A man walks over toward them dressed like a swat officer, and with a grin, "Right... right... right... on time... Ja... Ja... Jake."

Theo laughs, "Freddy, well I'll be shit, what brings your stuttering ass up here?"

"What, what, do you mean, what, what, brought me up, up, up, up, up, here? Jak, Jak, Jake brought me, up, up, here. Don't, don't worry about a thing, The, Theo. We'll round them, them, them, up."

Jake interrupts, "Enough already; I don't have all night." He turns to the girls and asks, "Did he say where he was taking the girls?"

Sherry answers, "I overheard him tell one of the other guys that you would know."

Jake thinks hard for a few minutes and then takes off running for one of the Blackhawks.

Theo yells, "Where are you going!?"

Jake yells back, "I know where he has taken them!" He jumps up in the chopper and yells at the pilot, "Lift off fast and turn south."

"Can't do it buddy, I don't have authorization."

Jake fires back, "I'll give it to you in one sentence and you'll never guess where the period at the end of that sentence is coming from. Now speed those eggbeaters up right now!"

"I said I can't do it without a…"

Jake pulls his 460, points it right at the pilot's head and pulls the hammer back, "I'm pretty sure I can fly this damn thing by myself, so I wouldn't push it if I was you. My daughter and another girl are going to die if I don't get there fast, so one more time; move it before I decorate the cockpit canopy with your brains." The pilot works the stick with shaking hands and the chopper blades increase and the loud noise drowns out every other sound as it lifts off, almost clipping some treetops as it disappeared into the dark sky.

Miles away in the old, abandoned silo, with battery-operated flood lights mounted against the inner walls, Jackie and Casey are tied together, back-to-back, on a three-quarter inch thick piece of plywood laid across the corn dust cover floor. Sitting ten feet away, on a bale of hay, is Rodger A.K.A Troy, wearing his red sheet without the hood and staring at them with his hands crossed and a gleam in his eyes. Jackie slightly turns her head, "When my daddy gets here, you'll gonna die shit-breath."

He laughs, "I'm the Dragon Bitch! What makes you think I won't kill him?"

"History, stupid ass!"

"Yeah, you're Jake's daughter alright. In a way, I feel bad about having to kill him. We went through a lot back in the old days. You better hope he gets here in the next thirty minutes or I'm gonna have fun. I'm going to rape you two over the next twenty-four hours, over and over and then strangle both of you with my bare hands. That will pay him back for what he did to me in Nam."

Casey with tears in her eyes, "What about me?"

"Well, I've been wanting to rape your ass for years, but it would have blown my long-awaited plans, and I can't very well leave you alive."

Jackie nods, "You're crazy, man."

He laughs, "That's what they say." He looks at his watch, "Time is running out for you girls." He stands and walks over to Jackie and takes a knee, "I'm gonna enjoy spreading your legs, bitch, seeing how important you are to Jake and all."

Jackie asks, "Why are you doing this?"

"For two reasons; one, as you say, has something to do with history and the other reason is, I like my stuff young, and the struggle drives me wild."

Jackie responds, "I can guarantee you, that the struggle that's coming this way is one you won't like."

He stands and walks over to the small opening and listens for a second. "I hear something girls." He starts laughing, "I hear chopper blades, and it sounds like its landing in the pecan orchard. I bet I know who's riding in it, and you can bet he's alone too. That Jake, he always makes a dramatic entry."

Jackie nods, "That's the Dragon Slayer bitch!"

"You are so right and he's as anxious to get me as I am him. I can taste the sweet odor of death running across that pasture."

Jackie snaps back, "The death you smell is your own, you freakin' pervert."

"I wouldn't struggle too much on that piece of wood dear, there's a surprise for your daddy under it." He turns his ear back to the opening, "I knew he would figure out this location. That Jake: he hasn't changed in all these years. He's one smart detective, but then he always was." He sticks his head out the opening to take a glance and suddenly he's hit in the mouth with a boot knocking him back inside and across the floor.

Jackie laughs, "That sounded a lot like the Dragon Slayer's cowboy boot. I would know that sound anywhere."

Seconds later Jake bends over and enters the silo with Big Bertha in hand. Troy quickly reaches into his pocket and pulls out a cellphone.

Jake smiles, "It's too late to call for an ambulance now, Troy."

Troy, "That's far enough, that's if you don't wanna see these two pretty girls spattered on the walls of this silo. This cell isn't for calling help."

Jackie yells, "He's got something under us!!"

Jake steps back a few feet and takes out a cigar. He places it between his teeth and lights it. "Okay Troy, I'm here now, let the girls go."

Troy stands and wipes the blood from his lips and with his left hand, tugs on a tooth. "I do believe you've loosened a few teeth."

"I take pride in my work. What's with the red sheet. So, you're the red Dragon; now let the girls go so we can get it on."

"I have a trigger, and one number from this cellphone will set it off, Dragon slayer. I wanna see you beg, so throw the pump down over there near the bales of hay and the 460 Rowland."

Jake throws them on the hay near the wall. "I'm not going to beg for anything. I've been in tighter spots than this asshole. You waited a lot of years to get me. What took you so long?"

"I had to take care of a lot of things before this day. You were never far from my mind, though."

Jake shakes his head, "I can't figure out why you went around your asshole to get to your elbow. All this was unnecessary."

"Sure, it was, I wanted to toy with you a little."

"You didn't have to kill those girls to get me up here."

"Actually, I was killing two birds with one stone. I like raping young girls; I just killed 'em for fun and then used it to get you up here and you took the bait. I've been killing young girls for years. About ten in all. I see you took care of my men."

"I can only take credit for two counting Miller. They are running down the rest."

"You look tired Jake. I wonder why you keep policing, when nobody really likes you.

"I'm not really sure; I don't do it to make people like me, and somebody has to rid the world of assholes like you."

"Why? Nobody appreciates what you do for them. Look what protecting citizens have turned you into, an alcoholic, foul mouth, arrogant, whore chasing, bitter man. You can't even stand yourself."

"You're right. I guess as long as there are people like you in this world, I'll keep on being what I am."

"You're a pathetic excuse for a police officer, just like you were a pathetic excuse for a Ranger. Too many morals. I will say this for you, when you had to kill, you never blinked an eye, or should I say, you're left eye blinked like crazy. Does it still do that when you get angry?"

"Yep! Not sure why it does that. A doctor once told me it was just a nervous reaction set off by anything that pisses me off."

Troy smiles, "Remember all the gooks we killed back in the old days?"

"Unlike you, I spend all my days trying to forget about those killings. The difference between you and I is, I killed because I had too, but you killed because you enjoyed it. You are one sick bastard. So where did Sheriff Ray fit into this picture?"

"He didn't know anything about the murders; him and Miller just took care of the drugs for me. I didn't know Ray had an eye for child porn. I was as surprised as you were when he blew his head off. I bet that was a mess. He sure took the attention off me."

"What did the drugs have to do with all this?"

"It had nothing to do with the killings, not a damn thing. The money did support my KKK plans."

"So, you killed your own son because you thought he could identify you?"

"I never thought for one second you would find that boy. I didn't want anyone to know I spawn a retard. I had Miller and Ray carry that out for me; just told them Bo was going to tell the authorities about the drug labs."

"You raped his mother and when the boy was born, you found out you had passed down those mental genes, so you strangled her. Then you raped the boy and tried to burn up any trace of him, but he lived and hid for years out there, living off dumpster food and whatever his grandmother took to him. Yeah Troy, you're one sick piece of work."

"That bitch had it coming. She wrote all that shit about me in that stupid diary you found."

"I told you on the phone I couldn't make out but a few words from the damn stupid diary."

Troy responds, "I never saw the diary, so I wouldn't have known that."

"Jesus Troy, I must admit one thing, you had me fooled. Sure, my hair stood up on the back of my neck when you were around and you had some familiar facial features, but I never had a clue until I saw the headstone at the cemetery. And then the picture of all of us on the nightstand in your bedroom… Bang!! It all came to me. How's your ass feel?"

"Flesh wound; it's all better now, thank you for asking. I killed the old bag because I knew eventually, she would say something that would make those gears start rolling in that head of yours. I didn't want us to meet prematurely. I was a decorated soldier, and you took all that away from me. The Rangers was my life."

"Bullshit; you raped that little girl and killed her parents all for a piece of young ass."

"Screw those people. She wasn't the first little gook whore I raped! You just happened to come in on that one."

"You should have been given 'death by firing squad' for that."

"Yeah, isn't the legal system a peach? I used Sherry to keep you busy enough to plan out your demise. I knew all along that you couldn't turn that stuff down. You didn't think I knew you and her was humping y'all's brains in the guestroom."

"Where to from here?"

"I'm not actually sure. I never thought we'd make it this far. I figured my men would take care of you and then they would kill Ann and Sherry, and I would rape these two over the next few days then kill them and carry on my life as the mayor. I guess you brought the ATF into the game and spoil my plans."

"What do you have buried under the girls?"

"Bouncing Betties with a remote blasting cape taped to one. Like I said, all I need to do is punch one button on this phone to set it off. So, if they moved off the piece of wood or I push this number, boom! So, you have five minutes to decide which is more important, your pride or their lives. I wanna see you get on your damn knees and beg for your life, you arrogant piece of shit. Now move away from that opening."

They rotate around the silo until Troy is standing by the opening.

Jake nods, "I don't understand; why don't you just lay the phone down so you and I can walk outside and end this? I can do to you in seconds what the judicial system couldn't do in years for you. Whatta say Troy, it will be like the old days except I'm older and you're sicker."

"You have three minutes Jake."

Jake shifts his eyes from side-to-side glancing around the open space looking for a way out of the situation. He stares at the phone real hard.

Troy smiles, "You now have two minutes...I'll do it! Now get on your knees, I wanna see the great Jake O'Malley beg like a pig and a coward."

"Playing the role of a cripple was smart Troy. No one would have suspected it. There were a lot of clues I didn't pick up on. I guess I'm getting too old for this crap like everybody says year after year."

Troy laughs, "Now Jake, don't underestimate yourself. You couldn't exactly keep your mind on the investigation and screw my wife at the same time. Somebody had to do it. I was getting it four times a week from her soccer players. That's right. I knew all along. Sherry was too much of a woman to go without it long. If it makes you feel any better, I never loved that whore anyway. It was just an easy way to get close to the young girls."

Jake glances over at the girls and sees them staring at him listening to every word. "I'll explain later."

Troy glances at his watch, "You have thirty seconds."

"You push that button, and you'll die too."

"So, what? I'm not going back anyway, so believe me when I say, I will push the number and kill us all. Now get on your knees and beg me to let them live!"

Jake looks into the girl's eyes and then slowly goes to his knees placing both hands in the corn dust mixed with dirt.

Troy takes a few steps forward, "That's it, Jake, now say; 'please Troy, don't kill them, forgive me for what I did to you in Nam.'"

Jake stares at the floor for a few seconds and then looks up at Troy. "Please Troy…" He hesitates for a few more seconds, "Please Troy, screw yourself, I should have killed you back then."

"Have it your way Jake." He pushes the button, and nothing happens. He pushes it again and still nothing happens.

Jake shrugs his shoulders, "You have no bars in here Troy. I've been here before and couldn't get a signal. Must have something to do with the shape of these round metal walls. You see troy the phone is in here and the tower is out there and in between is this silo wall. Instead of getting to the tower and bouncing back and getting to the Betties, the signal is just bouncing around in here."

Suddenly the pilot sticks his head in the opening and yells, "Hey buddy, how long do I have to keep my motor going? Aviation fuel isn't cheap you know!"

Jake yells at the pilot, "Get back and keep those blades rotating!"

Troy turns to the man as he takes off running, and then back at Jake. Jake throws corn dust in his face and runs at him, pinning him against the wall. Troy elbows him in the jaw and jumps for Jake's gun, but Jake dives for his red sheet, trips him up and drags him across the room. He stands Troy up, "This is for the four girls you killed." He snaps off a punch to his gut cracking a few ribs. He throws a punch to his head and Troy blocks it and comes up with a kick, catching Jake upside the head. Jake falls to the ground and blocks another kick in the face. He stands and pops Troy in the crotch, bending him over. He comes up with a knee and catches him between the eyes, knocking him to the floor. Troy struggles to stand. Jake, "This is for Bo." He drives a foot into his kneecap, breaking it instantly. Troy screams and falls to the floor again. Jake walks over to the girls and unties them.

Jackie says, "If we get up, those things will explode."

"Just sit tight." He stands and walks over to Troy, who's rolling back and forth on the floor holding his dislocated knee.

Jake shakes his head, "Worst than getting a tooth pulled without a pain killer isn't it." Jake pops him in the face a few times until it was a bloody mess and says, "I need your help."

Troy looks up through his swollen eyes, "You'll get no help from me you bastard."

"Oh, I think I will." He grabs him by the injured leg. Troy screams in pain as he drags him over toward the girls.

"You girls carefully slide your asses to the end of the board."

The girls slowly slide forward to the end. Jake drags him over and lays him across the center.

"You girls take off for that chopper and I mean fast." They run to the opening when Jackie stops and turns, "What about you?"

"I'll be along shortly." They exit the silo and run for the chopper with its blades slowly making its rounds. Back inside Jake lightly slaps Troy on the jaw, "I have to go now, this reunion really sucked."

He struggles to speak, "Please Jake, don't let me die like this."

"Don't beg; go out like a man." Jake takes out a cigar, places it between Troy's lips and lights it. "That's all I can do for you, sorry." He stands and starts to walk away.

Troy spits the cigar out, and in a loud broken voice yells, "If I gotta go, I'm taking you with me!" He rolls off the piece of wood and two bouncing Betties pop up knocking the wood over. They spin into the air three feet off the ground. Jake takes off making it through the opening before they explode, sending metal fragments through the wall, knocking out the floodlights. Shrapnel strikes him in the back as he tries to run like crazy across the pasture toward the chopper. The silo collapsed to the ground.

Jackie screams, "He's hit!!" The girls ran to him as fast as they could. He struggles to roll over and when he does, he's staring up at the full moon peeking through the pecan trees. The pain is almost too much to handle. Jackie bends over and places her hand behind his head, "Hold on Daddy, we'll help you to the helicopter and get you to a hospital."

He slowly turns his head, "Not this time baby girl. My back is full of metal. I love all y'all and fat ass Theo, so take care of him when I'm gone. Tell him I'm not around to keep him from doing stupid things."

Jackie starts crying and Casey joins in as she falls to her knees. He slowly places his hand on Jackie's cheek, "Don't cry for me sugar, you knew I couldn't live forever. I'm surprised I made it this far. Remember, you're an O'Malley. Hold that head up high and take no shit from no one." He closes his eyes and his hand falls in Jackie's lap.

Jackie screams, and then yells at the top of her lungs, "Not this time Jake O'Malley! Grab his arms Casey and let's get him to the chopper." They grab him and struggle to drag him across the field. Then the pilot runs over and throws him over his shoulder. "You girls get in the chopper, I'll bring him."

FINAL CHAPTER

Jake slowly opens his eyes then closes them. Minutes later, he opens them again and finds he's lying in a hospital room. He glances around at all the get-well balloons and flowers. Then with a gentle turn of his head, sees Theo lying in the bed next to him with a respirator attached to his face and struggling for every breath. His right leg is all wrapped up and in a sling.

Suddenly the door flies open, and Ann comes rushing in with her hands around Sherry's neck. She throws her over the bed and across his lap. She's screaming, "This with teach you to screw my husband!"

Sherry jumps up and dives across the bed again, grabbing her by the shoulders and slinging her against the wall. "I love him, and he loves me...so he's mine now!"

Ann fires back with a slap to her face, "Over my dead body bitch!" They fight from one corner of the room to the other knocking flowers and hospital equipment on the floor until Ann pushes Sherry over Theo's leg and then against the respirator, snatching the cord from the wall. Theo starts panting and grasping for every breath.

Jake in a loud voice, "Hey girls, you just unplugged Theo's thang-a-ma-jig!" They kept right on fighting, oblivious to Jake lying there. Ann grabs Sherry in a headlock and shoves her head into the door. Theo seems to be going into convulsions.

Jake grabs the bed control and starts pushing buttons trying to call a nurse for help, but there's no response.

Suddenly he wakes up in a cold sweat to an empty hospital room and sits up with pain running all through his back. He scans from one side to the other, but nobody was in the room with him. He looks over at the other bed and the sheets are pulled back like someone had been there, but it's empty now. He lays back down burying his head into the sweat covered pillow when he hears the door ease open, and Theo comes limping in on crutches with a bag of banana cream puffs under each arm.

He sees Jake's eyes open and with a smile, "Well good morning sleepy head. You won't believe what the machine down the hall is full of. It wasn't easy, I had to go through your pants for the money."

Jake wipes his eyes and responds, "Where am I?"

"You're in the hospital silly goose."

"What hospital?"

"The Alexander Medical Center."

"How long have I been here?"

"Two weeks. They dug enough scrape metal out of your back to start your own salvage yard. We'll call it Theo and Jake's Salvage Yard."

"You mean I'm alive?"

"Not quite…a piece of shape metal cut your penis off. You have no wee wee."

Jake quickly throws the cover back and checks himself out, only to find Theo screwing with him.

"When I get well, I'm gonna put my foot right in your ass."

"Hey, you want me to have the nurse get a fan for you?"

"Why?"

"You're sweating like a pig before a fourth of July barbecue."

"I was having a nightmare before you came walking in…. What time is it?"

"Ten minutes before visiting hours start. The girls are out in the lobby waiting to see you. Boy will they be surprised to see you awake."

"Have you talked with them yet?"

"Everyday. Ann is really pissed."

"Why? Does she know something?"

"She knows the nurses have been giving you sponge baths, and she doesn't like it."

"And Sherry?"

"She doesn't give you a sponge bath, but she's here everyday."

"Damnit Theo, do they act funny?"

"No, why would they act funny?"

Jake gives him a look.

"Oh that…I don't think Ann knows."

A voice is heard at the doorway. "Know what?" Ann was standing there with Sherry, Jackie and Casey behind her. They walk in and Ann repeats herself, "Know what Theo?"

"He was just asking if you knew he was awake."

The girls surround Jake's bed with Ann lifting his head up while Sherry turns his pillow over and fluffs it up.

Ann kisses him on the forehead and says, "For a while there we thought you went into a coma. You lost a lot of blood. They say if that helicopter wasn't there, you'd be dead."

Sherry winks at him, "Yeah Jake, you sure had us worried."

Jake closes his eyes for a second and doses off.

He opens his eyes and sees Ann leaning over kissing Sherry in the mouth with a lot of tongue action. Then Sherry runs her hands up Ann's skirt and rubs her between the legs. She gets so turned on she reaches under Sherry's skirt and rubs her between the legs. Then she goes down on her knees and spreads Sherry's leg apart and sticks out her tongue...

Suddenly Jake opens his eyes and sees everybody staring at the sheets.

"What the hell is wrong with you four?"

Ann leans over close to his ear, "I think the medicine is giving you an erection."

He turns to Sherry and the girls who couldn't take their eyes off the puptent rising under the sheets, "Sorry about your husband, Sherry, there was no other way."

"I didn't love him anymore. I'm in love with another man. A handsome man who knows how to take control of things; has the courage of a bear and the touch of an Angel; and he's well gifted in other areas, if you know what I mean. He sends goose bumps up my spine when he speaks."

He swallows the lump in his throat, "Well Sherry, he's one lucky guy."

Ann laughs, "If I didn't know better, I would think she's talking about my Jakey-poo."

Sherry smiles, "No Ann, it's a man a lot like him."

Ann replies, "He must be some kind of man, but everybody knows there's not but one Jake O'Malley."

Sherry reaches into her purse and pulls out a check.

He asks, "What's that?"

"It's a check for two hundred thousand dollars, and I have another bonus check from me for an additional fifty thousand. The Dragon Slayer has killed the Dragon."

"I can't take that Sherry, you'll be needing that for Casey's college, and the county can build a new stadium with the other."

"Nonsense, I have plenty. I sold the lumberyard and the seafood market. Casey and I have enough to last us a lifetime. I also have enough to build a new stadium."

Theo loudly clears his throat, "Excuse me, but there's two people in this room. Y'all do know I almost lost a leg here."

The girls giggle with Jackie and Casey jumping up on Theo's bed. Ann reaches over and pats him on the shoulder, "Donna's bringing you guys some homemade chicken and dumplings. I know how hospital food sucks."

Theo laughs, "Obviously you haven't tasted her cooking."

Ann shakes her head, "It's going to taste great; her mother came with her to help."

Theo swallows, "Somebody please find my damn pants, so I can limp my fat ass out of here."

Suddenly, a young, beautiful nurse wearing a short dress and legs-to-die-for, walks in the door, "Okay girls, times up, Jake needs his rest. We have a lot of tests to do later today."

With a disappointed look on the girl's faces, Ann says, "That's not fair, we just got here."

"Sorry, you can spend all day tomorrow with him."

The girls, being very disappointed, kissed Jake and Theo on the forehead and walked out the door one by one. Casey leans over after the others step out and kisses him on the lips, "I'll be waiting for your next trip to Fairmont." She smiles and walks out the door.

The nurse closes the door and locks it, slowly turns to Jake and gives him a sexy look, "I think it's time for your sponge bath."

She slowly walks over and pulls the cover back. "Wow!! The nurses on the third floor were not lying about this one. That has got to be the biggest I have ever seen."

Theo yells out, "How come he gets a sponge bath, and I don't? I guess I'll have to lick myself like a cat."

Jake gives him a look, "Always thinking of yourself, Theo."

"I was wounded too; it's not fair. They shot me three times in the leg. The Doctor almost didn't save the damn thing."

Jake turns to the nurse, "Can you give him something to make him sleep through my sponge bath?"

The nurse replies, "Sure."

Theo yells, "Like hell you say, if I can't have one, at least let me watch!"

The nurse responds, "Sorry Theo, it's against the rules and I have something special for Jake." She places some red lipstick on and smiles at Theo then draws the curtain between the two beds.

Theo yells again, "This is bullshit!" The light from the window had the nurse and Jake silhouetted.

He could see her washing Jake's large member, "He has other parts that need washing too, you know!!...This just pisses me off."

He could hear Jake whisper to the nurse, "Is there anyway possible you can get a nurse give him a sponge bath too?"

Theo, with a grin, "That's what I'm talking about. Looking out for each other; that's what it's all about. Jake and his Shadow!"

The nurse walks around Jake's bed and passes Theo. She opens the door and in a loud voice to the other nurses, "Motisha, can you come give Sergeant Williams a sponge bath?" She turns to Theo, "She will be in here in a few minutes."

Theo shakes his head, "Yeah, now we got it going on."

Minutes pass as Theo lays there listening to Jake moan and the nurse giggling. Suddenly, the door flies open and in comes a very large black nurse, weighing over two hundred and fifty pounds with buckteeth and sporting a large black mustache stretching across her upper lip. She's holding a sponge in her hand and yells, "Okay, who's bitching about a sponge bath!?"

Theo yells, "Not me, I'm very, very, very clean!"

"You just lay back stud-muffin, mama's not gonna hurt you."

On the other side of the curtain, Jake and the nurse could hear Theo...

"Ouch, that hurts; what the hell are you using for a sponge, a pinecone? Okay...okay, now, that really hurts!"

"If you'll be still honey, I can get this done. Now let's get that big black tool clean for ya."

"It's okay; I can get that...Oh shit!!...Wait a minute, you're too rough!!...Hey, that's totally uncalled for!"

"This will go a lot easier if you would quit squirming around."

"Damn woman, you're handling me like cheap luggage."

"Flip over so I can get that ass, sweet cheeks."

"My ass is just fine...stop! stop!!...Hey, you're gonna flop me off the bed...Okay, that did it, now you done went and made me squish my creampuffs..."

On the other side of the curtain, Jake is trying not to laugh because of his back pain, but is unable to hold it in. He looks down at the nurse as she gently and slowly wipes his member for the seventh time.

"This is so funny…"

Theo screams out, "Screw you, and the horse you rode in on!!!"

Two weeks later after being discharged from hospital, they leave Fairmont in their new black unmarked unit on their way back to Mobile. Jake's driving and Theo is leaning over against the window looking out at the miles and miles of pastureland.

Suddenly Theo looks across the field and sees a spotted cow that seems to have five legs.

"Oh, my G O D!! There it is, stop!!"

"There what is?"

He quickly turns his head towards Jake, "Go back I just saw the mysterious five-legged cow!"

"Nonsense Theo, it was a bull hung to the ground like me."

"Ok, I'm not a dairy farmer, but I have never seen a spotted bull. I know what I saw…. Go back, so I can get a picture to show all the guys at headquarters what almost got me hung."

"You are seeing things Coco. Are you still taking those pain killers?"

The End

E-mail: Lonemonkey56@gmail.com

Printed in the USA
CPSIA information can be obtained
at www.ICGtesting.com
CBHW021924221024
16140CB00020B/2